MELBURY SQUARE

COWARD-McCANN, Inc.

NEW YORK

MELBURY SQUARE

Contents

Contents

MELBURY SQUARE

BOOK I
MAUD

Chapter 1

It was that period just before dawn when the city was silent. The last tired cabby had gone home; the milkman had not begun his clattering round. The houses on the quiet Kensington Square were in darkness. Even the earliest-rising sleepy servant was not yet stumbling downstairs to light the kitchen fire. The only sounds were the intermittent hoot of an owl from an oak tree in the Square gardens and the dry rasp of fallen leaves as Guy Beauchamp sauntered unhurriedly to his mother's house, where he was now staying, presumably permanently, after his last travels abroad.

He had been to a party at the Rhymers Club in Fleet Street (where he had drunk an immoderate amount of beer out of a pewter tankard and smoked the traditional churchwarden pipe) to celebrate the acceptance of his first modest volume of poems. He was just twenty-two years old and had brilliant and logical opinions about a great many subjects. But that evening, aided by the beer, he had forgotten the world's problems, and his convivial mood was now passing gently into one of a pleasant euphoria. He found the owl's cry and the curling mist of this barely breathing dawn exactly suited to his romantic mood. Had he been in this state of mind earlier, he might have adopted his mother's suggestion and strolled across the road to watch the guests arriving for a masked ball at Holland House.

The prime minister and other notable political figures were to be there. As well as political guests, however, Lord and Lady Ilchester enjoyed entertaining a varied and rich society. The aristocracy, precisely mannered young men and beautiful young women in tiaras, would be well represented; it was possible there might even be royalty. There would certainly be a sprinkling of poets, musicians, writers, and painters. A circle of painters, following the lead of George Frederic Watts (one of the first of the Pre-Raphaelite Brotherhood) had made this part of London their territory. They had built large Gothic-style houses with studios facing north, where they painted their enormous classical or Biblical scenes and indulged in their scandals and feuds. Some of them though—such as the late Lord Leighton, with his bizarre tiled and fountained Arabian courtyard built in the entrance hall of his respectable Victorian house—were of the greatest respectability.

If any of this circle had been at the ball tonight, their fingers must have been itching to lift the masks of the younger women. Whatever they quarreled about, they had one thing in common, a penchant for discovering beautiful young women to sit as models for their paintings.

Guy thought of the serene and perfect face of Ophelia floating in the sluggish, swooning green water. Surely Millais' pulse must have quickened as he glanced from the canvas to his model. Had she lain in a bath of water for hours at a time, poor thing? It must have been something to see her rising at last, with her garments clinging to her lovely small breasts, her long hair dark against her white skin. That had been the artist's private view, fortunate fellow. One didn't get that at the Royal Academy.

Strolling along, deep in his reflections, Guy was suddenly startled to see a vision ahead of him that might well have been the actual model for Ophelia, a wraith in a long flowing wrap, who had materialized out of the mist. Surely it couldn't be a ghost conjured up by his romantic mood?

He stopped walking, fearful lest he should frighten the vision away. Even so, he fully expected it to dissolve in a moment.

Instead, a lively small animal escaped from the folds of the vision's skirts and gamboled off in the opposite direction.

"Han! Han, come back at once!"

The young woman, whose clear high voice definitely established her claim to being a human being, was using a key to open the gate leading into the Square gardens.

She swung the gate open and disappeared within, still calling, "Han, you bad dog! You must behave."

The little dog, a Pekinese, came frisking through the open gateway, and the gate clanged shut behind him and his mistress. Immensely intrigued, Guy peered through the railings, fascinated by what he saw. The young woman had spread open her cloak, revealing a ball gown, and with her arms flung wide, was waltzing around and around on the dewy grass. Her hair streamed in a dark generous cloud about her uplifted face. She paused a moment to kick off her shoes, then danced on, the little dog yapping at her heels.

Guy was an athletic young man. He set his hands on the railings, and with an effortless leap, he was over them and crashing into the branches of a shrub.

The sound made the girl stop. "Who's that? Who's spying on me?"

Her voice was startled, but not frightened. She watched as Guy made his way into the open.

"I wasn't spying," he said. "I was simply spellbound. You looked like Ophelia rising out of her watery grave."

"Ophelia!" The subtle change of tone told him she was reassured that he was no passing oaf. She even seemed to be diverted, for she gave a small laugh and, taking a dark object that had dangled from her wrist, fitted it across her eyes.

It was a mask shaped like a butterfly, with glittering sparks on its wings. Of course, that explained this mysterious abandonment. She had been a guest at Holland House. She had been dancing all night and drinking champagne. She was loath to go to sleep in the romantic dawn.

"Are you an admirer of Millais' work?" she asked breathlessly.

"A tremendous one. I say, that was clever of you to know that, by mentioning Ophelia, I meant Millais rather than Shakespeare."

The daylight was just sufficient to show the profile of this vastly intriguing young woman. How old was she? Seventeen? Twenty-seven? Guy's interest was growing faster than the daylight.

"I would prefer you to have meant Shakespeare. My father and I haven't much admiration for the Pre-Raphaelites. My father says they are all poseurs. But this isn't the time to have a discussion on art. I must go. Han! Han, come here!"

"You live in the Square?"

"Naturally. How else would I be here in the gardens?"

She was making a pretense of being in a hurry to go, one hand holding up her skirts from the wet grass, the other beckoning impatiently to the cavorting Pekinese. But Guy suspected she was dawdling. She was enjoying the unconventional encounter as much as he was.

"I live at Number Eleven with my mother," he volunteered. "At least, I have just begun to do so, since returning from abroad. Perhaps you've met my sisters?"

"No, we've just moved here. We've scarcely met anyone."

"Then may I introduce myself? I'm Guy Beauchamp. I'm about to begin work in my uncle's bank in the city, but I'm a poet as well." He had no notion of modesty after the evening's congratulations.

"Are you published?" The drawling, slightly mocking voice called for an answer in the same vein.

"Of course. I would hardly have mentioned my work otherwise."

"Oh! How vain!" She was teasing. He longed to see her face clearly. If only a small miracle would happen and the sun would suddenly be in the center of the sky! He wanted to see the color of her hair and her eyes. It would be stretching his luck too far to strike a match.

"Oh, I have plenty of vanity," he admitted amiably. "Was it a pleasant ball at Holland House?"

"It was quite wonderful." She sighed with pleasure. "I adore dancing. How did you know that was where I had been?"

"One doesn't often meet a beautiful, mysterious masked lady in the early morning. Won't you take your mask off?"

"Oh, I don't think we have reached that point in our acquaintance yet."

"Then will you tell me the color of your dress?"

"Green. I usually wear green."

"Is it your favorite color?"

"My father likes me to wear it. It matches my eyes. I have a very doting father, which is very fortunate for me. But sometimes I admit it can be the smallest bit tiresome."

She was certainly not over twenty, Guy decided. Her voice had too youthful a sound.

"Tiresome?"

"He watches me like a hawk. Dear Papa! A hawk watching a little harmless rabbit. A quite obedient rabbit, mostly. It's only occasionally that I creep out like this in the small hours. I say it is to give Han a walk, but it is also to establish my own identity. Do you know what I mean? Do you think me very bad?"

"Oh, beyond redemption I should think. Masked *and* with green eyes."

She gave a small gurgle that sounded like pleasure.

"Han, precious, we must go home."

The dog came scampering across the dewy grass, placing feathered wet paws on his mistress' skirts. She gave a little shriek of protest, and her mask fell off so that Guy could see what his quickened senses told him was a perfect face.

"We were the only people from the Square who were invited tonight," she said. He was sure now that she was as reluctant to end this encounter as he was. "That pleased Papa. He was able to indulge in his usual game of selecting a husband for me."

"I should imagine his task wouldn't be very difficult, from what I can see in this deuced mist."

"Oh, but it is difficult, because he has such high standards. Indeed, there aren't many places where he can play this game. A ball at Holland House, a soiree in Belgrave Square, the private view of the Royal Academy, a country house of sufficient prestige, even a royal drawing room—if you can imagine husband hunting under the queen's nose!"

Guy gave a shout of laughter. For all her obvious youth, this girl had a delicious, sophisticated sense of humor.

"I gather that your father is ambitious for you?"

"That is putting it mildly. And he would be furious if he could see me now. I think it better, Mr. Beauchamp, if we meet again, to pretend that this encounter never happened."

"We will meet again?" Guy said eagerly.

"I suppose it is likely, if you are going to live here. The Square isn't exactly a metropolis." Suddenly hugging her arms across her breast, she lifted her face to the lightening sky. Whatever disparaging remarks she had made about the Pre-Raphaelite painters, she looked remarkably like one of their dramatic, eerily beautiful subjects. "Isn't the dawn exciting! So untouched and unknown. I always get a little mad when I am awake at this time of day. God is giving us a new day, and anything, anything, can happen in it. Do you ever feel like that?"

"From this moment on, I shall never feel any other way."

"You said that as if you really believed it. Mamma says I corrupt people with my madnesses. You had better go quickly, in case I do it to you."

"This isn't corruption," Guy said, so intensely that the girl stopped to look at him.

For a moment their gaze was locked. Then, "Han! Han, come quickly!" she cried. "Home. To Nanny's hot milk. To bed. Back to earth."

Like a large butterfly, she had swooped across the lawn. Guy called with the utmost urgency, "You haven't told me your name."

She paused, looking back, giving that warm gurgle of laughter. "I really have the most absurdly appropriate name for this moment. I will give you two clues. A garden, the black bat night."

"Maud!" he exclaimed in delight.

The iron gate clanged behind her. Guy could hear her laughter all the way to the big house at the corner, where his mother had told him a fashionable portrait painter had come to live. His name was Sir James Lucie; he was a past president of the Royal Academy and an insufferable snob. He had an invalid wife and an only daughter. Maud. Maud, Maud, Maud . . .

Maud was still laughing softly to herself as she tiptoed up the stairs. What an enlivening encounter that had been! She had enjoyed it more than all the romance and artificiality of the ball. She and the strange young man had spoken the same language. He had completely and most satisfactorily entered into her euphoria. So few people understood her when that mood came on her. They thought her wild, eccentric perhaps, a little touched in the head. All last year, when long-suffering Cousin Harriet had chaperoned her at so many parties and balls, she had acquired the reputation of being unpredictable and fast, but gorgeous enough to be forgiven her indiscretions, and perhaps tamable.

Five young men had indeed, at separate times, offered to do the taming. They were all good matches, Cousin Harriet declared indignantly, but James Lucie thought no one good enough for his daughter, and Maud had heartlessly tossed them all aside. Dull! she had said. Where was someone she could *converse* with?

Had she just met that person? she wondered. She wished she could have seen the young man's face more clearly. But she would repair that omission soon enough since he was actually coming to live in Melbury Square.

With Han still tucked under her arm, she succeeded in negotiating the stairs without arousing anyone. On the landing, however, she was nearly caught. Her father's door opened. She shrank back against the wall, relieved to see that it was only Cora, the housemaid, who emerged. Cora was up very early. Papa must have rung for something. Maud hoped that he was not suffering an indisposition from too much champagne. He had a weakness for champagne. He thought it a noble drink.

She was conscience-stricken when she at last reached her own room, for there was poor Nanny, dozing by the cooling ashes of the fire. It was natural that she should wait up for the return of her charge from the ball. She would not have dreamed of retiring until Maud was undressed and in bed. But it had hardly been fair to keep her waiting that extra half hour while Maud indulged her desire to walk in the dewy garden, to listen to the owls, and to feel the dawn air on her face. Poor old Nanny, her face crumpled with sleep, her breath making a droning sound, like a fly caught in the globe of the night-light.

Maud shook her awake, and she started up, rubbing her eyes. "I must have fallen into a doze. No wonder, look at the time! Really, Miss Maud, you are a thoughtless young lady. Running off outdoors all alone like that. You might have met anybody. If I was to tell your father—"

"But you won't, will you, dearest Nanny? And I know that I am selfish and horrid. But it was so utterly wonderful in the garden; the air was so fresh and pure. Han loved it. And I met a poet." She began to sing softly as she kicked off her shoes. '*Come into the garden, Maud, For the black bat night hath flown . . .*' Nanny, do go to bed. You look ready to drop. I can undress myself."

"Before I give you your hot milk? I wouldn't hear of it!"

"Oh, Nanny! Champagne, followed by hot milk. When am I to be allowed to grow up?"

"When you stop doing such childish things. Now, off with this dress. I declare, the hem is sopping. That's a crying shame. Your shoes, too. They'll be ruined. Really, Miss Maud! And what's this about a poet you met? Or are you romancing again?"

"Don't scold," Maud begged. "I don't believe you were ever eighteen."

"I was, but I didn't go lunatic about it. There, I'll leave your hair loose for once. Otherwise, you won't get to sleep before the sun's up. Act first, think afterward. That's you, Miss Maud. Here's your milk."

Maud sniffed distastefully at the steaming milk, heated on a spirit lamp. "Would the world come to an end, or all my hair fall out, or something dreadful like that, if I didn't drink hot milk?"

Nanny's face creased ironically.

"I daresay you think the last-mentioned would be the greater calamity."

"Where did you learn those big words, Nanny?"

"In this household, Miss Impertinence. I'll call you at nine o'clock sharp. You know your Papa expects you in the studio at ten."

"Even Papa might like to sleep late this morning," Maud said, without conviction. Papa was a martinet where his work was concerned. Then he just must paint her with shadows beneath her eyes, because she would never be able to sleep.

What would it be like, she wondered, stretching luxuriously, to fall in love with a poet?

Chapter 2

It was nine o'clock before the house at 7 Melbury Square came to life the morning after the Holland House ball. Sir James awoke and leaped out of a tumbled bed, shouting for the servants. His wife had pointed out, time and again, that bells existed to be rung. But Sir James preferred to use his powerful lungs. He enjoyed shouting orders. He didn't care whether or not this indicated that he had been brought up in a house lacking servants. He never pretended to be what he was not. He had enough natural attributes, he frequently said, without depending on artificial ones.

"You answer him, Cora," Cook said, in the basement kitchen. "You know he always has Mabel in tears."

Cora tossed her pert head. "You've only got to show you're not scared of him, you silly thing," she said to Mabel.

"I can't help it," Mabel said. "He makes me go all atremble."

Cora was already halfway up the stairs, straightening her cap as she went. She wouldn't go all atremble, at least not from fear. But she never failed to enjoy seeing the master in his dressing gown, his yellow hair tousled. The excitement rippled up and down her spine. She found the wide shoulders and broad chest hidden by the rich brocade even more exciting than when actually visible in bare skin. If he pulled her to him, she would go weak in his arms. She had often wondered, and secretly hoped, whether one morning when she answered his shout, he would lock the door behind her and keep her there. But he was too discreet for that. She was allowed to creep into his room only when the rest of the house was asleep. She had nearly been caught by Miss Maud this morning. But if she had been challenged, she would have been prepared with an answer. The master had called for tea or brandy or something. Her quick tongue was one thing the master enjoyed.

Anyway, what was Miss Maud, fully dressed, doing at that hour? She was a chip off the old block, no mistake.

"Cora!" The voice bellowed again.

Cora tapped at the door and opened it to the loud "Come in!" As if he had never set eyes on her before, Sir James gave his orders.

"Hot water. Quickly. I want my breakfast on the table in fifteen minutes. And see that Miss Maud is wakened. That fire has gone out. Doesn't anyone know how to light a fire? Well, don't dawdle there. Be off with you!"

Cora's cheeks began to burn much more brightly than the sullen fire she had lit an hour ago. But when the master began to laugh, looking at her with his bold, bright eyes, enjoying the way he could upset her, she felt the tremors going over her again. It was no use; she was his slave. Bad, wicked, whatever Cook or Mabel would think her, she would go on having this desperate secret life until the master tired of her. As he would . . . Although sometimes she permitted herself to daydream that Lady Lucie would die and Sir James would declare their love to the world. Then it would be her ringing the bell and Mabel having to answer it. What a lark!

Sir James liked an ample breakfast. Grilled kidneys, eggs and bacon, kippers or kedgeree, plenty of hot toast, muffins, rolls, and a large pot of black coffee. He spent exactly an hour over it, reading the *Times* as he ate and making comments on the news to Maud, who always joined him at breakfast. His wife never came down before midday or midafternoon. They she lay on the drawing-room sofa until it was time for her to retire upstairs for an early night. Few words passed between her and her husband. A "Good morning, my dear" and a "Good night, sleep well," accompanied by a cool kiss on the brow. Sometimes, when Sir James was in an affable mood, he might comment on a becoming tea gown. Most of the time he behaved as if he didn't see his wife, as if she were a lifeless doll lying on the sofa, with neither ears to listen nor a tongue with which to speak.

A man like Sir James, Cook had been heard to remark, wouldn't have much time for delicate females. Strong, healthy men didn't like illness, didn't understand it. Which was a tragedy for poor Lady Lucie. But Cook, who had been with the family since Miss Maud was a small child, had her own idea that Lady Lucie didn't care for such rude health in men either. So perhaps it wasn't such a tragedy after all. And Cora, if she wanted to keep her position, had better keep her mouth shut about the master's occasional disappearances overnight and about the kind of young women who turned up to pose for his large allegorical paintings. An artist had to have models half-undressed. It was the fashion. The pictures sold for handsome prices and paid the servants' wages. And never mind if the creatures couldn't speak the King's English.

However, Cora had no need to be shocked. Those models were only extras. Miss Maud was Sir James' favorite model. The poor child must be thoroughly weary of sitting so many times. In a way, it was her bad fortune that she was so paintable. One of her child portraits hung in a ducal mansion, one was in the Long Island home of an American millionaire. It was said that Sir James could now charge three thousand guineas for a portrait, but his fame was as much due to his daughter's beauty as to his own skill.

Lately, however, he had abandoned painting her in that ravishing fashion of long-hanging red hair and sparkling emerald eyes. Since she had reached the age of seventeen, his portraits had become curiously prim and virginal, the abundant hair held back with a velvet band that resembled a coif, the expression modest and spiritual.

His current work was called "The Virgin," and it was intended to be shown in the summer exhibition of the Royal Academy. Miss Maud, far from wearing the rich colors she loved, was clad in a long white gown tied at the waist with a gold cord. A single lily was held in meekly folded hands. This lily, hothouse grown, was delivered every day by Harrods delivery van. It was to be hoped the supply did not run out before the portrait was finished. Everyone, including Cook, who had had a surreptitious peep at the half-finished work when the master was out, agreed that, although it was good, it was too pure and religious. If anyone was least suited to play the part of a meek virgin, it was the high-spirited Miss Maud. But some people (this rumor came from Lady Lucie's personal maid,

Bertha) believed that Sir James secretly couldn't bear the thought of his daughter's marrying. It was unnatural, the way he was so possessive of her. Although it was true that he had been much flattered by the courtship of the viscount last year, he had declared he had been only relieved that Maud had spurned him, because she was so young. There was plenty of time for even more eligible suitors to present themselves. He talked a great deal about the kind of man Maud would marry. It was his favorite subject.

Yet hanging that virginal picture in the Academy could be seen as a warning off. Or so Bertha said. But Bertha was apt to catch the fancies of her poor mistress.

Maud's mornings followed the routine that had existed ever since she had been a child. When she was dressed and before she went down to breakfast, she must pay her mother a visit. Nanny used to drag her reluctantly into the bedroom, whispering crossly, "Now, Miss Maud! You must learn to have thought for others. Your poor Mamma lying there. Kiss her nicely and don't fidget." But like her father, Maud had a distaste for illness, and she had always had to force herself to kiss Mamma's pale cheek, shutting her eyes tightly as she did so. Mamma made her think of fragile short-lived things like moths or fading flowers, crumpled and edged with the brown of decay, or a china doll with her big, infinitely tired eyes. Or of a limpet, because she would hold Maud's hand in such a tight damp clasp.

Although she was always beautifully dressed, in spotless nightgowns and bed wraps or graceful, ruffled tea gowns, and smelled of perfume, there was often an underlying odor of a damp sick unexercised body.

Maud, expected to adore her patient, brave mother, suffered shame and remorse at her revulsion. From an early age she had known that Papa felt exactly the same, this knowledge making a further bond between them. But whereas Papa could quickly escape from the sickroom, pleading engagements, she was expected to stay and amuse the invalid for an interminable half hour. In the evening, before supper, the time was increased to an hour. Her day's activities had to be related; she must show Mamma how well she could read from her latest storybook, or sing to her, or recite a poem.

Sometimes she sulked and was soundly spanked by Nanny in the nursery later. Sometimes a kind and generous mood made her try to make Mamma laugh. Then Bertha and Nanny clapped their hands, and the claustrophobic room with the hot fire and the dim lamplight (Mamma could not bear bright lights—perhaps, Maud was to reflect when she was older, because they would show too clearly the worn, lined face) seemed a triumphant place. Miss Maud could woo a lark out of the sky when she pleased to do so, Nanny admitted.

Last year, her coming-out year, had been particularly trying as far as these visits to the sickroom were concerned, for Mamma had wanted to hear every smallest detail of her daughter's activities. After the many late nights at balls, the endless number of luncheon parties, and the attendance at all the right events—Ascot, Henley, the Royal Opera, tedious cricket matches at Lords, the Fourth of June at Eton, the Oxford and Cambridge boat race, country-house weekends—Maud was frequently so exhausted that she almost fell asleep at her mother's bedside.

It had been a triumphant year, when she had discovered the powerful weapon of her beauty and had kept her heart comfortably untouched. The attentive young men had flattered her; she had acquired a reputation for being a cruel flirt, but no one had seemed to her more than a pale shadow of the kind of man Papa was, with his splendid presence, his amusing sophisticated outrageous conversation, his enormous vitality.

Lady Lucie's middle-aged Cousin Harriet, who had been summoned from Shropshire to organize Maud's season and act as her chaperone, said bluntly that James had ruined the girl. All that taking her about to his disreputable art gatherings when she was a child had made her precocious, disobedient, and worldly. It was Cousin Harriet's belief that if they managed to marry her without a scandal it would be a minor miracle.

But Cousin Harriet was impossibly old-fashioned. She still believed in the Victorian idea that young people should be seen but not heard. Maud was a chatterbox and apt to speak with the uninhibited deplorable freedom of her father. Cousin Harriet could only express profound relief that the girl had behaved impeccably at her presentation. The queen had actually had a short conversation with Maud about her famous father. He was to be invited to paint one of the hordes of great-grandchildren of the queen's late mother-in-law. Maud had made a beautiful curtsey. She had confessed that she had been more pleased by that brief conversation than she had been by any of the other excitements of her season or, indeed, by any of her offers of marriage.

On this morning after the Holland House ball, Mamma was particularly avid for information.

"I want to hear everything. Did the king and queen make an appearance?"

"Yes, but only for a little while. The queen looked beautiful, as she always does. She's awfully stately and royal, even if she is dreadfully dull, as they say. But the king is really much too fat. His face is purple. I'm quite sure he'll explode one day."

"Were you presented to him?"

"Yes, I was, because he wanted to dance with me. And do you know who looked awfully put out, that notorious Mrs. Keppel. She didn't need to be jealous; it's absolutely no joke, dancing with such a stout old gentleman."

Maud prattled on because her mother expected it of her. The truth or a little exaggeration of the truth, it didn't matter so long as that hungry white face was satisfied.

"After that I strolled in the orangery with a young man called Bertie something. What a lot of Berties and Peregrines and Reggies there are. I wish I could meet someone who was plain Jack or Fred."

"Darling, you do wander from the point. Who was this Bertie, and what did he have to say?"

"Almost nothing, but it was very romantic in the orangery. The oranges were like little yellow moons. I wish you could see Holland House, Mamma. It's very grand. Lady Ilchester told me about a white heron she saw fly over the garden last evening. She says a great variety of birds come to the woods, although now there are so many houses being built in the vicinity, the nightingales seem to have been frightened away."

"Never mind about the birds," Lady Lucie said impatiently. "Didn't this young man Bertie put his name in your dance program?"

"No. Our meeting was accidental. Accidental meetings are much the most fun, don't you think? Actually I had another one later with a young man called Guy Beauchamp. There, you see, I did discover his name."

Lady Lucie stirred on her ruffled pillows, not missing her daughter's deliberately airy tone.

"Who is he?"

"I don't know. How could I inquire into his background on such a chance acquaintance? But he did tell me he was a poet. Didn't you think meeting a poet rather a romantic thing to happen when you were a girl?"

"I never actually met one, that I can remember. At least not when I was a girl. I always thought poets were penniless and rather dissolute, like Lord Byron. But I doubt if Lady Ilchester would invite a penniless young man to her ball. Anyway, I think you were rather indiscreet to walk in the orangery with these strange young men. I am sure Papa didn't approve."

Maud sighed. "I do wish Papa were not so determined that I should marry a title." Then her eyes sparkled mischievously as she put her chin in the air and said in a high affected voice, "Lord Percival Snuffington Woffington of Woffington Towers is about to take the hand of Maud Lucie and embalm it forever in his musty old mansion."

"I don't think that's very funny, Maud. But I agree that your father is developing a greatly inflated idea of your importance. You have to remember that you are only the daughter of an artist and a poor silly invalid."

Maud bent over to give her mother a kiss.

"Actually," she said, "it's Papa who steals the limelight from me. I believe more people looked at him than at the king or the queen. I teased him about it. He really does look exactly as a famous artist should. I'm always so proud of him."

"It's time you grew out of this habit of adoration of your father," Lady Lucie said sharply. "It's rather childish, you know. As soon as you fall in love, you'll realize that. Now why are you in such a hurry to go?"

"Because I'm starving for my breakfast and Papa expects me in the studio at ten o'clock, as usual. Dancing all night is no excuse."

Lady Lucie frowned.

"I must speak to your father. It's high time he stopped painting you so often. He will be turning you into nothing but an artist's model."

"And I'll still adore him, whatever you say," Maud said serenely. "Even when I do fall in love."

When Maud had gone, Lady Lucie sank back with her all-too-familiar feeling of exhaustion. When had it begun, this fancy that Maud with her lively vitality took all the life from the room in just the way that James did?

The sterile quietness settled back. There was not even the sound of traffic, since it had been decided, on moving to the house in Melbury Square, that Lady Lucie's room should be at the back, overlooking the narrow, walled garden, away from the street noises, where she could hear the birds. Maud kept talking of the owls she heard in the tall oak trees in the Square gardens. They were too shy to come to this little strip of garden, but robins, finches, blackbirds, and the incorrigible sparrows flitted about here. Today, however, Bertha had closed the windows because of a cold east wind, and the lively chirpings were almost inaudible, almost a part of the silence.

Someone might realize sometimes, Lady Lucie thought petulantly, that the strident voices of street hawkers and organ grinders or the rattling of tradesmen's vans were necessary reminders that life still went on. Nevertheless, it was true that she was peculiarly sensitive to noise. Even the sharp tremolo of the muffin man's bell in the late afternoon, when she was ensconced by the drawing-room fire, sent her hands to her ears. And if Cora rattled the teacups when she brought in the tea tray, she was scolded for her clumsiness. Cora —one didn't quite like that girl. There was a sly boldness about her.

But servants were like that nowadays, or so Bertha and Nanny said. Badly trained, untidy, with a regrettable tendency to answer back. And their morals didn't bear speaking of. Times were sadly different from what they had been when the old queen was alive, Bertha repeatedly said. Everything had changed since she died, as if she had taken the virtue out of England. Well, you had only to remember the life the Prince of Wales had led. Hushed up, of course, now that he was on the throne. But what a world it was for a young girl to come out in, especially one as high-spirited as Miss

Maud, who didn't need any encouragement in naughty behavior.

Bertha might shake her head over Maud and Nanny defend her, but Lady Lucie understood her daughter all too well. She was simply a replica of her father. They both had that restless love for life and action, movement, talk, events, people. Lady Lucie could only grasp weakly at the edge of their activities, learning from long experience not to inquire too closely into her husband's, but still trying to keep her daughter under some kind of control.

Maud had grown simply too lovely since her season had given her polish and poise. Or was it the constant sitting for portraits that made her fall into those unconsciously graceful poses? James was quite insane, the way he painted the girl over and over.

But this was an old grievance that had been the subject of too many quarrels for too long. In vain, Lady Lucie had tried to get over it, or at least put it out of her mind. Since she was an invalid, it was natural that James should have taken over Maud's upbringing. But even had she not been confined to her couch, Lady Lucie suspected that the same manner of living would have prevailed.

James, like the Pre-Raphaelite painters whom he professed to disdain, had a fetish about feminine beauty. She was all too aware that when her own had begun to fade, in pregnancy, he had lost interest in her. Before that, he had painted her almost as obsessively as he was later to paint his daughter. He had said she had a delicate dryad beauty, and she had thought he married her for love. Eventually, however, she had had to agree with the suspicion her family had had from the beginning, that James Lucie, the good-looking, talented son of a humble potter from Staffordshire, was a snob of the first water. Lady Lucie came from an excellent old Somerset family. Her breeding and social standing could be nothing but an asset to an ambitious young man. Although even at that time James Lucie was beginning to be talked of as a portrait painter, his wife's dryad beauty, as he called it, had been far from his first reason for marrying her, but it had been a pleasant bonus while it lasted.

Which it had for a tragically short time. Recovery from a difficult pregnancy and a badly managed confinement was seriously delayed by Lady Lucie's discovery that her husband had already enjoyed his first mistress. He hadn't had enough patience to wait for her to get well. Shocked and disillusioned, she turned her face to the pillow and decided that she would not get well. She would accept and cherish the pain in her bones, which the doctor called a rheumatic gout, and her prolonged weakness.

She could not even turn to her baby, for the child was already possessed and utterly adored by her father. He saw so much of himself in this lively little creature that his ego was constantly satisfied. He worshiped vitality (a characteristic his wife was now permanently to lack) and shouted with laughter when the baby, precociously realizing her power, had a tantrum. He undermined everyone's authority and was never more pleased than when Maud was perpetually at his heels, an adoring shadow to such a splendid giant.

When his sentimental portrait of her, with her baby head bent over a daisy chain, was the picture of the year in the Royal Academy's summer exhibition, his arrogant satisfaction would have been trying enough even to a loving, sympathetic wife. Lady Lucie was no longer a loving wife, and far from sympathetic. It was at that time that she realized she hated her handsome, virile, egotistical, ambitious, and false husband.

He was vulgar, she thought. How strange that she hadn't realized it long ago. Vulgarity was even less forgivable than infidelity.

From then on, she sank into chronic invalidism, not, however, forgoing the pleasure of consulting new doctors and experimenting with new medicines. And exacting loyal and dedicated service from Bertha and Nanny, both of whom had been with her since Maud's birth. And using a subtle form of blackmail on her husband whenever she thought he deserved it. She had grown extraordinarily acute at recognizing the absent expression, the relaxed air suggesting recent satisfaction in love, the greater affability toward herself. It was then that, in her vague faraway voice, she demanded a new negligee or perhaps a piece of jewelry or a bibelot. She enjoyed collecting miniatures and small enameled patch- or snuffboxes. She imagined she was living a difficult life as intelligently as possible. Sometimes, in the early and dark hours of the morning when she couldn't sleep, she had moments of clarity when she fancied she had been running away from her too virile husband from the first night of their marriage. But this was not true, of course. It was he who had willfully and deliberately escaped her.

With Maud, however, it should be different. A daughter should belong more to her mother than to her father, especially when the mother was an invalid in need of love and affection.

So the unequal battle had begun in Maud's childhood and still continued. The last quarrel had been only a week ago, when Maud had refused an invitation to breakfast at the Duchess of Devonshire's because she had an unbreakable appointment to sit for her father every morning.

"James, it's you who wants her well married. How can this happen if she has to refuse invitations like this? And only for a sitting for a portrait. What sort of an excuse is that?"

"An unassailable one, my dear Lydia. Don't you realize pictures have to be submitted to the academy within the next month? My portrait isn't half-finished."

"Would the summer exhibition utterly collapse if there weren't a new portrait of Miss Maud Lucie?"

"No, my dear." James was determined not to lose his temper. He wore his consciously tolerant expression but paced about her room in the restless soft-footed way that made her feel diminished and feeble. "But I can safely say the public would be disappointed. Greatly disappointed."

"And what are you going to do when Maud is married? What husband is going to want her constantly shown off to the public?"

"Whoever marries her is going to be damned proud of her, if I am allowed a guess."

"You're ruining her, James. You're making her so full of her own importance she'll be unbearable."

"A touch of vanity never did a woman any harm."

"Just listen to her talk of the young men she despises."

"Quite right. Most of them are congenital oafs."

"No one's good enough for her, of course."

"No one is, in my eyes."

"When I was young, modesty was considered a girl's best asset."

The red-gold head, infuriatingly untouched by gray, was held at its most arrogant angle. "Modesty. An appalling disease. Not one even you suffered from, my dear." The cruel blue eyes held her. Another maddening thing was that she had never quite been able to forget how they had looked when full of tenderness. She sometimes glimpsed that look still, though never now for her. For Maud always, sometimes, incautiously, for another woman.

Her mouth tightened. "If you're going to stay, at least sit down. You make my head ache, pacing about like that."

"Then I'll be off." He stopped to give her his usual quick perfunctory kiss on the brow. "You know what's the matter with you, my love? You're jealous of your own daughter. Not that I blame you. A daughter like Maud." He laughed in high good humor. He had had the last word. It would compensate him for his enforced fifteen minutes in the sickroom. Poor Sir James Lucie, that splendid man, shackled to an invalid wife. Did he ever wish she would divorce him?

But no, he couldn't be so reckless. It would damage his reputation too much, even in these more relaxed days of King Edward's reign. It might take Maud from him.

And she—could she face the failure of being a divorced wife? That would possibly be more intolerable than her present existence. So she would accept the gift he would presently toss her and exhibit it carelessly at her next at home. "My husband spoils his silly useless wife ridiculously."

Lady Lucie rang for her maid.

"Bertha, bring me some fresh coffee. My husband has exhausted me, as usual. All that good health! It makes me feel depleted!"

"Yes, my lady, I understand."

"And draw the curtains. No, don't quite shut out the sun. Just a little less of that dazzling light."

"Very well, my lady. Are you going to rest?"

"Rest, rest, rest! Sometimes I think none of you know another word."

"Yes, it does get monotonous, doesn't it, my lady?"

Bertha was soothing, feather-pillow soothing, but sometimes Lady Lucie wanted more than an echo. What *did* she want?

She stirred fretfully.

"Who is about this morning? Have you and Nanny made any more acquaintances in the Square?"

"We haven't exactly made acquaintances, my lady. We've only passed the time of day with one or two. Pritchett from Number Eleven. Imagine, she has to do that whole house, with only a daily charwoman. They can't afford more help. The girls do their own room, of course, and some of the cooking. Mrs. Beauchamp pretends they like doing it. She's the grand one I told you about. The duchess of the Square she's called, for all she's got no money. She's spent most of what her husband left on her son, sending him to Oxford and then abroad. It don't seem fair that the son always gets the lion's share, does it?"

"That's the fashion, Bertha. It's how men like it to be, naturally. What is this pampered young man to do now he's had his education and his traveling?"

"He's just returned home to go into the city, into his uncle's bank. Rather a comedown, I should think, to be just a bank clerk."

"Perhaps he's to inherit the bank."

"Well, they do say the uncle won't put up with any nonsense, and that he's a bit of a miser, too. Fancy, with all those vaults full of money."

"Other people's money, Bertha."

"A good lot of his own, too, I'll be bound. They do say the family's all on her side."

"On whose side?"

"Mrs. Beauchamp's. The husband was only a major. Died fighting in some foreign place."

"Perhaps I'll decide to make her acquaintance," Lady Lucie murmured. She could sympathize with a lonely widow. "What are the girls like?"

"I fancy Miss Maud has spoken to them. They're quite ordinary, I'd say. One of them plays the piano. They're to have a season this year. Forgive me, my lady. I'm gossiping, and you've told me not to."

"No, go on, Bertha. It amuses me. Since we're to live here for the next few years, one ought to know something of one's neighbors."

Bertha needed no encouragement to go on. She had suddenly remembered that another young man had arrived in the Square, the great-nephew of the elderly colonel in Number 9.

"He's down from Oxford, where he was studying for the bar. He was in the Boer War and has a scar down one cheek. But they do say he's still quite handsome. Ninian Spencer. It's nice for his uncle to have him calling. Some company besides that smelly old dog. Then there's Miss Calcott in Number Four, been reduced to taking a lodger. She pretends the lady is an old family friend, but everyone knows she goes to business in a milliner's shop in Knightsbridge."

"Bertha, where do you hear all this gossip?"

"I expect my ears stick out, my lady," Bertha answered imperturbably. "I have a talent for it, Nanny says. You'll see all these people for yourself one day. When it's nice and warm, Nanny and I mean to take you into the Square gardens. We'll wrap you up warm, and you can take tea in the sunshine."

Lady Lucie sighed. "That seems very ambitious."

"Not a bit of it. It was the first thing I said when we moved here. Now my lady can get outdoors. You couldn't have sat in that sooty garden in Holborn, could you? But here it's different. Fresh and green. It'll be ever so nice. Miss Maud will come, too."

"Miss Maud has a great many affairs of her own. Too many to spare much time for a sick woman. Do you realize she danced with His Majesty last night? So we must put up with a few airs and graces. Don't get your bossy look, Bertha. Now go and bring me my coffee."

Chapter 3

AT NUMBER 11, there was no question of the mistress of the house not presiding over the breakfast table, nor was anyone, even the latest stay-out, excused from attendance.

Mrs. Beauchamp wore a dark-brown morning dress with stiffly starched collar and cuffs. Her gray hair was parted in the center and pulled back into a severely practical bun, her capable hands wielded the coffee jug, her observant eyes missed no aspect of her three assembled children.

Daisy hadn't combed her hair properly. As usual, she had lingered too long in bed and then had had to fling on her clothes without thought to her appearance. She had slovenly habits that must be corrected. She was also too plump. Her waist would need to shrink by two inches before she looked even passably well in the new season's fashions.

One had no complaints about the neatness of Honor's appearance, only about her absent, pensive look, which her mother was beginning to find decidedly irritating. What was wrong with her, always in a dream? She wasn't an adolescent; she was nineteen. If she wanted to find a husband this year, she would have to acquire a bit more vivacity and spirit. Like that Maud Lucie? No, that was going to the other extreme. Although Mrs. Beauchamp, who was essentially honest, had to admit that her dissatisfaction with her daughters this morning arose from the glimpse she had caught of Sir James Lucie (a spectacular, but surely rather a vulgar man) and his daughter leaving for the Holland House ball the previous evening. She had been returning, with Honor and Daisy, from a dull evening of cards just as the carriage stopped at Number 7, and the coachman climbed down to open the door for the young lady and her father. One of the streetlights had shone directly on Maud, illumining the famous red hair that had adorned so many portraits.

Sir James Lucie, seeing the approaching ladies, had given a deep bow. Maud had waved a friendly hand. Mrs. Beauchamp had nodded stiffly and hurried her daughters along—Honor elegantly slim, but exasperatingly retiring in manner, Daisy like a bouncing rubber ball.

Style was the thing these wretched girls must acquire.

And Guy, her good-looking son? He would have to realize that he couldn't make a habit of coming in at daybreak without disfiguring marks of dissipation soon beginning to mar his healthy young face. He would have to mend his ways next week when he put on the uniform of a respectable businessman. A bowler hat, a stiff white collar, striped trousers, a furled umbrella. Mrs. Beauchamp permitted herself the slightest of fond smiles. Guy had been an anxiety and a disappointment, failing his degree at Oxford and then spending too much of his inheritance, indulging in his passion for wandering about the world. He had no sooner returned from Europe than he had a hankering to go to the East and become a professional explorer like that scandalous Sir Richard Burton of the last century.

However, he did now seem to realize that sort of thing must remain a dream, and he had promised to settle down in his uncle's bank. One had had to make it clear to him that he had already had the lion's share of his father's modest estate, and something must, in all fairness, be done for the girls. They simply must come out this season. Mrs. Beauchamp was quite resigned to selling her last good piece of jewelry, a small coronet of diamonds which had been her mother's, to finance the necessarily extensive wardrobes the girls would require for their season. Although it was a pity about the coronet. Both Honor and Daisy should have worn it at their respective weddings. But how were they to have weddings if they hadn't a season? So the diamonds must go.

"Cares of the world, Mamma?" Guy's words made Mrs. Beauchamp abandon her obsessive thoughts.

"What did you say?"

"On your brow. Did you sleep badly?"

"I slept well, until dawn," Mrs. Beauchamp replied significantly.

Guy sighed. "Oh, lord, did you hear me come in? But I told you it would be a late affair. It was a celebration, after all. Have you read my poems yet, Mamma?"

"Yes, dear. They're very nice."

"Whew! That's damning with faint praise."

"I've told you, I don't understand modern poetry. Indeed, the only poet I have ever cared for is Tennyson, and I hardly think—"

"I'm another Tennyson?" Guy finished. He leaned forward, his face animated. "Speaking of Tennyson, I met the most gorgeous female on my way home this morning. Maud. Who is Maud?"

Daisy exclaimed, "Maud Lucie? Guy, did you really? Where?"

"In the gardens."

"In the dark, this morning! Whatever was she doing?"

"Taking her dog for a walk. She had been to the Holland House ball, she said."

"You talked to her?" Mrs. Beauchamp said.

"Why not? I thought she was a ghost, at first. One couldn't resist attempting a conversation with a ghost."

Daisy giggled. "Guy, you are absurd. But isn't she beautiful?"

"It was too dark to see clearly, but I guessed so."

"She's a picturesque young woman," Mrs. Beauchamp said repressively. "She takes after her father. One hopes she won't become as flamboyant as he is."

"How odd to take her dog out walking in the dark," Honor murmured.

"I would call that courage, not flamboyance," Daisy said. "What did you talk about, Guy?"

"None of your business, Miss Inquisitive."

"Those people are already changing the character of the Square," Mrs. Beauchamp said disapprovingly. "Carriages arriving at all hours, and those common-looking young women who call themselves artist's models. Not to mention the artists themselves, who are frequently the worse for drink if one can judge by their gait. As for Sir James Lucie, I can hear his voice clearly from my bedroom window when he speaks in his back garden. I'm afraid he's quite a vulgar sort of person. Everyone expresses sympathy for his poor wife."

"So you won't be leaving a card, Mamma?" Guy said.

"Oh, but she has. Haven't you, Mamma?" Daisy was certainly too ingenuous, too lacking in finesse, Mrs. Beauchamp thought crossly. "After the little princess went to Number Seven for a sitting for her portrait."

"Aha! Royalty!"

"The whole Square goggled out of windows. After all, it isn't every day that one of Queen Victoria's great-grandchildren visits here."

Mrs. Beauchamp dabbed her napkin to her lips.

"Daisy, why must you be such a rattle? Of course I have left a card, Guy. It was only common courtesy. I understand Lady Lucie is a charming person, but an invalid, unfortunately. She never leaves the house. The daughter has been too much under the influence of her father. She came out last season, but she didn't succeed in getting a husband. Some people say the father is too ambitious for her, and others that the girl is simply too fast."

"I would be fast, too, if I looked the way she does," Daisy said. "She doesn't have to care what anybody says."

"That's what you think, miss," Mrs. Beauchamp said tartly. "I may be old-fashioned, but I still maintain that a girl's good reputation is her most valuable possession. Looks or not. Walking in the garden in the dark and engaging in conversation with strange young men—"

"'Co-ome into the garden, Maud,'" Daisy sang under her breath.

Mrs. Beauchamp rang the bell sharply and rose.

"Come along, we've dawdled long enough. Pritchett wants to clear away. Guy, you haven't forgotten your uncle is expecting you at eleven? You know he doesn't excuse unpunctuality. Will you travel by bus or the underground?"

"I thought a cab—oh, very well, I expect I must begin the way I have to go on. I'll descend into the bowels of the earth."

"It would be much quicker," Mrs. Beauchamp said. "Honor, where are you going?"

"To practice, Mamma."

"There'll be time for that later. I want you and Daisy to do some shopping for me. And, I must mention this, could you play with a little less vigor? Miss Calcott was complaining yesterday that it goes right through her walls."

"I'm sorry, Mamma. The Beethoven Concerto needs—"

"Then you must play quieter pieces, dear."

Honor, about to answer, changed her mind and gave the smallest of shrugs.

"Anyway, there's no longer going to be time for all that piano playing. You know how much sewing we have to do. Miss Lavender is bringing your ball gowns for fitting this afternoon. Guy, isn't it nice, the girls have been asked to Laura Ponsonby's ball?"

"Ponsonby? Laura? Not the one with the squint?"

"I will not be made fun of!" Mrs. Beauchamp said sharply. "Laura has grown into a charming young woman, and her mother has taken a house in Belgrave Square for the season. So be kind enough to make a note of that date in your engagement book."

"I wonder if *Maud* will be there," Daisy hissed in Guy's ear. "Shall Honor and I find out?"

"Can you?" he whispered back eagerly.

"Of course. Apart from asking Laura—and she does have a squint still—Honor and I always pass the time of day with Maud when we meet her. She's very friendly." Daisy pulled him out of their mother's hearing. "Don't take any notice of Mamma; she's longing to get inside that house. She's heard about the murals in the studio."

Guy roared with laughter.

"Honestly, Daisy—"

"Well, no, to tell the truth it's Lady Lucie she wants to meet. She hears she's very well-connected. Now that you've talked to Maud, I expect we'll be invited any minute."

"Do you think so? You little minx, you're having me on."

"The irresistible Guy Beauchamp? Of course Maud will want you. She's a man-eater. Or so the gossip goes." Daisy nibbled at Guy's ear. "I only wish I were a man-eater, too. It must be so amusing."

By this time all the Square was awake. Dr. Burns, in Number 10, had already done two morning calls and, sending his coachman off for breakfast, was swallowing a quick cup of strong tea before beginning his morning surgery. He had been called only once to his new neighbor, Lady Lucie, when she had fancied herself suffering from a heart spasm, and there had not been time to send for her own doctor from Knightsbridge. He had asked her what she had eaten for dinner and had said bluntly, "Lobster soup followed by roast duckling is not to be recommended for a lady in your sedentary state."

"It was the smallest helping of each, Doctor."

"Enough to give you wind round your heart."

"Wind!"

"That's all it is. Your heart is as sound as a bell, and the pain has nothing to do with your rheumatic condition."

He wouldn't be called there again, he imagined, although some of these pampered invalids liked plain speaking. They didn't get enough of it. No one ever told them the truth. They fed on their own fears and their emotional insecurities and their carefully hidden loneliness. Their family escaped from them, and their servants either fawned on them or robbed them.

All the same, Dr. Burns suspected an underlying tough fiber in Lady Lucie. She might even, from sheer determination, outlast that tower of physical strength, her husband.

There were not many of this kind of patient in Dr. Burns' practice. This was the unfashionable end of Kensington, too far from the palace, the gardens, and the more stately squares. Dr. Burns had chosen it deliberately, with a shrewd sense of balance. He would acquire a few affluent patients, such as Lady Lucie, who would pay his bills, allowing him time for his real work among the genuinely sick, who could not afford to pay him at all. The people who lived in the workmen's cottages in narrow unfashionable streets or in rooms over stables in the many rows of mews. Washwomen with rheumatism in their fingers, bakers with flour in their lungs, children on poor diets who developed measles, diphtheria, rickets, consumption, or any of a dozen other serious diseases. Old people who could no longer work because of their bronchitis or their tired hearts and who were terrified of the workhouse. People for whom one square meal a day would perform wonders. Old Joe, the muffin man, doing the same round for thirty years, but now having to curtail the distance because of his gouty leg. Miss Lavender, professional dressmaker, suffering from failing eyesight, finding it more and more difficult to thread a needle and refusing to admit it; otherwise, what lady would engage her to make a new gown? Tom Bowles, cabby, suffering a spinal injury when his horse fell on an icy street, and with eight children to support. Mrs. Price-Jones who kept an idiot child in an upstairs room at Number 15 on the opposite side of the Square, allowing no one but the doctor to see the poor, snuffling moon-faced creature, and him not often. Children were afraid to pass the house in case that pathetic white face looked out. They thought it was a ghost.

Human tragedies. They were the people who earned Dr. Burns' sympathy and willing help. In his irascible way, Colonel Spencer at Number 9 earned it too, because he refused to indulge in self-pity. The colonel suffered from an old war wound, which became inflamed in damp and chilly weather, ached infuriatingly, and affected his temper. He slept badly and was not overjoyed with his new neighbors. The sound of Sir James Lucie's high-stepping grays in the early hours of the morning woke him from his difficult slumber, and the famous artist himself, flamboyant and conceited, was the kind of man the colonel heartily disliked. However, remembering what it was to be a gay dog, he had a more tolerant eye for the daughter. She was a high-stepper, like her father's grays. He enjoyed passing the time of day with her when they met in the Square gardens, he exercising his elderly spaniel and she with that bundle of nonsense she called Han. A pretty woman and a silly lapdog were an irresistible combination, however. The colonel had hopes that an encounter with Miss Maud Lucie would interest his nephew, Ninian.

Seven years ago Ninian Spencer had been wounded at Spion Kop, that disastrous battle before the tide of the South African War had turned in Britain's favor. One side of his face had been left scarred. He affected not to care. Some women liked ugly devils, he said. Beauty and the beast. He had made up his mind to send in his papers and leave the army.

His uncle had suggested that he might like to take up politics, as his young friend Winston Churchill had done. But Ninian had said his damaged face might scare off his constituents. In any case, he hadn't the necessary flamboyant personality. He had made up his mind to go to Oxford and then read for the bar. Later, when he was able to support himself, he would make a stab at becoming a serious writer.

Now he had achieved his first intention and had been established in chambers in Lincolns Inn for some time. He was still unmarried and secretive about his affairs with women. He must have some, damn it, the old colonel thought. He couldn't still be unduly sensitive about that fading scar down his right cheek. It was now the kind of disfigurement that women found attractive.

The advent of Sir James and Lady Lucie to the Square, with their dashing daughter, had roused an unsuspecting propensity for matchmaking in the colonel. Surely Ninian's reserve would soon be put to ruin and rout by that green-eyed beauty. He must persuade the boy to give up his chambers and come here to live. Or at least to stay for periods of time.

Besides, he wasn't feeling quite himself these days. He intended leaving Ninian the house in Melbury Square and his bit of capital. It wasn't much, but it would enable the boy to support a wife. Lately he had regretted not marrying. Queen and country had taken up too much of his time, and in the end, what reward did they give one? A fairly miserly pension, a row of medals, and an aching wound.

All the same, it was a damned shame that go of fever had made him miss riding with his company in the charge of the Light Brigade when he had been a fresh, keen young subaltern. It had been the great disappointment of his life. He still had a recurring dream about that memorable day and found himself sitting up in bed, shouting, "Charge!" whenever the sound of Sir James Lucie's carriage in the small hours clattered into his dream.

Perhaps living in such close juxtaposition with one's neighbors made thought carry. For at that moment, Maud Lucie, bursting into the dining room where her father sat at breakfast, was herself reflecting on the desirability of improving on her acquaintance with certain people in the Square, one in particular.

"Good morning, Papa. I'm sorry I'm late. The night was so short. The birds were singing before I fell asleep."

"And what kept you awake? Thoughts about some swain at the ball?"

"Oh, no, I didn't meet anyone there I would waste time dreaming about," Maud sighed, looking at her father with large innocent eyes. "I wonder if I shall ever fall in love."

"Time is speeding by, of course," Papa said. "Come and let me see if you have any gray hairs."

"Oh, you are a tease. You haven't any yourself!"

"I advise you not to look too closely." Papa ran his hand through his luxuriant golden hair, of which he was justifiably proud. Then he looked at his watch. "Hurry up, my girl. You have exactly fifteen minutes to have your breakfast."

"Oh, goodness! And I'm starving."

Maud helped herself liberally to kidneys and bacon and sat down. Presently, giving her father her most irresistible smile, she said casually, "Papa, don't you think we should give an at home to entertain our neighbors? Otherwise, they will think we are stuffy and stand-offish."

"So we are."

"No, Papa. You may be, but I'm not. I want to be friendly with the whole world."

"So who is it you particularly want to meet?"

Papa knew her too well. How would she ever keep a secret from him?

"There are two girls about my age at Number Eleven. I see them go by with their shopping baskets."

"And since when have you been interested in young ladies? Or is this part of your scheme to be friendly with the whole world?"

"You don't know how I've longed for a close friend of my own sex," Maud said earnestly. "I've never had one. You made me stay at home and have governesses instead of going to school. It would be different if I had had a sister. I passionately envy Honor and Daisy Beauchamp having each other. Of course, I may not care for them on close acquaintance—"

"Or they may not care for you," Papa said dryly. "I fancy the Misses Honor and Daisy will find you rather outside their suburban orbit. I have made you a woman of the world, haven't I, my angel? You haven't given Papa his morning kiss."

"But we could have a party, couldn't we?" Maud persisted.

"A tea party with your mother, certainly. I will beg to be excused."

"No, no, Papa, a proper reception."

Papa's golden eyebrows rose.

"Do I remember hearing that the Misses Beauchamp have a brother?"

"I believe they do have one who has just returned home from abroad." Maud's voice was admirably airy. "But he isn't the only member of the opposite sex living in the square. There's that crusty old Colonel Spencer. Han has formed a passionate affection for his fat elderly spaniel."

"As long as his mistress hasn't formed one for the spaniel's master."

Maud gave her delighted ripple of laughter. "Papa, you are absurd. Of course I haven't. Nor have I for the colonel's nephew, who has a scar down one side of his face and looks rather forbidding. Nor for Dr. Burns and various other people. I just think it would be pleasant to be on speaking terms with one's neighbors."

"And be invited back to endless dull functions?"

"You can be excused. They will know you have important affairs to attend to."

Papa took out his watch.

"Ten minutes to ten. Do you intend to eat your breakfast or not? No, I will not do anything so suburban as giving an at home for the neighbors. But you have my permission to judiciously select six or seven people to be included in the guest list for our next reception."

"May I? Oh, thank you, Papa!"

"Judiciously, I said."

"Yes, Papa."

"And because we are now living in a small square, it doesn't mean we have to love our neighbors, or live in their pockets, or become in any way personally involved with them. Prim young women with shopping baskets, indeed! They're hardly your sort of people. Have they ever danced with the King of England?"

"They're coming out this year," Maud said. "So who knows? And if you ask me, it's no great pleasure dancing with His Majesty. Breathing brandy fumes all over me. I'd rather—"

"Yes? You'd rather what?"

"Kiss you good morning, Papa," said Maud radiantly, throwing her arms round him. "And thank you again, Papa, for letting me have my party."

"Is this a new gambit, angel? My morning kiss withheld until a request is granted?"

"Of course it isn't. You always grant my requests, don't you?"

"I fear so. I'm a weak old man."

That was a familiar joke. They both knew how far from the truth it was. But it was certainly true that he could refuse her nothing.

Even her poet, if she wanted him?

Did she want him, or was he just a novelty, after the Reggies and the Percivals and the Algernons whom she was accustomed to meet? Had she been more bewitched by the freshness of the dawn and the spring stirring in her blood than by the unexpected conversation with a stranger?

The only thing to do was to find out these things. The process would be amusing and diverting, and that alone was important. According to Papa, life should always be gay and full of variety.

"Never allow yourself to be bored, Maud. That's the way to lose your looks."

She had had little chance of being bored in the circles to which Papa had taken her all her life. The studios of his artist friends, parties at the Café Royal, where once she had sat in the capacious lap of Oscar Wilde (but whose name she was now forbidden to mention), and endless Royal Academy functions where, with her spectacular long red hair, like a brilliant shawl, and her famous face, she was as much an exhibit as her current portrait.

Ruined by too much admiration and adulation she might be, as her mother said all too frequently, but bored she had never been. Life was one long excitement, because one made it so. Dancing on the wet grass this morning had been a delightful new sensation that might be repeated until it lost its novelty. Meeting her poet face to face would be her next diversion. Would she fall in love? That, too, would be a new sensation, and one for which she impatiently longed. It was ridiculous that at the mature age of eighteen she had not yet fallen in love.

Chapter 4

THE WIZENED figure in the armchair by the fire was no less than the aged artist William Holman Hunt. He had been assisted there by his attentive wife and was now the center of a small circle eager to hear every word that fell from his lips. Another circle surrounded the reclining Lady Lucie, who was dressed in an extravagant concoction of pearl-colored lace and ruffles. In the carefully arranged lights, she had a ghostlike charm. But, as was to be expected, the room was dominated by the splendid figure of Sir James Lucie. It was his confident voice and hearty laugh that was constantly audible, though occasionally he was out-shouted by old Colonel Spencer, in whom the champagne had aroused memories of mess parties preceding bloody battles.

The colonel had brought his nephew, Ninian, who was a silent young man with a remote air. Honor Beauchamp found herself having an uneasy conversation with him. She guessed that he didn't care for parties any more than she did. Going to war so young seemed to have given him another perspective on life. She was quite sure that anyone who had taken part in the Battle of Spion Kop could never be quite the same again. She made this remark tentatively and was rewarded with a gentle smile, although she noticed him touch the fading scar on his cheek.

"That's a long time ago. I'm not as bloodthirsty as my uncle, who eternally regrets not taking part in the charge of the Light Brigade. Apart from probably not living to tell the story, he's fortunate not to have those sort of memories to live with."

"Doesn't one ever forget?"

The young man smiled again, and Honor's heart gave a curious, agitated flutter.

"How unforgivable, talking about war at a party. How did I begin?"

"I think perhaps I started it. We were both agreeing that we didn't much care for parties."

"Were we?"

"I thought we were."

"I don't remember saying so, Miss Beauchamp. And isn't a young lady's life made up of affairs like this?"

"Unfortunately, yes."

"You don't look very happy about it."

"I have a whole summer of parties ahead. My sister and I come out this season."

"Which is your sister?"

Honor indicated Daisy, whose face was animated as she chatted vivaciously to a middle-aged gentleman wearing a flowing gaily colored cravat. One of Sir James' bohemian friends, no doubt. Mamma had predicted that this party would be too bohemian for words, but had not been able to resist the opportunity of making Lady Lucie's acquaintance and seeing the interior of this controversial household.

"She seems to be enjoying herself."

"Daisy's a great chatterbox."

"And you're not?"

He wasn't really interested, she was sure. He was only being polite. He had probably selected her as the least-flirtatious and least-demanding young woman in the room.

("You always look so serious, Honor," Mamma constantly complained. "You must smile more. Hold your head up. You're getting dreadful slouching shoulders from all that piano playing. Make the most of your good points. If you puffed out your hair, you would have quite a piquant look.")

"I'm a poor conversationalist," she suddenly confided with her compulsive honesty. "I really have only one ambition, and that's to play the piano."

"Can't you do that?"

"I mean in a concert hall."

She did have his interest now. At least, she was almost certain she did.

"You would prefer to do that than have a season of balls and parties?"

"Oh, infinitely. Why must it be so difficult for a woman to have a career?"

"Indeed, why? I'm sure there are a lot of things women can do as well as men."

"You try to convince people of that. Why, Mamma doesn't even like me playing Beethoven. She says it disturbs the neighbors."

"That's too bad." He smiled, but he wasn't paying her undivided attention any longer. She turned to see who he was looking at, and it was Maud, of course. Maud, who looked ravishing in pink silk, so daring, but so unexpectedly successful with that coppery hair.

"She's beautiful, isn't she?" Honor murmured.

"Beautiful? Oh, Miss Lucie? Yes, she's very picturesque. My uncle's rather smitten by her. I'm sorry, Miss Beauchamp, you were talking about Beethoven."

"It doesn't matter. I'm afraid I have to play very soon. Lady Lucie has invited me to, and Mamma said I couldn't refuse."

The dark eyes gave her that remote, gentle look.

"Why should you want to refuse? Can't you pretend this is your concert hall?"

Indeed, at that moment, Mamma was beckoning to her, and she found herself relieved to cease a conversation that was becoming awkward. She would take Ninian Spencer's advice and pretend that this was a concert hall and play with the greatest virtuosity. Never mind that most of the people preferred the sound of their own voices and would be waiting impatiently for her to finish. Young Mr. Spencer, she was sure, would listen attentively and be astonished by her skill. He had to be; otherwise, he was going to laugh at her for her foolish talk of being a famous pianist. Whatever had made her confide in him like that?

"Honor! You're to play your piece now." Mrs. Beauchamp added, her mouth close to Honor's ear, "Not one of your difficult ones. Something light and short."

Daisy would have to stop talking. Honor heard her high impetuous voice carrying right across the room. And Maud Lucie was laughing as she listened to something Guy was saying to her. More audibly than anyone else, Colonel Spencer was shouting at the crabbed figure of Holman Hunt, "Bless my soul, sir, the duke was worth a dozen of Bonaparte any day. As for Bismarck, I must insist that the fellow was nothing but a German swine."

"Hush!" said Lady Lucie imperiously. "Silence, everyone. Miss Beauchamp has kindly agreed to play for us."

With her unconquerable diffidence, Honor took her seat at the piano. But once her fingers were on the keys, the familiar alchemy took place. She was another person, confident, happy, transported. Deliberately, she disobeyed her mother, because she so badly wanted to make an impression on the remote young Mr. Spencer. She intended to play the last movement of the *Appassionata* sonata right through. And she did so, though when she finished and looked up expectantly, not hearing the polite spatter of applause, Ninian Spencer had gone. It seemed that his uncle had become affected by the heat of the room (or bored by the music?) and had had to be taken home. It was possible Ninian would return.

But of course he wouldn't. He had wanted an excuse to escape. Why should she imagine he cared for music anyway? And Daisy was hissing in her ear, "Whatever made you show off like that?"

Two other people were missing when Honor's piece finally ended. One of Maud's irresistible urges had come over her. By design she had been standing beside Guy Beauchamp, near the door, when Honor had begun to play. She had caught his eye deliberately. It was the first direct look she had given him.

Their meeting on his arrival hadn't really been a meeting at all.

"I'm so glad you could come," she had said to the young man who, in his correct evening clothes, was far more a stranger than the uninhibited person she had talked to in the dark. Formality had descended on them. They had exchanged a handshake, a quick inquisitive glance, and then the next arrivals were waiting to be welcomed. After that, Maud had found herself unexpectedly nervous. Supposing Guy Beauchamp didn't live up to her first impression of him. Supposing that romantic dream, nurtured for two whole weeks, did not match the reality.

"Then I shall have to give it up," Maud said to herself silently, as she talked dutifully to all of Papa's familiar guests before turning her attention to the strangers. Colonel Spencer and his nephew with the scarred cheek. He looked a difficult standoffish person. Ungay. That was Maud's word for all the young men who bored her. But she exchanged a few polite words with him and then was relieved to see that Honor Beauchamp, who looked a similarly serious person, seemed to be managing him very well.

Mrs. Beauchamp was a type with which she had become familiar during her coming-out season, the perpetual dragon with sharp eyes on straying daughters, a ramrod back, and a set of inflexible opinions. Was she really the mother of Maud's light-hearted, gay acquaintance in the early dawn? Of a poet?

At least Mamma was likely to approve of her simply because of her very respectability. What an odious reason for approving of a person! But it would be an advantage in this case, for Maud would be encouraged to make friends with Honor and Daisy, although she had doubts that either of them would fill the place of the close friend and confidante for whom she had told her father she longed. To be absolutely honest, she didn't much care for her own sex. Perhaps, as her mother said, that was Papa's fault. He had taught her to have an independent, original mind which went far beyond the bounds of boudoir and drawing room and made the usual conversation of fashionable young women inexpressibly tedious.

But it was also due to the fact that she aroused jealousy and resentment in most women. With her looks and her dramatic clothes (chosen by Papa) she was always the center of attention. Several debutantes, last year, had wept in secret because they had been outshone at their own balls by Maud Lucie. One couldn't not invite her because then her absence would be noticed by too many disappointed (and highly eligible) young men. It was rumored that she had had an indecent number of completely honorable proposals and had spurned them all. How dare she be such a wicked and heartless flirt? It was well known that her father thought no one good enough for her, but must she herself be so vain?

Perfectly aware of everything that was said about her, Maud smiled and held her head higher and didn't care a fig. Wait until she fell in love. Then she would show the world how single-minded and loyal she could be.

Now, as Honor began to play, people shuffled for chairs, but Maud, having caught Guy's eye, slipped out of the room and waited breathlessly for him to follow. If he didn't come, if he didn't interpret her signal, this was not to be her grand passion. If he did— She had not time to formulate that thought, for he was there already, the door closed silently behind him, his eyebrows raised questioningly, his eyes sparkling with anticipation.

She clutched his hand, whispering intensely, "You can't want to hear your sister play, can you?"

"Good heavens, no. I've listened to her all my life. Not that she isn't good. She's too good, poor Honor. But the piano isn't my thing."

"No, poetry is."

"You remember."

"Of course I remember."

"I began to wonder if it was all a dream. I'd had a bit to drink, and it really didn't seem probable that I had met a witch goddess in the dark."

"Witch goddess! How extravagantly you talk, Mr. Beauchamp."

"Guy. You called me Guy the other morning."

"That wasn't me, that was your witch goddess."

Maud moved provocatively beneath the lighted chandelier. "Am I prettier than she?"

"You're absolutely ravishing."

Looking at the young man, Maud was privately deciding, with deep satisfaction, that he was rather ravishing, too. Those tender brown eyes and the crinkly, well-brushed brown hair, the nice air of seriousness mixed with audacity. And he was articulate. Thank heaven for someone articulate at last, after all those stammering or speechless young men at hunt balls and champagne parties.

"But you don't want to paint me; you want to put me in a poem."

"You're laughing at me."

"Oh, no. A poem is welcome change, I assure you. Do you know, I asked Papa to persuade Swinburne to come this evening, especially for your sake. But he's become extremely eccentric. The trouble is with the bottle, you know. All the same, I adore his poetry. Don't you?"

"'They loved their life through and then went whither? And were one to the end. . .'" Guy quoted.

"'One to the end.' Isn't that romantic? 'All are at one now, roses and lovers . . .' Isn't he a seductive poet? Do you like Ernest Dowson, too? I once met him, although I can't remember what he said to me. 'I have been faithful . . . in my fashion.' Isn't that deliciously cynical?"

"What an interesting life you have led."

"Yes, I have. Thanks to my father. He's always said that things of the mind are just as important for girls as for boys. People say it's made me precocious. Do you think it has?"

"I'd use another word. Unique."

"Are you just flattering me?"

"Far from it. I can't think of another girl who could quote Swinburne and Dowson like that."

"Well, I've met them, which makes me more interested. There were others, too. That odd young man, Aubrey Beardsley. Everyone said he was so brilliant and what a tragedy it was he died young, but he gave me the shivers. There was something sad and unhealthy about him. He was like a very thin spider. Oscar Wilde, too, but Mamma says I'm never to speak of him and it's a great pity I ever met him, although I was only six years old. I remember sitting on his lap. He had a very large face and large soft hands, and he always made me laugh. They said he loved his own children, before the scandal."

Above the sound of the piano, there was a movement inside the drawing room. Maud whispered hastily, "We mustn't stay here. Someone will come out. Would you like to see Papa's studio?"

"Indeed I would."

"Then quickly, and don't make a noise or Nanny will hear and pounce."

"Have you still got a nurse?"

"Have I not! Hot milk, hair brushings, clean teeth, prayers. I've outgrown her ages ago, but she's so tiresomely devoted. Mamma says you don't dismiss good servants, you repay their loyalty. Anyway, Nanny's still useful. As a sort of watchdog she's useful! How I long to be free."

"You inspire devotion."

"I give her gray hairs. I make her old, sitting up for me night after night, and she tries to keep me a child. S-s-sh! That's her room, in there. She and Bertha, Mamma's maid, will be gossiping over their fire and their hot chocolate. Like old pussycats. There's one more flight of stairs. If you walk quickly, I've found they're less likely to creak."

"Experience," Guy teased, as they safely reached the top floor.

"You're perfectly right. I'm always escaping someone. Would you like to see my new portrait? Let's shut the door before I light the gas. If Papa sees even the faintest chink of light, he'll be up here in a flash."

"I can still hear Honor playing."

"Yes. Let's hope she goes on a long time."

The gas mantle hissed into a yellow blossom of light. Standing in the long chilly room with its stacked canvases and bare floor, the model's dais at one end and the colorful murals around the walls, Maud laughed with excitement.

"Isn't it fun being up here alone? It's almost as much fun as being in the gardens in the dark. How are you getting on in the bank with your uncle?"

"Let's say I endure the bank and my uncle endures me. In fact, he regards me with the greatest suspicion. Someone told him about my poems, and he's always coming up behind me, expecting to find me writing them under my desk."

"Instead of adding up figures? Poor Guy. How dull for you."

"But necessary, I suppose. At least my mother's pleased. She thinks I've settled down."

"And have you?"

"In two weeks? I've scarcely learned how to open a ledger the right way up. Aren't you going to show me your portrait?"

"Oh, yes. Here. It's finished. It's to be delivered to Burlington House tomorrow. So you may have a private view."

Maud whipped the covering off the picture on the easel, then stood back to watch Guy's face.

"What's the matter? Don't you like it?"

"I'm not sure."

"I can see by your face that you don't."

"I think it's that white dress. It's too pure. And that ridiculous lily."

"Ridiculous! Papa wouldn't like to hear you say that. It arrives by special delivery from Harrods every day and costs a fortune."

"It makes you look too angelic."

"Pure *and* angelic! Aren't I either?"

"I sincerely hope not. And I would never let you wear white. I would want you in brilliant colors always, violets, deep blues, golds, even crimson."

"With my hair?"

"You would look glorious."

"But not angelic?"

"I don't care for angelic women."

Maud let the cover fall over the portrait. Her heart was beating too fast. At first, she had been a little outraged and indignant. She was accustomed to admiration. Now she thought she was pleased. Certainly intrigued.

"Then let's not look at her. Papa would have hurt feelings. This is a very fine piece of work, like everything Papa does. I should be cross with you for criticizing."

"And I'm impertinent to criticize. It's not your father's skill as a painter I'm daring to say things about. It's a purely personal feeling I have."

She looked at him sideways.

"Critics should never allow personal feelings to intrude. It's one of the first precepts—"

"Good heavens, I'm not critical of you! I think you're perfect. Warm, human, natural. I only wish I knew why you had asked me here tonight."

"To see your face in a good light, of course."

"Do you like it? It's quite ordinary—"

She touched the tip of his nose with her finger.

"It's passable."

"Is that all?"

"Oh! So you are vain, after all."

"Not vain. Only wanting your approval. I wish you could admire me as much as I admire you."

"How do you know that I don't?"

"*Do* you?" The intensity of his voice made her stop smiling. Her heart began to beat furiously as some wild impulse made her say, "Naturally I have been kissed before. But never seriously. Guy," she whispered breathlessly, "kiss me seriously! I want to know what it's like."

He put his lips to hers and kissed her lightly.

"No, not like that. Properly."

"Are you flirting with me? They say you're an awful flirt."

"Don't speak suspiciously like that. Of course I'm a flirt, but this isn't flirting." Her arms wound around his neck. "Kiss me, Guy."

"The young man, I hope, will do nothing of the kind," came Papa's voice from the doorway.

It was his most lofty voice, calm, resonant, and magisterial. Maud had heard it used a hundred times on delinquent servants and had witnessed how it, accompanied by Papa's sternly flashing eyes, reduced them to jelly.

On the first syllable, she and Guy had sprung apart. But her chin had gone up in indignation and hurt surprise. How dare Papa speak to Guy like a servant!

"Papa, I don't think you have met Mr. Beauchamp. May I present him? Guy, this is my father."

"And is Mr. Beauchamp under a misapprehension as to where our reception is being held this evening?"

"Oh, no, sir," Guy said quickly. "This is all my fault. I asked Maud—Miss Lucie—if I could see your work, and she suggested coming up here. Only while my sister was playing the piano."

Surreptitiously, Maud's little finger curled around his. She wanted to hug him. He was being as calm as Papa, not in the least subservient or embarrassed at being caught in that kiss.

"You must understand, sir, that I have had rather a surfeit of my sister's piano exercises most of my life."

"So kissing your host's daughter is more entertaining. You young scoundrel, I ought to send you packing."

"Papa, that's unfair!" Maud exclaimed. "We only came up to look at my portrait."

Papa's angry eyes went to the uncovered painting on the easel.

"Is Mr. Beauchamp a critic of painting, perhaps? Then would he like to favor us with his august opinion?"

It was impossible to signal to Guy with her eyes, telling him it would be diplomatic to praise the painting. Papa's steely eyes were not missing her smallest glance, and anyway she was afraid Guy was too honest.

"To tell the truth, sir, I don't altogether admire it."

She had guessed correctly. He was too honest. Now he was making matters worse by going on to explain his reasons.

"I can't pretend to comment on the quality of the work, sir. I'm sure it's very fine. But Maud—Miss Lucie—seems out of character. My sister Honor suits that prim serious mood better, if you don't mind my saying so. And I always associate lilies with religious subjects."

He had done the irreparable thing, Maud realized in deep dismay. He had offended Papa. In middle age, used to adulation, Papa took offense easily and was not a good forgiver. What appallingly bad luck to have this happen at the beginning of such an exciting friendship! Now she was going to have to take sides.

Against Papa? But never in her whole life had she done that!

"Papa, do let us show Guy your last year's portrait of me in the peacock dress. He must admire that."

Her attempt at mending matters was too clumsy, for Papa's voice was now both offended and icy.

"My dear Maud, we are giving a party this evening, not an art lesson to an ill-mannered, and, may I say, extremely ill-informed philistine. If Mr. Beauchamp wants to see other examples of my work, I suggest he visit a few art galleries. And may I also suggest that viewing portraits does not entitle the viewer to the privilege of kissing the subject. I'm surprised at you, sir."

He turned on his heel.

"Oh, Papa!" Maud wailed, but Guy held her back, his fingers hard on her arm.

"I apologize, sir, for looking at your painting, when I can see you would rather I hadn't. But I don't apologize for being in the company of your daughter, since we are two grown people and have free will. I'd like you to know that I intend to see as much of her as she will permit."

Oh, Guy, you darling blunderbuss! Maud cried silently. *Why couldn't you have been quiet until I had taught you how to handle Papa?*

For after that rash and aggressive statement, it was going to take all her powers of persuasion to win Papa over. He simply must allow her and Guy to be friends. If he didn't, they would have to meet secretly. It was inevitable. Some sort of unspoken pact had been made between them in the last few minutes. Their little fingers were still clinging together, and her blood was tingling in an altogether curious and delightful way.

And Guy, contrary to bearing the look of a young man who had just been sharply put in his place, had his head up jauntily. He was quite unaware of the anguish and pain ahead if Papa could not be won over.

Chapter 5

MAUD LAY very quietly, knowing that her slightest movement would bring Nanny with her early morning tea, with inquiries as to when she would take her bath, what she would wear, what engagements she had for that day. These would be followed by frank comments about how she looked, whether her eyes were bright enough, whether she needed a tonic or a good dose of calomel or earlier nights or more exercise or a good blow in the fresh air.

One was that irritating devoted old woman's possession. One had no privacy. It was maddening. How one envied the freedom of Honor and Daisy Beauchamp, who drew their own baths, brushed their own hair, and absolutely looked after themselves—except for the sharp-eyed surveillance of their mother, of course.

I am a hothouse plant, she thought, opening her eyes and seeing that the clothes she had carelessly dropped last night had been tidied away and that crisply ironed underclothing was set out for the new day. What would it be like if she had to wash and iron her own petticoats and chemises or found that she hadn't a single clean blouse or a fresh pair of gloves? Or that her bath was not automatically filled with the right amount of lightly scented water of the correct temperature, or the bath towels unheated, or her bedroom fire unlit, or her breakfast unprepared? Would all happiness come to an end?

Maud threw back the bedclothes violently and sprang out of bed.

That was Papa talking in her head. "You're not going to, of course, my dear Maud, but if by any chance you did marry a bank clerk or a poor poet, or even a remarkable fellow who was both those things, you would have to make up your mind that there would be no more luxury . . ."

"Miss Maud! Why didn't you ring? You're up before Cora has lit the fire."

"I won't die of cold," Maud said impatiently. (What bliss it would be not to have fussing Nanny forever!) "Hurry with my bath, Nanny. It's a lovely morning, and I want to take Han for a walk before breakfast."

"Cook's had him out, Miss Maud."

"Then he shall have another treat. He might meet Colonel Spencer's spaniel. Imagine, what excitement!" Maud looked at Cora, arriving at the door with a bucket of coal. The girl was red-eyed and furtive.

"Good morning, Cora. Is something the matter?"

"Morning, Miss Maud." Cora bent over the grate, making a great rattling with the fire irons.

"Have you been having a quarrel with your young man?"

"No, Miss Maud."

"Who is your young man, Cora? You've never told me."

"I don't fancy anyone in particular."

"Don't you really? An attractive girl like you?"

"The master's in one of his moods, Miss Maud," Cora burst out, as if suddenly she couldn't help herself.

"Oh, dear. I'm afraid that's my fault."

Cora jerked her head up in surprise. "Yours, Miss Maud!"

"I don't expect it was yours, Cora. I upset Papa last night. I'll have to calm him down at breakfast."

"I heard you on the stairs," said Nanny sourly. "With that young man. I thought your Papa wouldn't be pleased. Your bath's ready, Miss Maud."

"Thank you, Nanny."

Maud snatched up her wrap and disappeared into the bathroom. Nanny looked at Cora.

"Well, fancy all that politeness. She seems pleased with herself this morning. She's got another man on her string, that's what."

"It's all right for some," Cora muttered.

"They're like moths around a candle," Nanny said proudly.

"Spoiled," said Cora.

"Loved," said Nanny. "She's used to love."

Papa was going to ask her not to see Guy again, Maud reflected, but he couldn't prevent a chance meeting. And a chance meeting was exactly what she was hoping for as she walked briskly through the Square with Han at her heels. It was inevitable that, living so close, she would encounter Guy occasionally. It would be easy enough to find out the time he left for work in the mornings and returned in the evenings. She had thought last night that, having seen him first in the half-dark, she merely wanted to see him clearly by gaslight, or candlelight, or whatever light was available.

Now she was greedy and wanted to see him again by the early-morning sunlight. Her fingers tingled as she remembered his grip. And the passionate kiss they had so nearly had. One day that kiss had to be experienced. That much she was very sure of.

"Come, Han," she said impatiently. "Don't dawdle. Oh, good morning, Mr. Spencer."

She had almost collided with Ninian Spencer, emerging from the gateway of Number 9. The tall young man paused, lifting his bowler hat.

"Good morning, Miss Lucie. You're out early."

"Aren't I? And I'm usually a dreadfully lazy creature. But it's such a beautiful morning." She lifted her face to the pale clear sky, breathing deeply, then realized, by the way the young man was looking at her, that he thought this was a feminine trick to show off her profile.

Hiding her irritation (why did all men think young women were constantly flirting?), she asked politely, "How is your uncle? I am sorry he was poorly last evening."

"He's better, thank you. He refuses to realize his limitations."

"What a wise man. I never intend to realize mine either."

This certainly was a serious young man, with his dark intense eyes and that faded scar down one cheek. A brush with death wouldn't make her so solemn. She would determinedly laugh all the more while there was time. But Ninian Spencer's look suggested that he thought her flippant and shallow. She wasn't used to this kind of criticism, even if unspoken.

"I'm not joking," she said tartly. "Anyway, how does one know what one's limitations are unless one experiments?"

"Indeed. You're perfectly right. If you will excuse me, Miss Lucie, I have a bus to catch. Thank you for a most enjoyable party last evening."

"Where do you catch your bus to?" Maud asked. Conversation bubbled out of her this morning, even though perforce with an unwilling subject. Because she was surreptitiously watching for Guy didn't mean that she wasn't interested in other people. She was plain inquisitive, Nanny said.

"To the law courts. I have chambers in Lincolns Inn."

"You're studying law?"

"I have just been called to the bar."

"How splendid. Congratulations."

"Oh, I'm a very humble member of the profession. I'm only deviling for Sir Herbert Browne."

"Ah, but you will be Sir Ninian Spencer one day."

The smile she received, fleeting as it was, had a certain rather shy charm.

"You must always be an optimist, Mr. Spencer. It's important."

He gave his tentative smile again, bowed, and walked away. She half closed her eyes and imagined him in twenty years' time, in his barrister's robes and wig, pleading eloquently for a prisoner's life. He would have a lean, hawk face. Exactly right . . .

Guy or herself in twenty years. That was impossible to imagine. She could only see them as forever young and in love.

Was she in love?

As she wandered along, dreaming, she heard the rumble of the horse-bus passing the corner of the High Street. Good gracious, she had made that wintry young man miss it. She imagined his look of annoyance and began to giggle. Serve him right for being so serious. Let him adapt himself to hazards. As she was doing now, deliberately dawdling in front of the Beauchamp house, pretending Han had a thorn in his paw.

"Han! There's nothing wrong with you," she said vigorously. "Come along. What a slow coach you are!"

The lace curtain in the front downstairs window moved distinctly, a dim form was momentarily visible. It couldn't be Guy's.

He surely wouldn't peep from behind curtains. Mrs. Beauchamp's? Old dragon eyes? Or Honor's? She was shy enough to peep and draw back.

Reluctantly, Maud moved on. Guy must have left for work, or he would have come hurrying out to pretend a chance meeting that she was certain he desired as much as she did. She certainly must find out his hours of coming and going. There was plenty of time. The spring was just beginning. Then there would be summer and endless hours of daylight for meetings, supposing Papa remained adamant.

But he wouldn't when she had used her wiles on him.

"Who are you looking at, Honor?" Mrs. Beauchamp asked from her place at the head of the breakfast table.

"It's Maud Lucie, Mamma. She's taking her dog for a walk."

"But I saw one of the maids out with the animal half an hour ago."

"Then it must be Maud who wants the walk," Daisy said. "What's she wearing, Honor?"

"A green cape with a hood."

"I suppose she looks ravishing, as usual. What a pity Guy isn't here to see her. Oh, my, I wonder if that's why she's taking her dog out, in the hope of seeing Guy."

"Daisy! What nonsense!"

"No, Mamma, it isn't nonsense, after the way she behaved last night. Why, if Honor or I had disappeared upstairs with a man—"

"I trust you would both have more sense. And I trust Guy will have enough sense not to be taken in by that young woman's flirtatious way. There's no doubt she is fast, as we had heard." Mrs. Beauchamp paused while Daisy watched her face with anxiety. Were they to be told that they were not to be on visiting terms with that absolutely fascinating creature? It would be too bad. Life with Mamma's judiciously selected friends was very dull.

"But Lady Lucie is an admirable person," Mrs. Beauchamp pronounced at last. "I wouldn't hurt her for the world. We will leave Sir James out of it. He isn't a man I could ever trust. I daresay his daughter takes after him. But for that poor sweet invalid's sake, we must be forbearing. Honor, do come away from the window. Peeping like a kitchen maid."

"I know who she's hoping to see," Daisy exclaimed. "A certain sinister scarred gentleman."

"Daisy, don't be ridiculous," Honor said, the color pouring into her cheeks.

"What are you making up, Daisy?" Mrs. Beauchamp asked. "A sinister scarred gentleman indeed! Where would Honor meet any such person?"

"But she did last night, Mamma. She had a long conversation with old Colonel Spencer's nephew. Where has the colonel kept him hiding for so long, Honor?"

"He hasn't been hiding. Daisy, you are a tease. Since he came back from the Boer War, where he was wounded, he has been at Oxford. Then he read for the bar and has recently been admitted." Honor gave this information in a factual but slightly breathless voice. "That's all I know about him."

"Well, do come away from the window," Mrs. Beauchamp said more mildly. "Is Mr. Spencer someone we can add to our list? Remind me to ask Guy about him."

"He's completely respectable," Honor declared, then blushed again at her vehemence.

"And completely unattached?"

"Mamma, how could I ask him that?"

"I daresay you couldn't, but it's information one needs to know. Well, Honor"—a vague indulgence came into Mrs. Beauchamp's sharp eyes—"perhaps you didn't entirely waste your evening last night."

But I did, Honor said to herself in silent anguish. *Because he didn't wait for me to finish playing. Even if he did have to take his uncle home, he could have come back.*

All the same, if Mamma added his name to the list of guests for hers and Daisy's ball and if he came and if she bit her tongue rather than talk about the piano and looked her absolute best in the dress Miss Lavender was making, perhaps he would write his name more than once on her dance program.

Perched on his high stool, his feet tucked around the legs, his head bent over a ledger, Guy found that under a column of figures he had written *"she walks in beauty, like the night . . ."* Hastily he looked for an eraser. Fortunately it was a pencil he had had in his hand.

Footsteps paused behind him.

"Mr. Beauchamp, you have the A to F ledger. Can you oblige me by telling me Mrs. Bishop's first name? It completely escapes my memory."

"Maud."

"Maud? Are you sure? That doesn't sound familiar."

"Oh, sorry, Mr. Wilson. It's Fanny Elizabeth."

"Hmm. That's nothing like Maud. Keep your mind on your work, young man."

Instead of ordering the carriage, Papa had decided to go by hansom cab to deliver the finished portrait to Burlington House. The horse clip-clopped along briskly. At Knightsbridge Green a ragged skinny urchin leaped on the back, clinging precariously by one hand. Papa waved him away, shouting that he had no luggage to be carried, but the grimy face with its stubborn grin remained, peering through the small square window, taking in Papa's prosperous clothes and Maud's green cloak with its fur-trimmed hood.

For once, Maud hadn't wanted to go on this ritual journey. But today had hardly been the day to break with tradition. Papa was superstitious about having her company when he delivered the portrait into the keeping of the academy and eventually exposing it to the comments of the critics and the public.

Not a word, so far, had been said about the previous evening. They were each being a little too polite, too stiff. She and Papa stiff with each other? It was unthinkable. Yet it was happening. But it couldn't go on for long. Papa would have some sudden broadside to deliver, and when the thunder and lightning were over, they would be friends again.

Maud glanced at him sideways, seeing his handsome profile, the long strong nose, the fuzzy blond eyebrows, the curving mouth, the healthily pink cheeks. She sighed a little and waited for the fireworks to begin.

"I thought we might have a light luncheon at the Ritz," Papa proposed quite calmly.

"That would be nice."

"Only nice? You don't expect five courses at the Café Royal after all that champagne last night? And we are dining with the Fortescues this evening."

"Oh, bother, I'd forgotten."

"Lord Randolph has a splendid cellar. And you know how his brother admires you. Or you ought to."

"He alone is enough to spoil one's appetite."

Papa tapped her knee with his gloved forefinger.

"Wicked. Wicked." He added, with casual deliberation. "Then I take it I won't need to worry about kisses on stairways."

"With Peregrine Fortescue!" Maud pealed with laughter. "Papa, how absurd you are."

"But it's not such a laughing matter when it's that young bank clerk, what's his name."

Maud stopped laughing.

"You remember his name perfectly well."

"Of course I do," Papa said affably. "He had the impertinence to to criticize my work."

"But not your daughter," Maud said slyly.

"Ah, that's another matter. I would be very happy for a thousand bank clerks to admire my work rather than my daughter. This young man has his priorities the wrong way around. Shall we say no more about the matter?"

"Are you forbidding me to see him?"

Papa gave his careless, charming smile, patting her hand.

"I can hardly do that, since we live a stone's throw from one another. I daresay you'll be passing the time of day. But I am asking you not to encourage a friendship, Maud. It would be unkind to the young man. Though a little unkindness would not be more than he deserves, the ignorant young oaf."

Maud withdrew her hand from her father's. "And if I disagree about not seeing him?"

"You mean if you disobey me?" Papa's blue eyes were too sunny to suggest more than the mildest threat. "But you never do, do you, my darling? Look, here we are in Piccadilly already. I suppose I must give a sixpence to that blackmailing wretch on the back. But don't let him lay his dirty hands on my painting."

There was the usual fawning over Papa in the offices of the Royal Academy, the usual discussion as to who would be exhibiting this year, Wilson Steer, Sargent, Leader with his endless pastoral scenes, old Holman Hunt if his hand had remained steady enough. The Pre-Raphaelites were thin on the ground nowadays. The great days of Lord Leighton's luscious "Garden of the Hesperides" and Millais' "Ophelia" and "Autumn Leaves" were over.

It was expected that, as usual, the current portrait of Maud Lucie would provide the most discussion. "The Virgin." Eyebrows lifted. That was rather different from last year's riot of peacock colors, wasn't it?

"One isn't always in the same mood," Papa said, a trifle brusquely. "Anyway, there it is, and my daughter and I have a luncheon engagement, so we must be on our way."

Luncheon in the splendor of the Ritz, and Papa chatting in his familiar, easy, amusing way. But it wasn't the same today. He didn't absorb her attention as he had always done previously. She was restless, impatient to get back to Melbury Square, perhaps to suggest tea with Honor and Daisy Beauchamp in order to talk about forthcoming parties and balls and to decide which of the sisters might be entrusted with secret missives. For Papa had made an edict which she couldn't possibly obey and which he couldn't justifiably expect her to. Dear short-sighted Papa. Didn't he realize how exhilarating this dangerous game he was forcing her to play might become? In the end, if he wasn't careful, he might really lose her. Someday there might even be no new portrait of Miss Maud Lucie hanging in the summer exhibition of the Royal Academy. The very notion was unthinkable.

Bethnal Green was a long way from Piccadilly, the sacred galleries of Burlington House, and the luxury of luncheon at the Ritz.

In the cramped, dark kitchen of a small, shabby terraced cottage in Smith Street, Cora's mother said impatiently, "What's the matter with you, girl? What are you sniveling about? You've got a soft job, living in the lap of luxury, while I break my back over the washtub day after day. What have you got that look on your face for? You scared of something?"

Cora hung her head, muttering that she was.

"Then whatever of? Is Cook a bully? I'd have thought you could stand up for yourself."

"So I can, with Cook."

"Then what is it?" Her mother's eyes, in her tired, clay-colored, long undernourished face, were suddenly sharp, suddenly knowing. "It's not the master! Oh, my God! Cora, you haven't—you aren't—"

Cora burst into noisy sobs.

"I'm not sure, Ma. I'm only scared."

"You little slut!" Ma's hand was raised, ready to strike. Something passed over her face, some far-off guilty memory. Slowly her hand fell to her side.

"I love him, Ma. He's that irresistible."

"Is big words what they teach you in that fine Square? You'd be bettering yourself, you said, going to work in the West End."

"So I was. I've learned ever so much. I know how to look after silver and linen and polish furniture—"

"Ha! You can do mine," Ma retorted, looking around the shabby room. "Come on, polish me silver salver! Do me crested cutlery! It strikes me you've learned more than how to clean silver. Then you'll tell him, won't you? Make him responsible."

"I told you I'm not sure yet."

"Then when you are. As you will be, I haven't a doubt. You've got the look already. I should have noticed it when you came in. So you'll make him pay. You won't have him sliding out of it and blaming the butcher's boy."

Cora lifted her head indignantly.

"He isn't like that."

"They all are, my girl, in that class same as any other. Must have their fun, but not their responsibility."

"Don't talk like that about Sir James. You don't know him. I'll be proud to have his baby."

"You can't live on pride. Nor can the baby. So you see you make him pay. Ask him how he'd like it if his daughter were took advantage of in that way."

Cora gave a crooked smile.

"She'd like it right enough if she got the chance. But that class, as you call them, Ma, don't get much chance. There are always all those chaperones about. Don't have much fun, young ladies don't."

"And where has your fun got you?" Ma asked spitefully. "After all the warnings I give you, too." Then she shrugged fatalistically. "Well, blood will out, I suppose."

"What are you telling me?"

Ma gave her gap-toothed smile, her eyes wry.

"How did you think you arrived, then? When did you ever see your Pa? He disappeared when you were little, I told you. Well, he weren't never around. And neither will your kid's be."

Cora's look expressed surprise rather than shock. Surprise that someone had ever desired this permanently tired, dried-up, bitter-tongued old woman. She had never been any different, as far as Cora could remember, with her reddened, rough-skinned hands, her straggling hair, her anxious eyes, and her constant smell of soap and wet clothes.

"Who was he, Ma?" she asked in plain curiosity. "Why did you never tell me before?"

"Because I wanted you brought up respectable, that's why." Reluctantly, but with a stubborn touch of pride, she added, "He were a footman to the Duke of Devonshire. He looked right handsome in his uniform. You don't need to be ashamed of your Pa. Except that he deserted us, the bastard. Never gave me a penny piece. So I'm telling you. Don't you let your grand lover escape in this way. Make a scene. Threaten to go to his wife. That'll make him see sense."

"She's an invalid, poor lady."

"I only said threaten, didn't I? All the same, go to her if you have to. Invalid or not, I'll make a bet she knows how to manage him." Ma was suddenly cheerful, giving the low chuckle that was rusty from infrequent use. "Well, don't let's be downhearted, love. On second thoughts, I believe we mightn't do so bad out of this, after all. Look in my purse. There might be a tanner for something to make life a bit brighter. We'll have to hurry. It's nearly closing time. And another thing. You take things as easy as you can from now on. Don't fill them coal scuttles too full for carrying upstairs. Lifting's the worst."

"But wouldn't it be the best thing if I lost it?"

"No, don't do that. That would be a crying shame. You might have an asset there in your belly. A real asset. You gets cunning in this life. Hard times makes you cunning. Trust your Ma to look after her little girl. Eh!" Ma gave her a playful push. "Being wanted by the great man. Fancy! Next thing he'll be painting your portrait!"

Chapter 6

Two DAYS later, it was suddenly full spring, and the Square gardens erupted into life. Nursemaids attempted to mind their charges and the gardener, old Bates with his stubble of beard, muddied fingernails, and short, strong legs sent marauding small boys flying from his newly planted flower beds. Garden chairs were drawn up in sedate circles, and as the warm sun miraculously lingered during the afternoon, the ladies came out to take tea. They wore wide hats to protect their complexions against such a sudden access of brilliance and carried shawls for protection against the cool wind that would almost certainly spring up.

This was the beginning of the pleasurable summer season, when the activities of other families, the growth and behavior of their children, and the fashions of the grown-up young ladies could be observed at first hand instead of from behind the curtains of front parlors.

At four o'clock precisely (it would be four thirty or five o'clock when the weather was warmer and the evenings drawn out), the maidservants, with flying cap ribbons, carried over the heavy silver trays laden with teapots enveloped in thick cozies, second-best cups and saucers, covered dishes of hot muffins, and the perennial dark, moist fruitcake studded with cherries like pieces of Chinese amber.

Because of the balmy weather, Bertha and Nanny had persuaded Lady Lucie to make her first journey into the gardens. It was like preparing for a journey to the continent, Maud thought. The bath chair had to be brought up from the basement, and Mamma lowered into its cozy nest of cushions. Then she had to have her parasol as well as her floppy leghorn hat, a cashmere shawl for her shoulders, and a rug over her knees. Smelling salts were tucked into Bertha's pocket and a fan, in case the unaccustomed heat was too overpowering, slipped into Mamma's hands. Maud must carry books and magazines and a footstool to sit on, close at hand. Cora was given exact instructions about the tea tray which must contain Mamma's favorite China tea with lemon, the almond wafers from Fortnum and Mason's, plenty of hot water, a bowl of sugar cubes (and not to forget the sugar tongs and the teaspoons).

When the procession had started, there was endless discussion about the best place for the invalid. Should it be in the full shade or the full sun? In the shelter of the rhododendron bank or on the open lawn, where the cool breeze could play on overheated cheeks? Within hearing of other groups of ladies or in discreet isolation, where a polite wave of the hand would suffice as a greeting to those people whom presently Bertha would identify?

Lady Lucie decided on the latter position, in the sprinkled shade of a young copper beech. Her parasol was erected and held by the faithful Bertha. She lay back, moving her fan languidly, occasionally sighing as if the short journey had exhausted her.

She was pretending again, Maud thought, hating the whole ridiculous parade, Nanny pushing the bath chair, Bertha holding the parasol, herself carrying books, footstools, rugs. If Mamma really disliked being an invalid, she wouldn't make such a show of herself.

Once, when her mother had been persuaded to attend a garden party at Lady Lister's, and Annabel Lister, a pert fourteen-year-old, had asked, "Which is your mother?" Maud had pointed to a slim graceful woman in a lovely flowing gown, standing admiring the roses. She had immediately been deeply ashamed of her deception. Why hadn't she wanted to acknowledge Mamma, who was pretty and elegant, even in her bath chair? She had had to avoid Annabel for the rest of the afternoon, in case she had been found out in her lie. It was difficult to know why she so resented Mamma's helplessness. The patient smile, the sweet, demanding voice, the alarming power beneath the gentleness. Delicacy, Maud resolved, was a weapon she would never use herself. She scorned and despised it. Yet the inescapable fact remained, that Mamma *was* delicate and an invalid. So here one was, as usual, fetching and carrying, sitting at her feet, quelling one's impatience to escape.

Today she couldn't escape, for she had no engagements of her own, and Papa, who would otherwise have wanted her company, had gone to Syon House to begin a portrait of the children of the Duke and Duchess of Northumberland. He would have to make several journeys before the portrait was finished, and his absence would have provided an ideal opportunity for Maud to have a clandestine meeting with Guy, if only Guy weren't at his bank. Maud hadn't set eyes on him since the party five days ago. It seemed impossible that he could live so close and remain so invisible. Every time she dressed, it was for his eyes. (The pink blouse or the white? The striped foulard, without a cloak in this warm weather? The new high-heeled shoes with buckles?)

But she had been unlucky. Even on Sunday, when she and Papa had attended morning service at St. Mary Abbott's church, she had been rewarded only with a glimpse of Mrs. Beauchamp's poker back, Honor and Daisy flanking her on either side. Irreverent Guy. Did he not go to church?

However, fortune obliquely favored her today, for just after Mamma had been comfortably settled, the garden gates opened and Mrs. Beauchamp, followed by Honor and Daisy and an elderly servant, swept in. It was almost as much of a procession as the Lucies had made, for Mrs. Beauchamp sailed forward like the figurehead of a ship, while Honor and Daisy and the servant were weighted down with chairs and cushions in her wake.

Mrs. Beauchamp's sharp eyes, scanning the scene, immediately discerned Lady Lucie. She bore down on the little group, uttering affable cries.

"My dear Lady Lucie! How good to see you feeling sufficiently strong to take advantage of the fine weather. May we join you for a few minutes? I promise not to tire you. Put my chair here, Honor. Daisy, have you my parasol? I see you have one, too, Lady Lucie. A wise precaution. One becomes so unaccustomed to the sun in this wretched climate of ours. Now, girls, don't stand there like statues. You and Maud must have a great deal to chatter about. I believe Laura Ponsonby's ball is the next occasion on which they'll all be meeting, Lady Lucie. And of course the girls expect Maud to come to their small affair in June."

Daisy was beckoning with her eyes to Maud. Maud's heart jumped foolishly. She sprang up.

"May we just take a stroll, Mamma, while you and Mrs. Beauchamp talk?"

"Of course, darling," came the frail voice. "Your young legs . . ."

Out of sight of their parents, Daisy pushed a sealed note into Maud's hand.

"From Guy. He said we were bound to run into you, but I've carried this for three days. I saw you at church, but there wasn't a hope then."

Maud thrust the note deep into her pocket. She didn't know how she was going to wait to read it. Her face was glowing.

"*Thank* you, Daisy."

Honor looked disapproving, but Daisy's eyes were sparkling with mischief.

"He's smitten by you, Maud. Did you know? He said he's called twice at your house, but he was told both times that you were out. He didn't believe it the second time. He said perhaps your father had given the servants instructions."

"It's quite likely," Maud admitted. "Papa is frightfully strict in some ways." Her fingers closed over the square of paper in her pocket, caressing it.

"It's hardly surprising," Honor said, but without rancor. "He wouldn't think Guy good enough for you. He isn't either. He has been a great worry to Mamma."

"But he is settling down now," Daisy said. "And if Uncle Lionel is pleased with him, he'll make him his heir and all will be well. Oh, bother, there's Mamma beckoning. She suspects we're having secrets."

"Which is true," said Maud.

"And it shows in your face," said Honor. "Keep your eyes down."

"*Why* can't we have private lives?" Daisy sighed.

"I intend to," Maud announced. "It will be easy enough." She raised her voice as they approached the seated women. "What are you wearing to Laura's ball?"

"My dress has blue bows," Daisy said. "They match my eyes,

Miss Lavender says." She rolled her eyes up in scorn. "Who makes your dresses, Maud? They have such style. Dear old Miss Lavender sews well enough, but she doesn't know much about style."

Unfailingly, her mother caught the words and said, "Has it occurred to you, Daisy, that the trouble might be more with your figure than with Miss Lavender? I'm afraid my youngest daughter, Lady Lucie, has too great a fondness for cream puffs and marzipan."

"Never mind, Mrs. Beauchamp," Lady Lucie replied sweetly, "if she has as busy a season as Maud had, she'll be much thinner at the end of it."

"Ah, Maud," said Mrs. Beauchamp.

"And here's Cora with the tea. Do join us, Mrs. Beauchamp. Cora will go back for more cups and saucers."

"I will," Maud exclaimed, and had gone before her mother could protest.

In the privacy of her room she snatched the note out of her pocket and unsealed it.

DEAR MAUD,

It looks as if your father has forbidden me the door, but I must see you. I dream of nothing else. I can't add or subtract, and I make great blots in my ledger columns. But I have written a poem, and it is, of course, about you. On Sunday afternoons I often stroll by the Round Pond in Kensington Gardens about four o'clock. I like watching the ducks. Do you?

Devotedly,
GUY

So it had begun. Maud was suddenly two people, one full of happy, crazy excitement, the other apprehensive and guilty. But she intended to repress that annoying second person and be completely happy.

The very next Sunday she and Guy sat on the hard park bench, their fingers entwined.

"Did you like my poem?" Guy asked as he finished reading it to her.

"It sounds vain to say yes when it's all about me."

"It's true."

"You flatter me too much."

"That would be impossible."

The shining water, the bobbing brown ducks, the little boys in sailor suits with their boats, the budding trees, the hazy blue sky —Maud had never before realized what an enchanted place Kensington Gardens was.

"Was it difficult to come?" Guy asked.

"No. I just told Nanny I was taking Han for a long walk because he's getting too fat. Papa was busy with the Sunday papers. Or taking a nap, most likely. I'll have to be back by five, though. Otherwise, they'll ask questions and read my face."

"Does this mean that I won't see you again until next Sunday?"

"If then. Papa may have something planned that I can't escape."

"Couldn't you stay out longer sometime? We could have tea somewhere."

Pouring tea for Guy in a small intimate teashop—the prospect was slightly naughty and infinitely alluring.

"I'll try. It would be heavenly. What time do you go to work in the mornings? I haven't liked to ask your sisters."

"I pass your house at fifteen minutes to eight. If I'm a minute later, I miss my train, and Uncle Lionel doesn't care for unpunctuality."

"I'll wave to you from my window."

"Will you really?"

"Yes. One wave will mean I can do what we've planned; two, I can't."

"And I'll raise my hat if I've given Daisy a letter for you so you can make an excuse to see her."

Maud giggled. "Isn't this all too silly! But I confess I think it's the greatest fun."

"Much more than fun," said Guy.

His fingers tightened on hers, and the blood surged through her veins in that alarming way again. She had to resist a desire to lay her cheek against his, longing for the touch of his flesh. With the smallest encouragement she would have thrown herself into his arms.

"Are you coming to Laura Ponsonby's ball?" she asked.

"I wouldn't miss it for a fortune. And that's saying something, since a fortune is my greatest necessity."

"Oh, money. Who cares about that?"

"People who haven't got it."

"I suppose so. But at least you're surrounded by it in the bank."

"All those sovereigns the tellers count out. That's just fairy gold." Guy sighed. "I'm a poor man, Maud. You know that, don't you?"

"I don't care in the very least."

"I love the fierce way you say that. But I have to admit that I've already had more than my share of my father's estate, and there's Honor and Daisy to be married and my mother to be provided for. Uncle Lionel says I shouldn't have spent so much traveling, but since he's never traveled farther than from London to Brighton in his life, he doesn't know what he's talking about. He simply doesn't understand how fascinating foreign places are."

"I'm sure they must be. I'd adore to see them. I've never been abroad, though Papa promises to take me to Paris."

"I'll take you! And to more exciting places than Paris. Egypt, the Nile, Persia, Baghdad."

"What wonderful names! Let's go to places like that! You could write poetry, and I could wear beautiful Oriental robes and have slave girls to brush my hair and perfume me."

"It wouldn't be quite like that." It seemed that whereas she was indulging in a daydream, Guy was perfectly serious. "Traveling can be uncomfortably hard work. Do you think you could ride a camel for hours at a time? Or camp in the desert in a sandstorm? I wouldn't be able to write poetry all the time either. I'd have to do pieces for the *Times* or the *Sketch* to pay our way. We wouldn't be tourists going to see the Pyramids. We'd get right off the beaten track. Why are you looking at me like that, darling?"

"I'm not sure whether you're serious. Are you playing a game?"

"Certainly not. I'm absolutely serious. I've already talked to editors and got preliminary commissions. I'm not just going to drift, as everyone thinks I am. I intend to be a legitimate explorer."

"Good heavens!" Maud gasped. "Me riding a camel!" She began to giggle. Then she said under her breath, "Papa would never agree."

"No, I don't imagine he would."

"Never."

"But you would, wouldn't you, Maud?"

"Would what?"

"Think it a great adventure."

"Oh, yes, yes. Just imagine, when we come back burned by the desert sun. We'd be a sensation in Kensington drawing rooms."

"I don't believe you do think I'm serious," Guy said reproachfully.

"Yes, I do, but not yet." Maud's voice was urgent. "Not today. It's too soon. Just being here with you—that's really enough to start with."

"Of course. I mustn't be so impatient. I always want things to happen immediately. People say I'm just a dreamer, but I'm not; I'm a man of action."

Maud sprang up restlessly. "Show me. Let's walk. If there weren't so many people about, I'd race you to the Bayswater side of the gardens."

Guy leaped up. "Who cares about people? I'll give you five yards start."

Han yapped excitedly, sensing the contest. Maud knew that Guy would easily outdistance her, but if she were not hampered by her long skirts, she would put up a respectable performance. Recklessly, she lifted them to her knees and fled away across the grass, Guy pounding in pursuit. She believed he wouldn't catch her after all. No, he was gaining on her. Fatally, she turned to look, and her shoe caught in a turf and she came down headlong.

She was laughing so much that she couldn't get up. Han was barking hysterically and licking her face. Guy was crying, "Maud, are you hurt? Have you twisted your ankle? It's all my fault. Here, take my hands."

Weak with laughter and breathlessness, she half struggled to her feet and collapsed into his arms. The kiss that followed was inevitable and far more ravishing to her senses than she had imagined in her most fanciful dreams.

That, she realized soberly afterward, was the moment the flirtation ended and the serious affair began.

It was really the nicest possible way to fall in love.

And Guy's dreams about leaving his uncle's bank and becoming an explorer in the East were more exhilarating than alarming.

"Miss Maud, how ever did you get all those green stains on your skirt? You'd think you'd been rolling in the grass."

Nanny's pursed-up face was full of suspicion and disapproval. Maud said lightly, "So I was. I got tangled in Han's lead and fell down."

Lies were easy, she was discovering, and much kinder than the awkward, uncomfortable truth. She would like to become an elaborate, gifted, and amusing liar. To protect other people's feelings, of course.

In the early dawn Sir James murmured into Cora's tangled hair, "I want you to do something for me, my dear."

Warm from love, temporarily forgetting her private anxiety, Cora said willingly, "Anything I can, sir."

"I'm not asking you to spy on my daughter, mark you, but it seems to me she's overexercising that lapdog of hers."

"What do you want me to do, sir?"

"Just keep an eye on her when I'm out of the house. Young ladies get too much freedom nowadays."

Cora got out of bed slowly. It was chilly away from the warm blankets, and there was no fire for her to dress by. Only a quick scrambling into her clothes and a descent to the cold dark kitchen to start the stove and put on kettles to heat water for the endless jugs which later she would have to carry upstairs. She was feeling queasy. Men never had to suffer that, did they? Men turned over in their warm beds and went comfortably back to sleep without a care.

Well, it was her own fault. She wasn't blaming anyone else. But now she understood what temptation was, and if Miss Maud was experiencing the same thing and secretly meeting a young man, Cora hadn't the faintest intention of betraying her to her father.

Lady Lucie turned the smooth Fabergé egg in her delicate hands. It was a lovely thing, lapis lazuli with a thin circlet of gold. It pleased her immensely. She would rather have this to look at and handle a hundred times a day than her husband faithfully at her side in her bed every night. Was that a dreadful comment on marriage? Was she an unnatural woman? No, she was just tired and too often in pain, and anyway he snored. She could hear his snores through the wall dividing their bedrooms. As well as other things which she had recently decided to hint at.

The egg, at this stage of her life, was adequate compensation.

"Thank you, James. It's quite charming."

"And valuable. So lock it up if you have any new servants in here."

"Darling, you know that no one but Bertha touches my things."

"I'm just warning you to take care. By the way, has Maud been neglecting you lately?"

"No more than usual. But I try to understand. Young girls have so much energy. She's always flying off somewhere."

"I hope she tells you where she goes."

"Of course. She's made friends with those two rather plain Beauchamp girls. And there's always Harriet, for whom she has such devotion. I can never understand why. I always thought my elderly cousin had as much charm as an onion."

"As soon as I have this Northumberland portrait finished, I'll take Maud off for a few days. We might go down to Brighton. Get some bracing air before the Royal Academy opens. You'll be coming to the private view, of course?"

"Would it matter if I didn't?"

"Of course it would matter," Sir James said testily. "Don't you want to see your daughter's portrait hung?"

Notwithstanding Sir James' pressure of work and Maud's new secret life, the ritual of breakfast together remained unchanged. Maud would greet her father sunnily, inquiring how he had slept and how the new portrait being painted at Syon House was progressing.

"Indifferently," he answered to both questions.

"Oh, Papa, I'm sorry. What's gone wrong?"

"It's this rigmarole of driving to work like a tradesman," he said in a testy voice.

"Isn't it worth a journey to immortalize the young Northumberlands?"

Sir James looked at his daughter sharply. That was the sort of double-edged remark the younger generation of critics was beginning to make about him. Sugar wrapped around a pill. But Maud, bless her heart, looked wholly innocent and admiring.

"I'd rather drown the little beasts," he grunted, and they both laughed merrily, and for a minute it was as it had always been. They were the closest-together father and daughter in the world.

"Well, my dear, what new conquest lately? You haven't been telling me."

"None, Papa."

"None? Are you losing your fascination? Do you need a particularly ravishing new dress?"

Maud suddenly got up and flung her arms around his neck.

"No, darling Papa. You spoil me."

"Hmm."

"Anyway, I told you I wanted friends of my own sex, and now I have them. Honor and Daisy Beauchamp and I gossip for hours."

"I don't believe it," Papa declared. "You and those two nonentities. You with your sophisticated mind, gossiping!"

Maud nodded calmly, the lie not altogether a lie this time. Daisy amused her, and she was genuinely fond of Honor, who had unexpected depths.

"You don't gossip with their brother, too, I hope," Papa said casually.

"Oh, no, Guy's always at that stuffy bank. He works very long hours."

"I'm glad to hear it. Even a profession without a future to it must be taken seriously. Now then, what about this dress? I had thought of making a brief visit to Paris and paying a call on Mr. Worth."

"Papa! Not a *Worth* dress!"

"Why not? You're old enough now to do it justice. I visualize something in emerald green, but we'll let the great man speak for himself."

Maud, to his surprise, burst into tears. She hid her face in her napkin and muttered something about not being worth it.

Sir James hid his uneasiness—tears and humility were both foreign to his daughter—and said chaffingly, "Now, now, my dear, I may be able to buy you a Worth dress, but I can't keep up with puns at breakfast."

"Just because he's buying you this dress—and really I don't understand the importance you females put on clothes—you don't need to feel so guilty!" Guy insisted.

"But I do," Maud said miserably.

"Then refuse to have it."

"Isn't that like a man! That would be worse! He would know I was out of my senses."

"Perhaps you are."

They looked at each other in the early sunlight. Maud had snatched ten minutes in the Square gardens before breakfast. Guy, in his city clothes, looked incongruous among the rioting spring flowers. Maud's lips trembled. A tear hung on her lashes. Guy put out his arms, and hidden by the big rhododendron bush, they went into a desperate embrace.

"What are we going to do?" Guy asked.

"What can we? I only keep on hoping I can make him change."

"You'll never do that, Maud. A Worth dress, a tiara, a title. That's what he has planned for you."

Maud fumbled in her pocket and produced an acorn, smooth and dry from a winter in her glove drawer.

"Look, I thought we'd plant this together, and when it's a tree, our grandchildren can sit under it."

"Maud! Of all the born optimists! You'd change the world. Or believe you could."

"Just make a small hole. Mark it with a stick. I'll have to tell Bates so he doesn't dig it up. There, Guy, that's the beginning of our tree."

Cousin Harriet, widowed and childless, lived in a house in Cheyne Walk, Chelsea, that was much too large for one elderly woman. She had never approved of her Cousin Lydia's marriage to James Lucie. It was far too bohemian for a conventional and rather timid creature like Lydia, and anyway, anyone but a lovesick girl would have seen that the man was not to be trusted.

All the same, Harriet, in her occasional soul-searching moments, admitted that she had been more than a little envious of Lydia. Her own marriage, completely respectable and approved by everyone, had provided her with twenty-five of the dullest years imaginable. When poor William lay dying, she had listened to the ticking of the grandfather clock outside the bedroom and realized that her own life, as well as that of her husband in the bed, was running away with that monotonous tick-tock. Slow, even, deliberate, and unpunctuated by events, either happy or disastrous, the unmemorable days were sliding by.

So she had made a spur-of-the-moment decision when that spectacular pair, Sir James Lucie and his daughter, Maud, came to pay their respects after William's funeral, and offered to take on the somewhat formidable task of Maud's coming out. Formidable, not only because the girl looked as if she would be the debutante of the season, but also because she had a rebellious look that would take some keeping in check. However, Harriet, by reason of poor William, who had been an eminent member of Queen Victoria's household, could provide Maud's entrée into the best circles.

She would also provide the fuss and feathers of her presentation finery, though presentations were not the nerve-racking affairs they had been in the days of the old queen. Queen Alexandra, with her carefully enameled face, her head tilted slightly in a vain attempt to hear, her eyes bravely hiding their loneliness, had none of the theatrical impact of the old widow in rusty black who had vacated the throne too late and too reluctantly.

Both James and Lydia had welcomed Cousin Harriet's suggestion —Lydia because she was unable to cope, James because he wanted his beautiful daughter to have the most splendid launching possible.

But what neither of them had expected was the friendship that had sprung up between Maud and Cousin Harriet. They found they had a similar sense of humor and a similar impatience with the more stuffy conventions. Not that Cousin Harriet neglected her duties as a chaperone. She was quite as much a martinet as Mrs. Beauchamp was going to be with Honor and Daisy. But she thoroughly approved of Maud's scorning the dull, anemic young men, no matter how eligible, and frankly indicated that she preferred her niece to marry a virile young man with brains and no money, rather than the other way around. She was glad Maud had not yet accepted an offer. In her opinion, eighteen was too young to marry, eager and anxious though most mothers were to get their daughters settled. The terrible faux pas of having an unmarried daughter in her late twenties was unlikely to happen to Lady Lucie.

But neither did she want an unhappily married daughter with three babies before she became of age. Anyway, Maud would do as she wanted to, whatever her elders planned. That was very evident.

Indeed, Cousin Harriet suspected that such a thing was happening already, when Maud appeared unannounced in her sitting room one bright spring morning.

"I walked all the way, Cousin Harriet. Mamma says I'm turning into an amazon. Oh, dear, it's so hot."

Maud cast off her shady hat, and Cousin Harriet rang for a jug of lemonade.

"What's all this, then? Have you suddenly found walking is such an agreeable pastime?"

"Papa's at Syon House all day, and I get so bored. The life of an idle young woman. What did you used to do when you were young?"

"We planned our days, my dear. We spent so many hours at our embroidery or our sketching, so many writing letters, taking walks, paying calls. As I remember, time went by pleasantly enough."

"I can't stand sewing."

"No, you're a spoiled young woman."

"I have too much energy. I must be doing active things. It's something to do with seeing Mamma on her couch. I feel I have to make the most of every minute. But apart from that, aren't you pleased to see me?"

"Of course, my lamb. Though I have a certain curiosity as to the reason for your visit."

"Mamma wants you to dine before Laura Ponsonby's ball. We're having a small dinner party. Only eight. Nobody of any interest whatever."

"Your mother has already written me to that effect," Cousin Harriet said dryly.

"Oh. Then you know that isn't really why I came."

"I do."

"It's only a little favor I wanted to ask. If you could pretend to invite me to tea on a Sunday or even to supper occasionally—"

"Pretend. Who is the young man?"

Maud colored, with only the briefest guilt. Then she leaned forward eagerly.

"He's wonderful, Cousin Harriet. He's good-looking and clever and witty, and he writes poetry, and I adore him. But just because he has very little money or prospects, Papa has forbidden me to see him, and it's so *unfair*. What can I do?"

"Except meet secretly?"

"Yes."

"And I am to aid and abet?"

"Darling Cousin!"

"What does your mother say?"

"Good heavens, I don't tell her! Anyway, even if she took my side, she'd never have the courage to oppose Papa."

"And you would?"

"I *have* to!" Maud cried in distress. "It's tearing me to pieces, but if he will persist in being so obstinate, what am I to do? Wouldn't you have fought for the man you loved?"

Cousin Harriet ignored such a hypothetical question.

"I don't approve of this, Maud."

Maud nodded meekly. "I hate being deceitful myself. But it's being forced on me. Papa really is behaving just like a Victorian father."

"Can't you be patient until he calms down?"

"Patient! While my life is slipping away!"

Cousin Harriet repressed a smile. "I'll have to meet this young man."

"I want you to."

"So if I ask you to tea next Sunday, it's understood that you are both to come."

"On the first occasion of course," Maud agreed, her eyes beginning to sparkle.

"And you promise to take my advice when I've formed my own opinion of the young man and the situation."

Maud's expression became suspiciously bland.

"Darling Cousin, you always give the right advice."

Honor Beauchamp had none of Maud Lucie's ingenuity. Maud could make events happen. Honor waited for them and tried to believe in a kind destiny. She knew that Maud and Guy were meeting secretly. She trembled for them and envied them. She hadn't the least idea how to contrive a meeting with Ninian Spencer.

So when it came by chance, she silently thanked the destiny that had not ignored her.

Ninian had been visiting his uncle and was just leaving when Honor came by with a heavier than usual shopping basket. He raised his hat and immediately offered to carry her basket.

"It looks much too heavy for you, Miss Beauchamp."

"That's my own fault. I took an extra book from the library."

"Are you a great reader?"

"I enjoy it."

"But not as much as music?"

"No, music is my great love."

She saw that he was looking at her quizzically.

"Don't say that as if it's something to be ashamed of."

"Did I? I suppose it's because everyone tells me I spend too much time at the piano. I get a little defensive about it."

"Don't do that. It isn't everyone who has a talent. People who have are fortunate. Cherish it, Miss Beauchamp."

"Mamma is hoping—at least Daisy and I are hoping—that you will come to our ball," Honor heard herself saying, then colored furiously, wondering whatever had come over her. Also, to her confusion, she found she had gone right past her gate.

Noticing this, Ninian was smiling. "Let's walk around the square and catch it the next time."

"I didn't do it deliberately!"

"I didn't really think you had. Geniuses are usually absentminded."

"Now you're teasing me."

"Not in the least."

But he was looking much less stern and ascetic. His eyes were gentle.

"What is your passion, Mr. Spencer? I mean, in the way that music is mine."

"Writing. I intend to write a novel."

"And also practice at the bar?"

"One has to eat. My first novel is certain to be a resounding failure."

"I refuse to believe that."

"Now you're being kind."

"No, I have faith in you," Honor declared impulsively and was again astonished at herself.

A look that was curiously like gratitude passed over his face, as if he were glad for an encouraging remark even from someone as unimportant as herself.

"You didn't tell me when your ball is, Miss Beauchamp."

"At the end of June. Shall you be in London, Mr. Spencer?"

"I shall be in London and delighted to come if you can bear with my ugly face."

Chapter 7

"The first, the third, the fifth, and of course the supper waltz—"

"No, Guy, you can't have all those," Maud exclaimed.

"Why not?"

"It isn't that I don't want to. But with Cousin Harriet watching—"

"She likes me."

"I'm not sure just how much," Maud said honestly. "Oh, *you* as a person, yes, who wouldn't? But occasionally she talks almost like Papa. About *prospects!* And the other thing is, Papa always wants to see my dance program the next morning. I can't let him see your name four times."

Guy took the program and, writing his own name, Guy Beauchamp, discreetly in the first place, filled the others with a scrawled "Hamish Drood."

Maud giggled helplessly. "Drood! What a name!"

"The mystery of Edwin, by Charles Dickens. This is the private mystery of Hamish, intended to baffle suspicious parents."

"Guy, you are crazy. Anyway, you must dance with your sisters."

"Honor, yes. But I fancy Daisy can take care of herself. Is that your Worth dress?"

"Oh, no, we have to go to Paris for that. Anyway, I want to keep it for Honor and Daisy's ball."

"If we're there."

"What do you mean?"

"Just that. If."

The potted palms and banked flowers, the overheated air, the smell of perfume and powder, the lilting music, the whirling couples (Daisy Beauchamp's cheeks were as pink as her gown), the immense amount of food in the supper room (cold chicken, turkey, hams, jellies, trifles, hothouse peaches and strawberries, champagne), the dark corners in the conservatory and on stairways, the snatched embraces out of the sight of chaperones' sharp eyes . . . It was a familiar world, but never before had it had such burning, beautiful excitement. For, in the darkest corner of the conservatory, Guy whispered, "Maud, will you marry me? Please, please, say yes."

The excitement was shot through with the faintest titillating sensation of fear.

"*How?* Papa will never—"

"I'll ask him formally of course, but I don't intend his refusal to stand in my way. He can't just get rid of me like that. I love you, Maud. Awfully, awfully. More than anyone else ever will."

"And I you," she whispered.

"Who is this?" Papa's finger stabbed at the ridiculous name, Hamish Drood . . .

"Oh, a rather amusing person." Maud kept her eyes on her plate of deviled kidneys, to which she now regretted helping herself.

"He must have been, since I see you danced with him three times. Horace Ponsonby?"

Now she was able to look up.

"Laura's brother. He was a dreadful bore. So serious. He's with a firm of stockbrokers in the city. He talked about investments."

"A good subject."

"But not at a ball, Papa."

"Guy Beauchamp?" Now it was Papa who wasn't looking up. His voice was deceptively mild. "I thought I had asked you not to see him."

"How could I cut him at a ball, Papa? That would have caused a scandal."

"I see you had the first dance with him, and here is this Hamish Drood again for the supper waltz."

Papa's blue eyes were probing now. "You seem to have been giving this young man an unfair share of your time. What is his family? What does he do?"

"I . . . really didn't discover, Papa. We were enjoying dancing too much to cross-examine one another."

"Are those kidneys not to your liking?"

"I'm not very hungry." Maud put her hand to her head. "I think I must have had a little too much champagne last night. May I be excused, Papa?"

"I think not. Stay where you are. We've only begun our conversation. Have another cup of coffee and explain to me why this mysterious Mr. Drood writes in a remarkably similar hand to Mr. Guy Beauchamp. A very childish deceit this, Maud. Whose idea was it, yours or Mr. Beauchamp's?"

The betraying color was in her face. Her recently acquired expertise in lying annoyingly deserted her at vital moments.

"Guy's," Maud admitted. "At least—"

"I'm glad to hear that. I wouldn't like to think my daughter had such an infantile imagination. Hamish Drood, indeed. Do you take me for a complete fool?" Papa suddenly flung the dance program across the table. His gaze was no longer benign. Bright sparks of anger danced in his eyes. Maud, familiar enough with his sudden anger, had seldom had it directed at her. She felt a shivering, devastating pain, which, however, was quickly followed by resentment that he should behave like this. How could he be so unfair, so unsympathetic, so deliberately opposed to her happiness? Didn't he love her, after all?

"You have disobeyed me, Maud."

"Yes, Papa."

"You have been seeing this young man."

"Naturally. Since we were both guests at the same function."

"I'm not referring to last night. I have had my suspicions for some time that you've been disobeying me. I was reluctant to find out the truth. But now I have."

"Oh," said Maud.

"Oh. Is that all you can say?" Papa banged his clenched fist on the table, making the cups rattle. "Is that all the respect you have for me?"

"It isn't a matter of lack of respect, Papa," Maud cried in anguish. "It's simply that you aren't being fair. You've judged Guy because he has no money."

"Money is important enough. You'll discover that before you're an old woman. But I've also judged him and am doing so again at this moment, because of his devious, secret, seducing ways."

"Papa! I won't have you saying things like that."

"He hadn't been in my house for half an hour before he was trying out his schemes."

"No, that isn't true! It was I who invited him up to the studio."

"Then I'm sorry to say that you're as bad as he is. I'll tell you again, and for the last time, I won't allow this to go on. You're my only daughter, and I have other plans for you. I absolutely refuse to have you getting a reputation for indulging in cheap love affairs."

Maud sprang up, her face hot with anger.

"This isn't a cheap love affair. It's the very opposite. Guy is coming to see you to ask permission to marry me."

"Then I'm afraid I won't be at home. Is there no limit to his impudence?"

"Do you mean that, Papa. Truly?"

Angry eyes looked into angry eyes.

"Every word."

"Then neither will I be at home, in a house that is becoming a prison."

"A prison? Those are your words, my dear, not mine. Remember that, if eventually I have to give orders to have you confined to your room until you come to your senses and give me your word of honor that you will break off your association with this young man."

She couldn't believe her ears. Locked in her room. She would be a laughingstock. Mamma wouldn't allow it. Neither would Nanny.

But would either of them dare oppose Papa in this mood, his cheeks roweled with dour determination, his eyes blazing fanatically?

"You're treating me like a child!" she exclaimed. "Or a lunatic," she added disbelievingly.

"Which is how you're behaving."

"Then very well. I'll stay in my room voluntarily until you change your mind. You won't even need to lock the door."

"Splendid. Do I have your promise? For what it's worth."

His contempt was too much. Maud burst into weeping.

"Papa, Guy and I love each other," she sobbed.

"No doubt you think you do. You're eighteen, and this young

man is less in his behavior. Married love must be adult and durable."

"Like yours and Mamma's?"

Papa's face tightened. Then he said, with infinite pain, "Maud, is this you? Or me? Speaking like this to each other?"

She couldn't bear to look at his tight gray face. She covered her own with her hands, crying passionately, "It's your fault, Papa. It's you who's ruining my life!"

She was deeply shocked by her ability to hurt her father. She kept remembering his shattered look of pain all that day, an endless day spent in her room, sometimes weeping, sometimes quietly brooding, sometimes raging up and down, Han perplexedly at her heels.

"You've got yourself in a pickle all right, Miss Maud," Nanny said. "Disobeying your Papa like that. He says I'm not to let you out of my sight. So don't you go getting me into trouble, too."

"I won't," said Maud. "I'm a voluntary prisoner. I don't intend to stir from here until Papa changes his mind."

"What will everyone say?"

"They can say the truth. That my father is an unjust tyrant."

"He only wants your good, Miss Maud."

"I might go on a hunger strike, too."

Nanny glowered. "I'll have none of that nonsense. Your meals will be brought up here, and you'll eat them and have the grace to thank Cora for the extra work caused. Oh, goodness gracious, you behaving like this, after the way I've brought you up and the way you used to worship your Papa. Whatever has got into you?"

The pain shivered in her again. "Be quiet, Nanny. Has anyone called asking for me?"

"I'm not permitted to say."

"What do you mean?"

"The master has given orders. No communication with the outside world while you're refusing to leave your room."

"Nanny, this is ridiculous!"

"You began it, Miss Maud, being untruthful like that. Grass stains on your skirt, and you said you fell over the dog. I might have known better."

She had made her rash ultimatum, and now she couldn't go back on it. She must stay where she was and stare at the wallpaper, or at her own forlorn face in the mirror. Or write in her diary or stand at the window, well back from inquisitive eyes, and watch the sunlight sliding over the Square. Somehow she must pass the monotonous days and wait for Papa to give her some way of getting out of this absurd contretemps.

The trouble was there was no way. For she hadn't the slightest intention of giving Guy up. Now, if he would still have her, she was utterly determined to marry him.

But her dreams, in the nights that were almost as long as the days, were dominated by Papa, with his painfully wounded gaze. She scarcely dreamed of Guy at all.

"Miss Maud!" That was Cora with her breakfast tray. "Are you feeling better?"

It was a polite fiction that she was ill. Not ill enough for a doctor, but merely suffering from a young girl's malaise, exhaustion after too much excitement.

"No, Cora, I'm exactly the same."

"Oh, dear, miss. I was wondering, so long as you're keeping to your room, I might be able to do errands for you. You know. Take letters and suchlike."

Maud shot up on her pillows.

"Cora, *would* you? You mean *secret* messages?"

Cora nodded. She was getting stout, Maud noticed. Her face had an overblown look. And there was an expression in her eyes that was puzzling.

"We're on your side in the kitchen, Miss Maud."

"Then you know all about it?"

"Lor', yes."

"Oh, bless you, Cora."

There had been nothing promised about not writing letters and smuggling them out of the house. She had already forgotten Cora's strange expression.

She wrote swiftly:

DEAREST GUY,

Don't attempt to see Papa in his present mood. He is being unbelievably stubborn, but so am I. I am a prisoner (suffragette style, though I am not chained to the bedpost) until I can persuade him to be more sympathetic and understanding. I am desperately unhappy, knowing how you must be suffering. And, of course, Papa, too, though that is his own fault. But be reassured, we will win in the end. Papa simply can't refuse me what I want. He never has before. Cora is going to smuggle this to Daisy and will bring back an answer. So write quickly—a long, long letter, to comfort your poor incarcerated Maud.

P.S. I stand at the window, feeling just like the Lady of Shalott, waiting to see you go by.

"Maud, whatever is all this nonsense?"

Mamma was actually alarmed enough to make the difficult journey up the stairs to Maud's bedroom. She collapsed into a chair, told Bertha to go and not come back until she rang, then turned her vague, distressed eyes on Maud.

"Is this a childish tantrum, or are you out of your mind?"

"If being in love is being out of one's mind, then I am, Mamma."

Mamma made an impatient movement. "Why must you and your father dramatize yourselves so much? You're both behaving exactly alike and, in the process, making yourselves extremely unhappy."

"Is he unhappy?" Maud muttered.

"Of course he is. In torment."

"I'm glad."

"I simply don't understand you, Maud. Once you could never bear to upset him."

Maud frowned, blinking back the furious tears.

"This is a question of my whole life's happiness. He must see— Mamma, can't you persuade him to be more reasonable?"

Mamma's thin, disgruntled face lifted. "When have I ever been able to persuade him of anything? When has anybody? He makes his own laws. You ought to know that. Besides, I'm inclined to agree with him over this matter. You can't be serious about wanting to marry this young man. No money, no position. You a bank clerk's wife!"

"You married a poor artist, Mamma."

"Which could be the very reason that I'm asking you to have some sense."

"But wasn't it worth while at the beginning, when you were

young and in love?" Maud begged. "Couldn't it have gone on being all right if you hadn't become an invalid?"

Lady Lucie turned her head away.

"Overromanticism is a great mistake. It never lasts. You'll learn, my darling."

"So I am not to be in love?"

"There are other, more reliable emotions. Admiration, friendship, good sense—"

"But that isn't living!" Maud cried in contempt.

"Neither is shutting yourself in your room in this ridiculous way. You'd better be careful. People will be saying you're unhinged. Like that poor child in the house across the Square. No doubt you've seen him at the window. Bertha's told me about the poor little ghost."

"Mamma, that isn't fair! That's as unfair as Papa. If that's all you have to say to me, I'd rather you didn't stay."

Mamma rose and made her halting way across the room to lay her scented dry cheek against Maud's. "Try to grow up, dear. I know it's painful. But it has to be done."

When Mamma had gone, Maud stood at the window and wondered if those cruel words were true, that her face frightened the children passing by. She was not moping and mowing, but she fancied she was already growing pale from her self-imprisonment. Privately, she was wondering how long she could keep this up without growing unhinged in all truth. Three days had been an eternity.

The strange thing was that for all the time she spent at the window she had never once seen Guy go by. Was he avoiding her? Had he decided the whole thing was too difficult and uncomfortable?

But that evening a note, swiftly transferred from Cora's apron pocket to her hand, sent her spirits soaring.

"*Thank* you, Cora. I'll never forget you for this."

"You may have to, miss."

"But I've just told you I won't."

"All the same—" Cora had her odd, secretive look again. Maud was going to inquire about it, then was too impatient to read her letter to worry about a servant's private thoughts.

Guy applauded what she was doing. Oh, thank blessed heaven!

Bravo, you adorable crazy girl. Now I know you really are the most wonderful person in the world, and I vow never to give you up. I am not in such good odor with my own family as my mother disapproves of what she calls "ill-advised persistence," and of course this has been communicated to Uncle Lionel, who is watching me like a hawk, as if he thinks I am going to fill my pockets with his sovereigns and decamp. I have even thought it prudent not to pass your house, so as not to further exacerbate the position until I have perfected my plan.

Yes, my darling, I have not been idle. I do have a plan. If we could bring it off, I would be the luckiest fellow alive. But I can't put it to you on paper. It is too dangerous. Besides, I must be able to watch your face as you hear it. So, here is the first step to be taken. I think I can persuade my uncle to let me have the afternoon off to attend the private view at the Royal Academy. Fortunately, he approves of culture and thinks there is plenty of room for improvement in my case. Could you call a truce with your father for this occasion? Since he, the famous artist, will be surrounded by people, surely we could contrive to meet for a few minutes. I will stand just within the doorway of the third gallery for the entire afternoon, if necessary. I love you, my angel . . .

Miss Lavender struggled with the two seemingly impossible meeting points, the eye of the needle and the thread of cotton.

"Oh, let me do it, or we'll be here all day," Daisy said impatiently. "You need new spectacles, Miss Lavender."

"Yes, Miss Daisy, I believe I do."

"Then why don't you get them?"

"I will when I get an opportunity. All you young ladies to be outfitted for the season. What time have I got to be running to eye doctors?" And with what did she pay their bills? Last time, her mother and herself had had to go without coal for a month. It wasn't that she minded chilblains, although they made her fingers clumsy for sewing: it was that her mother was eighty-three and felt the cold cruelly. Anyway, the doctor had said that her eye condition was progressive. How progressive? She was afraid he might tell her if she saw him again.

"Who knows, you might be making a trousseau before the season is over," Daisy said, and Miss Lavender sat back on her heels.

"Not yours, Miss Daisy!"

Daisy giggled in high glee.

"Goodness, no, I've scarcely spoken to a man yet."

"I did think you were rather young. Then is it Miss Honor?"

"I wasn't meaning her, though I can tell you there are straws in the wind. She's offered to read to old Colonel Spencer every morning, because he finds the print of the *Times* too small for his eyesight."

"That's a thoughtful thing to do, I must say."

"But can you imagine Honor tearing herself away from her piano every morning? She must have a very strong reason."

"In trousers, no doubt, Miss Daisy."

Daisy giggled again.

"You're very bright this morning, Miss Lavender. Yes, it's the colonel's nephew. I think he and Honor might be very well suited. They're the same type. Reserved. Though I believe the colonel can't understand why Ninian isn't more taken with Maud Lucie. But it's just as well he isn't, since my brother—oh, I'm not supposed to talk about this. Mamma's in a state. She'll hardly speak to Guy. She says she wonders how she ever thought he could keep out of a scrape for long and if Uncle Lionel washes his hands of him, then he must make his own way in future."

Miss Lavender calmly took pins out of the pincushion and continued turning up the eight yards of hem around Daisy's bouffant skirt.

"Would it be Miss Lucie's trousseau you were referring to? But I have never been engaged to do any work for her. I fancy I wouldn't be grand enough."

"That's what her father might think. He's an impossible snob. But Maud wouldn't. She's the greatest fun. I absolutely agree with Guy about her." Daisy lowered her voice and said rapidly, "Have you heard the rumor that her father has locked her in her room so that she can't see Guy? It isn't true, of course. She's staying there of her own free will until that cruel, hardhearted man gives them permission to marry."

"Good gracious!"

"It's time girls weren't so completely under the thumb of their parents," Daisy declared. "Look at men. They have all the freedom in the world. Guy traveled all over Europe before he was twenty-one. But here are Honor and I, dressed up like dummies, expected to marry someone Mamma approves of and never allowed to see him for five minutes alone. Scarcely even allowed a kiss."

"I daresay you'll manage, Miss Daisy," Miss Lavender observed. She wouldn't have minded being dressed up like a dummy herself. Handling lovely materials for so many years and never wearing anything but rusty black herself. She would like to be buried in a silk dress—the best French silk spun on the mills at Toulon.

"Oh, I'll manage, of course," Daisy said blithely. "I'm not pretty, and I'm too fat, and I talk too much, but—"

"Stand still, do, if you don't want a pin run into you."

"But I believe some men might like me. In spite of Maud Lucie. If she's still Maud Lucie by the end of the season."

It was the usual crush at the summer opening of the Royal Academy, but as always, Sir James Lucie contrived to make an entrance. He would never have admitted that half the flurry of their arrival was caused by his wife's invalid chair cutting a swath through the crowd. He undertook to push the chair himself on these occasions, as if Lady Lucie, in her wide-brimmed pearl-gray organdy hat and pearl-gray gown, were his most cherished possession. Or just one degree less cherished than his daughter, Maud, on his arm.

Maud had chosen to wear her favorite emerald green, with an enormous picture hat. She was as impossible not to notice as a peacock with a spread tail. Her father's fond smile gave lie to the rumor that the two were in the throes of a bitter quarrel. No more harmonious family group could be seen at this fashionable gathering on a hot May afternoon.

Reporters were clustering around.

"How do you regard your exhibit this year, Sir James?"

"It's for you fellows to regard it, not me."

"Isn't it a new image of your daughter?"

"I imagined we were discussing the quality of my work," Sir James replied blandly, "not its subject."

"With this sort of development, will Miss Lucie be a Madonna next year?"

The warning spark flashed, then was repressed in Sir James' sunny eyes.

"Who knows what form inspiration will take? Are you asking me to prophesy?"

Maud's fingers tightened on her father's arm. She couldn't help her pride in him on these occasions. One critic had once written that the opening of the Royal Academy's summer exhibition would never be the same without Sir James Lucie's histrionics. There were other picturesque artists of course. Holman Hunt had arrived wearing a shabby cape and leaning on a crooked stick. People said he had never been quite the same since that bizarre episode of painting a starving and thirst-ridden goat on the shores of the Dead Sea. The good-looking Sickert was there, and John Singer Sargent over from America, and a young man called Augustus John, who was being talked about. He also had flair and flamboyance, but he was young. The day still belonged to the golden-haired giant, Sir James Lucie, with his flightless moth of a wife and his spectacular daughter. His good fortune in having such a daughter had been discussed frequently over the years. Many people attributed his success entirely to her. But it could not be denied that he had given her generously to his public, from the days of her innocent childhood, through adolescence, to the full flowering of her beauty.

Though the damped-down pale virginal beauty this year was a disappointment, its artistic merit could not be questioned. It was a strange interpretation. Did Sir James really see that spirited beauty as a pale virgin?

Maud listened to the discussion growing louder as more people joined in. Mamma sat smiling her wistful, patient smile (presently the overheated atmosphere would make her feel faint) while Papa skillfully dealt with his impertinent, presumptuous critics. Maud found it easy enough to detach her arm from his to give him more freedom to gesticulate. Then she noticed the Marchioness of Londonderry, a favorite with Papa, approaching and in a flash seized her opportunity to escape. She would pretend later that the crowd had separated them. "You are too popular, Papa," she would say placatingly. "I couldn't get near you for thousands of people." She was elated, but also a little shocked that, at last, lying was becoming easy.

When she had gone downstairs yesterday morning and joined Papa at breakfast, it had been difficult to appear meek only because she had suddenly had an overpowering desire to rush into his arms. He had been so radiantly, transparently pleased at her appearance that she had wanted to weep.

"I'm not giving in, Papa," she had said at once. "I only thought that the private view tomorrow was nothing to do with our quarrel. We have a duty to our public—at least, you have and I—"

"And you are indispensable," Papa said in a great roar, throwing out his arms to gather her to him.

She avoided that, however. A feeling of acute treachery followed her first spontaneity. She backed away, saying distantly, "It's only a truce so that people won't talk. You must understand that."

"My dearest, bless you for your kind thought. But let people talk if they want to. Haven't we always been talked about, you and I? I'd have simply said you had the chicken pox. Sit down and have your breakfast. You look as thin as a matchstick. Haven't been starving yourself over that young man, have you? Well, it's better to do it now than later, if he got his wish and attempted to support you on his earnings."

"Papa, this is a truce."

"I apologize. I promise not to mention his name again unless some unfortunate circumstance forces me to."

He looked at her from beneath his golden eyebrows. "So that's up to you, my dear."

Now she was almost crying. How could she have known she would feel so treacherous?

"But nothing has changed, Papa. I shall go back to my room tomorrow after the private view."

"Shall you? How extraordinarily dull for you. Incarcerating yourself like a nun in a convent. Personally, I have had another idea. Since I've finished the Northumberland portrait, I thought we might have a few days' fresh air at Brighton. And not a moment too soon, by the color of your cheeks. I'll write today for rooms at the Old Ship. We'll stroll on the pier. I seem to remember you were once devotedly in love with piers, which I'm glad to say shows a slightly vulgar tendency which you inherit from me." He dabbed at his mouth with his napkin and bent his radiant gaze on her. "Your mother could never be persuaded to set foot on one."

His confident assumption that she would so easily come back under his spell, his careless dismissal of her real and anguished emotions restored her anger and her determination. Although he pretended he thought her grown-up, he was still treating her as a child. Perhaps he always would.

The lesson she must teach him was really long overdue, she thought as she slipped through the crowd to the place of rendezvous with Guy.

Someone spoke. "Isn't that Maud Lucie?"

"Who?"

"There. In the green. Doesn't look a bit like her current portrait, does she?"

One had to pause to look, not at the speakers, but at the portrait dominating the far wall of this gallery, surrounded by the crowd who inevitably gathered around the new James Lucie exhibit.

"A lily," said another woman doubtfully. "Do you think Maud Lucie recognizes that flower?"

"Jealousy, Sylvia, jealousy."

"But haven't you heard the rumor that she's having an affair and her father can't bear to part with her? This portrait is meant to be symbolic or something."

Maud moved on quickly, her gloved hand to her face to avoid recognition, the shaft in her heart. The crowd was thinner in the next gallery. They all seemed to be strangers, thank heaven. Why hadn't she worn a veil?

A strong clasp was on her arm.

"Maud, you idiot! Why must you look so conspicuous?"

"I'm used to dressing like this. Papa expects—" She saw that Guy wasn't angry, only highly tense and nervous.

"In the future your father can stop expecting anything of you," he said in a low urgent voice. "We're going to run away. I have the whole plan worked out. A friend of mine has a cottage in Wiltshire. We can have it until we are married. Then, when I've arranged funds, we can set out on our travels. I wouldn't dream of allowing you to come abroad with me until you have a wedding ring on your finger."

"Stop, Guy, stop! I can't keep up with you. You mean we're to *elope?*"

"The devil take it, Maud, everyone's staring at you in that gorgeous hat. Turn around and look at the paintings. Yes, of course we're to elope. What else can we do under the circumstances?"

"I don't know. I hadn't thought. Except that Papa will eventually relent, I'm sure."

"When we're middle-aged? Maud, this is now!"

"Yes, I know," Maud said breathlessly. "But eloping—"

"It will be perfectly simple. You'll slip out of the house tomorrow morning at six o'clock and meet me on the corner of the High Street. We'll take a cab to Paddington and catch the seven fifteen train to Salisbury. There'll be no one about at that hour. It will be quite safe. Though you'd better wear a veil. You can get out of the house unnoticed, can't you? You've always been clever at that in the past."

"Guy," she managed to interpose, "I'm under age. I need my parents' consent to marry."

"You're twenty-one as of now."

"But that's telling a lie. That's illegal!"

"By the time our secret's out your father will be happy to make it legal. We can be married again, in Westminster Abbey if you like. I say, did you ever see a sunset that looked like that?"

She stole a glance at his face. Her shock eased, and laughter began to bubble inside her. He was trying to look serious about a bad painting, but his excitement was so transparent that anyone who looked at him must be aware of it. Dear Guy, he looked so triumphant, so masterful that, as always, her adventurous spirit rose to meet his. Besides, it was quite a feat to be carrying off the virgin of the year. The irony appealed to her sense of humor. It was a perfectly delicious joke.

Maud dared to slip her gloved hand into his.

"Dearest!" His lips scarcely moved. But her fingers were stinging with pain as he squeezed them.

"Yes, isn't it a delightfully stormy sunset," she said gaily. "That poor wracked-looking tree. Guy, it's been so nice meeting you, but I must go now. Papa will be looking for me." She bent her head over her reticule, looking for a handkerchief. "Money?" she murmured.

He looked affronted. "That's hardly your concern. If I haven't enough, I really will rob the bank."

A small bag packed with one's immediate requirements. The rest of one's clothes could be sent on later, when Mamma and Papa had got over their shock and forgiven her or, alternately, washed their hands of her. Either way, they would not refuse her her wardrobe. Or she could buy another, one more suitable for traveling abroad.

How could she buy necessities without money?

Maud thrust that irritating wasp of a thought away but prudently unlocked her jewel box and took out her pearl necklace and a brooch, a crescent of diamonds, that had been left to her by her grandmother. She could wear both items inconspicuously when she left in the morning.

How was she to slip out of the house unnoticed? If Nanny woke and called after her, if Papa, still suspicious in spite of their supposed reconciliation (she knew by the way he watched her, as if he would like to look inside her skull), was wakeful and heard the stairs creak, if Han barked.

Beloved Han, how was she to leave him?

But of course she wasn't. He was coming, too. There was her excuse. Encountered on the stairs, her modest bag hidden beneath her voluminous cloak, she was taking Han for a walk. An emergency. Hadn't everyone heard him demanding to be let out?

Han was the hero of her life, the guardian of her happiness. He should have a small silver medal hung around his neck.

There was the letter to write, of course. That was the most difficult task of all.

DEAREST PAPA AND MAMMA,

Guy and I are being married tomorrow in the country. We promise, when you forgive us, that we will come back to London and have another wedding ceremony wherever you please. But, in the meantime, you force this action on us. We love each other and belong to each other. Please, please, forgive me and go on loving me.

MAUD

A tear dropped and blotted the last line. Bother, she would have to write it out again. No, she hadn't time. It was fully daylight, and Han was snuffling at her ankles. She had dressed in her plainest dress, thinking it best for traveling, but regretting it for a wedding.

Maud Lucie being married in bottle-green serge! A tiny voice sounded in her head. Wake up, Maud. Stop dreaming.

But she was wide-awake. And it was time to go.

Safely on the train, they couldn't stop laughing. Guy said, "Let's order breakfast, I'm starving," and then began laughing again. "If nothing is better than this moment, it will be worthwhile. Oh, Maud, my adorable Maud!"

"Did you see the way the conductor looked at Han? And I said, he isn't a dog, he's a person!"

"He isn't only a person, he's the arbiter of our fate, if you ask me."

"I plan to have a medal made for him."

"Not enough. He shall have a CMG at least."

"Guy?"

"Yes, my love."

"What do we do?"

He ignored the sudden uncertainty in her voice.

"I told you. We go into the restaurant car and get some breakfast."

"I mean later. Today, tonight, tomorrow, next week."

"Don't eat up our lives like that! Today we get a marriage license and make arrangements to be married at the earliest possible moment."

"You mean we can't be married today?"

"Well, I hardly think so. There's some stupid law about establishing domicile."

"For how long?" Maud asked tensely.

"I'm not sure. It may be three weeks."

"Three weeks!"

"But didn't you know that? I thought you'd know. Anyway, this cottage is miles from anywhere. We'll be quite private."

"But, Guy, I've only one dress!"

It was all she could put into words at that moment. The rest, the living together unmarried, in a lonely cottage—even though they intended to marry at the first possible moment—she hadn't thought of a cataclysmic thing like that. Guy hadn't told her. He hadn't had a chance, to be perfectly fair. Anyway, he would have swept her off her feet, she knew. But she would be getting a reputation like Elinor Glyn, or one of those fast women.

Who cared?

And Guy was laughing heartily at her typical remark. She had only one dress. Trust a female to think of that first. His high spirits were so compelling that she had to laugh with him. Why think of trivial details when they were so happy together?

And no one need know about the three weeks in the cottage. Unless they chose to be brazen about it. After all, what would it matter when they were married?

All the same, hadn't they been a little too impetuous and impractical? But how else could they have done this? Anyone less prejudiced than Papa would have seen from the beginning that they belonged to each other.

Was Papa reading her letter at this moment?

"What will your Uncle Lionel say?" she asked as once more her laughter died.

"Oh, I'll be thrown out of the bank. But I would be a horrible failure as a banker. I've made up my mind about that. Imagine living one's whole life listening to the sordid clinking of coins."

"Shall we have any to clink?"

"Dearest, you haven't a mercenary streak I didn't know about, have you?"

"A very slight practical one," Maud confessed apologetically.

"Well, of course we have to eat, and I have to buy my wife a new hat now and then, I know that. But as soon as I have all the necessary arrangements made, we'll be off on our travels. I'll be rich and famous before the year's out. If I'm not, I warrant your father will come around."

"What do you mean?"

"What I say. He'll never let his beloved daughter want for anything."

"But isn't it a husband's business to do that?"

"You're quite right, of course. I'll never let you want for anything if I can help it. That's a vow. But if you want the frills and furbelows you're used to, you may have to be a little patient. You may

have to rough it a little. You won't mind that with me, will you?"
He looked at her with so much anxiety, as if such a possibility had
only just occurred to him, that she had to say warmly that of course
she wouldn't mind. They had each other and were in love. Love
would more than compensate for a few economies and difficulties.

Guy Everard George Beauchamp, gentleman.
Maud Evangeline Lucie, spinster.
"Date of birth?" asked the clerk.
Maud hesitated. Then she said firmly, "I was twenty-one years
old on the fourteenth of January last. My father is James Edward
Lucie, and my mother Lydia Evangeline Lucie."
She went on answering the questions coolly, her fingers curled
tightly inside Guy's. She was wearing a veil, but the clerk's eyes
kept darting up to her face. He was curious naturally. A registry
office wedding for such a good-looking couple smacked of drama.
Maud's fears had materialized. The ceremony could not take place
for three weeks. And the cottage to which Guy hopefully took her,
assisting her out of the hired cab at the bottom of a deep-green lane,
turned out to have nothing in its favor but its picturesque situation.
It was dismally dark and damp indoors. The wide hearth of the living room was deep in soot; the larger cupboards held nothing but
a stock of candles and traces of mice; of the two rooms upstairs, one
had a double bed and spartan furnishings, the other was filled with
packing cases, broken furniture, and junk.
No dressing room, no bathroom, one of those dreadful primitive
places in the back garden.
Guy thought she should be entranced by the purple and white
lilacs hanging over the window, the hum of bees, the glint of river
water in the distance. He would go down and catch a fish for their
supper. He was a capital fisherman.
"Who will cook it?" Maud asked.
"That's easy surely. A frying pan, a little lard."
"Lard?"
"We'll have to go shopping, of course. The village is only half a
mile away. You make out a list while I get in some firewood. Tonight
we'll light all the candles and have a roaring fire."
"Oh, yes. How jolly!"

Her spirits were still oddly unreliable, up one moment, down the next. The prospect of dancing firelight and herself sitting on the hearth rug with her head against Guy's knees was entrancing.

She had never made up a shopping list in her life.

Tea. A cup of tea would be heavenly. That required milk. And cake. (One of Cook's rich dark fruitcakes . . .)

Eggs. It surely couldn't be difficult to boil an egg. Bread, butter, and cheese were simple. They couldn't starve on that. Some bones for Han. And Guy's fish. And an apron to protect her one and only dress.

"What tremendous fun," she said, writing busily.

"What?"

"Going shopping."

He put his arms around her and kissed the tip of her nose. "Bless you, you are a protected infant."

"Oh, I know your sisters would be a great deal better at this sort of thing."

"They've had to be."

"Guy, do they know about us? Where we are?"

"Good gracious, no. Though Honor—"

"Honor?"

"She knows I come down here fishing. But I don't think she would guess."

"She'd never give us away anyway. She has too much integrity."

"Yes, she should have been the man in our family. I'm sure Mamma thinks so."

"But if you were a girl, I couldn't have married you!"

This absurd sally so delighted them both that laughter seized them again.

"You adorable fool, Maud."

Again Maud's laughter died.

"It wasn't really such a funny remark. Come on, let's go shopping while the sun's still shining. Han needs some exercise after being cooped up in the train. Don't you, my poppet? And your master has to catch a fish for our supper."

The day was golden until evening. Then a cold wind rose, bringing a clammy mist. Guy had triumphantly brought home two perch and spent a laborious half hour in the backyard, cleaning them. He came in smelling of fish, and said it was time to light the fire. Maud could light the candles and set the table. They would fry the fish in the pan over the fire. The bottle of wine that Guy had added to their purchases was cooling in the well outside the back door.

It became gay, with the candlelight shining on the old oak table and the logs on the fire beginning to spark and sizzle. Maud stopped thinking about the double bed upstairs.

She sang softly as she laid the table and said that was what Cora always did. "Or sometimes she whistled. If she was sure Mamma and Papa were out of hearing."

"You're not a servant," Guy said, rather sharply.

"But here I am wearing an apron. Oh, dear, that chimney's beginning to smoke."

"It'll stop when the fire burns up."

"It must be the east wind. Ugh! It's making me cry."

Guy fanned impatiently at the sticks, and presently a stronger flame shot up. He carefully laid on logs, and a healthy blaze developed. He sat back on his heels. "There. Now for the fish. Have you put lard in the pan? Oh, more than that, that wouldn't fry a sardine."

"I'll learn," said Maud humbly.

"You don't need to. Do you think we won't have a maid?"

"Not for three weeks."

"No. Well."

But the pan held over the glowing logs seemed to be the unfortunate signal for another cloud of dirty gray smoke to belch out of the chimney. It enveloped the pan before Guy could snatch it away.

"Hell!" he exclaimed, looking at the soot-covered fish. "Oh, damnation! Oh, I'm sorry, Maud. I didn't mean to swear."

"Why not?" said Maud bleakly, her mood abruptly descending to its lowest state. "Isn't it something to swear about, that we now have no supper?"

"We still have bread and cheese and wine."

"Your beautiful fish are ruined!"

"Perhaps I could wash them."

Maud shuddered. "No, I couldn't bear it." She sat down. "I don't think I can bear it."

"Dearest, the world isn't coming to an end because our supper is spoiled."

Maud dragged at the fastenings of her apron and threw the garment on the floor. How could he be so unperceptive? Didn't he see her misery?

"It isn't only our supper," she cried passionately. "If we go on like this, everything will be spoiled."

Blinking his smoke-reddened eyes, Guy stared at her.

"What do you mean?"

"Three weeks of this! It would ruin the happiest marriage."

"But it's only a little discomfort. You'll have to put up with worse than this when we begin our travels. Where's your sense of humor?"

"I don't know. Perhaps I haven't got one."

"You don't think I mean to come upstairs tonight, do you? I'm going to sleep down here on that couch. I'll be perfectly comfortable. You can take Han to guard you, if you think a guard is necessary."

She searched his face, trying to decide whether he had just made that decision, judiciously. She was furious with herself for her own unexpected puritanism.

It wasn't puritanism; it was just distaste for what was obviously a damp lumpy bed.

"It's all so squalid!" she burst out.

His face fell ludicrously.

"I know it isn't quite the thing. Peter has let this place go to the pack. It didn't used to be like this. To tell the truth, I wouldn't have brought you here if I'd known. But now we are here—"

"Why didn't you tell me about the three weeks we'd have to wait?"

"I thought you'd know."

"How would I know? I've never been married before."

"The whole thing is your father's fault."

"Don't you start blaming Papa." She was angry now, pointing scathingly at the pathetic fish, the smoking fire. "He would never have brought me to a place like this."

"Naturally. He treats you like a princess. But I treat you like a woman." His face tightened in remorse. "Oh, Maud! I didn't mean it to be like this."

"I have only one dress," she cried furiously.

"Damn your dress! That's all you can think of, your wretched clothes. I suppose you want your Worth creation to be married in. You're as vain as a peacock."

She dug her knuckles into her eyes. They were smarting intolerably from smoke and tears.

"I thought you liked me vain."

"So I do, but—"

"Take me to a hotel, Guy. I'll stay in one alone until we can be married. Please! Don't let's spoil everything by trying to live this way. We'll only fight all the time."

He began to shake his head slowly, in disappointment and disbelief.

"All right," he agreed sulkily. "I suppose this was a mad idea. But I thought you would have entered into the spirit of it."

"If it's because you can't afford a hotel, I can pay for it myself."

"You mean send the bill to your father!"

She fumbled inside her bodice and unpinned the crescent of diamonds.

"No, I intend to sell this. I brought it for that reason."

"Maud!"

His shocked incredulity made her exclaim, "After all this, if you're still going to pretend pride—really, Guy, if we're going to be married, we've got to share!" He looked so stiffly disapproving that inevitably her sense of humor came to the rescue. "But not a double bed. Not yet. That's to be done properly, with clean linen and decent surroundings. I'm not being romantic, only practical."

"My witch of Melbury Square, practical!" he said wonderingly. "Who would have thought it? But you're right, of course. It shall be as you wish. Then we'd better go, if you can walk three miles in the dark. What about Han?"

"Poor sweet, he doesn't care for this smoky atmosphere any more than I do. Listen to him sneezing. Of course he can walk three miles. Better than I can since he doesn't wear high-heeled shoes."

Now that she had got her way, she had to be lighthearted and gay. She didn't know why she was illogically wishing that Guy had refused to do as she asked. She almost wished he had locked her in, as Papa might have done. She hadn't suspected that she had this secret desire to be dominated.

Chapter 8

It was too much to hope that the questions were over. Daisy, in tears, had at last confessed her part as go-between, carrying letters from Guy to Maud. Her resolution not to betray the runaway pair had vanished when she heard that Cora, the housemaid, had been dismissed for her part in the affair. Apparently, she had brazenly admitted her guilt and had declared that she would be glad to leave the house of a man who had a stone in place of a heart.

Since Daisy was not a servant, she could not be punished in this way. It was obvious, from the steely look in Mamma's eye, that some other form of chastisement would be devised for her.

Honor was saying nothing. She admitted that she knew Maud and Guy were in love, but beyond that, she had no knowledge of their plans or their whereabouts.

It seemed that Uncle Lionel was in a furious temper and had banned Guy from the bank forevermore. If by some improbable chance he became rich in the future, he would not even be welcomed through the bank's portals as a client. He was a selfish, unprincipled young wastrel, and his mother would do well to wash her hands of him.

Uncle Lionel and Sir James Lucie, in spite of their widely different personalities—the one so thin and dry that it seemed he would crackle like the parchment deeds in the vaults of his bank if touched, the other big, blond, deep-voiced, extroverted—got on famously. Perhaps this was because they had a common cause, to discover and destroy Guy Beauchamp while discreetly avoiding a scandal. It was essential for Maud's future that the disgraceful affair be hushed up. Lionel Beauchamp, that dried-up bachelor, agreed to this as emphatically as did Sir James, though his private opinion was that the girl must be as bad as his nephew and scarcely deserved to be whitewashed.

In Mrs. Beauchamp's opinion, that redheaded minx was much worse than her son and the rule of polite society, that a gentleman should chivalrously take the blame, ought to be revised rapidly.

"They *must* be found before they have gone through a form of marriage," she said, and when Honor protested that Maud would make Guy a very good wife, better than he deserved, she answered, "With her irresponsibility, her extravagance, her total disregard for propriety! How can you say that, Honor? She'll ruin Guy."

"I thought, by the way everyone was talking, that it was Maud who was ruined."

"Think how humiliating it will be for her to be dragged back," Daisy added.

Mrs. Beauchamp's lips tightened. "Can that girl be humiliated? She'll brazen it out. You'll see."

"Neither wife nor maiden," Daisy murmured.

"Daisy!"

"Well, that's what I heard Pritchett saying."

The damaged virgin. What a gaffe Sir James Lucie had made in painting that portrait. After marking it not for sale, he had been persuaded to change his mind and was allowing it to cross the Atlantic. It had become an embarrassing possession. His daughter had made a fool of him. Even if she returned as pure as the lily he had painted in her slender fingers, it would be difficult for the public to believe in this image of her again.

Colonel Spencer and other residents in the Square, who had no reason to admire Sir James Lucie's insufferable pretentiousness, thoroughly enjoyed the scandal, though the colonel had a good deal of sympathy for the lovers, and for Maud in particular.

"I knew the girl had spirit," he said to Honor Beauchamp. "I knew she was a high flier."

Honor bent her eyes over the columns of the *Times'* overseas news. It was almost a pleasant piece of escapism to read of troubles in Russia and Morocco, in order to avoid the interminable talk of

Maud and Guy. She had every sympathy for them. She was terribly afraid that, with the constant cross-examination that was going on, someone would guess that she knew more than she was prepared to tell. She only remembered that Guy had talked of getting fishing equipment and that he always fished in Wiltshire with his friend Peter Coates. This time there was every possibility that he was initiating his bride into the sport. For there was one thing about Guy that Maud would discover, he always followed his own desires. But perhaps if she loved him enough, they would be her desires, too.

Did she love him enough? Could two such headstrong temperaments survive together?

"I see that the Kaiser is planning another visit to England," she said sedately.

"What on earth has he got to interest him here now? His grandmother's dead. She was the only one who liked him. The king hasn't a good word to say for him. He's sticking his nose into our affairs, I'll be bound. I say, Miss Beauchamp, that terrible fellow Lucie isn't going to pursue the lovers, is he?"

"He would if he knew where they were. He's in a dreadful state. Mamma thought he was going to have a fit. What with him and Uncle Lionel descending on us—" Honor repressed a small giggle; it really had been funny, those two pompous, self-important men rendered so helpless, making their empty threats.

But it would not go on being funny, she suspected.

"Would you do the same yourself?" Colonel Spencer was asking, a frail gleam in his dim eyes.

"Run away?" Honor asked, startled.

"Would you defy scandal, count the world well lost for love, that sort of thing?"

"You're teasing me, Colonel."

"A crusty old bachelor shouldn't do that. Is that what you're thinking?"

What she was thinking was that neither he nor anybody would believe her if she said that she would count the world well lost for love. Even her beloved piano could be sacrificed. She would willingly live on a desert island without a note of music if Ninian were there, too.

But such a declaration, coming from a composed and apparently sensible person like herself, would be laughed at.

Nanny had hardly stopped crying for twenty-four hours. She blamed herself, she kept saying. How could she have slept so soundly as not to hear Miss Maud's departure?

"That girl can be as quiet and crafty as a burglar when she pleases," Bertha said sourly. "You've no call to blame yourself. I don't see how you could have done more for her, bar sleeping across her doorway. She's a bad one, and no mistake."

"Now don't you start calling her names," Nanny flared up. "She's only got too much life and high spirits."

"Takes after the master, although he'll never admit to her bad points. The mistress can see them, but what can she do? She was never allowed any authority over the child, she's said so a thousand times. Never marry a domineering man, Bertha, she says to me."

"You!" Nanny was not too far gone in misery to produce a scornful sniff.

Bertha tossed her head. "There's no call to be sarcastic. I chose to give up a life of my own to stay with that poor helpless creature downstairs. I'm the loyal kind. You too. Though it seems like your loyalty's gone unrewarded. And that Cora! Did you hear how she turned on the master? Shouted at him. Called him a heartless beast. He wasn't standing for any nonsense like that. Can you imagine!"

"I never cared for that Cora," Nanny said. "Common. I'm glad to see the back of her." She began rocking backward and forward again, her apron to her eyes. "When I go into Miss Maud's room and see her empty bed, I can't stand it. It's as if she's dead, as if she's been taken off and buried."

"Far from buried. She's having a high old time, if I know Miss Maud."

Nanny sobbed afresh. "To think how I've dreamed of her wedding day. The beautiful bride she'd make!"

"The master'll have her back, don't you fret. Do you really think he'll let a whippersnapper like young Beauchamp have his daughter? Her that's marked for a duke or an earl?"

"Not now," said Nanny starkly.

The two women stared at each other, the truth in their eyes.

"The master'll hush it up," Bertha said uncertainly.

"How can he? It's all over London by this time."

A good night's sleep in a comfortable bed and Maud's spirits had regained their usual ebullience. She bathed, dressed, and went down to breakfast, sweeping into the hotel dining room with such an imperious air that the elderly waiter bowed deeply and hurried to show her to a table.

"Not over there, over here," came Guy's familiar voice.

"Guy!" Maud cried joyfully.

It was as if they hadn't met for days. With the deepest pleasure, she studied his face, freshly shaven and rosy from his early-morning walk. It was a beautiful face, she thought with great contentment. His merry twinkle, his pleased grin at her astonishment, his young ardent look, all made the most delightful of visages. She would be very happy to sit opposite it every morning for the rest of her life.

"Did you sleep well?" she asked.

"Abominably. You were right about that bed. The mattress was stuffed with potatoes, from the feel of it."

"Then we must buy another one today. I can't have your nice shape ruined by three weeks on a sack of potatoes."

"You mean to stay in this hotel for three weeks?"

She nodded. "I must have Puritan ancestors."

"We're bound to be noticed."

"Who by? That nice old waiter? What have you ordered for breakfast? I have never been so hungry in my life."

"Eggs and bacon, grilled kidneys, toast and coffee. Is that enough?"

"Sumptuous. I gave the bootboy sixpence to take Han for a walk. And later"—she looked around to see that no one was watching—"I want you to take this and sell it for me. I'd do it myself, only I haven't the faintest idea how."

Guy took the diamond brooch reluctantly, closing his fingers around it.

"Do you insist?"

"Since I have elected to stay here, I do insist that I pay my own bill."

He frowned. "It's an expense I hadn't bargained for, I admit."

"Then do as I ask."

"You think I've managed this very badly, don't you?"

"I forgive you because you haven't had any previous experience. It would alarm me if you were too good at this sort of thing."

He gave a grateful smile and reached for her hand. It didn't matter that the waiter, coming toward them with a loaded tray, saw his movement. They were young and in love, and they had endured a night's separation.

"I signed the hotel register as Millicent Ealing from Putney," Maud whispered, and Guy snorted helplessly with laughter.

"Maud, you're priceless. What do you think they imagine you are?"

"A governess, I expect."

"What nonsense! A runaway heiress more likely."

"In this dress? Guy, you must bring me back enough money to go shopping this morning. And this afternoon, since it's such a lovely day, do you think we could go on the river?"

"What better occupation? Apart from marrying you."

"You mustn't be so impatient, Mr. Beauchamp," Maud said in a prim, governessy voice.

"Then may I have permission to proceed with my courtship, Miss Ealing?"

"Granted, I'm sure, Mr. Beauchamp."

Her husband's towering rage and then his furious unhappiness had exhausted Lady Lucie. She would have locked her door, simply for peace, if she hadn't known he would batter on it so loudly that the sound would reverberate down the whole street.

"It's your own fault, James," she pointed out uselessly. "You've handled the whole thing in the most stupid way."

"And what would you have done? Given them your blessing?"

"I would have remembered that Maud simply doesn't know what it is to be denied anything. By forbidding them to meet, you simply made her more determined to have this young man. You've thrown them into each other's arms."

"Poppycock!"

"It isn't poppycock. And another thing, whether you like it or not, now they'll have to be married."

"Never!"

Lady Lucie sighed. Her headache was growing worse by the minute.

"Speak to Harriet, then. Goodness knows, she's broad-minded enough, but even she says this isn't an episode that can be white-washed."

"If anyone dares to say my daughter's reputation is ruined, I'll call him out."

"For heaven's sake, James, you're not living in the Middle Ages. If you don't believe me, then you must wait and see how many of-fers of marriage Maud gets this season. Those two dull Beauchamp girls will do better, if I know anything. Get Maud and this foolish young man back and let them marry properly in a church. Then you'd better set him up in business, since it seems his uncle will have nothing more to do with him."

"He can go and live in the Orient, as far as I'm concerned," Sir James fumed. "I'll gladly give him money to do that, so long as he goes alone. I believe that's his ambition. He's a footloose wanderer, and he has the impertinence to think he can marry my daughter." He turned a face so roweled with anger and pain that even his wife felt a stirring of unfamiliar sympathy. "I can't stand this, Lydia. I must have Maud back. On any terms. No matter what it costs me. The young scoundrel can be bought off, I'm sure. Then I'll take Maud to Paris and buy her a new wardrobe, and when we come back, the whole thing will have blown over."

"You're being optimistic."

"Then, damnation, if it hasn't, we'll carry it off, Maud and I. Do you think we can't?"

"No, I'm sure you can, James, but how is this to be achieved since you haven't the faintest idea how to find Maud?"

"Oh, and James," she called as he strode to the door. Her thin nose quivered at the tip. The glint in her eyes was like ice stirring be-neath gray water. "I spoke to Cora before she left. I gave her a little money. I don't approve of girls in her condition being turned out on the street."

She looked up calculatedly. "I happen to need fifty guineas for a rather good miniature by Nicholas Hilliard."

"Good heavens, Lydia, are you mad?"

"Not as mad, or as careless, as you. I only gave the girl five guineas. I could hardly let her think I knew the truth."

"Good morning, Miss Beauchamp."

"Good morning, Sir James."

Sir James had stopped across Honor's path, raised his hat, and bowed. She was shocked to see how gray his skin was and the haunted look behind his smile. They said he was suffering tortures over his daughter. There was no doubt that this was true. Honor's sympathy, although not entirely engaged, was nevertheless stirred. It was true that her brother was a far from ideal husband for Maud and fair that Sir James should have wanted to put an end to the affair. It was just that his tactics were so overbearing, so stupidly Victorian. One had to take the side of the runaways.

"Are you in a hurry, Miss Beauchamp?"

Honor hesitated. Was this to be another cross-examination?

"No, not exactly, Sir James."

"Whatever you mean by that," Sir James said, smiling with all his considerable charm, "can you spare a few minutes to come into my house? I want to talk about Maud. We can be uninterrupted there. At this moment I'm sure a dozen people are saying there's that dreadful man trying to browbeat Miss Beauchamp just as he did his poor daughter." The haunted smile flashed again. "I have no intention of browbeating you, my dear."

"Very well. For a few minutes," Honor agreed reluctantly, wondering if Mamma was one of the people watching behind the front-parlor curtains. "But I can't tell you anything about Maud and Guy, if that's what you're expecting me to do."

"We'll see. Come upstairs to my studio. Would you like to see some of my portraits of Maud that aren't for sale? I have two in particular that I'm ridiculously sentimental and vain about."

They were beautiful, Honor had to agree. Romanticized, of course, but who better to romanticize than the glowing child with berries in her hair or the slender radiant creature in green silk, with a peacock feather fan.

"You don't need to make flattering remarks about my work," Sir James said. "I'd never have been what I am without Maud. She's been my lucky star, my gift from heaven. Without her, I'm nothing."

Honor could remember her own father only vaguely, as a stern abrupt man in a soldier's uniform. She had experienced great timidity with him. But he had disappeared from her life while she was still in the nursery. If he had lived, she couldn't imagine having this close intense relationship that Maud had with her father. She thought it would have stifled her.

"She must come back," Sir James said. "Even if I have to agree to what I still consider a most unsuitable marriage. I apologize. I realize I'm speaking of your brother."

"You mean you would give your consent if they came back?"

His gaze, hollow and forlorn as it was, yet seemed to Honor to have a certain shrewdness. Was he speaking the truth?

"I would, although it's against my better judgment. But I simply can't have my daughter eking out an existence. Probably trying to cook. Can you see Maud in an apron? Good God! They'll both be poisoned or starve to death." He attempted a laugh. "I'm even prepared to make them an allowance until this improvident brother of yours settles down in some remunerative employment. But they must be found and brought back before it's too late."

"Too late for what, Sir James?"

"For Maud's reputation to be entirely ruined, of course," he answered testily. "Don't you realize she's a minor?"

"They could have a quiet wedding," Honor suggested, her mind leaping ahead to the prodigals' return.

"Why should it be quiet? Let's have a blaze of trumpets. But first they must be found. Now, Miss Honor. I respect your loyalty, but it's doing no one any good. I'm perfectly certain you have some idea of their whereabouts."

Honor flushed, then went pale. She was acutely disturbed. Was she betraying Maud and Guy, or helping them, by divulging her only fragment of information? If Sir James meant what he said, it would be infinitely preferable to bring them home and let them have a conventional wedding and be decently provided for. Guy would thank her. So would Maud, eventually.

"My brother sometimes goes fishing in Wiltshire," she said slowly, at last. "In a little place near Salisbury. He did mention fishing equipment last week. That's absolutely all I know."

Sir James sprang up, his face transformed.

"Thank you, Miss Beauchamp. I'm infinitely obliged to you."

"But is that information enough to find two missing people?"

"When one of them looks like my daughter," said Sir James, with all his old confident jauntiness, "it's more than enough."

They simply didn't know how the money could have disappeared so quickly. Guy, with great astuteness (or so they had thought) had persuaded a jeweler to pay forty-five pounds for Maud's diamond brooch. She had insisted on his adding the money to his own, "our common purse" she called it, with naïve pleasure. But then she had had to ask him to pay the bill for the dress, hat, gloves, and shoes she had bought to be married in. Surely he couldn't want a shabby bride. There also had to be lingerie and a Swiss-lawn nightgown, which was all part of her rebellion against that squalid bed in the cottage. She wanted their wedding night to be perfect.

Guy said that he wanted this, too, but what with hotel bills and this three weeks of waiting and the fee he had had to pay the rector of a small outlying parish for agreeing to marry them in his parlor (the rector had been suspicious and dubious about the whole thing), money vanished like water down a drain.

"Then we must sell my pearls, too," Maud said.

She grew impatient when he protested. Wasn't that a bit hypocritical since the brooch had already gone? In the argument that followed—they both had tempers that flared quickly—it emerged that he had written several letters to good friends who would never refuse to help him out of a tight corner. The response to these had been less generous than he had hoped, but the loans, in addition to the remains of his father's legacy, were all they had on which to begin married life.

Maud was deeply shocked. He was so matter-of-fact about it all that it must be the way he and his friends always behaved. She knew that it was the accepted thing for fashionable young men to be in debt, but usually they had some prospect of paying their debts. Guy, she had to admit the fact, had none. Or none in the foreseeable future.

Why did sordid money problems have to spoil their idyll? The sunny afternoons on the river, drifting in a punt, chasing butterflies while Guy fished, the leisurely dinners by candlelight where they could hold hands unobserved, the delicious lingering kisses in a dark doorway near the hotel before she went upstairs and Guy set off on the long walk back to the cottage where he uncomplainingly put up with its austerity, the slight aura of danger and the tantalizing suggestion of immorality that sharpened their pleasure . . . not to mention the anticipation of their wedding night, which grew more urgent as the days passed and the good-night kisses grew more passionate.

She didn't care how much Guy teased her about her surprisingly conventional idea of what their wedding night should be. He hadn't expected her to be so conventional. But he agreed that these things mattered to a woman, and after all, it wasn't long to wait.

All the same—those shameful begging letters—for that was what they were, no matter how loftily Guy might describe them.

When they were married would he be writing one to Papa? The uneasy suspicion lurked persistently in her mind.

"How are you going to repay these loans?" she asked.

"I've told you. I'll have another volume of poems published shortly and also some travel articles. We can live on next to nothing in the East."

"But we have to get there first. Our fares—"

"Why are we always talking about money?" he interrupted impatiently. "Very well, give me your pearls, but only on condition that I replace them as soon as I'm in funds. You do believe me, don't you?"

She had to speak plainly.

"I believe in your intention, of course, but not in your ability to carry it out."

"Maud!" It was his turn to be shocked. His eyes, so full of burning sincerity, rested on her reproachfully. If she had loved him enough to defy her father and run off with him, how could she not trust him?

"First that horrid damp cottage, where you actually expected me to live! And now all this bother about money!" There were high spots of color in her cheeks. "Did you really think we could live on love? And a fish for our supper now and then?"

"You don't need to be so sarcastic about it."

"Well, I've never known an elopement so botched."

His expression turned to hurt sulkiness.

"I'm sorry to fall so far short of what you expected."

"Asking your friends to support us! Would it be my father next?"

"Oh, to the devil with your father! You have an obsession about him. Don't you realize it was absolutely essential for me to get you away from him as a first step? Maud! Where are you going?"

"To my room to rest. I have a headache."

"You never have headaches! Maud!" He was hurrying after her. "I didn't mean that about your father."

"I didn't know it was my father we were quarreling about," she replied distantly.

"Then dinner at the usual time?" he asked humbly.

"If we can afford it."

Sir James Lucie knew exactly what he was going to do. He did not need to have the craftiness of that modern and fashionable detective, Sherlock Holmes. He prided himself that his own wits were sharper anyway. A beautiful redheaded young woman with a Pekinese at her heels, probably in the company of a young man, would have been noticed whether the town be as big as Salisbury or as small as Taunton.

He intended beginning with Salisbury and doing a little discreet questioning, plus some skillful shadowing.

The essential thing was to interview Guy Beauchamp first, and alone. It was unfortunate that he could not give the young scoundrel his deserts. Persuading him to accept a sizable bribe could hardly be called punishment. He was going to be damned lucky— if one could relate the loss of Maud with luck.

It was as Sir James had guessed, the two runaways had been far from unnoticed in the quiet of a cathedral town. Of the row of cabmen at the railway station, two of them had driven the young woman with the red hair. A regular beauty she was. One had driven her to a hotel alone, and the other when she was in the company of a young man who had asked to be driven to a cottage near a stream three to four miles out of the town. Just the place for lovers.

Sir James, holding on to his temper and his dismay, made some more inquiries on the situation of jewelry shops in the town. And which was the hotel to which the young lady had been driven?

No, the services of Mr. Sherlock Holmes had not been required. Within half an hour, Sir James had spotted, in the window of a jeweler's shop, the diamond crescent which he had last seen pinned on Maud's slender young bosom, on her way to a soiree.

So his first deduction had been correct. That young cad had persuaded Maud to sell her jewelry. He expected her pearls and her turquoise earrings had gone the same way. The jeweler confirmd his suspicions about the pearl necklace. That and the diamond brooch had been brought in by a young man who said that he and his wife needed the money to travel abroad.

There was not a moment to be lost. Supposing, on receipt of the money, they had left. But no. They had come here to be married, and that would have to be accomplished first, if he knew Maud. She might be prepared to run off with a dashing lover, but she wouldn't be quite so reckless as to leave the country without a wedding ring on her finger.

Swinging his cane angrily, his face growing grimmer, Sir James made his way to the hotel the cabman had named.

A young lady alone except for her Pekinese dog? Did the gentleman mean Miss Ealing? The elderly receptionist was full of indulgence and information. Well, she was hardly alone. She was accompanied most of the time by her fiancé. He joined her for breakfast and left her in the evening after dinner, to go and sleep alone in his cottage. They behaved very correctly. The young lady had made herself a great favorite with the staff.

But why was a gentleman like himself asking questions? Had Miss Ealing run off from his employ?

Sir James snorted and again controlled his temper. Couldn't this dull-witted woman recognize a lady when she saw one?

A lady in this situation, living alone in a hotel and keeping assignations?

But at least it was clear that the two were not yet married. Obviously they had not been able to do anything about a special license. When the receptionist volunteered the information that Miss Ealing was in her room, resting before dinner, and should she be sent for, Sir James shook his head. His spirits were rising rapidly.

Now was the time to put his carefully prepared plan into action. It was fair to assume that while his love rested, Guy Beauchamp might enjoy the relaxation of his favorite sport, fishing.

A hand was laid on Maud's arm as, with Han at her heels, she crossed the foyer of the hotel. Han gave a joyful bark of recognition, then went into a series of cavortings and ecstatic yelps, so that Maud had to pick him up to silence him. This gave her the necessary moment to recover from her impulse to throw herself in surprise and joy into Papa's arms. She was thankful that she had spent ten minutes in removing all traces of tears from her face. She had wept for nearly an hour since leaving Guy. By using all her considerable willpower, she was now able to present a composed face to her father, who was looking his most handsome in a snuff-colored tweed jacket with a canary-yellow cravat. He was also, thank heaven, not angry. Or if he were, he was very successfully concealing the fact, for his smile was wholly friendly, his countenance benign.

"I seem to get more of a welcome from that pampered beast than from my daughter," he was saying.

"What are you doing here, Papa? How did you find me?"

"I had a clue here and there." He took the brooch and the pearl necklace casually from his pocket. "I bought these back for you, for instance. It seemed a pity for you to be deprived of your jewelry."

Maud gasped. "How did you know about them?"

"It wasn't hard to deduce that you would be short of funds with such an improvident lover. As for finding you, I persuaded the young man's sister to be a little forthcoming."

"Honor!" Maud exclaimed.

"Ah, now, you mustn't hold it against her. She did it for the best. But can't we talk somewhere where we aren't watched by ten thousand people?"

It was true that there were perhaps half a dozen pairs of eyes watching. Maud drew her father quickly into the deserted sitting room. She didn't want all her kind friends, the plump receptionist, the doorman, the elderly waiter, disillusioned by their dear romantic Miss Ealing. It would disappoint them to see her returned so abruptly and humiliatingly to childhood.

"I'm not coming home, Papa. You don't need to think that."

"But I do think it, my darling. And by the"—Papa drew his heavy gold watch from his waistcoat pocket—"by the six thirty, which will give you ample time to pack." He sat her in a chair by the window and went on. "You'll have to eat alone if you stay here tonight. By this time your impetuous lover has caught his own train."

Maud's incautious joy at the sight of her father left her. "Papa, what have you done?"

"Parted with a considerable sum of money. Enough to keep the young rascal in his beloved filthy East in comfort for the next five years."

"Five years!" Maud wailed. "Without me! Oh, Papa, no!" Her father caught her hands. His grasp was firm, warm, soothing, familiar. And safe. That treacherous thought was only half-formed.

"But you must have gathered his main intentions by this time, my dear. Granted he wanted you, but he wanted his ridiculous Sir Richard Burton vision of life more. It's easier to accomplish that unsaddled by a wife. Well, let us say, I managed to persuade him that that was the case."

Sir James stroked Maud's quivering hands, reflecting that young Beauchamp hadn't been too hard to persuade. He had been sitting on the riverbank, fishing, and had inappropriately landed a fine perch just as Sir James announced that he had come straight from his daughter with a proposition. It seemed she regretted the whole ill-planned affair and wanted nothing but to be safely back in London. He must, therefore, as compensation, accept from her father the large bribe that would give him all the traveling his heart desired. The Golden Horn, Baghdad, Samarkand. He could hire a magic carpet if he pleased.

Perhaps when he came back and they were both older and wiser, their possible marriage could be discussed more seriously. In the meantime, Maud was crying her heart out in a hotel bedroom. She wanted to go home, and that was that.

The wretched fish had flapped on the ground all the time and had expired only as young Beauchamp, with a fatalistic look on his face and a newly acquired cynicism in his manner, had taken the roll of notes. Far be it from him to persuade a lady against her wishes. All those taunts about a botched elopement. Besides, she was expensive, spoiled, father-ridden, and unexpectedly prudish. This was not the first time he had had doubts about his lovely bride-to-be. He seemed to have got his two dreams mixed. Maud or the East, not Maud and the East. One couldn't really imagine that delicious creature in a sandstorm. So if he didn't see her again and managed to get her face out of his mind . . .

"Go do your packing, my darling," said Papa. "And oblige me by putting on something more becoming. You look like a governess in that dreary garment you're wearing."

She had been convinced at last. Guy had gone. It was true that he had wanted the money more than her. Oh, her as well, if it had been possible, but it had not been. As Papa said, it was simpler to travel alone.

She sat in the train staring unseeingly at the flying countryside, the growing dark. She was deeply unhappy, bereft, disillusioned, and infinitely older.

She wished uselessly that she and Guy had become lovers. It would have been beautiful and right, and somehow it might have removed the sordid subject of money from their lives. At least, Guy simply could not have allowed money to come first after he had had her completely.

So it was all her fault. No, it was Guy's, for his vague dishonesty, his fecklessness, his habit of living in fantasies.

But it was hers for not completely understanding and sympathizing. . . .

It *couldn't* be all over, the bright and lovely dream!

"Maud, my dear."

"Yes, Papa."

They were traveling in comfort in a first-class compartment. Papa always cushioned the way with luxury and thoughtful care. Tonight Nanny would run her bath, exclaim over the state of her clothes, make her hot chocolate . . .

"You didn't—I mean, you were not yet married, so I take it for granted that you didn't share the same bed."

Maud lifted her furious unhappy eyes. She heard herself saying in a high proud voice, "Naturally we did. In that cottage we were quite alone."

Papa's eyes flickered away. Maud had never seen such a look of stark helpless shock on his face.

"But I didn't expect—"

"Yes, we did, we did, did!" she flung at him, bitterly enjoying his pain. He must be made to suffer, too.

The frail embrace, the rustling voice whispering sympathetic words in her ear, the familiar odor of expensive scent and illness—Maud didn't cry until she was in her mother's arms.

Then the bewildering desolation swept down and blotted out every emotion but misery.

"I loved him, Mamma. I did so love him."

"I know, dearest."

"How could he accept money instead of *me?*"

"Your father can be very persuasive."

Papa's manner now was a finely balanced combination of sympathy, reproach, and triumph, but underlying his calm, there was still his shock over her revelation. Why had she told him that cruel lie? Did she secretly hate him? But how could she, when now she was enjoying the balm of his lavish care and cosseting?

"Papa ruined everything," she sobbed into her mother's shoulder.

"Yes, he handled the whole thing very badly, I agree."

Maud lifted her wet face.

"Then you were against Guy, too?"

"You're so young," said the murmuring voice. "Now don't ruin your face by crying. Papa intends taking you to the Gilbert and Sullivan opera this evening, so you must be looking pretty."

"Tonight! I couldn't!"

"Papa thinks it a good idea."

"I know. It's a game called holding-one's-head-up-in-public," Maud said bitterly.

"You may even enjoy playing it." Mamma's eyes were too vague and unfocused to be cynical. "But first, I'm afraid Mrs. Beauchamp insists on seeing you. I find her an appallingly dull woman. But she sees the wisdom of us remaining friends, for the benefit of the gossips. Don't let her browbeat you."

"Her!" Maud's chin rose. "I count her as responsible for Guy being so—well, not entirely what I thought he was."

"Yes, parents need to be taught a lesson sometimes, don't they? Although, as one grows older, one may just find they were right." Mamma's fingers, white bones, gently tapped Maud's hand. "I wonder what sort of children you will have, my dearest."

Holding up one's head in public . . . It began with Mrs. Beauchamp, whose carefully chosen, scolding remarks seemed to have no effect whatever on the regal young hussy sitting opposite her. If anyone had done the seducing in this lamentable affair, she decided, it had certainly not been her son.

"If you prefer me not to associate with Honor and Daisy, please say so, Mrs. Beauchamp," the creature said. "But I assure you I won't contaminate them. After all, it was not some nasty disreputable outsider I loved."

Mrs. Beauchamp struggled to keep her temper.

"I have agreed with your mother and father that an open scandal is to be avoided," she said stiffly.

"Is the world run by gossips?"

Mrs. Beauchamp ignored this remark that suggested she might be intimidated. She was thinking only of Honor and Daisy and their coming-out season. What a time for a thing like this to have happened!

"You will, of course, see my daughters at social functions."

Maud bit her lip. Soirees, parties, balls, and no Guy, who had given such fresh and keen delight to these familiar things. Guy on his ridiculous flying carpet, following his dream, which, after all, had been more important than her.

She intended to be extremely cool with Honor, who had betrayed her. She had never found the gentle art of forgiving easy. She doubted if she would ever quite forgive Honor.

But facing her was very different from facing the steely eyes and outrage of her mother.

"I only told when your father promised to forgive you," Honor said with her desperate earnestness. "He said he would bring you both back and give you a proper wedding. Don't blame me because something happened to make him not keep his promise."

"I can hardly blame you for your brother's jilting me, can I?" Maud said, with hard flippancy.

"He didn't!"

But he must have. Or one might have to begin suspecting that Papa had lied to her . . .

It had been fortuitous for Papa that she and Guy had just had that wretched quarrel. That was why Guy had preferred to accept the bribe rather than a conventional wedding and afterwards the conventional life that Papa would have insisted on.

Was that how it had happened? She supposed she would never know. It was all over, and her heart was dead.

"Come on now, Miss Maud! Look a bit livelier. You're going to have a lovely evening at the opera, and next week your father's taking you to Paris. You don't deserve all this, I must say. Lor', this waist has got too loose. Didn't you eat when you was—"

"In that cottage with Guy," Maud said in her new brazen way.

"Oh dear, Miss Maud, I wish you wouldn't talk like that."

"Don't you believe me, Nanny?"

"Well, I must say your clothes hadn't seen much soap and water or a good iron. What was you thinking of, that a young lady like you could live without a maid?"

"Talking of maids, is it true that Cora has been dismissed?"

Nanny nodded, her lips tightened.

"But why?"

"She was in a certain condition, if you must know. I'd better tell you, or someone else will."

"You mean she's going to have a baby!"

"That's what I mean. It was beginning to show, something indecent."

"Who's the man?"

"That she's not saying. Like as not she doesn't know."

"Then we must help her."

"The mistress has seen to that."

"Oh, money. Money isn't enough. Poor Cora. That must be why she was so sympathetic to me and Guy. I owe her something for that, Nanny."

"You leave well enough alone, miss," Nanny said sharply.

It came to Maud that even a week ago Nanny would not have spoken so plainly to her. Cora's plight might have been hinted at, but not put into words. But now she supposed she had graduated into the world of sordid reality. The unmentionable cottage, where, if only Nanny knew, she had scarcely spent two hours, was the trouble. Even to faithful loyal Nanny, she was irredeemably tarnished.

Chapter 9

THINGS WERE back to normal at Number 7 Melbury Square when Sir James Lucie began painting a new portrait of his daughter in her Worth dress.

At least, he was doing so when she gave him time for sittings. She was less amenable about the old rules nowadays, for she was leading such a busy social life. Frenzied, one might have called it. She had struck up a friendship with a titled young man who drove one of the new noisy motor cars, a de Dion Bouton that roared around the Square like an engine of destruction and had even that monument of sloth, the baker's horse, old Dobbin, rearing in fright. She had also taken to early-morning rides in the row with another young man, untitled but rich.

While other young ladies were practicing their curtsey, she was off on more interesting activities, the archery contest at Strawberry Hill, the point-to-point at Cowdray Park, the fancy dress ball at Syon House. She seemed to be more popular than ever with the opposite sex, but if any offers of marriage eventuated, nothing was heard of them by that listening chorus of ladies, the chaperones. The foolish girl had thrown away her brilliant chances on an impetuous, unreliable young man, who had taken fright in the end and disappeared. Malicious rumor had it that they had actually gone through a marriage ceremony, so if she married again, she would be committing bigamy.

The girl was fast, wild, heartless. And a heaven-sent subject for the gossips. Honor Beauchamp declared that she wept a lot and had fits of melancholy, a difficult story to believe when one saw her whirling off on some new gaiety. It was said that she had sworn to her father she would never marry and that that strange ambiguous man was both dismayed and secretly pleased.

It was whispered even more shockingly that he was in love with his daughter.

Whatever the truth in any of these rumors—and there wasn't smoke without fire—Maud Lucie, instead of having the good sense to keep quietly out of sight until the scandal had died down, was exploding across the London scene like a firecracker. She would fizzle out. All these celebrated beauties with a suspect past did.

But Maud, on her nineteenth birthday, was far from being the social butterfly of rumor. She awoke with the now-familiar heavy feeling of melancholy. For once, she managed not to ask Nanny if the postman had been. There would not be a letter from Guy. There never would be, she had decided at last, after six weeks of hopeful anticipation. This bleak silence was the wisest thing, as everybody pointed out. The young man was behaving with good sense at last. But each day Maud thought that a little more of her heart dried up, fossilized. She was able to talk and laugh with convincing gaiety, yet with no feeling of emotion whatever. The young men who took her riding, driving, dancing were animated clotheshorses. Sometimes she touched their hands or their cheeks to see if their flesh was real. She had become a little mad, she thought. Only one friendship she had made gave her satisfaction. She had discovered where Cora lived and had visited her.

Cora was expecting her baby in two months, and she was enormous. As big as a circus tent, her mother said, but still the old aggressive Cora.

What did Miss Maud mean by honoring them with a visit? she wanted to know.

"I've been jilted too," Maud said.

"You!" said Cora unbelievingly.

"Men!" said her mother, who was small, dark, quick, an elderly flea.

"How did you find where we lived?" Cora asked.

"Cook told me."

"But I told her not to, if you asked."

"I did ask, and she did tell me. I persuaded her to."

"It's no business of yours, Miss Maud."

"Unless it's a lesson to her," said the little, sour woman in the background. "Her running off with a ne'er-do-well. You ain't caught yourself, are you, my lady?"

Maud shook her head.

The lower classes had too vivid an interest in begetting and dying. She knew that Nanny, too, had been watching carefully for the moment when she could go to Mamma, who would discreetly relay the profoundly welcome news to Papa. What a farce! But Cora's trouble was no farce.

"I came to see if I could help you, because you helped me when I needed it. Not that it did any good. It would have been better if I had stayed at home."

Cora's sulky face had a sudden sympathy.

"Fancy him letting you down like that. He seemed ever such a nice gentleman."

"It was my fault just as much as his. We kept quarrelling. But we had wonderful moments, too. I don't suppose I'll ever have such wonderful ones again."

"Oh, you will, Miss Maud."

"I've practically decided never to marry. But tell me about your—I mean, the baby's father. Why didn't he marry you?"

"That's a joke," came Cora's mother's tart comment.

"Ma!"

"Run a mile from trouble, men do."

"He couldn't marry me because he had a wife," Cora said shortly.

"Oh, Cora! Did he deceive you? Was it that handsome butcher's boy?"

"No one you'd know, Miss Maud. It's no use your going on asking questions."

Cora's mother sniffed loudly.

Maud said, "Then at least let me help you. Have you clothes for the baby? A cradle?"

"Everything I need."

"You have not, my girl."

"Ma!"

Maud looked around the miserable room, with its poor furnishings, the piled laundry basket in the corner, the ironing board, the heavy irons heating on the stove. She opened her purse and emptied its contents onto the table. Selecting enough to pay the cabdriver, she pushed the rest toward Cora.

"Let me help you, please. It'll make me feel someone wants me."

"You, Miss Maud!" Cora said, again without belief, not touching the small pile of coins. "Everyone wants you."

Maud ignored that, saying eagerly, "I like babies. It'll be fun. I'll come as often as I can."

Cora's eyes narrowed, it seemed suspiciously.

"What's it to do with you?"

"I need something to be interested in. I wish Guy and I—I wish I were having my own baby."

"For the lord's sake!" exclaimed Cora's mother. "You don't know what you're talking about," and Cora, sulky again, said, "I'm not exactly having one for amusement."

"Of course you're not, but truly I can make things easier for you." Cora's face was turned stubbornly away. "It's none of your business, I told you. I'll manage."

"But better with some help. I'll come again as soon as I can."

"Bringing hot soup?" Cora jeered.

The girl, Maud suddenly realized, was as hurt and quivering with sensitivity as she herself was. They were alike—jilted, unhappy, alone.

"I ain't even seen your pictures," said the mother suddenly. "Cora says your Pa's always painting you. I must say you are a looker."

"I told him he had a stone instead of a heart," Cora said, feelingly. "I mean, when he said he'd bring you back, no matter what."

Maud moved to the door. She found the tiny dark room unbearably stuffy. Outside was a narrow cobbled street, ragged children, dustbins, a shabby row of houses. A smell of soot and sourness. The cabdriver whom she had asked to wait had got down from his box to quiet his restive horse. She had a strong desire to ask Cora whether her moment of love had been worth the transition from Melbury Square to this.

"I will come again," she said, "whether you want me or not."

When she was away from the miserable house, she began to feel a tentative pleasure at the thought of sharing Cora's baby and her problems. She would say at home that Peregrine or Charles had

taken her slumming. Nanny would sniff at and recognize the East
End grime on her skirt. She had a nose like a bloodhound. Perhaps
she could say she intended helping at an East End mission. Lying
was becoming a necessary fantasy for her.

"Why didn't you tell her?" Cora's mother demanded.
"Because I couldn't. And if you ever do, I'll wring your neck."
"You'll have to tell her some day."
"I'll never. She's kind and good, and I wouldn't hurt her."
"Good! After what she's been up to. You're a pair."
"Who's talking?" Cora said wearily.
"Never mind pointing fingers. I wanted your life to be better than
mine. But you've played your cards all wrong. Letting him turn you
out like that."
Cora dug her fists into her eyes.
"Stop it, Ma."
"Well, didn't he? You could have stood up to him."
"And who would have been believed, him or me?"
"Then you'll have to take what you can from the daughter and be
grateful for small mercies."
"Oh, do shut up, Ma."
"And when the baby's born, you'll dress quiet, like a young widow,
and find a husband. No matter who. Just someone wearing trousers.
There's plenty about. Wedding rings, too. Plenty of women get
them. Why can't you?"

The lime trees in flower in Kensington Gardens, the lilacs, the
laburnums, the pink May making a delicious cloud of color. The
cream candles of the chestnuts, the blazing rhododendrons and
azaleas, the Japanese cherry trees, the matchless lawns like wild
silk, the cloud and sunshine days, the long blue dusks, umbrellas
replaced by parasols, then umbrellas again, in the sudden early summer storms.

The Trooping of the Color, with the stout king set solidly on his
horse, the wheeling regiments, their scarlet tunics a taut ribbon of
color; a royal garden party with the enameled queen moving among
her subjects, head tilted anxiously at the same angle as her parasol.
Henley and the regatta on the glittering river, the lawns smoking in

the sun after light, warm rain. Royal Ascot and the absurd array of fashion, gentlemen sweltering in morning suits and top hats, while the ladies, undressed in voiles and chiffons, floated about under their enormous floppy hats. Balls, the opera and the ballet, breakfasts at the Ritz or the Berkeley after a night of dancing, punting on the river at Oxford or Cambridge, depending on where one had the most beaux. A spectacular fireworks display in the gardens of Holland Park on Lady Ilchester's birthday. A spluttering, noisy motor race from Sloane Square down the Kings Road, the old royal route of Henry VIII to Richmond to visit his discarded queen, Anne of Cleves. All the nonsense and frivolity, the deadly seriousness and heartbreak, the triumphs and sheer exhaustion of the season.

Compared to some of the extravaganzas, the Beauchamp girls' ball was a fairly modest affair. It had been nearly ruined by Guy's defection, but with the combined determination of Mrs. Beauchamp and her brother-in-law, Lionel (who with a pained air and a refusal to believe in the appetites of the young had agreed to provide the food and drink), the ball became a reality. There had been many minor vexations, apart from the major one of Guy's absence. The necessity to invite Maud Lucie, whom one could hardly expect to have the good sense to be inconspicuous, had been one. Then Miss Lavender had spoiled Honor's dress by making it too tight. She had blamed the deplorable error on her eyesight, the extraordinary woman. Hadn't she been sewing for thirty years? After pretending no interest in the ball, Honor was now disproportionately upset. It seemed that she was a normal young woman after all and badly wanted to look her best on this important night. Then Uncle Lionel had fussed constantly over bills, and Daisy had become broody over a pale young man who was inclined to droop. She said his name was Bertie Sylvester. He wasn't exciting or romantic, but he seemed to like her because she made him laugh. Mrs. Beauchamp hadn't encouraged his being brought to the house. Daisy wasn't wildly attractive, but surely she could find someone less weedy than Bertie Sylvester.

A late June night and the ballroom in Lionel Beauchamp's house full of roses. It made a pretty setting for Honor and Daisy, who looked young and virginal in their white dresses, although Honor confided that she felt like someone about to sing in the choir at church. At nineteen, she was much too old for white.

Maud hadn't deliberately planned to outshine them. It was simply that she couldn't help it. Papa had bought her Worth ball gown and insisted that she wear it, not only to be painted in, but especially to the Beauchamp ball, since that was where inevitably there would be the most whispers. The dress was in a dull-purple rustling silk, infinitely sophisticated compared to Honor's and Daisy's conventional white. She wore a narrow gold ribbon around her hair and looked like a medieval painting.

Mrs. Beauchamp sighed. Couldn't that girl have let her daughters have the center of the stage on this, their special night? But no, there she was, as always, the cynosure of all eyes, accepting the first dance with Ninian Spencer, while Honor, still doing her duty in the receiving line, was looking stricken. Mrs. Beauchamp nudged her violently.

"Smile!" she hissed. "Hold your head up and smile."

This difficult feat would have been more possible if Honor could have heard Maud and Ninian's conversation. Or indeed if she had noticed the surreptitious passing of a letter from Daisy to Maud when Maud made her polite way down the receiving line. For there had been letters from Guy at last, arriving miraculously in time to wish his sisters a successful ball. One had been addressed to Mamma and one to Daisy. They had been posted in Cairo, from which place Guy was about to leave on an exploration of the Nile River. Shortly, he hoped, they would be reading articles which he intended writing for the *Times*. He was well and leading the kind of life he had always wanted to. No one was to worry about him.

Mamma had wept tears of relief; Daisy, secretive about her letter, had said it contained no further news. It was her letter. She tucked it into her pocket, and that was that. And at the head of the stairs of Uncle Lionel's grand house in Chelsea, she slipped Maud the tightly folded and sealed missive addressed "M."

Maud, with a murmur to Cousin Harriet that she felt her hair slipping, had escaped to one of the guest bedrooms and shut herself in. There she greedily read the tight writing, crowded onto one sheet of paper.

Was it just a game you were playing to amuse yourself? Did you ever love me at all? Or was it just the greatest lark to pretend to elope? I suppose girls like you get bored with your round of parties, etc., and this made a stimulating change until the novelty wore off. All the same, you should have told me you had written to your father and begged him to come and take you home and that you were crying your eyes out all alone in your hotel bedroom. I thought you might have been the kind of girl who could face hardships. But you weren't. You wanted your adoring father and your nanny and all that, as well as a husband. So I took the money your father offered, to punish him for making you what you are.

I don't blame you. I blame him.

I hope you will be happy when you marry a title and money, as of course you will.

I think of you a good deal; not even that villain, your father, can stop me doing that. Nor can he take your face out of my mind. I am sending this to Daisy so that I can be sure you will get it safely.

YOUR FAITHFUL HAMISH DROOD

Maud had always despised girls who, for one reason or another, took refuge in bedrooms at parties and refused to come out. She had somehow to get through this evening, with this bitter, cruel letter tucked in her evening bag. How could she blame Guy for hating her when he had been so misled? It seemed that it was Papa, clever, clever Papa, who had ruined their happiness.

It was terrible and unforgivable. She could never love him again. But Guy—dear foolish Hamish Drood—he too was hateful for what he had written. How could he believe those things of her? He was not to be pitied at all, for he was doing what he had longed to do, exploring strange places, seeing strange sights, even if he had to do it alone, while she was left to wither away in this meaningless pursuit of pleasure and gaiety. If this evening could remotely be inclined in that category.

She saw the admiration in Ninian Spencer's eyes after he had written his name twice in her program. This was hardly surprising.

There was always admiration in men's eyes when they looked at her. They were all boringly alike in their approval of her looks.

But it seemed that Ninian saw deeper than her polite social smile. "Why are you so unhappy?" he asked. He had a legal mind, she remembered. He was probing.

But she had exclaimed guiltily, before she could stop. "Does it show?"

"I think so."

"I have had some bad news."

"I'm sorry. Would a glass of champagne help?"

"It's hours till suppertime."

"Come and wait here. Leave it to me."

He expertly piloted her to a small alcove, half-hidden by a potted plant, and left her there. She stood with her back to the ballroom, not wanting to be recognized. She had an overwhelming desire to slip away, find a cab in the street, and go home, never mind the hue and cry. *Maud Lucie's run away again . . . Who with, this time?*

But neither did she want to go into that house in Melbury Square, where Papa would be waiting to greet her with his loving, treacherous smile.

A glass of pale-golden liquid was put in her hand.

"Careful! Don't spill it."

Her eyes widened.

"You've got a whole bottle!"

"And uncorked it without a sound. Let's go outdoors."

The old love of a prank stirred in her, then died. She swallowed the champagne quickly and said with determination, "Let's." And hesitated. "Shouldn't you be dancing with Honor or Daisy?"

"Later," he said, taking her arm. "I've found a back way out."

They went down a passage filled with furniture moved from the ballroom, past a vast kitchen where dishes were clattering (whatever did Uncle Lionel do, living in such a large house all alone?) across a small veranda, where Maud tripped over a stepladder and giggled helplessly, then into the small green oasis of an herb garden. There was a wooden seat against a feathery bush, a splash of light from the kitchen window, a glint of the river in the distance.

"Now," said Ninian, refilling her glass, "the thing to determine is how much of this to prescribe. Too little and it's wasted, too much and there'll be tears. The exact amount and you'll float through the evening with a suitably numbed mind. Do you know what your capacity is, Miss Lucie?"

"Maud," she said mechanically.

She waited and was surprised that he didn't say the inevitable "Come-into-the-garden-Maud." But this was Ninian Spencer, a different kettle of fish altogether. A sober, serious person, with a scarred cheek and probing eyes.

"Maud. I'm Ninian to my friends."

The cool drink was beginning to swirl in her head. To his friends. Did that include Honor?

"I think two glasses will be exactly right. Although I have a strong head, and I've been used to champagne"—her voice trembled as Papa's voice echoed "*A sip can't hurt her; she can't be left out*"— "since I was quite small."

She sighed and leaned back, breathing the warm herb-scented air. In a little while she could trust herself to speak calmly.

"I've just had a letter from Guy."

"That cad."

"No, it's he who thinks me a cad. Or caddess, if you don't think that's an appalling pun. It's quite a fall, from being a goddess to a caddess." She began to laugh, then stopped. "The fact is I was misrepresented to him."

Ninian Spencer was a dark shape standing over her. She was probably going to hate him later for being the witness to her hurt and shame.

"Is it too late to put this right?"

"Oh, much too late. Much, much too late."

"What a pity."

"Is it? Everyone said he wasn't good enough for me. Me! What's so good about me? Would I be anything without my father? Do people see anything but his image of me? When he dies, will I vanish, too, like a soap bubble? Pfft!"

She sighed again, deeply.

"But I adore him. I mean, I adored him."

"Your father, or Guy?"

"Both. And that's the crux of the matter, as you might say." She held out her glass. "Is there some more champagne?"

"A little. We'll have to go back soon."

She drank, then said sadly, "Now I have to hate him."

"Who? I'm getting bewildered."

"My father, of course. He's been quite unscrupulous in order to get his own way. Instead of my portrait, I believe he'd like to frame me and hang me on the wall. Safely out of reach of possible husbands."

"Surely he wants you to marry?"

"I don't know. I sometimes don't think so. Anyway, I've vowed not to. Listen! Isn't the music charming from this distance?"

"Charming."

"Who will you marry, Ninian? Honor?"

He made no answer.

"You should. She's nice and intelligent and predictable, and I could swear on the Bible that she's still a virgin."

He gave an unexpected and altogether surprising hoot of laughter. It needed only that for her self-pity to turn to euphoria. She laughed with him.

"And whether I am or not is the secret of the year."

"What an extraordinary girl you are!"

"I'm my father's daughter. Not particularly nice. I have my own way of taking revenge on people who hurt me. I can be quite remarkably horrid. Can I have more champagne? Or not?"

"Not, I think."

"Oh. A pity." She stood up, not quite steadily.

"Do you kiss girls in conservatories, Ninian?"

"And also in herb gardens," he said, bending his head and putting his lips against hers.

She drew back in a sharp, instinctive reaction, then cried remorsefully, "I didn't mean to do that. It was only—"

"That you were thinking of someone else." He took her hand. "Shall we go in?"

"I'm just a little drunk."

"I know. Just the necessary amount."

"I can hold my head up. You don't need to worry about that."

"Splendid."

"You're a nice person, Ninian."

"It's only my facility with a champagne bottle that you admire."

She did hold her head up. She laughed and talked too much and danced without ceasing. Once she caught Cousin Harriet looking at her with a frown, and once Honor's grave eyes, looking over Ninian's shoulder as they danced, regarded her perplexedly. But the evening was passing, and when someone trod on her skirt, tearing the hem, she said lightly, "Don't give it a thought. I never wear a dress more than once."

"But this is a beautiful dress. I haven't been able to take my eyes off it. Or you."

Who was saying this predictable nonsense? The young man with the pale square face, the slightly protruding pale blue eyes, and the foppish little fair mustache. What was his name? Henry? Harold? Horatio? *Horace!* Somehow that name rose to the surface of her mind.

Triumphantly, she said, "How perfectly charming of you. It's only a thing Papa bought me in Paris."

"Your father must spoil you."

"Oh, yes, he does. Quite criminally."

"But who wouldn't? I've thought about you ever since Laura's ball."

Ponsonby!

"Not wise of you, Mr. Ponsonby. I have a fatal habit of getting talked about."

"That's not surprising. Someone like you."

"Isn't it awfully hot? Do you think you could get me a glass of champagne?"

"And some strawberries?" He was overjoyed. He longed to serve her. Silly man with his silly mustache. But sincere. Never despise sincerity.

Cousin Harriet tapped her arm. "Maud, we're leaving."

"So soon!"

"It's much too late, by the look of you. Who's been giving you too much to drink?"

Maud felt her hot cheeks.

"That teeny little bit of champagne."

"Teeny! It's the better part of a bottle, I should think. You're being very foolish. You know you can't afford another scandal."

"Oh, yes, I can. The more, the better."

"Whatever are you talking about?"

"To please Papa. To keep unwanted suitors away."

"Maud! Come with me at once. We'll get our cloaks and leave."

"But Horace—"

"For heaven's sake, who is Horace?"

"A very kind man. Reliable. He's bringing me some strawberries and champagne."

"Then you must thank him and excuse yourself."

Nanny was waiting up, as always. She took one look at Maud and sucked in her breath.

"The best place for you is bed, as quickly as possible. Whatever have you been up to now?"

Maud stood swaying in the center of the room. She was no longer drunk, only desperately, deathly tired.

"You should be proud of me, Nanny. I didn't faint; I didn't have hysterics in the bedroom. And at least one man fell in love with me."

"Only one!" Nanny snorted.

And only a very minor one, with a milk-white face and earnest humorless eyes . . .

"And why should you faint or have hysterics, for goodness sake?"

"Lesser women would. So don't scold, angel Nanny."

"And the hem of your beautiful dress torn! What will your Papa say to that?"

"Oh, yes, Papa. Will you give him a message in the morning, Nanny. I can't sit for him, because I'm too tired and want to sleep forever."

"I'll get your hot milk," Nanny said worriedly. "You need it. You're not yourself at all. You've been partaking too liberally."

"Drowning my sorrows is what it's called." Maud yawned and tumbled onto the bed in her petticoat. "Oh, and Nanny, I'm taking some clothes to the East End tomorrow, for the poor. Pack a bag, will you? That old green serge that I hate—"

"The one you ran off in? Yes, I should think you would want to get rid of that."

"And anything else I don't wear. This too."

She kicked at the discarded ball gown, and heard Nanny exclaim, "Not your Worth dress!"

"It has a torn hem, and I don't care for it anymore."

"Miss Maud, you shock me! You really do. Your extravagance! Anyway, isn't your Papa painting you in it?"

"He'll have to manage without." Maud buried her face in the pillow. "It or me."

"What's that? Speak up."

But Maud was asleep. Nanny took a close look at her, shook her head anxiously, then pulled the blankets over her and turned out the light.

Cora looked at the beautiful dress incredulously.

"Lor', Miss Maud, whatever would I do with that?"

Her mother, peering over her shoulder, said, "What that cost would feed a family for a year. It's downright wicked."

"Yes, it is wicked," Maud agreed. "Cora can sell it, or wear it, or cut it up for the baby."

"Not for the baby! I won't have it wearing any of his things." The words were out before she could stop them.

In a completely quiet voice Maud said, "But it's mine, not Papa's. You did mean Papa, didn't you?"

"It was his money that bought it," Cora muttered.

Maud's fingers clenched around the edge of the table. Now there was no champagne to blur her pain. She believed she might actually faint.

"So it's his baby, Cora! He's the mysterious man you wouldn't accuse."

For once, the mother had nothing to say. She stood, iron held in her hand, listening.

Cora's head was hanging. She looked acutely distressed.

"I did accuse him, but I only got thrown out. I never meant you to know, Miss Maud."

"So this baby will be my half brother or sister. How extraordinary!"

"Don't take it like that, Miss Maud."

"But I'm taking it quite calmly."

"You're not. You look awful."

"He turned you out, Cora."

"That's what happens with fine gentlemen and girls that behave foolish like Cora," the mother said.

"Ma, be quiet!"

"But *Papa!*" Maud whispered.

Cora raised anguished eyes. "You understand, Miss Maud, don't you? Because you love him, too."

The iron plunged onto damp material, making a searing sound. Cora's mother said, "No man's that wonderful. You always find them out."

"Yes," Maud repeated slowly, like a lesson. "You always find them out."

"Was it a nice ball last night?" Cora asked, desperately breaking the silence.

"Yes, it was all right. Cousin Harriet said I drank too much champagne, and Nanny was shocked. I went to sleep in my underclothes. Cora, I wonder if the baby will look like him."

"We'll know soon enough," Cora said uneasily.

"I'll come most days now."

"Do you still want to?"

"Of course. I long to see the baby. Truly. And I don't blame you, I know how persuasive Papa can be."

Cora blushed again. "If it's a girl, I want to call it after you. I meant to ask."

"Maud isn't a very lucky name."

"I thought of Evangeline."

"Evangeline!" Cora's mother gave a loud sniff. "Ain't that too grand!"

"She'll need a grand name, Ma. She won't have much else."

"Yes, she will," said Maud. "My father will attend to that."

All the same, the interview was more harrowing than she could have believed possible. Treachery was the word for that handsome, tender, smiling face, although it grew subtly more perturbed.

"Maud, my dear, when you are more a woman of the world—"

"But you turned her into the street, Papa!"

"Please, please, don't sound like a bad melodrama. She was suitably remunerated. These girls know exactly what they're doing."

"And me? I knew what I was doing, but you had to turn it into lies and send Guy away."

"How do you know this?"

"I had a letter from Guy. He told me how you deceived him."

"My darling child"—Papa held out his arms in his familiar loving gesture—"it was for your own good. You'll realize that one day."

"And Cora's being turned out to have her baby as best she can is for her good, too?"

"Maud, Maud! You're too young. You'll learn to face the less pleasant realities of life."

"But, Papa, it's your baby! Don't you care about it?"

His voice was curt. "Don't be a fool." Then, with an abrupt gesture, he put his hands to his face. "You couldn't understand what it is to be married to an invalid. For twenty years . . ."

The suddenly haggard face must not touch her emotions. This vain, self-indulgent, selfish man had ruined her life and Cora's and had professed to love them both. Reality, he said. What else was she facing at this moment?

"If you don't provide for Cora, Papa, I'll tell her to bring the baby and leave it on your doorstep."

He stared at her for a moment as if he believed her threat, then said testily, "Of course I'll provide for her. I always intended to. Now stop looking like an avenging angel and tell me I'm forgiven."

Forgiven! But he didn't begin to understand the magnitude of his offense. How could he be so insensitive?

"Never, Papa. I can't forgive you. Oh, you don't need to be afraid I'll run away again. After all, where could I go to, now that I have no lover?"

"Lover? That was only a precocious adventure. I thought we had agreed not to speak of it again."

"You're interrupting me, Papa. What I was telling you is that I'll stay in this house—I suppose it is mine too—but I'll never speak another word to you that isn't absolutely necessary."

Papa put back his head and laughed.

"Bravo! Sarah Bernhardt couldn't have done better."

Maud stamped her foot. "I mean it! You've got to take me seriously for once. I'm telling you that if it weren't for Mamma, I really would never speak to you again."

Then she could hardly look into his naked eyes as he said slowly, "I trust you're not going to relate all this rigmarole to her."

"No, I promise not to do that. She may wonder why I don't sit for portraits anymore, but you must just tell her that I've been painted too often and that people are beginning to laugh at us."

"Maud! Not sit!"

"No, Papa. Never again."

Chapter 10

THE SUMMER lingered long enough for it to be possible to sit out-of-doors until the end of September. Lady Lucie was now a familiar figure in her invalid chair, with her lacy shawls and her tilted parasol. She was accompanied by her daughter much more than formerly. Maud seemed, unexpectedly, to have become a dutiful daughter, though the whispered rift between her and her father had not healed.

Sir James, it was said, was engaged in painting a great panoramic picture of the last days of Babylon, and Maud was no longer required to sit for him. A series of voluptuous young women came to Number 7 and posed in states of seminudity. Or so it was rumored. Anyway, Maud had less spare time since she had plunged so enthusiastically into charity work in the East End. There was another rumor that she had more or less adopted a baby there. Who would have thought her so maternal? Or so sympathetic toward the sufferings of the poor?

But she had changed remarkably since the scandal of her attempted elopement. The young men in their noisy motorcars had ceased to call at Number 7, and, even more surprisingly, their place had been taken by a serious and frankly dull young man, Horace Ponsonby. He brought or sent flowers at least once a week, and it was said that he had proposed eleven times.

What did Sir James make of that? Surely he would have preferred the much more dashing Guy Beauchamp as a son-in-law. He wasn't saying anything, and neither was Lady Lucie. The family at Number 7 had become almost as conventional as the rest of the Square. There was no longer any interesting gossip.

But it was certain that a lively young woman like Maud Lucie could not go about with that quenched look forever.

To everybody's surprise it was Daisy Beauchamp who had the triumph. She was to marry her amiable but far from sparkling Bertie Sylvester, who had turned out to be a lord, the eldest son of the Earl of Deepford. Plump, loquacious Daisy was to be a countess! It was said that her uncle was so gratified when he heard the news that he inadvertently committed himself to giving his niece a marriage settlement.

So Daisy had achieved the ardent desire of all debutantes (or their mothers), a brilliant marriage in her first season.

A short time before her wedding was to take place old Colonel Spencer died in his sleep at Number 9, a quiet death in a comfortable bed that he would have despised. A soldier should die on the battlefield, or failing that, he should at least put up a respectable struggle against this last enemy. Two days later, Honor Beauchamp, who had called with a spray of flowers to be laid on the old man's coffin, found his elderly spaniel dead in its basket by the kitchen fire. She had been fond of the peppery old colonel. His death was going to leave a blank in her life. As Maud enjoyed her charity work in the East End, Honor had enjoyed the chore of reading to the old man. More important, he had provided a link with Ninian, with whom Honor was secretly, but apparently quite hopelessly, in love. In spite of their fairly frequent meetings, he had never displayed more than a courteous friendliness.

She had never been able to forget the night he had danced with Maud, when Maud had got a little drunk. "That *disgraceful* girl!" Mrs. Beauchamp had hissed, but Honor had only been able to see how the two had laughed together. She had never been able to make Ninian laugh. At least not in that uninhibited way.

But now the colonel, his waxen nose poking up from his coffin, lay dead in one room and his faithful dog in another. Honor went down on her knees beside the basket and, holding one of the stiffened paws in her hand, wept with an overwhelming feeling of loss.

"What's this?" came Ninian's voice.

She hadn't known he was in the house.

He knelt beside her.

"Not Corporal! How did this happen?"

"I don't know. He's dead exactly like his m-master."

And then, not knowing whether it was by her action or his, she was in his arms, sobbing on his shoulder.

"It's all so sad!"

"Not sad at all. It's absolutely right. I wish we could bury them together."

"Couldn't we?"

"I'm afraid Corporal wouldn't be considered material for hallowed ground. Well, he won't mind, poor old boy." Ninian got to his feet and pulled her up. "Stop crying. It's not like you."

She wiped her eyes. "I shall miss them both dreadfully."

"But you'll have me instead, if I can persuade you to stand such a prospect."

"How . . . do you mean?"

"My uncle has left me this house. Could you bear to live in it with me?"

Now she had forgotten to be self-conscious about her tear-smudged face.

"You . . . are you asking me to marry you?"

"You sound astonished. Have I done it so clumsily?" He gave a half-smile, wonderfully tender. "And at such a time, you're thinking. But like Corporal's death being right, this time seems right. I know my uncle would have approved."

"You just thought of it now?"

"No, no, I've thought of it for a long time. But I didn't have a house to offer you or much money either. Now I still haven't much money, but I do have a house."

"Oh, I would adore it!" She had never spoken so impulsively or with such feeling in her life. She took Ninian's hand. "Let's go in and tell him."

"Uncle?"

She hesitated. "Do you think that's morbid?"

"Not morbid at all. Only he can't hear. Let's take it for granted that he knows."

"He always thought you should admire Maud Lucie."

"So I do. From a decorative point of view. I even kissed her once, but that was a mistake."

Why? thought Honor. *When?*

"And it's you I want to marry. This charming, serious little face." He kissed the tip of her nose. "Where will you put your piano?"

Her lips began to quiver. Now she knew this surprising conversation was real.

"Do you mean that about my piano? Mamma always said—"

"Of course I mean it. I'll enjoy it as much as you. I have to work a good deal in the evenings. You can play for me. Now listen," he said to her doubtful face, "I understand that a great part of you is your music. A creative person must create. So don't look at me so suspiciously."

"You'll promise to tell me if ever my playing begins to irritate you?"

"It never will. I have the slightest preference for Mozart rather than Chopin, but that is a minor matter."

She began to smile radiantly. Death had quite vanished from the house.

Daisy was cock-a-hoop, planning the big fashionable wedding that Uncle Lionel had agreed to pay for. It was the kind of wedding Melbury Square had thought Maud Lucie would be the one to have. Instead, it was plump Daisy Beauchamp who had made the catch of the season, which proved that looks weren't everything.

Honor, too, had made her less spectacular catch. In a way, the Square took Honor and Ninian to their hearts, since they were going to live there. They also liked Honor's modesty in insisting on a quiet wedding.

Where Daisy was suddenly too important to be dressed by Miss Lavender, Honor said that the faithful creature, with her failing eyesight, must make her wedding gown.

"It doesn't really matter, does it," said Daisy, "since you won't have all society watching you?"

Honor looked at her sister with surprise and some contempt. "I never thought you would be such a snob."

"Oh, I'm not, really," Daisy confessed. "I'm only doing all this for Bertie. He says his family expects it. He's such an angel I'd do anything to please him."

"Does he tell you he loves you?"

"Oh, goodness, yes. A hundred times a day. It gets quite boring. Why do you ask? Doesn't Ninian do that?"

"Of course. Though not a hundred times a day."

Honor knew that Daisy recognized the lie. Ninian had never said he loved her. She could never demand to know, in case he too lied.

He wanted to marry her. Wasn't that enough?

Miss Lavender's mother died in the late autumn, and Honor, horrified at the poverty of the rooms where Miss Lavender and the old lady had existed, made one of her impulsive decisions. Miss Lavender was to come live at Number 9 and look after Honor's clothes and the household linen. She could also go out dressmaking as much as her eyesight allowed. Honor intended to have only one living-in maid, so there would be plenty of room.

Until the babies came . . .

Miss Lavender's ailing eyes streamed tears. She had thought her growing blindness a well-kept secret, but of course, a thoughtful, observant person like Miss Honor would have noticed. She wished she could have told her mother, who had worried so much about her future. It seemed that death could be a friend to the living as well as to those taken, since the old colonel's death had brought Honor her happiness, and now, similarly, it had brought Miss Lavender security.

Nothing was ever all black or all white. It was a pity Maud Lucie couldn't learn that lesson. She had let her broken love affair and now her quarrel with her father turn her into a shadow of herself. It was said she intended never to marry, but to devote her life to good works. Well, that was just her extreme nature, flying from the heights to the depths.

It turned out that the baby in the East End to whom she was so devoted belonged to Cora, the disgraced maidservant. Cora was clever enough to know when she had a benefactress, for she had called the baby Evangeline, Maud's second name.

But she was also an opportunist, and when, suddenly, a chance for marriage came along, she took it. She intended going with her baby to live with her new husband in Leeds. Her mother would go, too, and Maud's interest in Bethnal Green would have to come to an abrupt end. One had to be sorry for her, then; she seemed so aimless and lonely. Maud Lucie, that golden girl, lonely! It was time she stopped being sorry for herself, found a husband of whom her father approved, and settled down.

Smoke poured from the chimney, the engine gave a series of monstrous chuffs, and the train began moving slowly out of the station. Maud ran forward and saw the figures behind the grimy window, Cora holding the baby up and flapping the little hand in farewell. Her face was almost obscured by her frilly bonnet; her blue eyes, Papa's radiant blue eyes, so surprising in that tiny innocent face, were screwed up as she prepared to yell in fright at the unfamiliar sounds. She was Papa in miniature, vociferous, demanding, engaging. And now she was going to be as lost to Maud as was Papa himself.

Life was full of pain and disillusionment.

But one had to be glad that Cora's troubles were over.

"Well now, perhaps you will stop holding me up to ransom," Papa said that evening.

"How did you know they had gone?" Maud asked.

"You'd be surprised at how much I know about my daughter's activities."

"Which daughter do you mean, Papa?"

A spasm of anger crossed the handsome face. Maud refused to let the fact that Papa was looking so much older disturb her. He couldn't have aged like that in only four months. Yet he had. The grooves down his cheeks were deeply set and permanent.

"I think we had better agree to close this subject. The girl's got herself a husband, thanks to my generosity. I've no doubt that a capital sum weighted the scales in the right direction."

"You would never have given her that if it hadn't been for me."

"No, my dear, you've been at me like a stinging wasp. It isn't like you, and I must say I don't find it enjoyable. But it's over now. The subject is closed."

"Is it? Don't you want to know whether your new daughter might not be as paintable as I was? Wouldn't you like to make another fortune through her?"

The bitter pleasure Maud got from causing her father pain secretly frightened her. What was she turning into? Could she never be softhearted and happy and carefree again?

"Maud!" said Papa with his infinite sadness. "Maud!"

"What you want," said Nanny, "is a baby of your own. Going all moody because that Cora has gone away. Good riddance to her and her brat."

"Don't call it a brat. She's a beautiful baby."

"Very well, then. I have nothing against an innocent baby. But you saw altogether too much of Cora. It wasn't right, Miss Maud. Now look, there's more flowers come from that poor young man you hardly ever even pass the time of day with. Pink roses this time. He must be spending a fortune on you."

"He's a stockbroker, Nanny. He just juggles a few stocks and shares, and hey, presto, he can buy a whole hothouse of roses."

"I don't expect it's as easy as that."

"No, but Horace is very astute. You have only to look at his eyes. Do you like him, Nanny? Tell me honestly."

"He's very polite and dependable and patient."

"Who wants someone *patient*, for heaven's sake!"

"You do, Miss Maud," Nanny said flatly. "Putting up with your tantrums. I declare I don't know why your Papa doesn't give you a good spanking."

"Papa has never spanked me in his life!"

"No, more's the pity."

Maud flung herself face downward on her bed.

"Oh, Nanny, life's so awful!"

"It's what you make of it. And if you ask me, you've sulked long enough. Mr. Ponsonby isn't what I'd have chosen for you, but he's a sight better than that wicked Mr. Beauchamp. I only hope a crocodile gets him."

"Nanny!"

"And how that pudding-faced sister of his can be having the sort of wedding you should be having, Miss Maud. Well, I do think you should stop glooming about and make something of yourself again."

"Nanny, the acorn Guy and I planted has sprouted. Is that significant, do you think? We planted a tree, but there's only me to watch it grow."

"That's life, Miss Maud. It has its milestones. And this particular one is well past."

"And I'm bored, bored, bored! I'm going slowly mad!"

Apart from the Beauchamp weddings and all the coming and going that entailed, nothing of great interest happened in the Square before midwinter. The leaves had fallen and the lavender mists begun. Old Joe, the muffin man, began to do good business again. No one wanted hot muffins in the summer, when the maidservants carried the elaborate silver trays to their mistresses in the gardens, but now fires were lit and the curtains drawn by four thirty, and the tinkling bell as Joe trudged through the Square with the heavy tray on his head, was a welcome sound.

Hard on his heels came the lamplighter with his long magical rod. One touch to the lamp and the yellow gaslight bloomed. The child in the upstairs room at Number 3 sometimes appeared at the window and clapped its hands at the sight. It was the only time it was known to show any animation.

But just before Christmas, there was a dreadful tragedy in that house. The mistress, a poor troubled harassed creature who had spent the last years of her life protecting her idiot grandchild from the world, was found dead in her bed. The discovery was made by Dr. Burns, who had been almost the only person ever admitted into that house. The boy upstairs, a big fellow of twelve with an oversized head and shambling body, was in a state of advanced starvation and had to be taken away to an institution. No one quite understood how such a tragedy could have happened under their very noses.

But now the white face pressed against the window would no longer frighten the children, which was a relief. Instead, the house stood empty. It seemed that the heir was somewhere in Australia and had not yet been traced.

The noise of traffic from the High Street was getting worse. The clattering cabs and tradesmen's vans were bad enough, but now they were joined by more and more sputtering, backfiring motorcars. Lady Ilchester, in Holland House, complained that the swallows were being driven away by the noise. She had so many birds coming to her lovely garden—cuckoos, jays, wrens, sometimes a passing heron. The trees were owl-haunted at night. Sometimes in June, nightingales sang, though not so often now. They, too, were moving to quieter places, though the lush green trees surrounding the old house gave an illusion of deep country. Perhaps the peacocks, on the terraces or wandering in the Dutch garden, screamed too much.

Late in November there was a ball in the large, new room which Lady Ilchester called the swannery. The new Lady Sylvester was showing off her wedding ring and the smartest ball gown from her trousseau. She and her husband were moving to their country house in time for Christmas, and they did not propose to spend much time in London thereafter. Daisy had always wanted to live in the country and intended to run her house efficiently and have as many children as possible.

Honor and Ninian Spencer were not at the ball, for the simple reason that they had not been invited. Both were perfectly happy about this, since neither of them cared for a social life.

A more surprising absentee was Maud Lucie, who had been invited, but who was remembering too vividly the aftermath of the last ball she had attended there and that mad, fateful dance in the Square gardens in the early morning. She had been young then. It seemed unbelievable that in nine months she could have become so soberly old. Her looks had deteriorated, too. She was thin-faced and pale. Papa wouldn't want to paint her now, even if she had consented to sit for him. Once she went up to the studio, when he was out, and looked at the portrait of herself in the Worth dress. The canvas was turned to the wall. She took it to the window and studied it, wondering if she had ever looked as animated and glowing as Papa had painted her. She put it back with its face to the wall and suddenly thought, in horror, that she was growing like Mamma, pale and repressed and lifeless.

This was what a man like Papa did to women.

She must escape him. She must escape from this house.

How? By giving in to Horace Ponsonby's insistent demands and marrying him? At least no one could be more different from Papa, except in the matter of worshiping her. And she had to admit that Horace's complete admiration was soothing after Guy's cruel treatment. Or was it that she had been so accustomed all her life to worship that it was necessary to her? Nanny said this. Nanny also said that marriage to Horace would be better than her present existence.

Either she made up her stupid quarrel with her father, or she married and left the house. She was selfishly making life intolerable for everybody.

Maud agreed listlessly, although she didn't agree that it was only her behavior that made life intolerable. For instance, it was infinitely galling to take tea with Mamma and her now-close friend Mrs. Beauchamp, listening to Mrs. Beauchamp's smug remarks about her married daughters. One wanted to drop a pinch of arsenic in her Earl Grey-with-lemon tea. One was ashamed to be so resentful of Honor and Daisy's happiness. Particularly Honor's, since had it not been for her, Maud would have been Guy's wife long ago.

And Papa, who could also be cruel since they were playing at torturing each other, kept making derogatory remarks about that dullard, her stockbroker friend. Was she going to keep the poor man dangling or send him about his business? Coyness didn't suit her.

Evenings spent in the dim, sweet stuffiness of Mamma's sitting room didn't suit her either. That was when, more than ever, she felt the life draining away from her.

"Read to me, Maud dear, if you haven't anything better to do."

"No, I haven't anything better to do."

"Trollope, do you think? Or do you find him too long-winded?"

Maud shook her head. It didn't matter how long-winded he was. Supposing Mamma had inconceivably asked to be read Swinburne's poems and she had had to come agonizingly to life?

There had never been another letter from Guy. If his mother had news of him, she obviously didn't intend to tell it to Maud.

Chapter 11

ACROSS THE breakfast table, Ninian said to Honor, "Let's give a dinner party. I want to entertain my godfather, Judge Hutchison. He's been very good to me. His wife died last year, and he's lonely."

Honor's heart jumped. She wished she were not so nervous about everything. This wish was followed by one even more fervent, that her nervousness was successfully hidden.

"Of course, dearest. Shall we ask anyone else?"

"A younger colleague of mine and his wife. Tom and Millie Ashburn. You'll like them. And someone for the judge."

"How old is he?"

"Oh—sixty, I should think."

"Mamma?" Honor said tentatively. She knew that Mamma, fretting in her now-empty house, was longing to be asked to something more exciting than tea or a light luncheon with her daughter.

"Good heavens, no. The judge may be old, but he still likes a pretty face. What about Maud?"

"Maud Lucie?"

"Do we know any other Maud?" Ninian got up, gave her an affectionate caress. "She'll decorate the table. And frankly I won't have you in a twitch at your first dinner party because your mother is watching."

"She isn't as bad as that."

"She's the judge and the jury rolled into one, and you know it. When shall we say? Next Wednesday?"

They had been married only a month. Honor had scarcely got the house organized. As a very junior barrister, no briefs had yet come

Ninian's way. Economies would have to be practiced for some time. Income from the modest capital the old colonel had left just paid the servants' wages—Cook, the housemaid, Lucy, who was only fourteen, quite untrained, and therefore cheap, and Miss Lavender, who also required only a pittance, since she had the inestimable boon of a room of her own in the attic.

Honor didn't mind economies. So long as she had Ninian at home in the evenings, working with his heavy lawbooks and his files while she played softly, anxiously inquiring from time to time whether her music disturbed him, she was completely happy. To be sure, the first night of their married life had not been a success. She had been so nervously exhausted, so afraid of her inadequacy, and so stupidly innocent that she had become as stiff as a poker. After a certain time, Ninian had kissed her gently on the brow, turned on his side, and gone to sleep. Or seemed to go to sleep, while she cried silently in the dark.

In the first daylight she had apologized so profusely that Ninian had begged her to be quiet. He had to kiss her in a prolonged way to achieve this, and then it had been better. Painfully, but with deep exultation, she became the wife of this reserved man, with his carved secret face.

After that, she took him gladly into her arms, though, because she too was an intensely private person, she was not sure that he knew how gladly she did welcome his embraces. She had learned, from that first night, not to talk. The gentle kisses and caresses after love were enough. Sometimes he took her face in his hands and looked at it. She knew it pleased him. She loved him deeply and painfully and was quite sure she would do so for the rest of her life.

But the dinner party—with three guests who were complete strangers, Maud, who would look devastatingly beautiful, a cook who was inclined to have her off days (when Honor suspected she had a weakness for cooking sherry), and a maid who would be clumsy, if nothing worse—was going to be an ordeal.

How helpless of her! Daisy, in her country mansion, wrote that she had already given dinner parties for twenty. But Daisy had a butler and footmen and a dozen maids and had scarcely to lift a finger. Though such a prospect, Honor reflected, as she descended to the basement to consult with Cook, would have scared her even more.

The dinner party at the newly marrieds, Maud complained, would be infinitely tedious. Nevertheless, that sour little grain of resentment that Honor should be happily married while she remained in her single state still flourished inside her.

Honor, the matron, should not be allowed to put on superior airs. Not that Honor would. She was much too self-effacing. Nevertheless, she would be the modest but proud hostess at her dinner table, and it was all too unfair. Honor the betrayer, Maud called her in her most resentful moods.

Maud wore a dress that looked its best by candlelight. The subtle bronze lights in the taffeta gleamed. She did her hair in a high swirl and applied a discreet amount of color to her lips.

Nanny, as usual, disapproved.

"You'd think you were going to Buckingham Palace, Miss Maud. It's vulgar to overdress."

"Am I overdressed?"

Nanny looked at the slim young figure in the stiff dark dress and reluctantly shook her head.

"I suppose it's just you. You take the eye."

"And you're a disagreeable old woman. I can't think why I love you."

Nanny's lips abruptly quivered.

"I do so want to see your babies before I die."

Maud looked at her in astonishment. She couldn't think why she had said she loved this annoying old woman.

"Now whatever makes you say that? I don't particularly want babies. And I'm only afraid you'll live forever."

She was glad she had taken trouble with her appearance. She needed that confidence to get through the evening, for she found herself suffering not only from resentment, but also from the sharp unfamiliar sensation of jealousy.

Honor had made the old colonel's house charming, and she herself looked charming in her simple ruffled white dress. Ninian must be proud of her. He, too, looked surprisingly impressive. That lean scarred face had a quiet authority.

The two were well matched. Maud's lips tightened. All she was here for was to enliven the evening for the elderly judge, who had a witty tongue and a decidedly lecherous eye. Therefore, she would do so. She would scintillate. She would make quiet Honor's party a success.

Though not from any altruistic motive.

She responded to the judge's sallies and made some of her own. She did a highly amusing imitation of a dowager duchess at a Royal Academy exhibition. She pretended modesty when the judge declared his pleasure at meeting the subject of so many famous paintings. She deliberately took the limelight from Honor and the other young woman, a mousy wife, just like Honor. Wives who, with their suppressed personalities, became shadows of their husbands were very misguided. She would be ashamed of herself if she ever allowed such a thing to happen to her.

"By George," she heard the judge exclaim to Ninian as the ladies left the dining room, "that's a wonderful woman!"

She didn't hear Ninian's reply. With Honor behind her, she couldn't linger, which was another annoyance to her.

Ninian walked her home, although it was only a few yards from door to door.

"Thank you for coming, Maud. I'm glad you've recovered your spirits."

"Without the help of champagne? Oh, I can act as well as the next person."

"Don't tell me you're still nursing a broken heart?"

"Do broken hearts ever mend? Don't you count me the faithful type?"

"The judge thought you a wonderful woman."

"Which is no answer to my question." She laughed and held out her hand. "Good night, Ninian. Tell Honor I thought her party was the greatest fun."

But Ninian didn't repeat those exact words to Honor. Instead, in answer to her anxious inquiry, he said that everything had been capital. Honor wanted a more explicit discussion.

"I think your judge enjoyed himself."

"Oh, absolutely."

"The Ashburns were rather quiet."

"They could hardly get a word in edgeways, with the judge and Maud. She was amusing, wasn't she?"

"Maud? Oh, yes. She always is."

"I expect she'll run a famous salon one day. She'll have to find the right sort of rich husband, of course. Your brother would hardly have fitted that part."

"No. I know that. But it does seem sad, if they were really in love with each other."

"I'd say Maud is much more angry than sad about that. She's a person who likes to get her own way, I imagine."

Why are we talking about Maud all the time? Honor wondered silently. She wanted Ninian to tell her that the dinner had been perfect, and she herself a good hostess. Had her clothes been all right? Had he noticed she had done her hair a different way?

His arms around her in bed reassured her. Yet she couldn't sleep. In the quiet Square the owls were calling. The old house creaked a little, spasmodically, as if the colonel with his lame leg were going up the stairs.

Honor lay still, afraid to move lest she waken Ninian. For the first time since her marriage, she wanted to be alone. Then she could have got up and played her piano until all her nervous excitement and uncertainty had ebbed away.

Early in February it snowed. Then it froze, and the streets became deep ruts of frozen snow and patches of black ice. To add to this hazardous state, one of the nastiest kinds of fog, evil-smelling and suffocating, came down. People who could stay at home did so gladly. Maidservants climbed up and down stairs with fresh coal for parlor fires, and the gaslights burned all day, dim moons of light in the fog-shrouded streets.

Dr. Burns, groping his way home, scarcely able to find his own gate, thought only in terms of a warm fire and a large scotch and soda. He would like to have been able to prescribe both these things to some of the patients he had seen today, gasping with bronchitis in damp rooms, with scarcely enough blankets on their beds, let alone the luxury of a fire in the grate. The English disease, breeding and proliferating in circumstances exactly to its liking—fog, damp, poor food, poverty.

Politicians talked of the golden Edwardian age. Let them visit some of the back streets of one of London's wealthiest boroughs. They were a pollution and a disgrace. Though it was ironic that even the king, living in wealth and luxury and chronic self-indulgence, didn't escape the prevailing disease. Perhaps there was a moral in that. Too much was as bad as too little.

One thing, when he was awakened in the middle of the night to go urgently to Number 7, Dr. Burns was certain that it was not bronchitis that had afflicted one of those well-cared-for occupants. Lady Lucie had probably been indulging in one of her too-rich dishes again, he reflected, struggling into his boots, thankful he hadn't to make a long journey in the fog and knowing he would speak his mind if the call were a trivial one.

It was far from trivial. Driving home by hansom cab from his club, where he spent most evenings since his estrangement from his daughter, Sir James had had an accident. The horse had slipped on a patch of ice, and the cab had overturned. The driver had escaped injury, but Sir James had been thrown out on his head and was still unconscious.

Concussion, Dr. Burns diagnosed. There was the possibility of a fractured skull, but it would be unwise to move him to a hospital at this stage. Nurses must be engaged, although nothing could be done about that until morning. He was willing to stay at the bedside himself, but Maud, who had been sitting at her father's side, holding one of his inert hands, said that there was no need for that. She would be with her father. There was no need for nurses, either, if the doctor would tell her what to do. Between her and Nanny, they would manage.

"I must be here when he opens his eyes," she said in a distraught whisper.

"It may be some time before he does that."

"Are you afraid I will fall asleep?"

No, that was the last thing he expected. Those enormous strained eyes, glowing like green lamps, looked as if sleep would never touch them again. So much for all that talk about her hating her father.

She followed the doctor to the door. He could feel her tension. Her slim body was rigid with it.

"This is all my fault, Doctor. If I hadn't been so beastly to Papa, he wouldn't have gone out on a night like this."

Dr. Burns patted her hand. She was a lovely creature, even with this dash of Lady Macbeth in her manner.

"He'll be fine, my dear. And the better for having you at his side when he opens his eyes. Send for me immediately if you're alarmed about anything. I'll be in first thing in the morning in any case."

He patted her hand as he went. She seemed to be a much more sensitive young woman than he had thought.

"Miss Maud, your mother wants you, to hear what the doctor said."

"I can't come, Bertha. Tell her Papa has no injuries except concussion. I must go back to him."

"You're not planning to sit up all night! Nanny and I can do that."

"Thank you, Bertha. But I intend to stay with him myself."

"Miss Maud!" Nanny was like an old sheep, wrapped in her flannel gown. "It'd be better if you was to let me and Bertha take turns. You've no experience."

"Don't *keep* me!" Maud cried. "I must go back to Papa."

She was there when the blue eyes opened in bewilderment, fell on her, and softened with pleasure.

"Maud!"

"Papa!"

The two words were enough. The past was forgotten. It had never been.

"What are you doing here? What's wrong with me?" His voice mumbled. "Feel as I've been hit over the head."

"You had an accident, Papa. You have a concussion."

"Maud—crying?"

"You mustn't talk. Close your eyes."

"Be glad to."

The heavy eyelids fell, making Papa's face sculptured and remote. He was so pale. He looked as he would when he was dead. Maud's tears flowed faster. She mopped them silently, feeling with intense relief the hard knot of anguish that she had carried in her chest for so long, dissolving. A quarrel with Papa, the most beloved person in the world? She must have been temporarily mad.

*   *   *

"Maud, where the devil are you?"

"Here, Papa. I only went out for a few minutes."

"I want you here with me."

"Of course, Papa. Are you feeling better?"

"Damned bedclothes are too hot. Take some off, will you?"

Maud laid her hand on his forehead anxiously.

"I think you have a little fever. Dr. Burns will be here soon."

"More than a little fever. I feel as if I'm lying in a desert. Vultures croaking over me." The blue eyes opened, twinkled dimly. "Don't look so anxious. I'm as strong as a horse. A good deal stronger than that old crock that fell last night. Pitched me out on my head. I've only caught a chill." His hand groped for hers. She could feel the fever in it. She must send a message to Dr. Burns to hurry. But she couldn't leave the bedside while her fingers were held in that hard grasp.

"Who's that sawbones? You mean the shabby little Scotsman next door?"

"He was the nearest. He came at once. If you don't like him, we can send for someone from Harley Street."

"No, no. No fuss, Maud. I've only had a bump on the head."

It was more than that, however. It appeared that after the accident Sir James had lain in the snow for some time, with only his greatcoat spread over him, until a passing motorist had been prevailed on to bring him home. The cabdriver, who had frequently driven Sir James, assured the police that the gentleman would prefer to go to his own home. Which was a good thing since, with the bad weather, the casualty wards of the hospitals were overflowing.

Dr. Burns put away the thermometer and beckoned Maud out of the room.

"A slight touch of pneumonia, Miss Lucie."

"That's dangerous, isn't it?" Maud was deeply alarmed.

"Not at present. But it can be. I would really advise a trained nurse."

"No. Papa wouldn't be happy. He wants me. I can do everything a trained nurse would do."

"I don't doubt it," Dr. Burns said, looking at the intense, dedicated face. "But you can't stay awake permanently."

"My old nurse will help. I'll have a bed made up in Papa's room that I can rest on."

"Then will you follow my instructions faithfully?"

"Faithfully."

Mamma, helped by Bertha, made her slow, shuffling way to the bedside. Her face, between the heavy loops of faded hair, was like a white candle.

"James, how are you today?"

"Capital." His voice wheezed. "Be out and about soon. What are you doing here, Lydia? Where's Maud?"

"Here, Papa."

"Don't let your mother stand about. Help her to her room."

In the passage, a tear slid down Mamma's pale cheek.

"He doesn't want me."

"He's too ill, Mamma."

"He's not too ill to want you." The large gray eyes, misted with tears, were haunted by the old defeat. "Call me if he's worse. He'll want me then."

The doorbell rang constantly. News had spread of the famous man's illness. At times there were four or five of Papa's friends in the drawing room, sipping sherry, talking to Lady Lucie, who suddenly found herself strong enough to entertain. She even found a secret pleasure in it, since James' daunting shadow no longer hung over her.

"Miss Maud," whispered Nanny. "Mr. Ponsonby is asking for you again. Shall I send him away?"

"Yes, I can't possibly see him. He ought to realize that."

"He's brought red roses. In February! He must have money to burn. Or else no sense. Although he looks like a young man with a great deal of sense. I suppose love makes him lose it."

But Maud wasn't listening to Nanny's inevitable comments on another suitor. She thought Papa was breathing a little more easily. But the radiant flush of fever remained on his cheekbones. A blond stubble had grown around his jaw. He looked like a disheveled Viking. Sometimes he gave her a lucid gaze, but more often, distressingly, his eyes were clouded and confused.

Now, after Nanny's visit, he said quite clearly, "Who's this unfortunate fellow you're dismissing, Maud?"

"Horace Ponsonby." She was so delighted at his coherent voice that she laughed. "He's terribly faithful and persistent. I imagine he'll still be calling in ten years' time."

"You must marry, Maud."

"Of course, Papa. One day."

"Not one day. Soon. Having those two plain Beauchamp girls get ahead of you. It's damned humiliating."

"You mustn't talk anymore."

His hand made its familiar groping movement for hers.

"My fault, Maud. Should have let you have your poet. Love in a cottage. Would you have been happy?"

"No!" Maud lied loyally.

"I thought I was doing the right thing."

"I know, Papa. That's all over now. I've forgotten it."

The dulled blue eyes looking up from the pillow had a painful intensity.

"I must be honest. If I can't be honest on my deathbed—"

"Papa!"

His lips twitched. "Joke, Maud. But I admit I couldn't bear losing you. I doubt if I'd have let even a duke carry you off. I wanted to keep you forever. But you can't embalm beauty. So find a husband soon. Someone who won't nag you about that escapade of yours."

Maud knew what he meant. The vexed subject of her virginity. She must tell him the truth about that and relieve his mind. But suddenly he was asleep, his mouth slightly open, his cheeks sunken, his breathing shallow and harsh.

"Miss Maud, Mr. Ponsonby is here again. He might as well sleep across your doorway. Shall I send him away?"

"No. Stay with Papa a few minutes."

"You'll see him now!"

"That's what I said."

"But look at yourself. You haven't had your clothes off for twenty-four hours."

"I don't think he's come to see my clothes."

Horace Ponsonby was pacing up and down in the downstairs sit-

ting room. He turned eagerly when Maud came in and looked at
her with concern.

"My dear girl, you look fagged out."

"I've been sitting up all night."

"Must you? Aren't there others—" His confident, slightly hectoring voice faltered as he met the blaze of her eyes.

"You don't seem to realize. This is my father!"

"I do understand, Maud. I mean, is he as bad as that?"

Maud nodded and began to cry. She was so tired, so anxious, and
Horace with his neat mustache, his well-ordered face, his absolutely sincere concern for her, although the most unlikely of ha-
vens, was indisputably a haven simply by being there at the right
time. His arms about her were more comforting than she could have
imagined. She laid her head on his shoulder and let her tears dampen
the good broadcloth of his jacket.

"You should be resting, Maud. You're worn out."

"I wanted to thank you for your roses. And for calling so often. I
do appreciate it, although I haven't seemed to."

"I'm a patient man."

"Yes, I know that."

"A persistent one, too."

"Perhaps your persistence ought to be rewarded."

She felt his body stiffen.

"Maud!"

"I'm not saying anything. But would you mind—what Papa calls
my escapade—wouldn't you want to know—"

"Never, Maud, never! I trust you! Good heavens, I would be a
cad not to." He held her away from him, looking at her with his
severe serious eyes. "Haven't I proved that by wanting to marry you?"

"Yes." She sighed. "Yes, you have, Horace darling. I must go
now." At the door, she looked back at him wildly. "But Papa isn't
going to die, and it will all be different."

"How? What do you mean?"

She had gone. He thought she was distraught and hysterical and
unaware of what she said. Understandably so, for her father's accident seemed to have brought about an almost too ardent reconciliation. Comprised of guilt on both sides, of course. But that would
calm down when the old man recovered. Or died.

Either way, there seemed to be hope for him, and he was jubilant. He was utterly obsessed by Maud. She was beautiful, unpredictable, tantalizing, both tender and cruel—possibly she had a streak of her father's ruthlessness. His parents and his sister thought it would be the greatest mistake for him to marry her. But he intended to if, by some supreme miracle, he got the chance.

It was early morning, and Papa was better. He asked for a scotch and water and swore peevishly when Nanny gave him unadulterated water.

"Where's Maud?"

"She's coming. She's just managed to get a few hours' sleep. She was worn out. Could you take a little beef tea, sir?"

"I believe I might. Oh, Maud. Maud, I've been lying here thinking that it's time we had a motorcar. No more being pitched out of hansom cabs on my head. I'll sell the carriage and get a Rolls. What do you say to that?"

Maud, washed and dressed and twice as awake now that Papa was actually talking about the future, exclaimed enthusiastically, "How perfectly wonderful! Can I learn to drive?"

"Certainly not. Much too dangerous. We'll have a chauffeur. We'll go on picnics in the country. When the larches are out."

"Oh, Papa, how divine!"

"Yes. It will be nice to see another spring. I'll paint you in a large hat, wandering in a meadow of deep grass. Queen Anne's lace and scarlet and white poppies—"

"Papa!"

"Yes, my darling."

"I told you a lie about Guy and me. We didn't sleep in that bed. It was much too lumpy, like a sack of potatoes." Maud's voice was high with laughter and hysteria. "Wasn't it too ridiculous?"

She thought he said, "Good God, why didn't you?" The golden eyebrows certainly lifted in delicate irony. Then his voice was clear. "Don't even become anything so dull as a good woman."

The awful thing was that the coherent flash didn't last. Maud wondered if it had actually happened, as she hung over one side of the bed, Dr. Burns over the other.

The figure with the blue, distorted face and the rasping, choking breath was no longer Papa.

But it was. For fragments of sentences came.

"Maud . . . must marry . . ."

"Yes, Papa, I'm going to."

"Going . . . to?"

"Horace Ponsonby. I told him yesterday."

"The good . . . dull . . . stockbroker . . ."

"But you want me to marry him, don't you, Papa? It makes you happy to know this?"

"Such . . . an end . . ." The glazed blue eyes suddenly opened wide. "I must be buried in Westminster Abbey," Papa said in a strong voice and died.

The straw that had been laid in the street outside the residence of Sir James Lucie in Melbury Square was swept up before the funeral.

It was a grand funeral, even though its destination was not Westminster Abbey. Sir James Lucie, Royal Academician, was taken to Mortlake, just like any other Kensington citizen, and that had to be good enough for him.

Soon enough the trees in the square were budding, and the winter was over.

BOOK II

MAUD AND HESSIE

Chapter 12

By 1917 the little oak tree in the Square gardens was several feet high. Maud used to point it out to Hessie on the rare occasions when she joined the child and Nanny for tea on a fine summer afternoon.

"Did you and Daddy plant it, Mother?"

"No. I've told you before, Hessie. You don't listen."

"She never listens to anything, does Miss Hester," said Nanny.

"It was I and another man I knew. Before I met Father. We were very young."

"Where is the man now?" (Nanny was quite wrong. Hessie listened to every word that fell from her mother's lips. She knew, however, how much Mother enjoyed recounting this old story, so she simply pretended not to have heard it.)

"He's dead, sad to say. He was drowned in the Nile River several years ago, before you were born. He was a great explorer, and a poet."

"Did he never see his little tree?"

"No, never."

"Did you love him, Mother?"

"Yes, I did. We wanted to be married once, but there were reasons why we couldn't be."

"If you had married him, would he have been my father?"

"I expect so, darling." Mother's gaze at Hessie was critical, as always, and perplexed, as if she couldn't understand how she had come to have this child.

"Oh, well," she finished fatalistically, "if Guy hadn't been drowned, I expect he would have died in the trenches. Almost everyone else has."

But there still seemed to be plenty of officers in uniform to come to Mrs. Horace Ponsonby's on Sunday afternoons. She said it was her war effort, entertaining them, taking their minds off the horror of the front line. She also worked in hospital wards, changing bandages, carrying bedpans, making cups of tea. More particularly, she volunteered to sit beside the dangerously wounded, holding their hands and helping them fight their pain. She had a gift for giving herself in this way, radiantly and cheerfully. But afterward, she would come home looking white and thin and tired and refuse to listen to Nanny's protests.

"If they can get shot to pieces in France, I can hold their hands when they are dying. It's the very least one can do. Besides, they like me, poor loves."

"Well, of course they do. You put so much of yourself into things. You wear yourself out. The master doesn't like it. And there's Miss Hester, scarcely sets eyes on her mother."

"Nanny, because you're eighty and have been here forever, it doesn't give you the right to run my life." This was an old argument.

"Seventy-eight, if you please, Miss Maud. And I'll try to keep you in order till my dying day. Someone has to."

The idea of someone as beautiful and confident and loved and as grown-up as Mother being told what to do by Nanny was astonishing to Hessie. All the same, it was true that Nanny was the only one whom she did occasionally obey. Not Father, not Grandma, certainly not her daughter unless she was in one of her indulgent moods, when Hessie could demand anything. Those wonderful days when she came home with her arms full of presents for everyone. She adored giving presents, even the most trifling things, wrapped up with silver paper and ribbon. Those were the times when Hessie dearly loved her mother.

There were other times when she hated her. She knew well enough that she, Hessie, six years old and like her father in appearance ("She has a face like a white cabbage" she had once heard her mother say), was not loved as other children she knew were loved by their mothers.

She had to snatch at scraps of affection and forget the rebuffs.

She spent as much time as she was allowed to with Nanny. Her governess, Mademoiselle, terrified her. She smiled just before rapping Hessie's knuckles with a ruler; she pinched secretly when there were other people in the room and Hessie could not cry out. Sometimes, she stumbled about the room, and her breath smelled strange. Once, in the middle of the afternoon, she fell asleep at the schoolroom table, and snored loudly.

Hessie had never dared tell her mother about this strange behavior. She was afraid that if she did, Mademoiselle would pinch her until she was black and blue. Anyway, Mother tried not to dismiss servants, as it was so difficult getting new ones while the war was on. "We have to put up with lower standards," she said constantly.

If Father had been home, it would have been different. But he was at an army camp on Salisbury plain, teaching young men how to be soldiers. Everyone said how lucky it was that his eyesight wasn't good enough for him to fight in the trenches. He would come home safely at the end of the war, and everyone would be happy. Although sometimes Mother seemed upset that Father couldn't go overseas. It was pretty dull for him just being an instructor, and there was no chance to win promotion or decorations doing this. Perhaps she wanted to hold his hand in the hospital when he came home wounded. Certainly it would be nice if he were a hero.

Hessie's haven in the house in Melbury Square was Grandma's room. Grandma was a complete invalid. She lay in bed, propped up with pillows, her fine white halo of hair and her bedjacket with ruffled lace making her look like a piece of thistledown that might float away. Her voice was high and frail, her eyes full of love for the silent child who wandered about her room, brooding over her treasures. From a very early age, Hessie had shown an instinctive reverence for these small exquisite *objets d'art*. Things that not even elderly Bertha was permitted to touch could lie in the plump careful baby hands. No one but Hessie was allowed to lift the glass-topped table and take out the jewel-colored miniatures. Ladies and gentlemen with stiff lace collars, pink cheeks, and snow-white curls, children with rosy smiling faces. All so pretty. None as plain as Hessie. She played a game, imagining herself to be the golden-haired laughing child or the elegant lady with the sloping white shoulders or the soldier in the red jacket. Who would she be today, she would think, as she tapped on Grandma's door, waiting for the whispering voice to bid her come in.

She might have told Grandma about Mademoiselle's pinches; only Grandma had enough pain of her own. Her twisted hands dropped and spilled things. Sometimes she was too tired even to smile. Hessie understood. She was such a peaceful child, Lady Lucie said. So different from Maud. But Maud had had a tirelessly energetic father who had permanently ruined her character by his spoiling, and now Maud could never sit still for two minutes either. Thank goodness Horace was different. He was extremely kind to his daughter, and fond of her. He would have been even kinder and have given her more wholehearted attention if he had been able to overcome some of his infatuation for his wife.

Maud Lucie's wedding to Horace Ponsonby was perforce a quiet one since the Lucie household was still in mourning. The bride looked wan and *triste* in pale lilac with black velvet trimmings.

"I wasn't a real bride," Maud was to tell her daughter some years later. "Everything was too sad."

"But you and Father wanted to be married," Hessie insisted. Her romantic heart should have had a more fitting receptacle than her square solid breast, her remorselessly earnest eyes.

"How did Father ask you to marry him, Mother?"

"He didn't ask me. He simply said 'When will we be married?' And if that wasn't very romantic, it was honest. You know Father isn't one for pretty talk."

"So did you put on your lilac dress with the black velvet and go to a church at once?"

"Well, no, we had long arguments to begin with. I wanted to live here, in this house, where my darling Papa had lived and where there was Grandma and Nanny and Bertha to take care of. For one thing, there wasn't too much money for Grandma. Papa left me his paintings, but I couldn't sell them. It would have been like selling part of him. Hessie, I warn you, don't love your father too much. It can make life very complicated."

Hessie did love her father very much. She wisely kept silent about that.

"Didn't Father want to come and live here?" she asked in her practical way.

"No, he didn't. He was very against it. But he gave in when he finally realized that we couldn't neglect Grandma, and we couldn't run two establishments. Besides, he wanted to please me."

It was an upsetting time to remember. Maud had found that Horace's stubbornness, which had seemed to be rocklike, had suddenly crumbled, and he had promised to do exactly as she wished. She saw that she would always be able to manipulate him, and she was afraid. She didn't want to be strong and ruthless. But if Horace allowed her to go on defeating him, she would grow worse and worse. It was inevitable. She would turn into one of those hateful women who bullied their husbands and whom nothing ever pleased.

She must constantly remind herself of Horace's good qualities and begin to love him.

She had never for a moment not intended to keep the promise she had made to Papa on his deathbed. She had only to wait a short decent interval before it could be carried out.

Most people agreed that Maud Lucie, with her dubious past, had made a better catch than she deserved. Horace Ponsonby was a thoroughly respectable young man, with a good brain and good prospects in the city. If he could persuade his dazzling young wife not to be too extravagant, he had the ability to build up a modest fortune.

That was before the war, of course, before the stock market was shaken to its foundations and the taxes became crippling. When Horace went into the army, Maud had at last agreed to sell some of her father's pictures.

But to the surprise of the art world and to Maud's furious resentment, the demand for works by James Lucie, RA, was negligible. Death had unkindly made him unfashionable. Maud sold two paintings at ridiculous prices and withdrew the remaining six. Three others she never intended to sell. Two of them had been Papa's favorites, the peacock one and the one of her in her Worth dress. The third was too personal ever to be exhibited to the public. It must have been painted during the unhappy estrangement between Maud and her father and was nothing more than a series of charcoal sketches of her face, drawn over and over. She had found it after her father's death and had sat with it in her hands, repeating an old joke, "Who do you think you are? Leonardo da Vinci?" her eyes hollow with misery.

So there were still nine paintings by James Lucie decorating the studio which, just before the war, Maud had turned into a lavishly furnished reception room. It was there that she held her Sunday afternoon at homes. Her friends had responded to her old magnetism and had come willingly. Strikingly dressed, Maud had been an amusing and successful hostess.

But that was before the war and before Hessie's birth had put a temporary stop to the fun of being a young matron and mistress of a house. Somehow Maud had never expected a baby from one of those nights of what was supposed to be love in the big double bed in Papa's bedroom.

What other room in the house could they have had? This was the main bedroom and intended for the master and mistress. Its windows faced over the Square. The handsome William Morris wallpaper didn't show the least sign of wear. It was a comfortable, even a rich room, and Horace had no reason to be displeased with it or with his bride, who waited for him with her long red hair hanging over her shoulders. He could hardly believe his good fortune, even though he was completely aware that she had already had her own way in every detail. Later he would assert himself. But now he only wanted to please her. He prayed devoutly that he would be able to do so that night.

Maud found herself perfectly calm. So now she was about to do this thing she had boasted she had done with Guy. But she couldn't allow herself to think of Guy. For it was Horace panting above her. His mustache tickled her nose, and she sneezed. This seemed to excite him unbearably, for almost at once he hurt her quite severely. She only just managed to control her cry of pain. She let him collapse on top of her, murmuring incoherent thanks into her neck. What was he grateful for? She had done nothing but endure what the marriage service had exhorted her to do. She expected it would get better with practice. It must do, or what was the hold Papa had had over Cora, and why did Honor's eyes follow Ninian everywhere?

One would have to be philosophical. One was certainly not going to give way to tears or despair or wonder what desert one had strayed into because of a rash emotional promise to a dying man. She could hear a nightingale beginning to sing. It was so rare that one came to the trees in the Square now that it must have been a serenade for her wedding night. It was a happy omen. She *would* make her marriage a success.

With this determination, she fell asleep and was only awakened because Horace was sitting up exclaiming, "The old fellow's here!"

"Who?"

"Your father."

"Horace, you're dreaming! Shall I put the light on?"

"No, no," he muttered, falling back on the pillow. "I must have had a nightmare."

"Not a nightmare, a dream."

But Maud put affectionate arms around him as they settled to sleep again. She hadn't guessed he would be so sensitive to his surroundings. It was hopeful. There were other hopeful things, too. She would begin to entertain, first refurbishing the studio and making it a suitable setting for Papa's paintings. She was unaware that already Hessie, the smallest seed, not even the size of the acorn she had once planted, lay within her. Nor that Hessie on birth ("Can we call her Hester, Maud? It's my mother's name") would be the image of Horace, even to the colorless eyelashes.

So that she had to struggle hard with herself to love her baby and not think all the time of the blue-eyed lost Evangeline, whom she had wholly adored.

She had never really succeeded in either thing. Neither did she succeed in enjoying her husband's embraces. The forbidden memory of Guy's tender gaze and hard, lean body came too often to her. This act of love would have been totally acceptable and completely ravishing with Guy. She knew that now. She was almost certain her father had known it, too.

She had moments of panic, when she wondered how to endure all the years ahead. Horace's ritual before departing for the city, for instance, the final inspection of himself in the mirror, his sedate kiss on her cheek (the passionate grunting blind kisses were kept for the nights in the big bed in Papa's bedroom when she was desperately ashamed of herself for being afraid of conceiving another cabbage-faced child), the rear view of his stocky figure, with its permanent accessories, the bowler hat, pigskin gloves, and rolled umbrella, going down the short path to the front gate. Would this go on until the fringe of hair beneath the bowler whitened, the compact figure thickened, and the umbrella had to be used as an unobtrusive walking stick? She couldn't even contemplate the thought.

Because she had found that there were no surprises in Horace, no hidden beauties or even interesting vices, that aroused her love or sympathy. Everything he did and said was maddeningly predictable, and the high pure glow of self-sacrifice that had at first filled her, giving her an image of herself with which she could live after the terrible grief of Papa's death, had long ago vanished.

She, the divine Maud, the toast of so many Royal Academies, was now a quite ordinary wife and a far from successful mother.

She was almost glad when the drums began beating in Europe, and suddenly the war had begun.

Hessie was a timid child, though she tried to hide this characteristic, as she hid others of which she was ashamed, such as her habit of crying too easily and desperately attempting to conceal her tears. She was afraid of Mademoiselle, whom she saw as someone who was all sharp spikes, thin nose, long thin teeth, pointed chin, meager, bony body, and those scissorslike pinching fingers.

Another terror was the empty house on the opposite side of the Square. Hessie was extremely loath to pass this house even in daylight. The bushes grew up around the never-opened front door, and it was said that the white face of the idiot child who used to live there sometimes pressed against the upstairs window. When the owls hooted at night, Hessie thought of that forlorn child. It was one reason why she was afraid to go to sleep in the dark, though that was now a rule. No more night-lights, Mother had said. A great girl of six had to be brave.

And dearly as she loved Honor Spencer with her gentle sad face, she wasn't entirely happy in her house after dark either. The servants said the old colonel climbed the stairs with his lame leg, making them creak. Honor smiled and said perhaps it was true, but that the colonel had been such a dear person that it was pleasant to hear him.

It was company. She was lonely now that her husband was in France. It would have been different if her baby had lived. He had been born, by a strange chance, in the same week as Hessie. They would have been practically twins. His name had been James Edward Everitt, but he had lived only two days to bear it.

"I used not to be able to go past your house in case I heard you crying in your perambulator," Honor told Hessie.

"Didn't you like me?" Hessie asked in her belligerent way.

"Only because you could cry and my baby couldn't. I wasn't very sane at that time."

Hessie didn't know what sane meant, but she did know she was selfishly glad that that tiny ghost, James Edward Everitt, wasn't around. If he had been, Honor wouldn't have had so much love to spare for her.

For Honor did love her. She had said so.

"Even though I look like my father?" Hessie had asked diffidently.

"Because you look like yourself."

And Hessie got the impression that Honor was glad she didn't look like her mother, which was surprising. Other people almost always said, "What a pity she doesn't take after her mother!" and until the time of Honor's declaration, she had wished it herself. Now she was less discontented with her lack of grace.

Another of Hessie's fears was old Mrs. Beauchamp. It was almost impossible to believe that that terrifying old lady, a stout figure always dressed in black, had been the mother of the beautiful young man who had wanted to marry Mother. And also was the mother of Honor, who was so gentle, and of the plump, bossy, self-important Countess Daisy, who occasionally visited with her four children, Lord Sylvester, the Honorable Marcus, Lady Grizel, and Lady Edith. "And another coming!" Mother had exclaimed in horror, though how she could see the mysterious fifth child following behind all the bags and baggage that were an inevitable part of Countess Daisy's arrival, Hessie couldn't imagine.

One could never be sure that Mrs. Beauchamp wouldn't be at Honor's, sitting squarely in the wing chair in the drawing room, punctuating her remarks with taps on the floor with her ebony-knobbed walking stick. Alternatively, she might be at Grandma's bedside when one burst in, forgetting to knock, as sometimes happened.

Then Hessie would be frozen to the spot, and Mrs. Beauchamp would make a remark, as if she were deaf or didn't understand the English language. "She's getting too big to behave like that, Lydia. Doesn't that French mamselle keep her in order? She's too busy going out with the army, I expect. Really, I can never believe that child is Maud's daughter. It's certainly not a face to sink a thousand Royal Academies." Then she would give her sharp bark of laughter. Her pleated chin sank into her high black collar. She had a little curved bird's-beak nose with which she might be expected to peck at any moment.

"Don't be unkind, Agatha. Hessie has a dear little face."

But Grandma's voice, or alternatively Honor's voice, was ignored by this nasty old woman, who could often be met sallying out around the Square.

Once Hessie had accidentally bowled her hoop right into the advancing black skirts and had been petrified. The strange thing was that Lady Grizel and Lady Edith could clamber all over her, to the mutual enjoyment of the three of them. But Grizel and Edith were remarkably stupid countrified children.

Chapter 13

MOTHER SAID, "Now write a list of the people you want to come to your birthday party. We'll have tea in the gardens if it's a nice day. Cook will make you a cake. Don't you think that will be fun?"

Hessie sucked her pencil and wrote, "Father, Mother, Grandma, Honor, Nanny." Then she stopped. She was a funny child, she was constantly told. But she simply didn't want other children at her party. She simply didn't like people of her own age. They were too silly. She knew those awful Sylvesters were staying at their grandmother's, Mrs. Beauchamp's. If they came to her party, it would be ruined.

Mother read the list and exclaimed, "But this is all old people, darling. Don't you want your own friends? You'll have to ask Grizel and Edith and their brothers. It would be so rude not to. And what about your other playmates in the Square?"

She had no other playmates. Which showed how much Mother knew about her.

"I don't really want a party," she said.

"But of course you do. You are a funny child. I have a new dress for you. It was meant to be a surprise, but supposing we take a peep?"

Mother was laughing and persuasive. Hessie could never resist her in that mood. She always hoped that this time it would last forever. It wouldn't, of course. It would change, like an English summer day, to chilliness or storms. But she could prolong it now by looking at the dress and showing pleasure. Unfortunately, she could never be anything but honest, and the white muslin dress with the lace insertions and the blue sash was surely not for a stout, plain child.

"Will I look nice in it?" she asked agonizedly.

"Of course you will." She heard the repressed exasperation in her mother's voice. "I thought this was the kind of dress you would like."

It was really meant for Evangeline, Hessie thought silently. Evangeline was the mysterious child from whom a postcard used to come once every few months. Postcards from Birmingham or Morecambe Bay or Blackpool, always with the same message scrawled on the back, "Love and kisses from Evangeline."

She was just a child Mother had once known, Mother had said in answer to Hessie's questions. She was a few years older than Hessie. She must be quite old now. This had been borne out by the message on the last postcard: "Joe says no more of these, Vangie is getting too old and beginning to ask awkward questions, Sorry, Cora." But old as Evangeline was, Hessie was certain Mother had been thinking of her when she bought this fussy unsuitable dress.

"Nanny will put your hair in curling papers," Mother went on. "Then you'll look pretty."

Hessie thought of the uncomfortable night to be spent in the hard knotty curlers. Her straight hair always came out of curl almost immediately.

"Will Father be coming?" she asked.

"He's promised to do his best to get leave. Now you really must write an invitation to the Sylvesters. And to their mother and grandmother. Don't pout, Hester. I don't particularly want the grown-ups either, but at least you won't have to sit with them as I will. You children can run off and play. And remember that you're a lucky girl to be having a party when there's a war on."

The party day started well, after all. Father arrived home in the middle of the morning. He hugged Hessie, who had run into his arms.

"Happy birthday, my darling. Would you like your present now or at the correct time, in the middle of the celebrations?"

"*Now*, please, Father."

She opened the bulky parcel to discover a palette and brushes and a row of enchanting little bottles of oil paints.

"Father—" she began rapturously, then saw Mother, wearing the neat gray coat and skirt that she wore to go to the hospital, standing in the doorway.

"Hester, what have you got there? Oil paints! Horace, whatever sort of a gift is that for a seven-year-old?"

"I thought you'd be pleased. After all, she is the granddaughter of James Lucie."

"And can't draw a line."

"Well, never mind. Let her make what daubs she likes. It seems to me modern paintings are only daubs anyway."

The excitement had gone out of the gift. Hessie closed the wooden box and quietly went out of the room. But she deliberately aggravated her hurt by stopping in the passage to listen and hearing Mother say, "Really, Horace, you do do some strange things. Such an unsuitable present. Even if she is Papa's grandchild. You know she doesn't take after him in the least. She's far more your child than mine."

"Therefore she should be given a manual on the stock exchange?" Father said. "Well, aren't you going to tell me you're pleased I got home?"

"Of course I'm pleased, you old bear. Don't sound so sulky. And Hessie will be delighted. She worries me; she's such a solitary child. She doesn't seem to make friends. And, Horace, I'm terribly sorry, but I've simply got to go to the hospital this morning."

"Must you? Can't someone else? You're looking fagged out."

"No, I've promised. There's a poor private in the Welsh fusiliers. He's only eighteen, and he's lost both legs. He won't live. I know he won't. They seldom do. But I seem to be able to reach him when no one else can."

"Maud, isn't this too harrowing?"

"Who for? It's not me who's dying."

"Doesn't he have any family?"

"In the north of Wales. So I'm his mother and his sister and his sweetheart. Is it true that the war is going to be over soon?"

"It must be. If it goes on much longer—"

"Everyone will be dead but you and me," Mother cried passionately.

"Oh, God, Maud, I never wanted a safe job."

"Neither did I, if it comes to that. I must fly now. Go up and see

Mamma. She's getting so vague. A new face sharpens her up a bit."

"You'll be back this afternoon?"

"Of course," Mother said in astonishment. "It's Hessie's party."

Hessie, listening, prayed her mother wouldn't arrive back from the hospital with a white face and reddened eyes, too tired to eat and too restless to stay still. She gave too much of herself, Nanny kept saying. "She's drained, Miss Hester, that's what your mother is. Those poor young men love her too much, and she loves them back. If this war isn't over soon, I wouldn't like to say what will happen."

"To Mother?" Hessie asked in acute apprehension.

"To us all. Them Huns would like to put a bullet through the lot of us. I'd just like to get my hands on that Kaiser. I'd throttle him."

But the sun shone in the afternoon, and the war seemed a long way away.

The Honorable Marcus boasted that he had seen a zeppelin flying over London last night. The moon had been shining, and he had looked out of the window and seen this great whale swimming through the sky. He was making it up of course. He was angry that he had been in the country and had missed the zeppelins when they had come over.

The grown-ups sat in a circle in the sunniest part of the garden. A tablecloth had been spread on the grass, and Ada was scurrying back and forth with laden trays. There were so many cups and saucers needed, not to mention all the food, and the silver teapots and hot-water jugs, the milk, and the silver sugar bowl filled with sugar lumps. Considering how long the war had been raging, they were having quite a spread. Still, it was Miss Hester's birthday, and Cook had been saving up the dried fruit and the candied peel for the cake for a long time.

It looked for a little while as if the mistress was going to be late, which would have been an awful shame, for poor Miss Hester had eyes like saucers and the master sat glumly trying to answer the questions that rattled like gunfire from old Mrs. Beauchamp.

However, she came at last, running over the grass, still dressed in her sober gray coat and skirt, looking as tired as Ada had ever seen her. Almost plain, with her cheekbones sticking out and circles round her eyes. But she tried to be merry, bless her heart. Ada had been at

Number 7 for five years and would have been prepared to die for the mistress, cranky as she could be at times. But when she was happy, the house came alight. There was no other way to describe it.

"I'm not late, am I? I tried to get a taxi, but I couldn't. I had to come on the bus, and it just crawled." She dropped a kiss on Horace's neatly brushed head, then wrapped Hessie in a warm embrace. "How's my birthday girl? You look sweet in your new dress. Don't you think so, you boys? Come along, be gallant. Is everyone here? Where's Honor?"

Honor, at that moment, was coming through the garden gate. She had a tall man in khaki at her side.

Daisy sprang up. "Why, it's Ninian. What a surprise. Did Honor know he was getting leave?"

"Didn't say a word to me," Mrs. Beauchamp grumbled.

The pink in Honor's cheek suggested that she, too, had had a surprise. She came hurrying up, holding Ninian by the hand and exclaiming breathlessly. "He just walked in. He has a whole week's leave. I simply can't believe it."

"I can't either," said Ninian. "I crossed over from Boulogne this morning." He shook hands with everyone and with Hessie especially, wishing her a happy birthday. Hessie, who didn't care for him being home since that meant Honor had much less time for her, had to admit that he had a nice strange face, thin and scarred and hollowed and quiet. She didn't know him very well and was shy of him. He and Honor sat down in the circle, and everyone began talking at once. Ada was dispatched for another cup and saucer. Questions were asked about the front, something was said about prisoners and wounded and killed, and Mrs. Beauchamp exclaimed sharply, "Children, go and play."

Hessie, resisting being tugged by Grizel and Edith, saw her mother get up and go over to Ninian.

"Come see my tree," she said, as if she were giving him a present.

"Maud, it's a perfectly ordinary tree," Father said.

"But it has a future. One simply has to contemplate things that have a future. It will live longer than any of us. I find that most peculiarly comforting."

Hessie was whirled away by the Sylvesters, but she looked back to see Mother and Captain Spencer standing close together, earnestly contemplating the little tree. Some obscure impulse made her climb the gnarled branch of the spreading rhododendron bush, a favorite refuge, and suddenly the four Sylvesters were stamping and howling beneath it, pretending to be wolves. "And you're a puppy dog, and if you come down, we'll eat you."

The noise they made was terrifying. It shivered down Hessie's spine. One of the boys shook the branch on which she crouched, trying to topple her off it. Her new white dress was streaked with sooty dust. Oh, dear, she had forgotten to be careful of her dress. But what did a stained dress matter, compared with those ravening mouths beneath?

"Go away!" she sobbed. "Go away, leave me alone!"

"Hessie's crying. Hessie's a crybaby. It's bad luck to cry on your birthday."

"Children! Children!" came Countess Daisy's voice. "Come get tea."

Like a storm abruptly stopping, the noise ceased. The four horrid creatures catapulted away, and soon Hessie deemed it safe to slide down the bush. She looked at her ruined dress, then across the lawn to the little group of people, Mother and Captain Spencer sauntering slowly back and Father standing with a cup and saucer in his hand, forgetting to pass it as he stared at them.

That was the moment when the dark cloud came down on Hessie. She hadn't wanted this party, and she wasn't enjoying it. Therefore, the sensible thing to do was to leave it. She would go home to Grandma, who had been left all alone. Grandma wouldn't scold her for having a dirty dress or for being rude to her guests. She would play with the miniatures, perhaps being Lady Hamilton welcoming Lord Nelson home from battle, just as Mother was welcoming Captain Spencer by showing him her own special tree, offering it to him like a gift.

There would be a fearful row, of course.

But Grandma said with her air of dim pleasure, "Have you come to have tea with me, Hester?"

"Yes, Grandma."

"Aren't you supposed to be having your birthday tea, Miss Hester?" came old Bertha's tart voice.

"Is it your birthday, dear?"

"Yes, Grandma."

"Someone should have told me."

"I told you several times this morning, madam."

"I must find a gift for Hester."

"You have one already wrapped, madam."

Bertha placed the small package in Grandma's twisted hands, and Grandma smiled and said, "What is it, Bertha? I've quite forgotten."

"You'd better let Miss Hester unwrap it and see."

"Yes, of course. Come, Hester, this is your birthday gift."

Hessie held the small silver egg in her hand, and tingles of pleasure went over her body. The day stopped being a calamity. Whatever happened now, she had this perfect moment with Grandma, in her nest of pillows, giving her vague tender smile, and the delicious egg lying cool and heavy in her palm.

"It's Russian, I believe," said Grandma. "Not Fabergé, though."

Hester had frequently seen and coveted the beautiful blue Fabergé egg with its golden belt.

"Did Grandpapa give it to you, Grandma?"

Grandma's mouth was sucked in thoughtfully.

"Yes," she said at length. "He did."

Some little time later the door burst open, and Mother came in.

"Hester! Oh, just look at your dress!"

Hester backed away, feeling the comfort of the egg in her closed palm.

"*Must* I go out again, Mummy?"

"Don't take her away, Maud. She's having a nice visit with me."

"But she has guests. She's being very ill mannered. Run upstairs and change your dress, Hessie. Mademoiselle will help you. I expect you back in the gardens in ten minutes. Mamma, you mustn't encourage her. She mustn't run away from things. She'll turn into a recluse."

"What is a recluse?" Hessie asked Mademoiselle, to postpone the moment of returning downstairs in a clean but ordinary dress.

"It's a nasty, dirty old person," Mademoiselle answered. As Hessie hesitated at the top of the stairs, she flapped her hands at her and said, "Shoo! *Vite! Vite!* You bad girl!"

Dragging her feet, Hessie had to descend. One flight, two flights, and suddenly there was Father in the hall, putting out his hand to take hers and whispering, "Quickly! Before we're caught."

Out in the street, she managed to gasp, "Where are we going?"

"Down the High Street for tea. Which would you like, cream buns or chocolate ice or both?"

"Oh, Father!" she panted in rapture. "How scrumptious."

She would adore him forever, his kind jolly voice, his conspiratorial little-boy smile, his eyes with their naughty shine. He was enjoying the forbidden treat as much as she was.

Yet one small worry nagged her. She could still see Father, as still as stone, watching Mother no longer tired and wan, no longer thinking of that poor dying soldier, talking to Captain Spencer.

"What would the young lady like now?" the waitress asked. "Chocolate layer cake, cherry cake, fudge cake?"

But Hessie, to her shame, was feeling a little sick. She couldn't even finish the delicious cream bun.

In their bedroom, brushing her hair with short, sharp strokes, her angry eyes looking back at her from the mirror, Maud said, "Really, Horace, you puzzle me. It was bad enough, Hester behaving so rudely, but she was overexcited, and she's only a child. One can make certain allowances. But for you to take her off like that. Why ever did you do it?"

"To give her a treat."

"But she was having a treat. Hadn't I gone to a lot of trouble to arrange a party for her?"

"And you never bothered to find out that she hates the Sylvesters."

"What, John and Marcus? And those two simple creatures, Grizel and Edith, just like their mother."

"Well, she hates them."

"Then she must get over it. We can't have a child who is antisocial."

"Is that a crime?"

"No, it isn't a crime, but it will make life even more difficult for her."

"Even more?"

"Well, the funny little thing is practically a misfit already."

"Like me?"

Maud recognized the stiff, offended voice—it was all too familiar —and sighed.

"Darling, who said you were a misfit? But it's true that Hessie takes after you. I can't see the smallest part of myself in her."

"Is that why you don't love her?"

Maud's mouth tightened. Her temper had become extremely touchy lately Her moods changed from low depression to exhilaration. She was working too hard, she was thin, she had this conviction that all nourishing food should be kept for the sick and wounded brought home from France and for children. She practically starved herself, Nanny declared worriedly. It was ridiculous that a woman of twenty-seven with a child should have a twenty-three-inch waist.

Maud tied the sash of her dressing gown around that waist now, as she stood up to face her husband.

"That really is a double-edged remark and a very unkind one. You suggest (a) that I don't love my child and (b) that I don't love her because I could only love my own qualities in her."

"Now, Maud, you're talking like an encyclopedia. That's more my kind of thing, as you've told me often enough."

"Then I must have caught it from you. Horace, what are you doing? I thought you were staying overnight."

Horace was methodically putting articles in his rucksack. His only sign of anger was the line of his mouth beneath his neatly clipped mustache and the way his square pale-skinned hands trembled slightly. Nothing, of course, would make him lose his neatness.

"Sorry, my dear, I can't."

"But you told me you had leave."

"Did I? Must have been a slip of the tongue."

Maud slumped wearily into a chair.

"You never make a slip of the tongue. Tell me, then. Did you imagine I was flirting with Ninian Spencer?"

Horace replied evenly, "I didn't imagine. I knew. So did Honor. That wasn't worthy of you, Maud. I know you can't help flirting, it's part of your nature, but Ninian Spencer had barely set foot in his house, and I thought it was a bit hard on Honor."

Maud leaned forward with an intense movement.

"But didn't you see his face? The nightmare in his eyes? Perhaps I've seen that too often in eyes of the boys I help to nurse. I begin to look for it. In Ninian, it was so plain you would have had to be blind not to see it. He's on the edge of shell shock, and if Honor doesn't recognize it, I do. So I talked to him about trees."

"Was that all?" The surliness, the everlasting suspicion were suddenly more than Maud could bear.

"Horace, I will not be cross-examined in this way. You make my life impossible. I think your jealousy is psychopathic."

"Perhaps." Then suddenly Horace shouted, "Why, for God's sake, did you marry me?" Standing absolutely still, his arms stiffly at his sides, he sounded as if he were barking an order to a platoon of soldiers. He was ridiculous when he was angry. Ridiculous.

"Because I promised my father on his deathbed. And if you didn't realize that years ago, you didn't know much about me."

Maud was saying at last what she had never quite allowed herself to say over these eight years of exacerbated nerves, resentment for being the victim of her emotional nature, and the feeling of being caught in a lifelong trap. Was this the time to admit the truth at last? She didn't know. She was so tired of her dishonesty.

All the same, had she gone too far?

"Horace—"

"Well, I always knew we never had this room to ourselves," Horace said, the flatness of discipline back in his voice. "Your father is always here." He began to do up the buckles of his rucksack. At the same time Lady Lucie surprisingly rapped on the wall.

"You two—are you quarreling on Hester's birthday?"

Maud sprang up in guilt and shock. How much had Mamma, over the years, heard in this room? Papa and his servant girls? She and Horace arguing or Horace making his panting love? What secrets houses held!

But she had never rapped on the wall before. One had thought that her thistledown head, sunk in the pillows, was both deaf and blind. Oh, God, what a day this had been!

She had only to close her eyes to see Honor and Ninian walking over the grass, hand in hand.

"No, Mamma," she answered. She lowered her voice, "Horace, I never knew you felt like that about this room."

But Horace, his rucksack over his shoulder, was walking stiffly out the door. She must have shocked him more than she had realized. He wasn't even going to say good-bye.

Remorse swept over her. She flew down the stairs after him.

"Horace! Horace, wait, please!"

She caught up with him at the front door.

"You know I can never bear you to go in the middle of a quarrel."

"Because of my feelings or your conscience?"

She almost lost her temper again.

"Oh, for goodness sake! I never mean more than half the things I say. You know that."

"But something drives you to say them. That's what bothers me." He took her by the shoulders, holding her in a tight grip. "Whatever the reason you married me—and I always knew it was something to do with your father—you did marry me, and that's final. I'll never give you up."

Maud was trying not to tremble. She always trembled ridiculously after a quarrel.

"Darling, that's not a very gracious way of accepting my apology."

"Was it an apology?"

"It was meant to be. You know I'm not good at that sort of thing."

Abruptly his head went down on her shoulder.

"Maud!" he whispered. "Maud!"

Then, just as suddenly, he released his grip and had gone, the door banging behind him.

From the top of the stairs Hessie called in outrage, "Has Father *gone?*"

"Yes, darling."

"What did you *do* to him?"

Maud swung around, the relieving anger hot in her cheeks.

"I scolded him, as I'm going to scold you now. Both of you running away from your guests like that. It was disgraceful."

"Is my birthday over now?"

"Yes."

"I'm glad," Hessie shouted, "I'm glad a hundred times."

After love, they lay silently. Honor's anxious mind pondered the unfamiliar violence in Ninian's lovemaking. But there were other things to ponder on, too. The conversation at dinner.

"Whatever did make Maud marry a man like that?" Ninian had asked.

"It was on the rebound from Guy, I think. But Horace is an awfully decent person."

"Decent? Is that a quality Maud enjoys?"

Honor looked at her plate.

"What do you think of her, Ninian?"

"I think she's a lovely creature. Fascinating. I've always thought so. I once kissed her, but she was thinking of someone else, so it wasn't an experience I treasure in my memory. I should think life with her could be rather unpredictable."

"Yes. To say the least."

"One might need some of Horace's dour and dogged qualities."

Honor smiled, since Ninian, watching her with his dark, sunken eyes, seemed to expect it of her.

"Yes, perhaps. But they have Hessie."

"A dour and dogged little girl. Is she really Maud's daughter?"

"That's what everyone says. She's a dear child when one gets to know her. A very solitary one. I don't think Maud realizes that her governess bullies her. One doesn't quite know how to interfere."

"I should think one doesn't interfere."

"But a mother should know those things herself," Honor said indignantly.

"How much did your mother know about you?"

"Well—I suppose—"

Ninian came around to drop a kiss on the top of her head. "You were a secretive child, just like Hessie. Let's go up early, shall we?"

She knew that her face became too vulnerable, too revealing.

"Yes. You must be tired."

"Not that tired."

Nor did it seem so by his vigorous and impatient lovemaking. She tried to convince herself that he was thinking of what she had said about Hessie (she must have let her own loneliness show too much) and was trying to give her another child, even though the doctor had said that such a thing was impossible. He must have thought she envied Maud. So she did. Maud had a living child.

She was also fascinating, and a fascinating woman haunted a man, no matter what he said or did to convince himself that this was not so.

Abruptly, in the darkness, she said, "What made you marry me, Ninian?"

He didn't answer for a moment, but lay still on his own side of the bed, not touching her. The bed seemed wider than it used to be. Perhaps it was because they had both grown so thin.

Then he said, "Because you were such a peaceful person."

"Were? Am I not any longer?"

Again the pause, not of hesitation, but of only half attention. "Of course you are." He turned, feeling in the dark for his cigarettes. "Do you mind if I smoke? Are you sleepy?"

"No."

"Would you like to play something for me?"

"Now?"

"Is it too much trouble?"

"Oh, no. Only—"

"Play the *Moonlight* sonata."

"Do you want to talk about the war, Ninian?"

"No. Just play for me."

She sat up, shivering as the bedclothes fell off her naked shoulders. For the first time in her life, she was reluctant to go downstairs to her piano. Who, or what, would inhabit his thoughts once she was out of the bed?

"Put on a dressing gown. Don't catch cold."

But his voice was absent, his thoughts already following some path unknown to her.

Chapter 14

In October, tragically, since the war was over a month later, Countess Daisy's husband, Bertie, was killed.

For some unaccountable reason, Mrs. Beauchamp invited Hessie to tea. Hessie pleaded with everyone to make her excuses, but no one would. She must go, since Mrs. Beauchamp appeared to want her. One must humor the bereaved. The Earl of Deepford had only been her son-in-law. The person she had never stopped grieving for was her own son, Guy. But he had died long ago. If he hadn't, he might have been Hessie's father, which was odd to think of. Perhaps that was why Mrs. Beauchamp wanted Hessie's company now.

So she had to eat seedcake, which she detested, while Mrs. Beauchamp sat behind the silver teapot and the polished copper kettle on its little spirit lamp and talked in her constant, complaining voice.

"Things will never be the same, you mark my words. Not just because poor Bertie has gone, but because a war like this can't be recovered from. All the best young men have gone. We're left with the weeds. And what sort of a nation will they make? Tell me that."

Hessie strove for an answer, but could think of nothing to say. Weakly, she allowed Mrs. Beauchamp to put another piece of the nasty seedcake on her plate.

"Bless me, you're a quiet child. You're very different from Daisy's mob. And now poor Bertie will never see the new baby."

The new baby, a girl, had been called Melinda. Hessie was extremely puzzled as to why Countess Daisy had bothered to get another baby while her husband was away. Perhaps she had wanted to surprise him.

"All those girls to find husbands for," Mrs. Beauchamp worried. "It won't be as easy as it was. I had to sell my diamonds to get Honor and Daisy off. But now I predict there won't only be a shortage of money, but of men. Even you will find that when you grow up. If there isn't a shortage, the quality won't be there."

But Hessie didn't intend to marry and said so. Mrs. Beauchamp gave her cracked laughter, showing her long yellow teeth. "Now how have you come to such an important decision so young?"

Hessie hung her head, not answering. How could she tell Mrs. Beauchamp that she didn't think marriage was a very happy state, at least not what she had seen of it in her own home. And also, she was afraid her husband might have to be Lord John (now, importantly, the new earl) or the Honorable Marcus. People always said, "How are your little titled sweethearts, Hessie? Which one is going to marry you?"

The small dark parlor was stuffy, and Mrs. Beauchamp had her familiar smell of lavender water and unaired clothes. Hessie was glad when Pritchett came to take away the tea things.

She was ashamed of herself for being glad, for Mrs. Beauchamp thanked her for coming in quite a gentle way.

"We've had a nice conversation together, haven't we?" It had all been on the part of Mrs. Beauchamp, but Hessie nodded politely. "Come and shake hands, then. Goodness gracious, how did you get that nasty bruise on your arm?"

Hessie hastily covered it with her hand.

"I fell down."

"Doesn't look like a fall to me. Looks more like a pinch. A vicious one, too. Have you been punished for something?"

"I didn't do anything!" Hessie said indignantly. "At least, I only couldn't get my spelling right. I find spelling awfully difficult," she added, surprised that she could confide in Mrs. Beauchamp.

"Ah," said Mrs. Beauchamp. She nodded her head several times. "Well, a misspelled word now and then isn't too important. Needlework, music, dancing, French. Those were the things that mattered in my day."

That was how her mother found out about Mademoiselle. At least, Hessie guessed it was, for suddenly Mademoiselle was packing her box, and Mother was making inquiries about suitable day schools. She had decided that it would do Hessie good to mix with children her own age. Later, she would go to boarding school, but just now the small school the other side of Holland Park, run by two sisters, the Misses Peebles, seemed suitable.

She walked Hessie down Melbury Road, pointing out the houses that had belonged to the artists who had been famous when Grandpapa had been a young man. The red-brick outlandish places where William Holman Hunt, Sir Luke Fildes, George Frederic Watts, and Lord Leighton had lived.

"They were called the Pre-Raphaelite Brotherhood. Papa used to say they were terribly pretentious. The best thing about them was the beautiful women they painted. He used to take me to have tea with Mr. Holman Hunt. You never saw a house filled with so many strange treasures."

Hessie had a vision of Grandpapa, that tall, splendid man Mother talked about so much, holding his daughter's hand, marching down this tree-bordered road. Everyone would turn to look at them. "I used to wear a green velvet jacket and carry a white fur muff," Mother said, adding to the brilliant picture in Hessie's mind.

It was an era that was past. Even Holland House, that great gray mansion that Hessie longed one day to enter, was losing its influence in this modern Kensington, with the motorcars roaring up and down the High Street and the little cozy shops being pulled down to make room for large department stores. Mother talked about the balls there used to be at Holland House before the war, when the king and queen were guests and all the ladies wore their grandest gowns and masses of jewels.

One could occasionally hear the screech of a peacock and see smoke drifting from the tall chimneys that rose above the green woodland, but that was all passersby could know of the great house.

Hessie sighed. Mother made the past sound so romantic, so hopelessly lost. Now she was a soberly dressed matron, taking a dull little girl to school. It couldn't be what she had expected, after talking to kings and queens.

One of the nicest things, to Hessie, was that Honor had begun giving her piano lessons. After school, which, after the first petrified days, was not too unendurable, Hessie rushed into Number 9 and began her lessons. It was obvious from the start that she had little talent, but Honor didn't seem to mind. She enjoyed Hessie's company, she said. After the lessons, when the weather was fine, they would sit in the paved garden at the back of the house and have glasses of ginger ale and biscuits with pink icing.

There was a little pool at the bottom of the garden, and by some miracle a frog had appeared in it. It was an endless fascination to Hessie to sit absolutely quiet and watch for the frog to hop onto a lily leaf, an added triumph if she was still enough for it to begin to croak.

Hessie would have liked to stay at Number 9 much longer than she did. But Ninian would arrive home and want quiet because he was tired after his long day in court, and besides, he was writing a book. Not that Hessie made as much noise as the frog. However, it seemed that her presence, even when silent, was disturbing. Ninian was still recovering from the war, Honor explained. He was nervous and irritable, his face all lines, his hair quite gray. Hessie was in awe of him. He either said something sharp and clever to her or didn't appear to see her. But he had insisted that he couldn't stand finger exercises, so Hessie went home on his arrival.

Anyway, by that time Father would be back from the city, and he would expect a conversation with her before she went upstairs. And there was Grandma, who looked for a good-night visit, which sometimes stretched into an hour or more. Life was extremely busy, but it now had an orderliness that pleased Hessie's methodical nature. Her once-long list of special and private requests to God in her prayers at night were now reduced to two, that the Sylvesters wouldn't come to stay with their grandmother and that Mother and Father wouldn't quarrel.

At last, the haunted house on the other side of the Square was occupied. Real children's faces looked out of the upstairs windows, the garden was cleared of weeds, and the door painted a daring shade of red.

There were other changes, too. Dr. Burns was found dead in his bed; he had had a bad heart for some time and had told no one about it, visiting his patients until the last day of his life. Pritchett, Mrs. Beauchamp's faithful housekeeper, had developed acute rheumatism and could no longer climb the steep stairs from the basement to the top of the house. She would ring a bell when Mrs. Beauchamp's breakfast tray was ready, and Mrs. Beauchamp would have to come down and get it herself.

Then, as if the privations and anxieties of the war had worn out all the old people, Miss Lavender, completely blind now, fell down the stairs in Honor's house and was taken to a hospital with a broken femur. She was not likely to live, chiefly because she no longer wanted to. She lay in a half coma, muttering something about a silk dress. She was worrying about one she imagined she was making for a debutante, Honor thought. Poor faithful old soul. When she died a week later, she was buried in her plain cotton nightgown.

Quiet as she had been, like a blind mouse in the attic, she was extraordinarily missed in Number 9. The fumbling tap of her stick now joined the colonel's limp on the stairs at night. Honor told herself she was growing fanciful. She had developed a habit of playing the piano late at night, partly because Ninian found the sound soothing as he worked in his study, partly to hide her loneliness. Somehow she and her husband had lost touch. (Had they ever been in close touch?) Their conversation was polite, like that of friends. Certainly not like that of lovers. Ninian gave her his courteous, remote smile. His face, creased and haggard, was almost ugly. She couldn't get used to his gray hair. The steel helmet had done that, he said. He was lucky his hair hadn't all fallen out. How would she have liked a bald husband?

But had she a husband at all?

Perhaps he wondered if he had a wife, for she knew that a part of her had died with her infant son. And the remaining part was now so inhibited by the distance that had grown between them that sometimes she felt almost as much a ghost as the old colonel and Miss Lavender. If only Ninian would get back his quick, lively spirit, she would get back hers.

In the meantime, she found her chief pleasure in Hessie's visits. Funny earnest little thing, she would never make a pianist, nor would she ever quite overcome the misfortune of having such a beautiful erratic mother. But Honor and she could help each other. Only someone who had been acutely lonely could guess at the loneliness of others. They met on familiar ground.

Time was perplexing. Nanny was eighty, an enormous age, Hessie thought, yet she didn't seem as old as Grandma, who was only sixty. Although that was a great age too. Nanny was a hopping, perky sparrow with fading feathers, as tart and domineering as ever, missing nothing, while Grandma seemed to grow smaller and farther away every day. Bertha was old, too, and had a sister in the country whose cottage she would share when the mistress "passed on." She talked a lot about the expected pleasures of country life, though never in Grandma's hearing.

Nanny was kind enough to Hessie, but it was plain that she still considered "Miss Maud" her real charge. She was delighted that the master was home again and things back to normal, with dinner parties and theater and shopping expeditions. Miss Maud had been looking dowdy, if such a thing could be believed. She had worn that drab coat and skirt for her hospital visiting for much too long. It was nice to see her being extravagant again, her face bright with the fun of having bought a perfectly nonsensical hat. It was nothing but a large bunch of violets, but it would be pretty for the private view. Papa would have liked it, she said.

There was a new hat for Hessie, too. Hessie must accompany her mother to the Royal Academy and learn about paintings.

Hessie wrote in the new five-year diary that Father had given her for her eighth birthday: "Went to the Royal Academy and looked at hundreds of pictures. The one I liked best was called 'Miss Marion Abercrombie with Lapdog,' but Mother said it wasn't a patch on Grandpapa's portraits and the Royal Academy was very dull nowadays. All the same, lots of people talked to us; they all said how pretty Mother looked in the hat with violets and how much they missed the usual portrait of Maud Lucie, as it was always such a talking point. (What is a talking point?)"

They also asked, though Hessie did not put that in her diary, where Horace was. He didn't care for art, Maud said; besides, he was terribly busy.

"All those rich stocks and shares?"

"Not always so rich," Maud said, and laughed, and then an ugly old woman with a nutcracker face, Lady somebody, said, "Maud, this *can't* be your little girl!" And then, "It's no time since you were that size and your father used to bring you. You were both so beautiful the place was absolutely illuminated."

"Hessie is learning to take an interest in art," Maud said. "Papa couldn't have a grandchild who didn't enjoy paintings."

"But who won't figure as a model, I take it?"

"She wouldn't have the patience. Would you, Hessie darling? All those tedious hours of sitting. They say that the Augustus John is the picture to see. Shall we go look for it, Hessie?"

Standing, looking at the picture, were Honor and Ninian.

Hessie gave a cry of joy and seized Honor's hand.

"Do please come and look at Miss Marion Abercrombie with me. Her lapdog looks just like Han, though not so old."

"Will you excuse us, Maud?" said Honor, laughing.

"Of course. I think Miss Marion Abercrombie is an obnoxious creature. This is much more interesting. Do you think so, Ninian?"

"Fascinating. But it's very different from your father's technique. Very different from his subject, too."

Maud studied the portrait.

"She's rather beautiful, in an austere way. Her bones show. I quite like that. Anyway, fashions in beauty change."

"Do they?" Ninian was looking at her with his disturbing eyes. Maud realized that she had always found them disturbing because of their perception. A sort of controlled awareness. An intensity and an absence of happiness.

Did her own eyes show that deficiency? she wondered. And why should gentle, quiet Honor make her husband unhappy?

"Fashion," he said in his ironic voice. "I never follow it."

"How sensible of you." Because he was looking at her with too much of that uncomfortable intensity, she went on, "Goodness me, I have just realized this is the gallery where I once agreed to elope. The great scandal in my life. I was only nineteen. It wasn't so laughable at that age."

"But it is now?"

She shrugged. "It's ten years ago, Guy is dead, and I—"

"And you can laugh at anything?"

The slight sting in his voice made her retort flippantly, "I'm nearly thirty. I'm older and wiser, as they say."

"And you're wearing a very charming hat. Fashions in beauty or not, you can still hold your own, Maud. My great-uncle, the colonel, you remember him—"

"Of course. He was ill and took you away from our party. Wasn't that the night you first met Honor?"

"It was. But it was you my uncle talked about. He couldn't understand why I didn't admire you as much as he did. To tell the truth, I did. But Honor was the kind of wife I wanted. That's ten years ago, too."

This was an astonishing and fascinating conversation, entirely unexpected. Maud was lured by, but resisted, its danger. She wanted to ask if Honor was still the kind of wife he wanted, but prudently said instead, "I hear that you're writing a book."

"Yes. I find I care a great deal more for literature than for the bar. I dislike pleading eloquently for unmitigated scoundrels."

"So, if your book is a success, you will give up the bar?"

"I'd like to. At present I'm compromising. I scribble in the evenings, and Honor plays the piano."

"It sounds a very compatible arrangement."

"Compatible. That's a significant word."

"Is it? It's one Horace taught me."

"As allied to marriage?"

"I suppose so."

He looked at her again with that intent look. She thought he was going to start cross-examining her, but instead he said surprisingly, "I go look at your tree sometimes."

"Do you, Ninian? *Do* you?"

"Now why should you get excited about that?"

Why should she? She was bewildered by the pleasure she felt.

"That little tree means a lot to me. It's part of my life. Do you remember, I showed it to you that day you came back from France and were feeling so terrible. I got to recognize your look because I had seen it so often on the boys in the hospital."

"You were very perceptive."

"Well—once you administered champagne to me, and once I showed you my tree."

"And once I kissed you, and you didn't like it."

"Oh, you shouldn't have minded. I wasn't myself."

"Then perhaps we should try again?"

She laughed merrily. "You almost look as if you intend to attempt the experiment at this minute. But not, I hope, with that critical look in your eyes."

"Have I a critical look? I was only wondering if you were still so absorbed in yourself."

"Why do you say that?" she asked, wounded.

"Isn't it true? I don't see how it can't be, since you've been taught to love yourself from the moment you were born."

"That isn't my fault. And it really isn't true." To her surprise, she was pleading. "I know I'm hateful sometimes. For instance, I didn't realize Hessie was being bullied by her governess until Mrs. Beauchamp told me. I could hardly forgive myself."

"Well, there you are, you see. You were too self-centered to notice what went on under your nose."

"You're treating me like a prisoner at the bar."

"But you forget, I plead for prisoners at the bar."

"I don't need you to plead for me," Maud said sharply. "I really think you ought to make amends by discovering some of my good points. I do have some. Now I must go find my daughter."

"And I my wife," he said absently, his gaze still on her. Suddenly, with a strange leap of her heart, she sensed what he had been doing. He had been flirting with her in an oblique way, throwing down a challenge which she knew she had every intention of picking up. It would be stimulating, amusing, enlivening. Nothing was better for a woman's looks or good spirits than a slightly dangerous flirtation. Even Horace would benefit from it, since she would be so much better-tempered.

"I've promised Hessie I'll take her to tea at the Ritz," she said. "That's what Papa and I frequently did. Indeed, I often go there alone because it reminds me of Papa. I know I'm too sentimental. Morbidly so, Horace tells me. Oh, there are Honor and Hessie now. What did you think of Miss Abercrombie, Honor? Isn't she a smug creature?" She noticed the way Honor was looking at her, with those dark too-aware eyes, and added gaily, "Hessie, it's quite time we went and had our tea. Even I have had enough pictures for one day."

"Well, what were the pictures like?" asked Horace perfunctorily over dinner that evening.

"Ordinary."

"When will you stop being prejudiced, Maud? Your father wasn't the only artist worth looking at."

Usually Horace's slightly hectoring tone, which had lately become a habit with him, annoyed her intensely. This evening she scarcely noticed it and answered amicably, "You're perfectly right, darling. I do try to tell myself exactly that. There was an Augustus John that I admired very much. It was strong and interesting. I expect he would call Papa a romantic. And there was a lovely Sargent. You see, I did look at some pictures."

"Hessie said you talked to the Spencers."

"Yes, Honor and Ninian. It was quite a surprise to see them. Apparently everyone in this Square isn't a philistine."

"I hear Spencer is neglecting his practice to write."

"You say that disapprovingly."

"Well, I think the man's mad. Does he want his wife to starve?"

"Some writers make money."

"Perhaps ten percent of them."

"Oh, you with your percentages. How do you know Ninian isn't going to one of the favored ten percent?"

"Is it likely? A man of his age, changing horses in midstream. He must be nearly forty."

"Then it's time he followed his heart's desire."

"Don't talk like a romantic schoolgirl. I'm sorry for Honor. A woman needs security."

"There are other things."

"Of course there are other things. Security is one of the important ones. If you hadn't got it, you'd notice soon enough."

But later he said, "I suppose I should have gone with you. Did everyone look at you with that bit of nonsense on your head?"

He was looking at her now, and she recognized the signs, the wistfulness, the half-ashamed ardor. He would want to make love to her when they went to bed, and she hated herself for having brought him to the humiliating state of having to be ashamed of his desire. She was heartless, cruel, cold, frigid. And knew she could not change as far as Horace was concerned. And that, contrarily, she would dislike him even more if he ceased to want her, because that would be an unforgivable insult.

All the same, it had got to the point where she would have to plead for separate rooms. She couldn't go on having him in Papa's room constantly. Now and again, of course. She had to remain his wife. But not night after night until the end of time.

Even after ten years the front bedroom was overwhelmingly Papa's, with the green-patterned William Morris wallpaper making the room like a bosky dell, the turkey-red rug on the floor, the Queen Anne tallboy, the severely plain bedcover and curtains. Maud had even bought Horace a set of toilet articles similar to Papa's. She had scarcely realized she was doing it. She had been so grief-stricken for so long. But now she understood what she had been about. She had been setting the scene that would eventually make her marriage intolerable. Horace had been an intruder, and still was.

She was afraid that Ninian Spencer had been right when he had said that she was completely self-centered. And he obviously was not going to accept her oblique invitation to tea at the Ritz since he never appeared there when she sat taking her tea alone. She must have misjudged his intentions after all.

The thought was infinitely depressing. The more she reflected on it, the more confused her feelings became. Disappointment, indignation, resentment, and beneath these exterior sensations, panic and fear. She would have to experience being spurned one day; she was growing older all the time, but to grow old without having known real love was the most outrageous thing she could think of. *That* for Maud Lucie! Papa would turn in his grave. Or would he?

She was sure that she herself would expire of boredom if her life went on in its present fashion, Horace working over his company balance sheets at night and Hessie announcing flatly that since she couldn't practice at Honor's because Ninian came home and wanted quiet, she must have a piano to practice on at home. Hessie, with her unwavering logical gaze and her sensible statements, was sometimes as hard to endure as Horace with his obsession for figures and percentages.

Nanny said, "That child has more sense in her little finger than you ever had in your whole body, Miss Maud. But I must say it makes for dullness," she added.

The terrible agonizing war, when she had been needed and loved and appreciated, had kept her sane, Maud realized. What a reflection that was on her present existence! Something had to happen. She would stop dreaming and make something happen.

"Maud, this account from Harrods—"

"Yes?"

"Do we need a new dinner service?"

"But of course we do. I can't give our guests cracked plates."

"I hadn't noticed any cracked plates."

"You don't look."

"Crown Derby, hand-painted in a maroon and gold design, with gold-leaf edge. One hundred and fifty guineas."

"It's an investment. It will be an heirloom."

"Who for? I fancy Hessie's tastes will be more simple."

"More's the pity. But her children may conceivably take after me. Heirlooms are for grandchildren and great-grandchildren."

"This one, I imagine," said Horace with his relentless look, "is for no one but yourself."

"Well, of course it is," Maud agreed disarmingly. "I so enjoy nice things. It's in my blood. Papa was always buying treasures for Mamma. She adored them, too. And think of their value now. And how dull not to have the best things!"

"You're very lucky you've been able to have them. Eighty percent of the world can't. And do remember that the stock market is tricky at present. The bottom may fall out of it at any moment. A world-wide depression is predicted."

"You've said that ever since I've known you. Old pessimist." She dropped a kiss on the top of his head. She was feeling cheerful. Extravagance was having its usual euphoric effect. "We'll give a special dinner party to show off our new plates."

But the next time Maud went shopping she took care to buy a present for Horace, which he accepted with a helpless sigh. However, he liked the bottle-green velvet smoking jacket. Secretly it made him feel a dashing fellow. Maud was always so clever with presents. But it was a luxury. That was the difference in their natures; Maud believed luxuries were a necessity, and he knew for a fact that they were not.

Nevertheless, he consented to wear the jacket when, that winter,

Maud gave a succession of dinner parties that began downstairs and finished in the studio, with people sitting about on the floor and the gramophone playing the latest records. In the dim lights, the portraits of Maud glimmered, making it seem that she was in several places at once. There was no doubt that the portraits added an extra dimension to parties at Number 7 Melbury Square.

Maud's Sunday afternoons, too, were becoming famous. She had considerable flair as a hostess and enough flamboyance to make her more than just another good-looking woman in her thirties. Poets, artists, ambitious young politicians—all began coming to Number 7. It was like the old days. The Square might be shabby after the war, the houses old-fashioned, with their dark steep stairways and cold basements, and good servants, apart from those growing old in faithful service, a vanishing race, but at least the Ponsonbys still contrived to live in style. And Maud's new idea, to have the studio redecorated in the style of her father's famous "peacock" portrait, was an inspiration.

She planned to have emerald-green walls, green and blue rugs on the floor, a lot of lamps with golden shades, and an enormous jardiniere of peacock feathers. The raised dais where the models had sat would be turned into a throne, its back shaped like a peacock's spread tail. The peacock portrait would, of course, hang in the most dominating position. And anyone who dared to murmur that James Lucie was hopelessly sentimental and out-of-date would most certainly never be welcome again.

It was useless for Horace to protest. This cult his wife had of enshrining her father was becoming an obsession. He hated the whole thing and could do nothing about it. Neither did he care for the kind of people who were coming to the house. Bohemians, crackpots, adventurers—like that fellow Maud had once wanted to marry, now fortunately deceased. He had nothing to say to them. They spoke another language. He took to going to his office on Sunday afternoons, enjoying the quiet of the deserted building and the deserted city streets. Maud said that if he was so buried in his work, he must be making his fortune.

There were different kinds of obsessions. He certainly regarded his as healthier than hers.

After the quarrel over the absurdly pretentious peacock studio,

Horace was angry enough to accept Maud's suggestion of separate bedrooms. He moved into the small room next to Hessie's and for a few nights felt nothing but relief.

Then the old gnawing longing came back. The jealousy and suspicion. He should never have married Maud. He had always known it. They were absolutely incompatible.

But although living with her could be hell, letting her go was a sheer impossibility. If she put him to the test one day, she would find that out.

There was an article in the Sunday *Times*. Horace read it out at breakfast.

"Successful barrister-turned-author Ninian Spencer (41), living in a modest Kensington square, more accustomed to seeing a client walk free from the dock than to seeing his words in print, has written a novel about a fictitious *cause célèbre*. *Prosecution* is listed for publication in the autumn. The author's wife, who is an accomplished pianist, provides mood music while her husband writes. In addition, there is a frog in the lily pool in the garden and, perhaps, a ghost in the attic. All this has obviously provided a successful climate in which to write what is expected to be the season's best-selling novel."

Maud sat silent, exploring her feelings.

"A successful climate. What tosh these fellows write," Horace said. He sounded irritated. He had once said that ninety percent of writers failed, indicating that Ninian Spencer would be one of the failures. He never liked to be proved wrong.

Maud sprang up, deciding that her dominant feelings were pleasure and excitement.

"How perfectly wonderful for Ninian. I must ring him and congratulate him. Now I'll have to forgive him for never coming to one of my Sundays. He has simply been working too hard."

"Well, don't fall all over him, persuading him to come because he's suddenly famous."

"You ought to know me better than that. I'm not a lionhunter. Actually, I expect to be the lion—or lioness—myself at my parties." Maud's voice was flippant. "That's why Ninian despises me."

"Despises you! Are you cracked?"

"No. He told me so once. He thinks I'm vain and selfish and egotistical. Which is all perfectly true. I'm a horrid creature. Who knows that better than you, my darling?" She gave her radiant smile. "But I must ring him up, nevertheless. Success might even make him a little egotistical himself."

Honor answered the telephone.

"Oh, Maud. Ninian's out. Actually, he went out to escape the telephone. So many people have been ringing."

"I wanted to congratulate him. He's been an awfully dark horse."

"Has he?" Honor's precise, honest voice was a little troubled. "He just worked on his writing. It was no secret."

"Well, it's kept him hidden away for too long. You too. Hessie's the only one of us who ever sees you."

"You know that we're not party people."

"Which doesn't mean we have to avoid each other."

"We're not doing that."

"Then come one Sunday afternoon and learn to do the Charleston. It's the greatest fun."

"Yes. I'll tell Ninian."

"By the way, Honor, how is Hessie getting on with her piano lessons?"

Honor's voice lost its cautious quality and grew warm. "Oh, she works so hard, bless her heart—"

"But she hasn't much skill, has she? You don't need to mind my saying so. I have to listen to all those plodding finger exercises. Isn't it waste of time for her, Honor? Shouldn't she be studying something she has more aptitude for?"

"Oh, no, she enjoys it. Really, Maud."

(*You were the person who betrayed Guy and me. If it hadn't been for you, I would have married Guy and, who knows, he might still be alive. At least I would have known what real love is. So why should you have a husband you love and this ridiculous devotion of my daughter's as well?*)

"Let's talk about it, shall we? Come this afternoon with Ninian. We'll find a quiet corner while the rest dance."

"Maud, are you blackmailing us?"

Maud looked at Ninian, her eyes opened wide in astonishment.

"Good gracious, do you have to be blackmailed to come to one of my afternoons?"

Ninian laughed. Maud decided that she wasn't and never had been in love with that spare haggard face. But there was no doubt that it intrigued her. Besides, it was irritating to meet a man who resisted her charms. It made her determined to overcome his resistance. She could feel that strange excitement and elation again, a tingling all over her body. Perhaps she was in love in a way she didn't recognize.

"Honor said something about your stopping Hessie's piano lessons."

"I didn't say I had decided to. But it would be only practical. The child has no ear for music, just as she can't draw a line. She isn't a creative child. So she must concentrate on other things."

"Why? Will she have to earn her own living?"

"Goodness me, I hope not."

"You mean she'll have a season and find a husband?"

Maud bit her lip. Privately, she had always found it difficult to imagine Hessie as a debutante.

"Of course she will," she said firmly.

Ninian laughed, his strange face crinkling into a thousand lines.

"Maud, I never thought I would be able to accuse you of being old-fashioned."

"Are you going to tell me my failings again?" Maud asked, with airy sweetness. "Because if you are, I really must say it's rather rude of you."

"Not this time. We're talking about Hessie, remember? If you want her to be a successful debutante, then she'll need to play the piano, won't she, and perhaps sing a little and converse in French? All the Victorian virtues."

"What's wrong with them?" Maud asked, nettled.

"Nothing. They're charming in their own way. But the war and Mrs. Pankhurst and others have rather blown such things out of the window. However, if you think they should still be persevered with, then Hessie must go on having her piano lessons, mustn't she?"

"Beast!" Maud began to laugh. She was always a generous loser in an argument. "You're too clever. Tell me what your book is about."

"It's about a man who commits a murder for a woman."

"Really! How fascinating. This woman must be a *femme fatale*."

"She is."

"Could you commit a murder for a woman?"

"God, I hope not."

"Then can you successfully imagine such a thing? Doesn't a writer have to put himself completely into his character's mind?"

"Yes. But sometimes I think that creating intense complex situations and emotions on paper gives the author a kind of immunity from them."

Ninian with his quiet wife . . . An immunity from love?

"That," said Maud, "simply must be a fallacy."

"Must it?"

"I thought a writer had to have infinite experience in order to write."

"But stopping short of murder?"

Maud saw the quizzical look in his eyes.

"You've been teasing me!" she exclaimed. "You knew I was trying to show off intellectually."

"Were you?"

"Of course I was. I wanted to impress you."

"*You* impress *me!* But it's always been the other way around, you know . . ."

Hessie, who was allowed to please herself whether or not she attended the Sunday afternoons and who almost always chose not to, came up to the studio after hearing Ninian's voice on the stairs. She thought Honor must be there, too. She was hovering on the edge of the crowd, looking for her, when she heard Mother saying, "But surely you've seen that portrait of me before?"

"I have, but I've never been able to compare it so directly with its subject. There's something wrong with it."

"What?"

"I'm not sure. A look in your eyes that isn't there any longer."

"Oh, well—Papa painted it just after my own very small unimportant *cause célèbre.*"

"When you eloped?"

"When I tried to. That gorgeous dress, you might note, is a Worth model. Dear Papa bought it to console me."

"And did it?"

"Don't be stupid."

"Yes, that was stupid of me. Because it didn't take that look out of your eyes."

"Well, that came of my recent shattering experience. Though I might say the experience was much more mental than physical, in spite of what people thought."

"Wasn't that an omission?"

She met his eyes candidly.

"Of course it was. And a great mistake. The look you see in my eyes is regret. After all, I was going to be hung for a sheep anyway, so I might as well have deserved my punishment. Hessie! How long have you been standing there?"

"I just came in."

"Well, don't lurk, darling. Talk to people."

"I was looking for Honor."

"She didn't come," Ninian said. "She had a headache. Why don't you go along later and cheer her up?"

In life it seemed that the same things happened again and again. Mother and Ninian standing close together and still, as they had once before, beside Mother's little tree in the gardens. And Honor sitting in her favorite garden chair beside the little pool with that faraway look in her eyes. Perhaps she was waiting for the frog to pop up.

"I came to see if your headache was better."

"Yes, it is a little." Honor smiled, her eyes crinkling at the corners in the gentle humorous way that Hessie loved. "Why are you sounding so aggressive?"

"I don't like you to have a headache."

"Silly!" Honor's voice was loving. "The telephone rang all morning. That's what gave it to me. I'm very old-fashioned. I wish telephones hadn't been invented. Once people used to deliver little polite notes to each other. That was much more civilized. And why aren't you at your mother's party?"

"Because I don't choose to be. I'm allowed not to go if I don't want to. I think parties are boring."

"So do I."

"Ninian doesn't."

"Oh? I rather thought he did. I'm glad he's enjoying himself."

"Has the frog come out?"

"Not today."

"He must be asleep. What is physical experience?"

"Physical—oh, something to do with one's body. Why ever do you ask?"

"Mother was saying—I heard someone saying. It doesn't matter. It isn't anything."

But it was, mysteriously, something important, for pain had flashed in Honor's dark eyes. Hessie couldn't help noticing. She was acutely aware of every expression on that loved face.

"Grandma, what does physical experience mean?"

There was the smallest stir of the cobwebby head on the sparkling white pillow.

"What an extraordinary question, Hester dear!"

So it was something bad. She had thought so all along.

"Where did you hear it?" came the faint voice from the pillow.

"At school."

"Good gracious, what an unsuitable school. I must tell your mother."

"No, it wasn't at school," Hessie said hastily. "I remember now, it was someone at Mother's party."

"Little pitchers," came Bertha's voice in the background.

"I might have known it would be in this house," said Grandma.

Chapter 15

As it happened, those were the last words Lady Lucie spoke. A little later that afternoon Bertha found her unconscious, slipped down from her pillows with one of her soft, weak rheumatic hands lying defensively across her face.

She had had a stroke. She died two days later, without recovering consciousness. When they carried her out of the house, Maud imagined they were carrying away only a bundle of expensive invalidish clothes, smelling of lavender water overlaying mustiness. That, she realized with profound sadness, was all her mother had ever been to her. Whose fault was it? Her own? Papa's? No one but Bertha, over these last years, had seen Mamma's body. One wondered if she had ever had one. She could have been a mermaid with a tail, Maud thought, for all one had known of her. *I have never even seen her ankles,* she thought. Had they been slim and pretty? One only knew her slight form becomingly arranged on couches or in her invalid chair and, of late, concealed permanently beneath the bedclothes.

With Papa and Cora (how many Coras?) in the next room.

Poor Mamma. And poor Papa. Now they were lying in enforced proximity until the last trumpet.

And poor me, Maud thought, twisting her hands at the graveside. *With my healthy and ardent husband, whom I shudder away from. Is there something wrong with me? Am I Mamma over again? Must I think so much about that sort of thing . . .*

Hessie had insisted, most unsuitably, on going to the funeral. A square, stolid figure in her neat gray overcoat and sailor hat, she stood beside Maud. When the first earth fell on the coffin, she made an instinctive movement, not toward her mother, but to the person on her other side. It was Mrs. Beauchamp, who looked stout and tired and old. Hessie slid her hand into that wrinkled one, knowing that they were grieving together.

Maud, noticing the movement, was upset. She had thought that Hessie disliked that severe old woman as much as she did herself. She must have been wrong. What with the unreasonable affection the child had for Honor and now, apparently, for Honor's mother, it seemed that the Beauchamp family was more important to her than her own. It was time she became her age, which after all was only nine years. She must get over her obsession for old people and make more friends with her contemporaries. Even Nanny was probably bad for her, but there was nothing one could do about that. Nanny was a fixture—and a remarkably alert and vociferous one in spite of her eighty years.

What would Papa have made of a child like Hessie? *My little white cabbage*, Maud thought wryly, and suddenly knew that she wanted a son. The longing struck her acutely. After Hessie's difficult birth, which she had been unable to forget, she hadn't wanted another child. But now, with the earth falling on Mamma's coffin and the lettering on Papa's headstone sharply black on the white marble, it was necessary and urgent to begin something. A golden-haired, straight-backed, arrogant little boy.

But Horace would only give her another white cabbage, if she could conceive from him again, which didn't seem possible. She put up her hand to conceal the pain and hopelessness that made her face contort. Hessie thought she was crying and pressed against her in anxious sympathy. Horace took her arm and murmured, "It's all over, Maud. Time to go."

Her family. Two strangers leading her away from her real family. How dreadfully alone she was.

Lady Lucie's estate consisted of her collection of miniatures and bibelots. Enough were to be sold to provide a legacy of one hundred pounds for the faithful Bertha. The rest were left to Maud and Hessie: the Meissen, Chelsea, and Derby porcelain figures, and the lapis lazuli Fabergé egg to Maud; the miniatures to Hessie.

Hessie could hardly believe her good fortune. She had thought that, with Grandma's death, all the beautiful fantasy world that had

existed in that quiet room had gone forever. But now the miniatures actually belonged to her. She could keep them in her own bedroom and take them out and dream over them whenever she wanted
to. No one could forbid her. She was so astonished and delighted
that she sobbed half the night, Nanny reported. The tears were for
her grandmother, of course, although Hessie insisted, odd child that
she was, that she wasn't unhappy, that she was very, very happy now
she had all these friends, Lord Nelson and Lady Arabella Stuart and
Boy in Blue and Miss Francesca Martin with the pink bonnet ribbons and the rest.

An only child was a mistake, Nanny said. They grew into themselves.

"Except in my case," Maud said. "But I had Papa."

The house seemed extraordinarily empty without Lady Lucie,
even though she had been confined to her bedroom and as quiet as
a ghost. Especially now that Bertha had packed up and gone to her
sister in the country.

Ada, Cook, and Nanny were the only servants left. The way
things were nowadays, when Nanny went, and Cook too, for she
was in her seventies, one would have to rely on daily help. A woman,
improbably named Mrs. Thrale, came in every morning to do what
she called the rough work, scrubbing the steps and the basement and
the bathrooms. She was common, Ada said, and she quarreled with
Cook, but this was something one had to put up with. The time was
coming when the mistress herself might have to polish the silver and
lay the table. Servants were getting above themselves. It was sad.
The times were deteriorating.

Old Joe, the muffin man, had died long since, and no one had
come to take his place. Tea with hot muffins in the early winter
dusk was a thing of the past. And the gaslamps in the Square had
been replaced by electricity, so the lamplighter, too, was a vanished
figure. But every spring, to Hessie's delight, the lavender seller, a
stout countrywoman with a stentorian voice, sang her song in the
Square:

> Will you buy my sweet blooming lavender,
> Sixteen blue branches one penny . . .

Ladies fair, make no delay,
But buy my lavender fresh today . . .

You will scent four handkercher
With my sweet blooming lavender . . .

Will you buy my sweet blooming lavender,
Sixteen blue branches one penny . . .

Hessie, imagining herself one of the ladies fair, always rushed out to buy the sweet-smelling blossoms and afterward laid the sprigs carefully among her handkerchiefs and underclothing. The lavender woman, with her weather-beaten face (a gypsy, Nanny said disgustedly), always had a friendly smile for her. But it was a little upsetting when the price went up to twopence, then became as high as sixpence. Profiteering, Nanny said. Those gypsies knew what they were about. But her father said it was only a sign of the times. Everything was getting more expensive.

Maud wanted a car. It could be garaged in one of the mews' stables, which were now seldom occupied by horses. She would learn to drive. But Horace was worried, as apparently he always would be, by the state of the stock market, and said that if Maud insisted on having a car, she must buy it herself. She could sell that Fabergé egg, for instance. It should fetch a fair price in Sotheby's. Or one of the remaining pictures of her father's. He had been dead long enough for his work to be coming back into favor. Who knew, she might be sitting on a fortune?

"Wouldn't it please *you* to give me a present?" Maud asked.

"My dear girl, what do I ever do but give you presents? That ostrich-feather thing you hang around your neck, for instance. I expect I'll be getting the bill for that any day."

"They're the latest thing," Maud said. "Don't you like me in it?"

"Of course I do. You'd look beautiful in Mrs. Thrale's woolen muffler, and you know it."

"Then don't be such an old bear. After all, I might have bought sables. But I'll never sell Papa's pictures, so don't ask me to," she added.

All the same, the Fabergé egg, smooth, richly blue, exquisitely fashioned, did make her feel uneasy. Once Mamma had said, "One thing is certain, Maud dear, Horace will never buy you a thing like this." She had thought Mamma was referring to Horace's closeness with money, but later another interpretation had come to her. The egg had been a reward for condoning Papa's infidelity; Mamma had known that it was unlikely Horace would err in the same way.

Would she mind if he did? She would be indignant and angry, of course, but her heart would not be touched. What did touch her heart nowadays? The house was so silent after Hessie had gone to school and Horace to his office. Ada and Cook talked in the basement, but upstairs Nanny dozed by her fire, and Maud was alone and filled with desperation. One would not have believed the house could be so empty after Mamma's death. And empty it would stay—until what?

Strangely, Maud found her restless thoughts turning more and more to Evangeline, who would now be twelve years old, a schoolgirl with a long golden pigtail and Papa's merry blue eyes. If she could never have the son she suddenly longed for, she must see Evangeline again. The desire became a compulsion. Surely such a thing should be possible. The child was her half sister. What possible harm could it do if they met? It had never been fair of Cora's husband to take the child completely away. Perhaps she was living a deprived life in Leeds. A visit to London could be a great adventure for her, and she could be a companion for Hessie. It would be good for Hessie, and the house would have some life in it again.

The more Maud turned over this idea, the more it obsessed her. She was determined to trace Evangeline. She couldn't think why she hadn't done so sooner. But how was she to set about doing so?

She picked up the telephone directory and looked up a number. This, too, was a scarcely evolved thought, entirely spontaneous. She dialed the number of the office of Ninian Spencer, Barrister, Lincolns Inn.

"Mr. Spencer is in court," a clerk's voice said in answer to her inquiry. "Can I take a message?"

"Yes, please. Tell him Mrs. Horace Ponsonby would like to make a business appointment with him as soon as possible."

"I'll give him your message, Mrs. Ponsonby."

"Perhaps he'd telephone me when he comes in."

"Can I have your number, Mrs. Ponsonby?"

Maud replied, feeling foolish. As if Ninian didn't know her number. And why had she stressed the word "business" in that guilty way? Or did it only seem guilty to herself, not to the owner of that cool voice at the other end of the wire?

And why, for that matter, did she want to see Ninian in his office?

Because she would not do so in front of Honor, that was why. And it really was a business appointment. Ninian, with his legal knowledge, would know how to set about finding a lost child. Horace wouldn't have the faintest idea how to begin. Anyway, she had absolutely no intention of telling Horace her scheme, least of all divulging Evangeline's parentage.

She liked him sitting behind his desk, grave and businesslike, his eyebrows lifted in faintly anxious inquiry.

"What is it, Maud? Are you in trouble?"

"No, no trouble. It was awfully good of you to see me quickly, Ninian."

"I was worried when I got your message. I thought it must be trouble."

"No, it's a private matter that frankly I didn't want to discuss in front of either Horace or Honor."

"I'm a barrister, Maud. Shouldn't you go to your solicitor?"

"No, not for this. It's quite personal. It's about an illegitimate child of my father's. I want to trace her whereabouts. I thought you could tell me how to."

Ninian leaned forward.

"Tell me about it."

The story of Evangeline, the enchanting baby whom Maud had adored. Telling it made tears come to her eyes. Why had she never felt for Hessie as she had for that little lost creature? She remembered the soft baby plumpness and warmth. Her arms felt achingly empty.

"I so long to see her again. I feel there are so many things I could do for her."

"Such as a coming-out season?" Ninian said in his dry ironic voice.

"Perhaps even that, later. But at present just to teach her things, give her a happy time, get to know her again. Hessie needs a companion."

"No, Maud. It won't do."

"Why won't it do?" Maud's voice was sharp and affronted. "I only want to be generous. I should never have allowed that man Cora married to take Evangeline away so completely. He even stopped the postcards Cora used to send to me."

"And wisely. What do you want to do? Confuse the child? Take her out of her environment and make her discontented? Remind her of her illegitimacy?"

"You sound just like a magistrate. Is this another way of telling me how selfish I am?"

"So you are, you know. Admit that you're not thinking of Evangeline's good, but of your own pleasure and amusement. How old is she now? Twelve? An impressionable age to be taken out of a working-class background and indulged in luxury."

"Luxury in Melbury Square," Maud said tartly. "You know we couldn't live more simply."

"With that gorgeous peacock room? Maud Ponsonby's folly. Did you know that's what the other people in the Square call it? But let's keep to the subject. I'm sure it wouldn't be impossible to trace this girl, but I strongly recommend that you do nothing about it. Apart from everything else, who are you going to say she is?"

"Oh—a second cousin or something," Maud said airily.

"Hessie will want to know more than that."

"Nonsense. She's much too young to be curious."

"Hessie was never young. Don't you even know that?"

Maud clenched her hands angrily.

"Why do you always criticize me? Am I so bad, so awful? Then how can you bear sitting talking to me?"

He contemplated her, as if pondering her words, then unexpectedly sprang up. "I can bear more than that. I'm going to take you out to tea. Will you come?"

His eyes were glittering. It was as if he had suddenly come to a momentous but inevitable decision. Without waiting for her to answer his invitation, he rang a bell on his desk, and when his clerk appeared, he said, "I'll be out for an hour or so, Mr. Seaton. What's the time? Four o'clock. It's hardly worth coming back. Well, Maud. Where shall it be? The Ritz?"

"Do you realize"—he went on out into the street as he hailed a taxi and followed her into it—"that one's whole life can be shaped on the course of a few minutes?"

"This few minutes?" Maud was completely bewildered by his change of mood.

"No, I was thinking of that night we had champagne at Honor and Daisy's ball. If I had refused to let you go back indoors then, if I had run away with you—but you had just run away, hadn't you? It all seemed a bit much to suggest you do it again. I could have kidnapped you, I suppose. I've often thought about that."

"Did you want to?" Maud asked in astonishment.

"I think I did. Only I had the sort of logical mind that saw through to the end of those melodramas. The excitement over, the disillusionment setting in. Hadn't you just had one example of coming down to earth with a crash?"

"But, Ninian, there was Honor! You were just about to propose to her. You must be making all this up."

"Not a word of it, Maud my darling. Not a word."

His hand lay over hers. It was cool and dry and should not have produced such a fever in her veins.

"I'm a deliberate sort of man. A stickler for the right circumstances. They weren't right at that time. You were indulging in your broken heart, and I was damned sure I wasn't going to be secondbest in your life. Even if you would have had me. Honor seemed to be the right wife for me." He paused. "And was."

"But not now?" Maud asked cautiously.

He shook his head. "It's not her fault; that's the bad thing. She's so innocent about it. I could never leave her."

The taxi was negotiating the traffic at Piccadilly Circus. Maud's surprise at this conversation began to turn to pleasure.

"So you listened to your great-uncle after all," she murmured. "About me."

"I didn't need to listen to him. I had my own eyes."

At the Ritz the waiter bowed and smiled at her, showing her to the table she preferred.

"Your usual, madam? And sir?"

"I don't have a usual," said Ninian. "But I'll have madam's, whatever it is."

"Ceylon tea with cream, hot buttered muffins," said Maud.

"I might have known it would be something perfectly splendid."

They faced each other across the small table. Maud's lips began to quiver and tilt upward.

"And I once gave you such a broad hint about coming here."

"I know. Actually, I did come twice, but you weren't here."

"Oh, I'm sorry." Maud was astonished at the depths of her desolation. What trivial thing had she been doing on those afternoons when he came here seeking her? "All the same, you took an awfully long time to decide to come."

"Don't make flirtatious remarks. This isn't a flirtation. Or if you think it is, I might as well leave you right away."

"I'm stupid. That sort of thing is my natural language. It's a h-habit I should have grown out of." She was stammering a little. She couldn't think what else to say. She had thought a great deal about Ninian, but she hadn't let herself think about love. About being in love.

Or had she, subconsciously, thought of nothing else?

The waiter brought the tea. They sat back to allow the tea things to be arranged on the table. The muffins were in a covered silver dish. Maud lifted the teapot and found that her hand was shaking.

"I love you, Maud."

"Oh, dear, I've spilled the tea."

He took the teapot out of her hand.

"And you showed me this afternoon that you loved me."

"This afternoon? How?"

"By all that fantasy about wanting to bring back your father's illegitimate child. You don't really want that. You wanted a way of telling me that if your father could indulge in love affairs, so could you."

"Ninian! What a thing to read into—" She stopped, realizing guiltily that he might just possibly be right.

"After all, your husband could have told you how to go about finding the child."

"Horace! But I'd never tell him about Papa!"

"That's my point."

She stared at him, her eyes wide.

"So that's how you assumed all these things—that I love you and you love me."

"Assumed?"

She felt her cheeks warm.

"Are they true?"

"They've been true since that day I came home from France and you showed me your tree. You knew then as well as I did."

"Then why have we waited so long?"

"I had to get my book published and have it a success. That's going to give me freedom."

"You mean financial freedom?"

"Yes."

Maud nodded slightly. "Horace is the same, too. I'm sure he'll never give me a divorce."

"I didn't mention Honor."

"No, but I can guess what you're not saying."

"We read each other's thoughts too well."

"Honor has her music," Maud said. "And Horace has his balance sheets. Often he never looks at me or speaks to me. All the same," she added, with inescapable honesty, "part of this, about Evangeline and coming to see you today, was because I was so bored. I've been nearly dying of boredom. I had to make something happen."

"But it had happened, Maud darling. That's what I'm telling you."

She sighed with relief. "Yes, so it had. I was afraid I was just being wicked and irresponsible, making secret meetings like this a pattern of my life. Guy and I used to meet secretly, you know. It was so divinely wonderful; it's addictive, I'm sure. The danger and the forbidden part. Perhaps I just wanted a love affair with those extra dimensions."

"This is me, Maud. No one else."

She smiled slowly and tenderly. She touched his cheek with her forefinger, not caring who saw.

"Feel how my heart's going like a sledgehammer," she whispered. "No, you can't here. What a pity. But you can feel my pulse under the table. There. Isn't it racing?

"You don't need to count it," she added in a moment, though not drawing her wrist away from his probing fingers.

"It's jumping all over the place, Maud. I think you might be ill. What can I prescribe?"

She did take her hand away then, her gaiety dying.

"What indeed?" she said disconsolately. "I don't love Horace, but I truly don't want to hurt him. Neither do you want to hurt Honor, and you can't have a scandal in your position."

"My position doesn't matter. I'm going to give up the bar. A writer can be as scandalous as he chooses. It even helps him to be successful."

Confused thoughts raced through her mind. She and Ninian making love. In bed together. But there would have to be a bed. Where? Once before she had been defeated for lack of a bed. But that couldn't be allowed to happen this time. She was older, wilier, much, much less innocent.

Her own room, with Hessie at school, Horace at his office, Cook and Ada having their afternoon off, Nanny upstairs, but deaf and helplessly drowsy in the afternoons.

All the same, she said, "No scandals, Ninian. They hurt too many people."

He nodded, not speaking.

"It was because of that early scandal that I made such a mess of my life. There was all that time when I cherished my broken heart and wouldn't speak to Papa, and then I couldn't bear it when he was dying, so I promised to marry Horace to please him. I was so numb then; I needed someone to look after me. I really thought Horace was the person. I suppose he was, for a while. But in the end it turned out to be terribly unfair to him."

"I don't know about unfair. He's the lucky fellow who's had you all these years."

Maud shook her head. "No, that isn't true. He's never had me. I can't even conceive from him again. Isn't that strange? Perhaps I can't from anybody, of course."

His hand pressed hers painfully beneath the tablecloth.

"We could have a son."

"Oh! How did you know? That's what I've been longing for." She thought she was going to cry. She began to fuss over the teacups. "You've let your tea get cold. Let me give you some more. And you must eat a muffin. Otherwise that nice waiter will give evidence in court. 'On the said day I served the defendants with tea, but neither of them touched a thing. They just held hands under the tablecloth and looked ever so romantic.' Is that the right court language?"

"Except that the words would be 'respondent' and 'corespondent.' And having tea in a public place would not constitute evidence."

"Respondents can't have sons. Or are very unwise to." Maud shivered, very slightly, suddenly crying, "Ninian, let's be happy! Otherwise I'll die."

"We're going to be happy. We're going to take this a step at a time. For instance, as soon as you have finished your tea, I'm going to take you for a slow taxi ride through Regents Park. We might walk in the flower garden."

"What a lovely idea!" Her face sparkled, and as Ninian looked at her, she made the profound discovery that it was only truly satisfying to be admired when one also admired the admirer. But she must have always known that. Papa must have taught it to her. It was another inevitable pattern of her life, such as the irresistibly delicious one of illicit meetings with a lover.

"Anyway," she said, "I'm a very bad mother. Poor Hessie knows that."

"Hessie adores you."

"Does she? In small patches perhaps. Let's go buy her a wonderful frivolous present. Now."

"Maud! You're not so guilty already!"

"With Hessie I'm always guilty. I've never truly been able to love her. She's so solemn and dull. I look at her and know that Papa would never have wanted to paint her. Never."

"What an unfair standard to have! You really can be heartless, can't you?"

"That's what I'm telling you. I'm a bad mother. So it's actually a good thing that we can't be allowed to have a son. Isn't it?" Now she had begun to cry. "But I have to live. I haven't lived for so long."

"Crying in the Ritz isn't exactly living."

"It's a beginning." She was mopping her tears. "I feel most terribly alive at this minute. Happy, and frightened, and full of remorse about the people who might be hurt."

"If we're careful, we don't need to hurt anybody."

"I just don't think we can be that lucky . . ."

*   *   *

Hessie undid the wrapping paper, uncovering the large box of chocolates tied with blue satin ribbon. The lid was quite beautiful, patterned with pansies, her favorite flower. She had never realized her mother knew that.

But her pleasure was cautious, as always. A suspicious look in Nanny's eye had diverted her attention from Mother's smiling, glowing face. Nanny was thinking: *Why is the child suddenly being given such an expensive unsuitable present; what is Maud up to now?* At least, Hessie was fairly certain that those were Nanny's thoughts, which would later be put into words. So what was Mother up to? Was she going to announce that she was sending Hessie off to boarding school? Or to spend that long-threatened holiday with the Sylvesters at Deepford. (Hessie had already avoided that dreaded visit twice by contriving to be deplorably sick on the morning of departure.)

But nothing was announced. Mother simply went on looking gay and happy, and that night at dinner, which was usually a silent meal, she laughed and talked a lot. Even Father was surprised.

"You seem to be in good spirits tonight, Maud."

"Yes. I've been thinking we live much too dull a life, and you work far too hard. Why don't you take Hessie on a visit to Paris, the way Papa used to take me? Those have always been some of my most treasured memories. I don't see why Hessie shouldn't have similar ones."

Hessie sat rigid. This couldn't be true. It was too great a pleasure to be happening to her.

Father must have been thinking the same thing, for he was staring at Mother in the greatest surprise.

"You can't be serious, darling. At a time like this, when the French franc—"

"Oh, never mind the French franc or the English pound, or anything. I'll give you this trip. I'll sell the Fabergé egg."

Now Father was looking thoroughly suspicious. Like Nanny, but in a different way.

"What are you up to, Maud? You've always refused to sell the egg —well, anything—"

"If you also mean Papa's pictures, you know I can never sell those. They're all I have left of him. The egg was only made in a famous

Russian jeweler's workshop, and it doesn't mean a thing to me sentimentally. I'll put it in Sotheby's. The valuer of Mamma's estate told me I should get three or four hundred pounds for it if I sold it at auction. So you and Hessie can have your trip, and I'll amuse myself while you're away by having Mamma's room turned into a sitting room. I've been wanting to do that for a long time. It's the sunniest room in the house."

She was talking too much, Hessie thought uneasily, even for Mother at her gayest.

"Why don't you come with us to Paris, Mother?" she asked.

"I've just told you, darling. I want to do Grandma's room. You know how happy I am when I'm redecorating. Besides, I want you to have your father to yourself, the way I had my father."

"If I agree to do this—" Father began, and Hessie interrupted involuntarily, "Oh, Father, *please* do!"

"If I do, Maud, I really do wish you would come, too."

"No. You have Hessie alone. You'll both love it."

Father stared, his eyes puzzled.

"Then no more peacocks, Maud. I do ask you that."

"Peacocks? In Mamma's room? Oh, goodness me, no. I promise you."

At breakfast, after reading his letters, Ninian said to Honor, "Would you have any objection to my having a small studio somewhere?"

Honor looked up, showing her surprise that was not yet alarm. "A studio? Whatever for?"

"To write in, of course."

"But, darling—haven't you been able to write here?"

"According to Nick Palmer"—he tapped the open letter beside his plate—"yes. My book's quite a success. Ten thousand copies sold, and he's doing a reprint of five thousand. That's very good for a first novel. I believe I'm going to make my fortune," he added lightly.

"How nice!" said Honor. "How very nice for you!"

"For you, too, I hope."

"Well"—Honor carefully cut the top off her egg, which she was afraid she wasn't going to be able to eat—"not if you find you can't work in the house with me in it."

"Now I didn't say that."

"Then what can you mean? A studio to write in, to be alone—"

"That's it. I'm one of those writers who need absolute solitude. Even hearing Cook rattling dishes in the kitchen—"

"Or me at the piano?"

"Not you. You know I enjoy your playing. But Hessie's touch, you must admit, isn't the most talented."

"Then Hessie mustn't come while you're home."

"But you enjoy her coming."

"Oh, yes, I do. I'm devoted to her. But she can still come only when you're in court."

Ninian sat back.

"That's the point, Honor. That's what I'm trying to tell you. I'm giving up my office. I'm going to do nothing but write."

Honor, hoping she was concealing her dismay, tried to speak objectively.

"Is this wise? After only one book?"

"Wiser than splitting myself into two people. Nick Palmer agrees with me absolutely. He says I must do it."

"Nick's only thinking of the money he can make from your books."

"Not entirely. He understands the psychological angle. After all, he knows enough of this curious breed of people he makes a living by. If my other job were undemanding, it would be different. But it isn't. I thought you would understand that, Honor."

The faint reproach in his voice brought back that familiar niggling ache in her breast. If she hadn't understood him, it was only because he wouldn't let her.

"I do," she said quietly. "I know that writing has always been your real love, and of course, you must go on with it."

"I've given this decision a great deal of thought."

"I only didn't realize this house wasn't suitable to work in."

"I can't be home twenty-four hours a day. I want to go on keeping regular hours. Neither can you go about on tiptoe all day. We'd get hopelessly on each other's nerves. Anyway, that's what I plan to do, and I'm sure you won't notice any difference. It will be exactly as if I had gone to work."

"I suppose it will."

"Then don't look so tragic about it."

"I'm not good at change," Honor said defensively.

"But this isn't change. All that happens will be that our income comes from another source."

"When do you propose to make this change?" Honor stubbornly went on using the word.

"Within the next month. I have to clear up at the office."

"Then you've already told everyone!"

"Not everyone. Only my associates."

"Only not your wife," Honor murmured.

"I wanted to have it all absolutely clear in my mind first."

"You didn't want to discuss it with me?"

"I *am* discussing it with you."

"But only after you've made up your mind. I don't call that a discussion; I call it an announcement. An ultimatum," Honor added, testing the word.

His face was too sensitive. She saw the anxiety spring into it. She had always tried so hard to spare him all kinds of anxiety. Perhaps she was too maternal, less a wife than a mother. Perhaps that was the trouble.

"An ultimatum. Don't be so melodramatic. That isn't like you. Are you so opposed to the idea? I know most people will say a man with a wife has no right to substitute a certain income for a gamble."

Honor sprang up, exclaiming, "Oh, no, everyone's entitled to a gamble. If my mother had allowed me to have the career I longed for, I would have been a gambler myself. Oh, no, Ninian, I don't oppose your gamble. I sympathize with it. Really I do."

His eyes softened in the way she loved.

"Then why the long face?"

"Only because you feel you can't work at home. But I'll understand that, too. And you don't need to worry about money. I didn't mean to tell you this, because it seems wrong to anticipate a legacy, but Uncle Lionel called here the other day. He's eighty-one now, and he has a bad heart. He told me he means to leave me most of his money. There'll be a little for Mamma, but she's getting old, too, and Guy's gone, and Daisy's rich already. So I suppose I'll be an heiress. You can afford your gamble, my darling."

Contrarily, Ninian didn't seem as relieved as he should have been. He muttered something about never living on his wife's money;

then some other thought went through his mind, and he looked calmer.

"Congratulations, darling. It will be nice for you to own a bank vault or two. I must be off. Good heavens, it's nine o'clock, and I'm due in court at ten."

"Ninian—have you found this place yet?"

"No. I haven't begun to look. I've been telling you first."

"Can I help you look?"

Did he hesitate? He had turned away, and she couldn't see his face. She simply couldn't go on convincing herself that he hadn't grown much too quiet lately. Secretive and closed in on himself.

"I don't want to bother you."

"It wouldn't be a bother. I could arrange the furnishings."

"They'll be simple. Only a desk and a chair and a bare wall. Nothing distracting. I've the theme of my next book worked out, did I tell you?"

Suddenly his voice was so alive and enthusiastic that Honor was ashamed of herself for her selfish depression. This was what Ninian wanted to do, so how could she oppose it? Now he wouldn't need to shut himself away in the evenings to work. He might even give up his long silences and talk to her again. He would be creatively fulfilled and happy. She of all people should understand that.

All the same—she wished that he could have worked at home. It was a failure on her part that he couldn't. Another failure, like the one that kept him out of her bed.

Chapter 16

IT WAS the first time they had kissed—if one dismissed that badly timed affair at the Beauchamp girls' coming-out ball so long ago. There had been a world war since then. It and its aftermath made that night of chaperones and virgins and formal waltzes and innocence seem to be in another century.

Apart from having longed for this moment, it was doubly exciting because they were alone in the quiet house. There was a delicious air of risk and secrecy about their meeting, although it had been carefully arranged.

The servants, even Nanny, who had been persuaded to go on a rare visit to a niece in Putney, were out. It was midafternoon, a sleepy time, when few people were about. Even if Ninian's call at Number 7 were observed, it didn't matter too much. Maud wanted to ask his advice about the refurbishing of her mother's bedroom. She had been having trouble with decorators, and her husband was away.

It was a flimsy excuse. They hoped they wouldn't have to tell it to anyone. After weeks of discretion they were suddenly hopelessly indiscreet.

There was no doubt this knowledge added to the wild excitement of their kiss. Maud drew back from Ninian's arms, breathless and dizzy.

"Let's go up to the studio. No, come and see Mamma's room first. It's only half-finished. I'm waiting for the carpet to arrive. I've chosen William Morris wallpaper, of course, to go with my own bedroom. It's in shades of green. I want it to look as if the garden comes into the house. I'll have lots of pot plants on the windowsills. It will be a sort of miniature conservatory."

"You're talking too much, Maud."

"I always talk too much when I'm happy or nervous or sad. I just always talk too much, that's what it is."

Their footsteps echoed on the uncarpeted floor. The bed where Mamma had lain for so long, the mirror that had reflected her ashy face, her wardrobe of ruffled clothes, everything that reminded one of her had gone. Yet the scent of lavender water seemed to hang in the air.

Maud wrinkled her nose uneasily. Could Ninian smell it, too?

The house seemed oppressively quiet.

"I'll have my writing desk here. And my sewing table here."

"Do you sew?"

"Of course I don't. I was never that well brought up. But Papa once gave me a dear little Sheraton sewing table that I like to look at. He never meant me to use it for its correct purpose, of course. And in this corner I intend to have a sofa and a sofa table so that I can breakfast in here. I'll be terribly extravagant and have Ada light fires on cold mornings."

"This will be an innovation?"

"Breakfasting alone? Oh, yes." Maud looked at Ninian with serious eyes. "I've planned it. Horace won't miss me. He buries himself in the morning papers."

"And your bedroom?"

"It's next door. Come and see it. Horace has a room upstairs, next to Hessie. We decided long ago that we both slept better alone. I should think that's one of the least acknowledged facts of marriage."

In the big bedroom they kissed again, going spontaneously into each other's arms. Ninian began to pull the pins out of Maud's hair, burying his hands in its richness, saying he had always wanted to do this. Then, with quiet purposefulness, he felt for the buttons of her blouse.

After a moment, she assisted him. Suddenly she wanted him to hurry. She couldn't wait for the feel of his hands, those long nervous hands she admired, on her breasts. Her head was spinning; she gasped with startled pleasure when his fingers touched her erect nipples.

I had to be thirty years old before this revelation came to me, she was thinking. *What a tragic waste of time!* She was overcome by the most overwhelming urgency. Subsiding gently onto the bed, she reached for him.

"Take off the rest of my clothes," she whispered. "Let me take off yours. If you must know, Maud Lucie is in reality an elderly virgin. Oh, yes, it's true. In spite of Hessie."

"You're talking too much again," he said, struggling with the fastenings of her skirt. A hook caught, and he tugged at it impatiently. "I'm going to tear this off you. Do you mind?"

"Mind? What's a skirt?" She was laughing helplessly, and he began to laugh, too. When her skirt fell off, they rocked in each other's arms.

"Maud, you're a zany."

"What's a zany? It sounds lovely. I can't stop laughing. Love should be made to laughter. I've just discovered that. Don't you agree? Oh, what's that?"

She pushed him away, abruptly tense and listening.

"What? I didn't hear anything."

"I thought I heard someone rapping."

He hastily straightened his clothes and went to the window.

"It wasn't at the front door," Maud said. "It came from Mamma's room."

He turned, his face questioning.

"There's no one in there. We looked not five minutes ago."

Maud pushed her hair back, trying to pin it up. She was confused and uneasy. She suddenly felt indecently naked, with her blouse undone and her skirt lying on the floor.

Mamma's sharp ears, so tuned to Papa's infidelities, were still listening, although she was in her grave.

What a crazy thought! Crazy or not, it was not to be lived with.

"This house is haunted!" she cried. "Ninian, I'm sorry. It wasn't a good idea."

He looked at her with his reflective eyes.

"It's not the house, it's you. You're parent-haunted."

"It isn't the right place," she said miserably. "Couldn't we go into the country and find a haystack or an empty barn?"

He began to smile.

"Anyone less suited to lying in a haystack I have yet to find. I think a flat on the Chelsea embankment is the only solution."

She flung herself at him.

"Ninian, you haven't found one!"

"I have actually. But I can't move in until next week. Can you wait until then?"

"I shall have to. Because this house—it was a mistake. This was Horace's bed, too, if you must know."

He sat beside her, taking her hand.

"Aren't we going to be much good at adultery?"

"Oh, we're going to be supreme. Don't you worry."

"Then why are you crying?"

"I don't know. That's me. I'm idiotic. What was that lovely word? Zany. I just hope Hessie's having a good time in Paris, since I sent her there for this reason."

"Next time," he said, handing her a handkerchief, "send your mother and father, too."

Actually, Hessie was having a superlative time. There had been the dizzying excitement of going to the top of the Eiffel Tower, and the equally dizzying pleasure of sipping a glass of wine with her *omelette champignon* at a street café. Les Deux Magots, a famous café, Father said. Also, the walk through the Luxembourg Gardens, around the circle of the stone queens, standing ashen and silent against the dark trees, the dutiful visit to the Louvre—since Mother would be sure to ask if they had been there—and the more absorbing visit to the Bourse, where Hessie found herself unexpectedly fascinated by the proceedings. Since she seemed so interested, Father said he would make a point of taking her to his office when they went home.

They had to look for a gift for Mother. Hessie pressed her nose against shopwindows, gazing into the small Aladdin's caves of jewelry, perfume, scarves, lengths of silk. The week simply flew. The chestnuts dropping their amber leaves along the Champs Élysées, Notre Dame as dark as the inside of a tomb, the fat chambermaid who turned down Hessie's bed and spread out her cotton nightgown and called her Mamselle, the terrific importance of staying up late to dinner, wearing her best dark-blue silk dress and reading the menu without any assistance from the waiter or from Father, whose French was very funny indeed. He used to suggest that Hessie ask for the bill, *l'addition s'il vous plaît,* which she did in fits of giggles.

Why ever hadn't Mother come on such a divine holiday?

But Hessie was glad she hadn't. It was so peaceful, just Father and her. For the rest of her life, she knew that Paris would be her favorite city. "When I was in Paris," she would be able to say the next time she saw those ghastly Sylvesters. "No, it wasn't to improve my French. It was to go to the Bourse with my father."

The very odd thing was the change that had taken place in both Mother and Honor while she and Father had been away. Hessie was aware of it at once.

Mother was vague and dreamy. True, she threw her arms around Hessie warmly, saying, "You're wearing your clothes differently, darling. And your pigtails are quite French. What did you do? Go to all the art galleries? Didn't you simply adore the Renoirs?"

Hessie looked hastily at Father who said calmly, "We didn't spend all our time in art galleries, Maud. Hessie's a bit young for too much culture."

"Then what else did she do?"

"She learned to drink wine and count French francs."

Of course, there was a twinkle in Father's eyes, which Mother failed or chose not to see.

"How utterly unsuitable. Is this true, Hessie?"

"Yes, and I learned about stocks and shares and dividends and capital gains and calls and op— What was it, Father?"

"Options."

"Horace! Well, couldn't you have done that with her in London, if you must?"

"I shall later," said Father. "Hessie has a good head for figures. Well, Maud, you're looking splendid. Have you missed us?"

"In only a week? I haven't had time. I've been so busy with my decorations. Come and see."

Grandma's room had been completely transformed. It looked very pretty, Hessie had to admit, with the green walls and white curtains, and the brilliantly colored begonias in terra-cotta pots on the windowsill.

"It's going to be my sitting room," Mother said.

"What a luxury that is for someone who never sits for more than two minutes at a time." Father's voice was good-natured, however. He put his arm around Mother's waist. She stood a moment, slightly frowning, then slipped away, giving a little manufactured cough and saying not to come too close, she had a cold. Father's face became expressionless. After a moment he turned and went out of the room. Hessie was about to follow him when Mother called to her to admire the little Victorian rocking chair she had found. Hessie looked at it briefly. She had already decided that she much preferred the room as it had been, dark and stuffy and cluttered with Grandma's treasures. Changing it had, in some extraordinary way, changed Mother, too.

Honor hadn't been doing any house decorating, unless she had been helping furnish the flat Ninian had rented to write in. However, she said she hadn't, because he had preferred to fix it himself. He only wanted a desk and a chair, he said.

So something else had caused the guarded look in her eyes.

"I missed you," she told Hessie.

"Really, did you?"

"Really I did. The week seemed awfully long. Did you have a wonderful time?"

Where Hessie, from experience, had told her mother only a little, lest boredom show in her eyes, everything was poured out to Honor, the Metro, the cafés, the alarming taxi drivers, the kind chambermaid, the rolls and coffee for breakfast, the Louvre, which was far too big and made her legs ache, the statues of the queens in the Luxembourg Gardens, and last but not least, the Bourse, where she had begun to understand about stocks and shares.

"But Mother thought that was very unsuitable," she finished.

"Hessie," Honor was looking at her hard, her thin face serious, "what are you going to do when you grow up? Is there anything you badly want to be?"

"A stockbroker," Hessie answered promptly.

"Oh, dear, that won't do, I'm afraid. Women can't be stockbrokers. You'll have to choose something else. Make up your mind soon what it's to be and begin to learn it. Don't let anyone stop you."

"Like you wanted to be a concert pianist?" Hessie said shrewdly.

"Yes. You see, some women need more than marriage. If they haven't children, or if—" Honor stopped. Her lips tightened. Hessie watched her agonizedly. She couldn't bear Honor to be unhappy. Was she thinking of her dead baby?

"This hangover from Victorian times, that girls of our class don't work, is all nonsense. You learn a profession, Hessie. You'll always be thankful you did."

Mrs. Beauchamp had grown almost as stiff in her joints as poor Pritchett. But she could still stump along the street as far as Honor's, an immense figure in her old-fashioned black velvet toque and long black coat.

"What's this nonsense about Ninian having to move to Chelsea for peace and quiet? Are you playing the piano too much? Do I need to ask? It's a wonder you haven't worn your fingers out long ago."

It was useless, at this late stage in one's life, to wish once again that one's mother had a sympathetic and comforting bosom on which to pour out one's fears and unhappiness. Honor replied in her usual contained way, "Ninian has always enjoyed my playing. But now that he's writing full time, he has to work a great deal harder, and he must be alone. That's a necessity for a writer."

Mrs. Beauchamp gave her familiar snort. "If you ask me, he's mad, giving up a profession on the strength of one success. Personally, I couldn't get on with his book."

Honor smiled a little. "Never mind. He doesn't expect a fan-mail letter from you."

"People will talk. You know that, don't you?"

"Don't be silly, Mother. Ninian is only going out to work each day as he has always done."

"They'll say he's keeping a woman in that flat."

"Ninian! Oh, Mother!"

"You may laugh. But no man's perfect, I can tell you. You'd have done better to spend more time on your husband and less on Beethoven and Mozart." Mrs. Beauchamp rose. "Well, that's all I wanted to say. I haven't told Lionel this, I might add. He's got old-fashioned ideas. Remember how horrified he was about Maud and Guy."

"Good-bye, Mother. Come again when you have more cheerful news."

Mrs. Beauchamp's caustic gaze softened to the faintest extent. "Honor, you always were a dreamer. I told you you'd manage your life badly. You want more of Daisy's practical nature. By the way, she's coming up next week and bringing the girls. We might arrange an outing and take Hessie. I like that child. She has an amazing amount of sense, considering she's Maud's daughter. I have her in mind for one of Daisy's boys."

"Mother, she's only ten!"

"She could be a countess. I'd like to do that for my old friend Lady Lucie. I shouldn't think Maud would be averse to it either, although she threw away her own chances and ruined my son."

"Hessie detests both John and Marcus," Honor protested.

"She'll get over that. They're good-looking boys."

"She doesn't want to be a countess; she wants to be a stock-broker."

"What an extraordinary idea! I hope you're not encouraging her, Honor. Look to your own life, that's my advice."

How could she look to it when she didn't know where she had gone wrong? She simply didn't know. Ninian with a woman? Her mother hadn't needed to drop that prickly thought into her mind. It had been inevitably there. But she had dismissed it determinedly. Ninian hadn't changed except to be, perhaps, a little quieter and less communicative. He was still gentle, affectionate, courteous. If he was absent in manner, it was because he was already absorbed in his new book. He hadn't been happy as a barrister. He was happy as a writer, so she would be happy with him.

She most certainly had no intention of turning into one of those suspicious wives who looked for lipstick or powder smears on handkerchiefs or shirt collars, who read private diaries and tried to unseal letters.

If, by any remote chance, Ninian was guilty of infidelity, she preferred not to know about it. One could pretend things not talked about had not happened. One could make oneself live in a dream world, which might be cowardly, but she knew of no other way.

Maud now spent her mornings in her sitting room, taking breakfast luxuriously by the fire, still in her negligee, writing letters and answering invitations, and generally behaving like her Victorian forebears, whom she had once professed to despise. She called goodbye to Horace from the top of the stairs, but Hessie was commanded to present herself to her mother, to be looked over before setting out for school. Her hair ribbons were retied, her hat straightened, and her satchel examined to see that she had her lunch box and her books.

Sometimes these visits were prolonged while Hessie was put through a cross-examination about her friends or her scholastic progress. Although fidgeting and fearful of being late, Hessie loved these moments, when her mother's brilliant green eyes were fixed on her with the most anxious interest and the famous long red hair hung loose to her lap. She preferred them to the times when she was given only the most perfunctory examination, because her mother was writing a letter (which she had covered with her little silver-topped blotter), and her expression was soft and far-off. The nice thing was that lately Mother always seemed happy.

And her bout of extravagance this time didn't end with the new room. She announced that she was going to buy the car she had long wanted and that she would learn to drive. If Horace couldn't or wouldn't afford a car, she would sell her mother's porcelain. She had had it valued, and it was worth at least five hundred pounds. Better to sell it before something got broken. She herself had never cared for what she called small fidgety things.

During the process of putting it up for auction in Sotheby's, she got into conversation with picture experts, and the suggestion was made that she should arrange an exhibition of her father's paintings. He had been dead long enough for interest in his work to be revived. An exhibition would undoubtedly do much to increase the value of James Lucie paintings.

The idea was so compelling that Maud seized on it with enthusiasm and excitement. She owned several of Papa's best works; other works could be borrowed from art galleries and private collections. Such an exhibition would be a wonderful dedication to Papa's memory.

Life, after such a long barren period, was suddenly almost too full. It was rich and satisfying, as it had been when Papa had been at his zenith and she his faithful companion and disciple.

The driving lessons in the red Chevrolet and the exhibition arrangements were gratuitous extras that provided a plausible explanation for her happiness. That, of course, lay in the austere and river-smelling flat on the Chelsea embankment.

Maud loved the view from the low windows. There was a window seat just wide enough for her to sit with her arms wrapped around her knees, her cheek against the pane, as she watched the barges and small craft going downstream. Looking like the Lady of Shalott, Ninian said.

"You're a medieval creature, you know, in spite of those short skirts. And in spite of that car outside. Do you have to park it right in front of the house, and did it have to be such a spectacular color?"

"I hate subterfuge," said Maud.

"My dear darling, it's a little late to object to that."

"I know, but I have to make my protests. Anyway, I couldn't have taken a taxi here every day. That would have been more suspicious."

"So you come by fire engine instead. Idiot. Are we going to bed?"

"Have you done a good day's work?"

"I didn't lift my head all morning."

Maud sprang up, laughing, tender, excited. "Then certainly we are going to bed."

First there was the audacity of making love in the afternoon, with the curtains drawn back to the sky and the river; then there were the sounds that Maud found so compelling, the hooting of tugs, the lap and suck of the water against the river walls, the cry of seabirds. Timeless things, with a fascinating melancholy that had also disturbed Whistler and Rossetti and Turner when they had lived on this part of the embankment. And earlier, that man of dour integrity, Sir Thomas More, and his family and friends.

Ninian had shown great perception in wanting to have her here

—if the intention to find a place in which to make love to her was a greater purpose than writing his book, and she suspected it was.

She knew that his quivering body in her arms was totally hers, as hers was totally his. They emerged from love soft-eyed and vague, talking in blurred whispers.

Guilt was a thing that couldn't possibly come into anything that was so nearly a miracle.

Chapter 17

By a coincidence which Maud regarded as symbolic, they both had notices in the *Times* on the same day, Ninian for his new book and Maud for the exhibition of her father's paintings, which had taken nearly a year to organize. Apart from various art galleries and private houses in England, some of the paintings had come from America, one from Australia, and one, of all unlikely places, from Japan.

Of Ninian it was said: "Mr. Spencer, who has had the courage to give up a promising career at the bar to become a full-time writer, has obviously made the right decision. His new novel is more than a worthy successor to his first. He seems to have gained in perception and warmth, as if he has discovered that not all the human race deserves to be on trial."

And on the James Lucie exhibition, the art critic wrote: "One tends to think of the late James Lucie, RA, as purely romantic. But the romanticism overlies a high degree of professional skill, as one can see by a collection of the works of this artist now on show in Leighton House, Kensington. Who remembers with nostalgia 'The Peacock Girl' and 'Gathering Primroses,' pictures that were Royal Academy highlights in those old spacious days before the war? These and many others are part of this exhibition, which has been arranged by the artist's daughter, Mrs. Horace Ponsonby, who was the subject of many of his paintings. And this makes one reflect on the tragedy of Lucie's premature death. I, for one, would like to have seen what he could have done on canvas with the mature good looks of this famous beauty of the last decade."

"Who is this fellow?" asked Horace. "What did he go to see, the pictures or you?"

"He makes me sound old and passé," Maud complained.

"Well, I must say growing older seems to agree with you."

"You mean I've stopped being extravagant," Maud teased. "It's true. I've only bought one new dress in the last three months, and that's for tonight's soiree. But don't be too optimistic. I've simply been too busy lately. I might go back to my old bad ways."

"Oh, they weren't entirely bad. Maud—"

"Not just now, Horace." Maud was halfway out the room. "I must get Hessie off to school. And I want to get the doctor in to look at Nanny. She doesn't seem at all well, although she'll never admit it."

"Damn it, I never see you, what with that ridiculous morning room of yours, and we haven't had an evening alone since goodness knows when."

"Darling, arranging the exhibition has taken every minute. You know that. Don't scold. I'm happy when I'm busy."

Horace looked reluctantly at her glowing face.

"Anything to do with your father makes you happy," he grumbled.

Maud agreed amicably. "Yes, it makes Papa seem alive again. But it must please you that there's a growing demand for his pictures. Mrs. Alastair Bruce was offered two thousand pounds yesterday for the one she has, and it's not nearly as good as mine."

"Does it matter? Since you don't intend to sell?"

"No, I do not, Horace. But can't you think of my pictures as the equivalent of your precious stocks and shares? They're a much more stable asset."

Horace's mouth drooped gloomily at the corners.

"I sincerely hope so. Because, if I know anything at all, there's a depression coming."

Maud said that Hessie must go to the soiree. She didn't need to stay late. Countess Daisy, who was staying with her mother, was going and taking her boys, who were now quite old enough to escort Hessie home at a suitable time.

"When I was your age, I'd have had to have Nanny. Think how

lucky you are to be allowed out with two handsome young men. Don't glower, Hessie. Be nice to them. It isn't so long until your coming out, and think how useful John and Marcus will be then."

"I don't intend to come out," Hessie said, but silently.

There was no sense in breaking that particular piece of news to Mother yet. Who knew what might happen in the next six years, an earthquake or a war, or something cataclysmic that would put an end to stupidities like balls and presentations to the queen and all those fripperies that were simply a waste of time. She intended to be an accountant. With Honor's help, she had found that this was possible for women. She already had a book called *Elementary Bookkeeping* that she studied whenever possible. She would much rather be doing that tonight than going to the soiree, where once again people would look at her and say, "Maud, this great girl *can't* be your daughter!"

Still, that was life, as Nanny said.

"You're not a patch on your mother, Hester, but that's life. Still, you look very nice in your brown velvet. Hold up your head, and remember to make conversation. No one can abide a tongue-tied child. I hope Miss Maud remembers to come and show herself to me before she goes."

"She came, Nanny. Ten minutes ago."

"Oh! Did she? Are you telling the truth? I can't have forgotten."

But Nanny obviously had forgotten, as she forgot everything nowadays. The only thing she didn't do was think that Hessie was Maud as a child. That was too unlikely even for her darkening, groping mind.

Maud found it immensely flattering, the way people had responded to her invitation. Though why shouldn't they? Papa had been famous, and she wasn't unknown herself.

Nevertheless, the streams of well-dressed people arriving at Leighton House were very satisfying. She stood, with Horace unwillingly beside her (this was not the sort of occasion he enjoyed, though he would not have forgone his position at his wife's side) at the top of the stairs, welcoming her guests. She knew how well she looked in the green silk dress, an almost exact replica of the one she had worn in the peacock portrait. Green was still her color and would continue to be while her hair remained so richly red. She had it done in a luxuriant twist on the top of her head, emphasizing her high cheekbones and slender neck. Her mature beauty, the critic had written. But maturity, which could last from thirty to eighty, Ninian said, could be the most attractive time for a woman.

He hadn't seen her in her peacock dress, however. She was waiting for his arrival, perfectly aware that she would make a gratifying impact on him. It was pleasant greeting all these people, some of them old friends of her father's whom she hadn't seen for years. But she secretly only cared about Ninian being here tonight and seeing her against her true background, the rich dramatic frieze of Papa's paintings. It would be like illustrating for him her childhood, girlhood, and early maturity, all in one colorful scene.

Lady Ilchester, the Duke and Duchess of Northumberland, the president of the Royal Academy; Mr. Augustus John and his beautiful wife, Dorelia; Sir John Lavery, Mr. A. J. Munnings, the Beauchamp family in a solid block, Mrs. Beauchamp in black brocade that made her look like a funereal piece of upholstery; Daisy, almost as stout as her mother, badly dressed, placid, and complacent; Honor, too thin in a surprisingly chic brown chiffon (it looked like Molyneux—did Honor go to Molyneux now that her Uncle Lionel had died and she had inherited thirty thousand pounds?); Hessie at Honor's side, clutching her arm. Why did Hessie have so little self-confidence? Behind her came the Sylvester children, the young Earl of Deepford and his brother, the Honorable Marcus, red-cheeked, a bit countryish; and the three girls, Lady Edith, Lady Grizel, and Lady Melinda, who all looked like their mother.

Maud shook hands with them, smiling brilliantly, waiting to greet Ninian bringing up the rear. But he was not there. After the Sylvesters, there were strangers pressing up the staircase. Not strangers, of course, but everyone suddenly became a stranger now that Ninian did not seem to be there.

"Some urgent work." Maud realized that Honor had lingered to speak to her. "He sends his apologies. You know what he is when he gets buried in his work. The rest of the world doesn't exist."

The rest of the world? But surely she was not included in that anonymous company?

How casual, how ungallant, how unforgivable that he should

send her this late message—and by his wife! As Maud continued to greet guests, her temper mounted. She must have said the right words, for people smiled and complimented her. Horace didn't give her any warning nudge. But it was amazing that her disappointment, her feeling of slight and humiliation, and her rising anger did not appear on her face. How *dare* Ninian behave like this to her?

Hessie drank half a glass of champagne, and immediately her head whirled. She frankly enjoyed that sensation. It gave her the courage to slip down the staircase and stand in the deserted hall, half of which was made into an indoor courtyard, Arabian in style, with colorful tiled walls, a mosaic floor, and a dear little tinkling fountain in the center. She bent to dabble her fingers in the cool water and made up a fantasy, that Honor's frog, which disappeared in the winter, came here and lived indoors in great comfort and luxury. Perhaps he turned into a prince . . .

"So that's where you are," came Marcus Sylvester's voice behind her. His voice was breaking. It came out gruffly and with that bullying masculinity that had always terrified Hessie.

"What are you doing down here? Waiting to meet someone?"

"Of course I'm not. Who would I be meeting?"

"A boyfriend, I suppose. You're old enough, aren't you?"

"Don't be silly. I'm only twelve."

"Is that champagne you're drinking?"

Hessie looked guiltily at her empty glass and nodded.

"Then if you're old enough to drink champagne, you're old enough to have a boyfriend."

"Well, if I did, it wouldn't be you," Hessie retorted bravely.

"Wouldn't it then? For that remark I'm going to kiss you."

"*Kiss* me!" Hessie exclaimed in astonishment. "You are not! I'd rather kiss a—a frog."

Marcus' face reddened. It seemed that Hessie's words had actually stung. This gave her the courage to add, "You've always bullied me. But I'm too old now to be bullied. So just leave me alone."

Quick as a flash, Marcus' hand shot out and took her by the wrist. "Not before you've kissed me." His grinning face was close to hers.

"It's time you learned about kissing, Hessie Ponsonby. You can't run away and climb a tree this time."

Neither could she. But the old panic had gripped Hessie. She tugged furiously to escape his grip, and when this was not possible, instinct made her take the only other possible action. She raised her left hand and gave Marcus a hard slap across the cheek. He stepped back incautiously, in angry surprise, and the next moment had toppled into the fountain, pulling Hessie on top of him.

A tremendous hoot of laughter came from the stairs. The Earl of Deepford and his sisters were watching. As Hessie climbed, dripping and humiliated, from the slippery pool, the little group on the stairs increased. Mrs. Beauchamp and Countess Daisy were there, exclaiming loudly. Then Father came, quickly followed by Mother. Everyone stared in astonishment, while Hessie stood dripping and shivering, wishing uselessly that she had been able to drown in the shallow water. Her dress clung to her, showing the budding breasts of which she was still extremely sensitive. Perhaps Marcus' trousers clung to him in a similarly revealing way. She couldn't look. She was petrified into silence, feeling that she was standing naked in public.

Then Father's voice came, loud and reassuring.

"Bless my soul, it's only been a slight accident. Have any of you ladies got a wrap I can put around the child? Then she must go home. I'll take her."

"Oh, poor Hessie," said Mother, flying down the stairs. "What an unfortunate accident. Don't worry, darling. Worse things will happen before you're grown-up. What were you and Marcus doing anyway?" Her voice was kind enough, but Hessie was well aware of the impatience she was feeling for her stupid and clumsy daughter. Once again she had been a great disappointment. Why did things always go *wrong?*

It was comforting to be hustled home by Father, Marcus, in his wet clothes (he had disdained the offer of a coat), following sulkily behind. Marcus would never forgive her. But neither would she forgive him, so that was all right.

She was going to study to be an accountant. Like Father, she was going to escape into the fascination of complicated rows of figures that had to be balanced. Figures couldn't laugh at one or care if one was clumsy or tongue-tied or didn't care to be kissed. After tonight she was absolutely determined to turn her back on the social world.

"Don't worry," Father said. "You've made your mother's party. Everyone will be laughing their heads off." He opened the front door and gently pushed Hessie inside. "They enjoy practical jokes, that lot. Not that this was meant to be a joke, was it? If that boy was responsible, I'll skin him alive."

"He only wanted to k-kiss me," Hessie stuttered, shivering violently. "It's n-not that I'm too young to be k-kissed. It was only that I d-didn't want it to be him."

Father seemed, suddenly, to be struggling not to laugh. Was he joining the enemies? But abruptly he put his arm around her shoulders and said, "Treat every kiss as a compliment, lamb. That's what your mother would do, and see how well she manages. Now run along upstairs and have a hot bath before you go to bed. Take my advice and don't mention this to Nanny, eh? Avoid fusses, when you can."

"Father, I love you!"

He held her against him closely, in an embrace that seemed a little desperate. "I know, lamb. We have each other, haven't we? Well, I'd better get back, but we'll be home soon, your mother and I."

Sleep, for Hessie, was impossible. She longed to sink into darkness, where the dreadful humiliation of the evening was forgotten. But as the minutes went by, she became more wide-awake and more physically uncomfortable. In spite of the hot bath she had taken, she thought she had caught a chill. Her head ached, and she felt feverish.

She hoped Marcus was suffering similarly. The memory of his jeering face made her writhe. She passionately hated him and all his kind for their insolent superiority and their awful sense of humor. Schoolboys. If she ever fell in love, it would be with an older man who knew how to treat a woman.

What seemed like hours later, the front door banged, indicating that Mother and Father were home. Now Mother would come up to see her, Hessie thought confidently, and ask her how she was and reassure her that she hadn't spoiled the party.

But there was no step on the stairs. Another door banged. Then all was quiet, and Hessie knew that Mother was not coming. She blinked back tears, put on the light, and got out her miniatures. However, even their special alchemy failed tonight. She shivered over the pretty pastel faces, and felt sick, and finally knew she had to wake up Nanny. In spite of her great age, Nanny still knew the things that comforted. She would fill a hot-water bottle and make a soothing drink. Her brisk voice, used to half a century of calming crotchety children, would say, "There now, Miss Hester, go to sleep. Things will look different in the morning."

Once Nanny had sat up for homecomings, Mother had told her, even if it was until dawn. But one couldn't expect that now that she was over eighty. She must have her sleep.

Not sleep like this, however.

Hessie stood beside Nanny's bed, looking at the light shining on the immensely old, immensely still, carved-ivory face. Suddenly she screamed.

"Mother! Mother!" She was flying down the stairs in her night-gown. "Mother, come quickly! I think Nanny's dead!"

And then came the ultimate disaster of that dreadful night. Mother was not in bed, or in her bedroom, or in her sitting room. It didn't seem as if she were anywhere in the house.

Hessie's screams had aroused not only Father, but also Ada and Cook in the basement. Ada held Hessie tightly in her arms while Father went up to Nanny's room, then came hurrying down, grim-faced, to phone the doctor.

"Is it true, sir?" Cook asked nervously. "Is she gone?"

"I'm afraid so. Ada, get Miss Hester's dressing gown. She's shivering. And did either of you, by any chance, hear Mrs. Ponsonby go out? She doesn't seem to be in the house."

"No, sir. I heard you come home, but nothing else." Ada said this, and Cook confirmed it.

Father said, "Never mind, the immediate thing is Nanny. Probably my wife couldn't sleep and is walking in the Square gardens. She's done that on previous occasions."

"I'll put me coat on and go and look," Cook volunteered.

"Ring Honor, Father. Please ring Honor."

"I don't fancy your mother would be there, Hessie." Father's face was pale and frowning.

"Just tell her," Hessie begged. "She'll come."

This was true, for Honor came immediately, arriving just before the doctor. Cook returned to report that the gardens were empty and that the mistress' car was gone.

"She must be taking a drive to calm herself down after all that excitement, sir. She was that pleased about the exhibition. I've never seen her so pleased about anything. Have you, Ada?"

Ada was crying softly. She was still young and found death a great shock. Poor old Nanny, dying all by herself. After a life spent in the background of other people's lives, it didn't seem fair that she didn't get a bit of a fuss made over her on her deathbed.

The doctor arrived then, and after disappearing upstairs for a short time, he came down to say that nothing could be done until the morning. It was two o'clock. He would get in touch with the necessary people at daylight. He touched Hessie's tousled head.

"This young lady might be the better for a mild sedative. Where's her mother?"

"We had a small affair tonight. She's driving some of the guests home." Father, meeting nobody's eyes, made this reasonable statement quite calmly.

Honor's arm tightened around Hessie.

"Have you something with you, Doctor? I'll see she takes it."

"Not until Mother comes home," Hessie wanted to say. How could she rest until she knew Mother was safe? Father, she guessed, felt exactly the same. Hessie hadn't realized that she would disapprove strongly of Mother's unpredictable behavior. But hadn't there been something about Mother and Honor's brother meeting in the Square gardens in the early dawn, after a ball in Holland House? Who had told her that? Grandma? Nanny, perhaps?

How could that old scandal matter now? Mother was middle-aged, even though she still looked beautiful. She would never be meeting a man.

And of course she wasn't, for just after the doctor left, the hall door opened and closed softly. Then, realizing that all the lights were on and everyone awake for some reason, Mother burst into the drawing room.

"What's wrong?" she exclaimed. "Why is everyone up? I only went for a drive." Her hair was untidy, as if the wind had been blowing it; her cheeks were flushed. She looked brilliantly lovely. "You haven't been looking for me, have you? I needed some fresh air. I was still so excited after the party. I would never have slept."

"Nanny is dead," Father said flatly. That was all.

"Nanny! Oh, no! Oh, poor Nanny!" Then Mother just stood there, her arms spread out against the door, like a butterfly pinned there, caught after its flight . . .

In spite of the shock of her return to a house unexpectedly ablaze with lights and poor Nanny dead upstairs, Maud could not bring herself to regret the reckless hour she had just spent with Ninian.

He had been very angry with her. He had told her that she was never to come in the night like that. The only reason he hadn't gone to her soiree was that he couldn't stand seeing her with her husband correctly at her side, putting on an act for all the snobs. He hadn't thought her a snob until tonight.

And she had not thought him so rude and a boor, she retorted. And a coward. If he could not have come to her very special important memorial to her most dearly loved father, then he couldn't love her. Could he? Because he completely failed to understand her. So they had better part.

"Very well," said Ninian curtly. "What are you waiting for? You have a car."

"How will you get home?"

"Walk."

She couldn't bear his stiff, offended face. His eyes were glittering. He looked as if he hated her. And she was in her lovely dress, waiting to show it to him.

"Oh, Ninian, for God's sake! I didn't know you sulked."

"I don't sulk."

"Then don't let's just stare at each other. Either I go or we make love. There's no in-between."

"I'm glad you realize that," he said slowly. "So are you going?"

"No."

"Then we have no alternative, have we?"

"I wanted to show you my dress."

"Your dress is very effective in its correct place. That isn't here."

He took her in great haste, before she had her dress half off. It was flung over her face, and she nearly smothered. Not that it mattered for a few moments. The violence of her feeling made a small thing like lack of breath almost unnoticeable. But at last, as they lay still, she had to cry out for air, and he immediately lavished his disarming tenderness on her.

"Maud! Did I hurt you? I'm sorry."

"You didn't hurt me, but if you did, you're not sorry, and I'd hate you if you were." She stared up at the dark shape of his face. Her voice shook. "It was utterly marvelous. Say it was for you, too."

He buried his face in her shoulder. After a long time he said, "You'd better go. You might be missed."

"You too."

"I don't think so. Honor doesn't notice."

"Neither does Horace."

"Or are we all pretending?"

It wasn't until after Nanny's funeral that Horace said anything more about that night. Maud had hoped he had accepted her explanation and put the episode out of his mind.

However, he had not. He came into her bedroom, where she was taking off her dark dress and the hat with the little black veil, and said flatly, "You never looked like that for me, Maud."

"When? What do you mean?"

"The night you came home late, after your party. You hadn't been out driving alone, had you? You had been with your lover."

"My lover!"

"You never looked all soft and flushed like that for me."

"Horace, you're talking nonsense. You're making up fantasies. Like Hessie with her miniatures."

"Not like Hessie. And not fantasies. Stop pretending, Maud. I'm not blind. Do you think I wouldn't notice the difference in you? I'd have to notice that, even if I only cared for you a little. And unfortunately I care for you a great deal, so I watch how much you laugh, or the color you have, or your vagueness. Do you mean to say you haven't realized how vague you've become?"

"I'm more settled. Happier. I'm older!"

"And losing your memory?" Horace said sarcastically. "Don't insult my intelligence. I might just be a dull fellow messing about with figures and scrip certificates; I don't paint, I don't write, I'm not artistic, but I do know when my wife changes. Now I'm not even welcome in my own bed. Or was it ever my bed?"

Maud sat down at her dressing table and put her head in her hands.

"Don't talk to me like this just after Nanny's funeral," she reproached him.

"But I did wait until after the funeral. Credit me with that."

Maud was silent a moment. Then she made an abrupt decision. She was tired of being dishonest.

"So what then, Horace? You really believe I have a lover?"

"I know you have. You've always flirted. But this is different."

"Then will you divorce me?"

He winced, a sharp spasm of pain crossing his face as if, although he knew of her unfaithfulness, the actual admission was unbearable to him.

"No," he said. "I have absolutely no intention of doing that. You're my wife, and I happen to believe in the marriage vows."

"It suits you to believe in them," Maud retorted.

"Perhaps it does. It also suits me to preserve our home, not only for myself but for Hessie. I won't have her hurt by a broken marriage. I simply won't. So get that into your head. And of course, there's always the chance you'll tire of this fellow."

"Oh, Horace!" Maud said remorsefully. "Don't build hopes on that."

"Then at least promise not to run off with him." Horace's face had grown red. "If you do, I'll kick up a great stink. I'll lodge an enticement suit."

"I won't run off with him," Maud said in a low voice. "I can't."

"Why? Because he won't? That must be a change for Maud Lucie, not getting what she wants."

"Horace, don't be so bitter. I haven't been Maud Lucie for years."

"You've never stopped being her. You were certainly never Maud

Ponsonby. But I don't blame you. I blame your father. You're his creation. You've never really belonged to anyone but him. He only agreed to your marrying me because he was dying, you told me that yourself. But even then, it was because he knew I was no real threat to his ownership."

The pain shivered through Maud. Was this true? Was she pretending to herself that she hadn't known it all along?

"Then why did you marry me?" she asked.

"Because, damn it, I wanted you under any conditions. Even those. And they're worse than another man in your life, I can tell you that. Fighting ghosts. Your lover will find this out, too."

"No," Maud said vehemently. "No."

"Well, all the same, you're my wife by law, and that's how you'll remain. I deserve that much, Maud."

She bent her head, unable to look at him. She had preferred his anger to this sudden unnerving humility. Of all things, she couldn't stand him to be humble.

However, it seemed as if the painful conversation was over, for he had turned to go. In the doorway he paused.

"Maud."

"Yes?"

"You used to say you could never bear me to go in the middle of a quarrel."

Now he was adding wistfulness to humility. Was it a trick?

"It's different now," she said briefly, not looking up.

In a moment the door closed. She could hear his footsteps going down the stairs. They were slow, elderly. Oh, God, what had she done to him? Was she what he accused her of being, a monstrous, heartless creation of Papa's? It was so unlike Horace to talk like that. Which proved the harm she had done him. But was she to be forever blamed because she couldn't love him?

She saw her face in the mirror, the day's strain giving it a slightly famished, ethereal look, her cheekbones too prominent, her eyes like green glass. It was not Papa's voice but Nanny's that spoke to her. "Handsome is as handsome does, Miss Maud."

"Ninian," said Honor carefully, "if you're not going to come home all night, couldn't you let me know? I worry."

"I don't have a telephone in the flat. I told you. I won't be interrupted."

"Then isn't there one near? In a pub or somewhere?"

"Yes, there is. But I forget. If I go out, it breaks my line of thought. I'm sorry, love. All artists are selfish, but none so selfish as I."

There was a woman, of course. But Honor still reasoned illogically that if the question were never asked, the woman would not exist. At least she would remain unreal. Even if she were Maud. As Honor was almost certain she was.

Ninian could not be blamed for falling in love with someone so much more vital and alive and lovely than she was. Why had she been made so shut in, so contained, so utterly unable to lose her temper and shout her angry suspicions? At the beginning Ninian had thought he wanted someone quiet and peaceful, but now he had found he had made a mistake. She wouldn't despair. He might eventually find he did want quiet and peace, after all. She had to struggle constantly with her great fear that he would leave her altogether, instead of every day and the occasional night. All the same, she thought there was love for her in his eyes as he watched her now. At least it was a great gentleness, if it was not love. Perhaps that could be made to be enough.

"Ninian," she went on in her composed voice, "if you are going to be away so much, it makes me very dull. Would you mind if I took some more piano pupils? Hessie is getting so busy with other things now."

Ninian gave her a long, thoughtful look. Then he came across and rumpled her hair in his old affectionate way. "Of course I don't mind. Take as many pupils as you like, if it makes you happy."

It wouldn't make her happy. But that random gesture of affection helped a great deal. She was still somewhere there inside him.

Chapter 18

"HESTER," said Miss Pringle in her calm, emphatic way, "is one of our most studious girls. It seems to me that she is not only ideally suited to a career, but that she needs one."

Maud crossed her legs, knowing the headmistress' eyes settled on, then flicked away from the display of slim silk-stockinged knees. It was easy to read what she was thinking. Frivolous mothers often had serious daughters. Then the object, surely, was to make Hessie less serious; otherwise, what in the world was ahead for her? To be an accountant? Maud had never heard such nonsense in her life. She was still feeling abnormally sensitive after the shock of Hessie's ultimatum: "If you don't let me study, I'll run away."

Such a threat was childish, of course. The fact that it had been made was what hurt. And Hessie, solid, stocky, and aggressive, almost looked capable of carrying it out. One could only hope that, adolescence over, she would lose this humorless intensity and grow more feminine.

It was infuriating, however, to find Miss Pringle on Hessie's side.

"Are you suggesting, Miss Pringle, that Hessie isn't likely to marry?"

"I'm doing nothing of the kind, Mrs. Ponsonby. Hester is a warm-hearted girl, even if she does tend to put up emotional barriers. That only comes from shyness. Credit me with enough experience to be able to read a girl's character."

"I wasn't saying—"

"But your daughter has a good brain, and what I am saying is that she may not find marriage sufficient in itself."

Maud, who didn't care for being interrupted as this unexpectedly suave woman had just done, found herself irritatingly on the defensive.

"I wouldn't object to her having an interesting hobby. Now if she took after my father and could paint, or if she had a talent for music or even wanted to become a nurse. But accountancy! Really, Miss Pringle, I must say I'm surprised that you encourage her."

"Have you not heard of the emancipation of women, Mrs. Ponsonby?"

Stung, Maud retorted, "Good heavens, yes. I regard myself as completely emancipated. But that doesn't mean one doesn't remain feminine. Does it?"

Deliberately, she stared at the thin gray-haired, bespectacled woman in her severely tailored coat and skirt. She slightly adjusted her smart little cloche hat and shrugged back her sable necklet. She knew that the movement stirred a faint fragrant scent, the one Ninian liked her to wear. Then she was impatient with herself for thinking that the calm, matter-of-fact Miss Pringle would even notice her tactics, let alone be affected by them.

The time had come not only for plain speaking, but for Hessie to be removed from this school. One should have discovered its undesirable influence long ago. (Once, she remembered guiltily, she had been unaware for too long that Hessie's French governess practiced small cruelties.)

All the same, although she might rout Miss Pringle, when faced by the solid front of Horace and Hessie combined, she was forced to compromise.

She looked at them as if they were two strangers who had incomprehensibly strayed into her life.

"Very well, I will agree to Hessie taking these lessons. What are they?" Distastefully, she studied the prospectus Hessie had thrust at her. "Bookkeeping, economics, mathematics. Good heavens! So long as she promises in three years' time to have a season and learn a few social graces."

"Oh, Mother!" Hessie burst out. Her last attempt at social graces, when she had fallen into the fountain at Leighton House, was still seared in her memory.

But her father pressed her arm.

"I think that's a fair promise to make, Hessie. So long as we can swing a coming-out season, Maud. One never knows—"

"Now, none of that, Horace." Maud was good-tempered again. She had won what she considered to be the most important point. "You know how well you've done out of those South African—what were they? I never can remember the names of shares."

"They were gold mines," said Horace briefly. "A gamble not to be recommended to widows and orphans. If it hadn't come off, you wouldn't have got your sable necklet, and we'd have been in Queer Street."

"But it did come off, and you're much too clever for it not to come off. I'm not going to let you worry me by your gloomy predictions again. They never happen. I really believe you take this pessimistic attitude simply to keep me from being too extravagant."

"You were never taught money sense, that's your trouble, Maud. Well, I can tell you there is a depression coming. I've predicted it for long enough. I wish I could be wrong, but I fear I'm not. That's why I've been trying to accumulate some liquid capital. But if anything happens to me, you and Hessie will be all right. You've got this house and a fortune in pictures."

Maud gave a satisfied smile.

"So haven't I been right to keep them, after all? Ever since that exhibition the price has gone on rising. Not that that makes any difference to me, because I never intend to sell any of them. I've told you so often enough. I couldn't live without them. That month they were on show in Leighton House I was utterly miserable. The house was naked without them, as if its soul had gone."

"Now you're being fanciful again," Horace said impatiently. "A house doesn't have a soul. And you'd surely sell them if you were hungry."

"Not even then. What an extraordinary thing to say!"

"I'm a bad mother," Maud said remorsefully, in the airy much-loved room looking over the river.

"You've said that before. And of course you are. All beautiful egotistical women are."

"I've always felt guilty because I couldn't love Hessie properly.

She's such a funny dour creature. I simply don't understand her. Would it have been better if she had been pretty?"

"Then you would have hated her for being your rival."

"Oh, Ninian! Am I as nasty as that?"

"I suspect so. I love your nastiness."

Maud took out a pocket mirror and studied her face, frowning anxiously at the fine lines around her eyes.

"I can still sit on my hair," she said irrelevantly.

"Show me."

"You know very well—" She raised her eyes. "Now?"

"Yes, now."

Maud took the pins out slowly, her heart beating with warm delight. She existed only for his admiration, she thought. If ever his face remained cold at the sight of her, she would wither away and die. He was ruthless in a quiet, utterly determined way. How could he have treated Honor like this if he were not? Or her? Yet his other side was all that wonderful serious tenderness that again operated for Honor as much as for her. This curious split personality was intriguing and utterly absorbing. Apart from his body, which she loved so passionately. His body would have been enough, even without his mind. Together, they ravished her.

"Ninian, supposing we had been able to marry. Would we have been happier?"

"No," he muttered, his hands and his lips in her hair.

"Why?"

"Too much familiarity. This way, we have the heights and the depths. Nothing in between. It suits our characters."

"It suits yours, I know. But mine, too? I can't tell you how often I think it should be you I hear walking about the house instead of Horace."

"Do you really want it to be me? To give up this? To find each other tetchy and bad-tempered, to live through bad colds and hacking coughs and striped pajamas and nourishing creams and hairpins and damp bath towels—do you want me to go on?"

"That's marriage."

"Boring for people like us."

"Yes, I suppose so." His fingers were exploring, and Maud's body was beginning to quiver with the familiar, irresistible pleasure. "I must have been born immoral."

"You were."

"But with a conscience, too," Maud sighed. "So awkward."

"Stop talking about a conscience just now, will you?"

"Hessie mustn't be hurt, that's all."

"Hessie will understand one day."

"But it's always too late! I understand Papa now, but what's the use when I can't tell him so?"

At the unimaginable thought of lying in her grave while Hessie, middle-aged and tolerant, spoke kindly about her, Maud flung herself into Ninian's arms. He was right. The heights and the depths were what gave life this almost unbearable poignant happiness.

After love, the quiet austere room was so exactly right. Ninian would make coffee or pour a drink while she sat curled on the window seat, watching dusk gather over the slow-flowing river, the dipping seabirds, the blackened barges, the smoky buildings on the opposite bank. Sometimes she thought it was a dream, the whole lovely thing.

She could not allow herself the weakness of feeling sorry for either Horace or Honor. Instead, she despised them for condoning what was happening. Horace certainly did so. Honor might still have been unaware, although one could hardly think so when one saw her averted thin face. But Honor had once betrayed Maud, and Maud hardened her heart. Even if she had loved Honor, she could not have stopped this wholly unstoppable miracle.

The times were subtly changing. The elaborate tea parties in the Square gardens, when the capped and aproned maids carried the heavily laden trays, were a thing of the past. Not that Ada wouldn't willingly have brought tea for her mistress, but now such a thing would be ostentatious. Few people in the Square nowadays could afford live-in servants. Several houses stood empty for want of buyers, and there was a new, entirely different generation of children playing in the gardens. Children whose manners were not all they might be. Respect for their elders no longer seemed to be taught to them. Perhaps it was old-fashioned.

Maud deplored this new generation in much the same way as old

Mrs. Beauchamp did, though she would have been startled if she had realized that her ideas of good behavior in the young were the same as that narrow-minded stuffy old woman's. She surely wasn't going over to the side of age. She was only thirty-nine and was convinced that she still had twice as much vitality as the young, certainly twice as much as her own daughter. She kept to her habit of taking walks in the garden in the early morning or the late evening, when the dew was on the grass and no noisy children drowned the birdsong.

Anyway, had she wanted to have a tea party as in the past, whom would she have invited to it? Mrs. Beauchamp retained a polite friendship simply because she was fond of Hessie. Honor for the same reason. Maud, aware of this, shrugged her shoulders. Hadn't she always been a subject of suspicion and disapproval?

She was on nodding acquaintance only with the rest of the occupants of the Square. They kept changing, and she simply hadn't time to get to know them, even had she wanted to. What had she in common with dull businessmen with dull wives and families?

How did she know they were dull? Horace asked in his maddening pedantic way, and Maud answered illogically that she simply hadn't time to find out. Let them talk about her if it amused them, that fast Mrs. Ponsonby, with her short skirts and her long cigarette holder and her smart car, behaving like a flapper when she had a nearly grown-up daughter.

What they actually said was that when Maud Ponsonby wasn't looking at herself in a mirror, she was looking at the different images of herself in her father's portraits. She must be very vain, but with justification, for in early middle age, she still made heads turn.

The saleswoman in Harrods indicated this by her significant glances from daughter to mother when Hessie was trying on a succession of dresses that looked depressingly less than their expensive price on her too-plump figure. She was trying valiantly to diet, but her weakness for cream buns was always her undoing. She got so hungry. Although she had an idea that she would be less hungry if life could be more simple. She ate when she was anxious or worried or lonely, all three states of mind much too familiar.

"It would need to be let out here and there," the saleswoman said tactfully, and Mother exclaimed humiliatingly, "But this is a size sixteen. It's enormous. It would almost fit two of me."

"But madam has a wonderful figure," the horrid woman purred.

"My daughter will have a good figure, too, when she loses all this puppy fat." One of Mother's most endearing habits was that she would never allow Hessie to be criticized. Why should she, indeed? Hessie was her own flesh and blood, an extension of herself. How had she ever come out of that lovely slim figure? Hessie wondered frequently.

"Hessie dear, I think we had better postpone buying your wardrobe for a few weeks. I'm going to put you on the most severe diet and count every crumb you eat. You do want a pretty dress for Edith and Grizel's ball, don't you?"

The ball was two months away. Hessie dreaded it. It was to be held at Claridges. There would be another one at Deepford later in the summer, when John, the young earl, came of age, but Countess Daisy liked the idea of her daughters having their coming-out ball in London, because that was where she and Honor had had theirs. It had been such a triumphant time, the beginning of their happy futures. Their mother had had to sell her diamond tiara to dress them for their season, but what an investment it had been!

Hessie had heard this story many times. Privately, she found the merits of Mrs. Beauchamp's investment doubtful, for Daisy had lost her husband in the war, and Honor, for all her self-contained front, had clearly not been happy for a long time.

However, the status of marriage and respectability had been the necessary achievements. What a comment on society, Hessie said passionately to her friend Albie Smithers. She would never be bound by such narrow rules.

Albie, indeed, was one of the reasons for her lack of willpower in dieting. He shared her fondness for cream buns, currant buns, toasted buns, any kind that were sufficiently filling. In his case, however, eating was not so much a compulsion as a necessity. He was thin and hollow-cheeked and permanently hungry from an insufficient diet at home.

He and Hessie had begun to meet for tea at the Lyons café on the corner after class every Wednesday and Friday. Those were the only two days Albie was free. For the rest of the week, he helped the janitor sweep and tidy classrooms. The small sum he earned paid for his schoolbooks and kept him in clothes. Just. Hessie knew for a fact that he lined his leaking shoes with brown paper and that he did not possess an overcoat.

There was nothing she could do about that, but she could pay for the teas out of her own pocket money. She had had to fight a battle with Albie's pride in this respect, until she had had the brilliant idea that he keep a record of the weekly expenditure. In a small notebook he made columns headed "Owing to Miss Hessie Ponsonby" and entered the date and the sum meticulously. The entire amount would be repaid when he had finished his education and got a job. It was a debt of honor. Looking into those honest gray eyes staring with such intensity out of the hollowed face, Hessie knew that it would certainly be repaid. Unless, of course, they married and automatically wiped out the debt.

She would be eighteen in March. She had first talked to Albie when she had stayed late in the classroom one afternoon to finish a profit-and-loss account and balance sheet that was absorbing her. She hadn't noticed the tall thin boy with his broom until, satisfyingly, the last figure added up and the beautifully tidy set of accounts was complete.

"Hello," she said. "Aren't you in this class?"

"Yes."

"Then what are you doing with that broom?"

"Can't you see? Sweeping. It's what a broom's for."

His prickly aggressiveness rather pleased her. He could be as rude as she could. For the first time, she noticed his shabby clothes and his gauntness, and without asking, she knew why he was sweeping the classroom. His parents were poor, and he had to earn money to be able to come to school. They probably thought he should be doing a job and bringing home money. He must have had to struggle to stay at school. He must want to learn very much.

With a tact which she could display when necessary she said, "I'm sorry. I'm in your way. I'm going in a minute. I could do this at home, but I like working here better. It's lonely at home."

He was interested now. He didn't mind talking about her.

"Why?"

"Because I'm an only child. My father's at work, and my mother goes out a lot."

"Where do you live?"

"Kensington. Where do you?"

"Limehouse."

"Have you got brothers and sisters?"

He gave a derisive laugh. "Gawd. What do you think? Seven. You'd think me mum and dad had nothing else to do, wouldn't you?"

"Are you the eldest?"

"No, I'm in the middle."

"What's your name?"

"Albie Smithers. What's yours?"

"Hessie Ponsonby."

"Gawd!"

"Why do you say that?" Hessie asked frigidly.

"It's a bit la-di-da, ain't it? Are you rich?"

"No."

"You live in Kensington, don't you?"

"That doesn't mean one is rich."

"Oh, does it not?" He imitated her voice very cleverly.

"No, it doesn't, and you don't need to be like that."

His angular jaw stuck out.

"I'd say you was rich compared to us." He brandished his broom fiercely. "That's why I'm doing this, to get money to buy me books. Me dad's mad enough as it is, me not going to work and earning a wage."

"Why aren't you?" Hessie asked interestedly.

"Because I have me own plans. I have to learn figures and accounts. I'm not going to work in the docks all me life, like me dad and me brothers."

"And then?"

"What?"

"After you've learned how to keep accounts."

A totally unexpected and touchingly shy look came into his eyes. "I'm going to have a shop. Me own. Somewhere in the country."

"What kind of shop?"

"A general store. You know, where there's tea and sugar on one shelf and cigarettes on another, and those big glass jars of toffees, and knitting wool, and birdseed, and whatever you fancy."

Surprised, Hessie found herself liking his enthusiasm.

"You'll need money to buy this shop."

"I know. I'll get it. Bit by bit. I'll start by taking a lease. But in the end I'll own it." He began sweeping with such vigor that dust flew. He was almost as thin as the broom handle.

Hessie began putting her books away methodically. She said loudly, "I'm hungry." When he didn't stop his work, she went on, "I'm going to the Lyons corner house for some tea. Why don't you come?"

"Haven't time. Thanks a lot."

"I don't like going alone. I get stared at. Oh, I know I'm nothing much to look at, but I still get stared at."

"You're all right." The broom moved vigorously. "Quite nice actually."

"I'll stand you a tea, Albie. Honestly, I wish you'd come."

"And be a gigolo!"

Hessie's mouth dropped open. Then she began to giggle. "Me with a gigolo! How do you know about gigolos? That's the funniest thing I ever heard. Anyway, they only go for thin old ladies, not fat young ones. Do come, Albie. You can pay me back when you get your shop. We can keep accounts."

So that was how it began.

They had been meeting for more than a year by the time Hessie's dreaded coming-out season arrived. Their café encounters had extended to country walks and the very occasional extravagance of a cinema. To her mother, Hessie said that the country walks were organized by groups from the school (imagine having Mother probe into her friendship and scaring Albie into fits), but to her father she had confided that sometimes a boy from her class took her out. He was absolutely to be trusted, she assured Father, and so was she. No, she couldn't bring him home yet. It might rather spoil things. Didn't Father understand?

He did indeed. He squeezed Hessie's hand and told her to have a nice time. She must be a bit lonely at home.

"He's from the East End," Hessie blurted out.

There was a sudden flicker of amusement in Father's eyes. He didn't often look amused nowadays. He mostly looked sad.

"That needn't be against the lad. I trust your judgment, my dear. But I imagine your mother might find him *persona non grata* at the big events this summer."

Hessie giggled. "Don't be silly, Father, I couldn't drag Albie to them, even if he were asked. He shares my contempt for that sort of thing. He says it's an awful waste of time, apart from anything else."

"Sounds a sensible chap. But try not to disappoint your mother, Hessie. She's going to a lot of trouble for you. And if it comes to that, I don't want my money wasted."

"Father, I love you."

The familiar formula satisfied them both. Hessie confided to Albie that whereas her relationship with her father was absolutely uncomplicated, her feelings for her mother were muddled and forever changing.

"Sometimes she's maddening, and sometimes she's adorable. On the whole, though, she's maddening. She's one of these egotistical women who doesn't really see beyond herself. She's never begun to understand me or even tried. But that's because I've always disappointed her, and she's a bit embarrassed about me. I'm not pretty. I don't shine socially. I'm just a failure. I always drop things when I'm with her, or get tongue-tied, or something. She gives me the most awful inferiority complex."

"She sounds horrible."

"But she isn't. She's absolutely gorgeous, even though she's over forty."

"I'd like to see her."

"Yes, I wish you could. But I've told you, if I bring you home—"

"Gawd, nothing would make me set foot in your house. But couldn't I sort of hang around the Square at a time when she's going out? You must know the times she goes out."

"I don't. She's very erratic. Half the time I don't know where she goes. I don't think Father does either. She has artists she befriends. She goes to tea parties and shows and things."

"I'll come to the door selling matches."

Hessie giggled. "Ada always answers the door."

"Servants! Gawd!"

"Don't say it like that. We only have Ada and Cook, who's due for the workhouse at any moment."

"You'd send her to the workhouse!" Albie exclaimed, shocked.

"Albie, don't be daft. You're talking like Charles Dickens. No, but we might have to find her a decent sort of home. Father's been looking into it."

"Then your mother will have to do the cooking with her lily-white hands."

Hessie frowned. "You're not being very funny. It just happens this has been my mother's way of life, and it's coming to an end, and it's rather sad. Oh, I expect we can find another cook, but she won't be the old-fashioned kind. And don't you start telling me that servants were put upon in the old days, because Cook has been happy with us for thirty years, and why would she have stayed if she hadn't been?"

Albie was giving the faint crooked grin that she liked.

"I'm only pulling your leg, love. But you're a bit mixed up, aren't you? Defending all this servant lark and hating being a deb. Though I must say I'd hate being a deb."

"You are an idiot."

"Laugh then. Don't look so down."

"I am down when I think of this summer. I dread it, I dread it, I dread it!"

"Then run away."

"If only I could."

"Money's the problem." She saw that he was serious. She felt breathless. She had never known how she could part with Albie when she left school, which would be very soon. These talks had come to mean a great deal to her. She loved his wry humor and his honesty. She also enjoyed looking after him, scolding him when he came out in a thin shirt without a jacket in cold weather, telling him he needed a haircut, cosseting him when he had a cold. He did the same for her. He admired a dress or disliked it, he preferred her hair done simply, and also assured her, without a trace of flattery, that plump girls were nicer than thin ones. They were more restful, jollier, less vain. Lack of vanity was one of Hessie's strongest characteristics. She enjoyed being told that it was a virtue.

They were friends, very good friends. They had never met each other's parents, seen each other's homes, or kissed.

Nevertheless, now he was suggesting that she run away, and she didn't know whether he meant to come with her or not. If she could ever do a thing that seemed so enormous to someone of her timidity.

"I'm going to get a job," Albie said.

"When?"

"At the end of term. You'll be leaving to do your deb stuff. I'll get a job and start saving money; otherwise, I'll never get me shop."

"How long will it take?"

"I dunno. I'd have to be twenty-one before anyone would give me a lease. Saving to buy, I'd be about thirty-five."

"That's forever!"

"That's the way it is."

"I'll be getting a job too," Hessie said after a while. "When this awful season is over. Albie? Can we go on meeting?"

"Sure. Why not? If you're not ashamed to be seen with me."

"Albie Smithers, don't you dare say such a rotten thing!"

He shrugged. "Wait and see. Anyway, I'd still like to see your mother."

He did this, unknown to Hessie. She nearly had heart failure when he told her afterward.

"You mean you lurked about our front gate!"

"The street's free, isn't it? You've got a nice house."

"But did you see my mother?"

"I saw her. She came out and got in a red car. A nice job."

"But Mother?"

"She's all right. For someone that age. Classy. I wouldn't know what to say to her if I met her, though. She's got marvelous eyes."

"Yes," said Hessie. "And hair. Everyone notices her hair."

"Don't sound so gloomy. You're all right yourself."

"I look like my father. He's the nicest person in the world, but you could never say he was good-looking."

"She looked right at me," Albie said. "She's a smasher, all right. But I wouldn't like to oppose her."

"Now you understand," said Hessie gloomily.

"That you have to do as she says? No, I don't. I said I wouldn't like to oppose her, but I didn't say she couldn't be opposed."

"If it came to the worst."

"Yeah," said Albie. "Think about it."

Chapter 19

Maud's oak tree was now high enough to throw a very respectable shade. She had had her own special garden chair placed beneath it, and she now sat very upright, like a queen on a throne rehearsing the girls in their curtsey.

As always, the trees, lush with late-spring leafiness, blurred the constant rumble from the High Street. The noise was getting worse than ever, now that the big stores were replacing the small cozy Georgian and Victorian shops, which, with their bow-fronted windows and crooked doorways, were disappearing forever. The double-decker red passenger buses roared by every half minute. Tradesmen, driving vans instead of peaceful old Dobbin on a leisurely round, spread their own noise and gas fumes. Soon one wouldn't be able to breathe or hear oneself speak. Mrs. Beauchamp maintained that the noise in her youth, with organ grinders, barrow boys, and clattering carriages, had been just as bad. It was hard to believe.

But the Square gardens still provided their oasis of fragrant quiet.

Maud related, as she had done a thousand times to Hessie, how, when she had been presented, Queen Alexandra had had quite a long conversation with her about her latest portrait, painted by her famous father, but she hadn't heard a word of Maud's answer. She had been almost stone-deaf, poor thing.

Lady Edith and Lady Grizel smiled politely. Hessie sighed with boredom, a fact which Maud did not miss.

None of the girls, Maud thought, had the faintest chance of being the debutante of the year. Edith and Grizel's prospects of a successful season were good enough because of their title, but poor Hessie's were dim. The child simply wouldn't try. She hadn't kept to the diet Maud had so carefully planned for her. Quite clearly, she gorged on buns and cakes after school, the result being a thirty-inch waist. Although none of the three girls was madly graceful, Hessie's curtsey, in spite of practice, was still the most uncertain affair. One could easily imagine her falling flat on her face in front of the queen, probably deliberately. She really was the most infuriatingly difficult girl.

"Try again," Maud commanded in her clear imperious voice. "Imagine that I'm the queen. She's not a terrifying person, you must remember. She's just tremendously regal. And that's a matter of training and discipline. Any of you girls could be the same if you tried hard enough."

Daisy and Honor were there also, and old Mrs. Beauchamp, wrapped in her gray velvet cloak, like an enormous mushroom, sat a little distance away, surveying the tableau through her ivory-handled lorgnette. Edith and Grizel, cheerful round-faced girls like their mother, didn't know how to wear clothes, but they chattered and laughed vivaciously, and even without the mystique of their title they would probably be snapped up in their first season. Hessie, on the other hand, looked as if she were going to the guillotine.

Maud sighed. "Darling, why didn't you put on your high-heeled shoes? Those flat things—no wonder you stumble! Remember, you'll be managing a train and coping with your fan, too."

"If you think I'll ever be regal!" Hessie muttered.

Edith and Grizel giggled, and their mother said placidly, "Oh, Maud, it's not the end of the world if anyone does trip. I should think the queen would rather enjoy it. It must be awfully dull if all those lines of gels are perfect." Daisy had picked up an affected way of speaking. "I remember I stood on the hem of my skirt and thought disaster had struck. Anyway, after my gels' ball Hessie will be more used to society. You've let her sit over her books too much, Maud. Oh, and did I tell you, we're hoping a certain personage might be coming."

"Not the Prince of Wales!"

Daisy nodded smugly. "Certainly his brother, if not him as well. Isn't it exciting for my gels?"

Maud concealed her resentment. "Daisy, I do believe you have designs on the throne! For whom? Edith or Grizel?"

"Don't be absurd, my dear. I only regard this as a social triumph."

"Oh, indeed." Maud's expression was dreamy. "Hessie will be able to tell the young man—whichever one turns up, of course—how once her mother danced with his grandfather."

"Honor," Hessie said in a low urgent voice, "can I come see you later? It's important."

Honor gave her gentle, absent smile. Even for Hessie, she was always a million miles away these days.

"Of course, dear. Come now. But just for ten minutes, because I have a pupil at eleven. Maud, Daisy, I have to go, I'm afraid."

"That girl will wear her fingers down to the knucklebones on her piano one day," Mrs. Beauchamp said querulously. "No wonder Ninian gets out of the house. Well, I warned her when she was Edith's age. I said you can't have a career and keep a man. Thank goodness you two don't care for the piano. What do you do in your spare time?"

"Ride, Grandmamma," said Edith.

"Hunt," said Grizel. "I could hunt every day of the year."

"Good heavens!" said Maud.

"Well, it's better than poring over figures the way your gel does," Daisy said mildly. "That I call quite unfeminine."

"Honor," said Hessie desperately, "I want to run away."

"Of course you do," Honor answered in her quiet voice. "I did, too, at the beginning of my season. But I got through it, and so will you. Then you can be free."

"Mother will expect me to be engaged to John or Marcus at least, and preferably John, since he's the earl."

"And you only want to have your career?" said Honor gently.

Hessie blushed. "Not only that. There's someone I like. I've never told Mother."

"He's not suitable?"

"In Mother's eyes? Oh, goodness, no. He comes from the East End."

Honor's face seemed to close.

"Don't tell me any more, please."

"But why? Aren't you interested? I thought *you* would be interested."

Honor met the young accusing gaze with a hint of anguish in her own. "It isn't that I'm not interested. But the fewer people who know about secret plans, the better. Once, with your mother, I knew too much. She's never forgiven me. Now, darling, I have to go. My pupil will be arriving."

"But *Honor—*"

"The sooner you learn to stand on your own feet, the better."

"I won't," Hessie shouted at Honor's retiring figure. "I'll fall on my bottom in front of the queen. If the prince asks me to dance—*if* —I'll stand on his royal toes. I'll—I'll—oh, Honor, you've deserted me!"

So she had to do it alone. Since school was finished and Albie had said nothing about meeting again, she sent him a telegram. "MUST SEE YOU. DESPERATE."

Albie answered, after a long tortured week: "All right, just this once. But it won't work, you know. It will have to be at night because I've got a job. How about seven o'clock at our Lyons next Monday. And what's wrong? Have you tripped over your train?"

Hessie had planned exactly what she was going to say. She had rehearsed it a dozen times. But when she saw Albie waiting outside the familiar café, she did something entirely unrehearsed. She put her face up to his and said breathlessly, "Kiss me!"

"What?"

"Kiss me, you dope."

He did so, tentatively, on the cheek.

"Is there something wrong with you?" she hissed.

"Wrong? With me!" He caught her to him and kissed her hard, pressing her lips painfully against her teeth. She hadn't known that kisses hurt; she thought there must be better ways than this, but the important thing, the totally wonderful thing, was that she hadn't been revolted.

How could she have been, when the lips were darling Albie's? All the same, she had had to be sure.

"What's wrong with *you?*" he grumbled.

"Nothing. I'm quite normal, thank heaven. I've only been kissed once before, and that was so horrible that I had to see that it wasn't my fault."

"So you're making me a guinea pig."

She laughed with the most extraordinary feeling of happiness. "Don't you like it?"

"Of course I do, but it's a bit public here. Let's go down on the Embankment or somewhere."

"Anywhere," she said.

"Cor, what's got into you? Who was this chap who kissed you?"

"Just one of the horrible Sylvesters. The Honorable Marcus."

"One of them chinless wonders!"

"He isn't exactly chinless. He's quite good-looking. If you admire that sort of looks. Albie, will you marry me?"

He stopped dead, staring at her.

"Have you gone off your nut?"

"Far from it. Now I know I don't mind being kissed, I think I might make quite a good wife. So I've decided to sell the miniatures my grandmother left me and buy you a shop—buy us a shop—and we'll live happily ever after, and I won't need to have a coming-out season."

He backed away from her. "You blithering idiot! How much do I owe you already? All them teas. Fourteen pounds one and sixpence. It'll take me a year to pay for them at the wage I'm getting."

"They can't be fourteen pounds. They're only seven pounds, I'm sure."

"You see! You won't even let a chap pay for his girl."

Hessie began to laugh, but her breath caught in her throat. She was afraid she was going to sob.

"Albie, I love you!"

"Well, I love you, too, but that doesn't mean I'm going to let you keep me."

"But if you don't—how many years will we have to wait to be married?"

"I dunno. About ten."

"Ten! We'll be middle-aged! Oh, don't be so stupid. I never thought you would be so stupid."

"Nor you. You're eighteen, and I'm nineteen. We're minors. Who's going to marry us?"

"We'll get our parents' consent."

"Fat chance."

"My father will agree if I talk to him. Don't worry about that. Actually, I think my mother will, too. She'll be glad to get rid of me. I only embarrass her. Curtsey to the queen! Oh, Gawd!"

His slow, crooked smile began.

"You're beginning to talk like me, did you know?"

"I'm glad."

"Hessie Ponsonby. Honestly! If I tell me mum and dad I'm marrying someone called Hessie Ponsonby, they'll split their sides."

"Let them."

"You're only doing this to get out of this coming-out lark. That only lasts a few months. Marriage is forever."

"I know." Hessie slid her hand into his. "That's why I want it."

"You are a funny—" He peered at her in the half-dark. "Truly, are you serious?"

"Only if you love me."

His fingers clenched hard around hers. After a while he said, "How much do you reckon those miniatures are worth?"

"Four or five thousand pounds."

"*What!*"

"That's what the insurance company said. We could go somewhere in the country and have a magnificent shop, couldn't we?"

"With a quarter of that. You could keep your favorite ones, couldn't you?"

"Yes, but I won't need them, you know. I only needed them to make up stories about when I was lonely or unhappy. And that's absolutely all over."

After the short arid ceremony was over, Horace took Maud's arm and led her out of the registry office. They followed the bridal pair, Hessie wearing the simple dark-blue dress and coat she had chosen herself, clinging proudly to the arm of that thin, gaunt, common boy, who Maud simply could not believe was her son-in-law. He was a good lad, Horace said. Horace, of course, would be on Hessie's side. But even he was looking a little bewildered and unhappy at this moment. Probably because he hated to part with his daughter, who was going to live somewhere in the depths of the West Country and run a village store. It was all so crazy and so typical of the sort of disappointment Hessie had been all her life.

Not that she could help it. One had to be fair. This was the way she had been made, this strange cuckoo daughter—dour, dogged, stubborn, gauche, suburban. And so impossibly young to be a bride, to be Mrs. Albert Smithers.

There had been no use in opposing her. Maud had realized that at once. When Hessie had stated calmly that she would run away and live with Albie if her parents refused their consent to her marriage, Maud had pointed out that running away was a foolish and mistaken thing to do. And she ought to know since she had done it once.

"But that was different, Mother," Hessie said, with her uncomfortable perception. "You didn't really want to elope, did you? Your heart can't have been in it, since you allowed yourself to be brought back. I would never be brought back, unless I was carried unconscious on a stretcher."

"Hessie, for someone who's usually so sensible, you do have the most melodramatic ideas." Maud was irritated by the feebleness of her answer. But she had been startled. Hessie seemed to have realized something that just possibly might have been true. If she had actually succeeded in marrying Guy, she would have been torn with remorse for Papa's pain for years afterward. No, perhaps her heart hadn't been in it.

All the same, she did genuinely want Hessie's happiness, and if it lay with this odd young man with his shabby gaunt intensity, then she had to accept the fact. Anyway, Horace would not have allowed her to do otherwise. He said flatly that Hessie had enough sense to know what she wanted and young Albert Smithers seemed a good reliable lad, never mind his background.

"And you needn't think I'm going to wear a train and walk down the aisle at St. Margaret's Church, Westminster, Mother. We don't want a wedding at all. We're going to be married in a registry office."

"Good gracious," said Maud faintly. "Whatever would Nanny have said?"

Mercifully, after the young couple's departure, the bridegroom's parents couldn't, or wouldn't, stay for any false celebrations. Mrs. Smithers, as thin, gaunt, and knobble-boned as her son, reminded Maud of Cora's mother. And that was another world. The father was a gray, quenched person, awkward in his best suit. They both obviously regarded their son's good fortune with uneasiness and suspicion. Hessie alone they might have accepted, but Maud, even though she had worn her simplest dress and flattened her rich hair beneath a little green velvet toque, was still much too sophisticated for them. They said they had to catch the next bus back to Limehouse. Their eldest daughter was living at home and expecting a baby at any minute. Her husband was one of the growing list of unemployed, so it was lucky Albie was leaving home. It made more room.

Again Maud thought of Cora's mother and, inevitably, of Cora and Evangeline. How strange that her own daughter should bring back memories of that bittersweet past. Was Evangeline married? One hoped her wedding hadn't been a furtive affair like this one.

"Well, that's over nicely," Horace said, jerking Maud's arm.

"Nicely? I don't see how you can be so smug about it. Hessie will be talking Cockney before she knows it."

"She'll enjoy having a shop. Keeping the accounts. Besides that, they're in love. Didn't you see the way they looked at each other?"

"Yes, I did," Maud admitted reluctantly. "I suppose, to tell the truth, I didn't really want to see it. It made me feel such a failure."

He glanced at her quickly.

"With Hessie," she added.

"Stop thinking of yourself for once, Maud."

"Am I always doing that? Is that why I failed? She just never seemed to be my child."

Horace gave a short sigh.

"Never mind. Not all women were meant to be mothers. Nor, because you've had a baby, does it mean you automatically love it. Well, are we going home? It will be a bit flat, won't it? Would you like to go somewhere gay for dinner?"

"Gay?" she said doubtfully.

He sighed again. "All right, let's go home."

*   *   *

That decision proved to be a mistake. Although Hessie had never been a conversationalist, she had been the third person at the table, the buffer between two people who had nothing more to say to each other. Faced with a wilderness of nights like this, Maud chattered resolutely.

"Can you imagine the gossip in the Beauchamp house tonight? Well, at least Hessie's the first off this season, even if it's to the wrong man. Do you realize it's Edith and Grizel's ball next month? I always think of them as Honor and Daisy over again. I must be getting old. At least we can save the cost of a ball gown for Hessie, if that's any comfort to you."

"Frankly it is. Frankly I don't know how I would have paid for the season you were so determined she should have."

"Oh, Horace, not the threatened depression tonight, please."

"It's not threatened, it's here. Didn't you hear Smithers say his son-in-law was out of work? Well, he's not the only one. There are thousands now, and there are probably going to be millions."

"I'm not ignorant, Horace. I know about the soup kitchens. But there have always been soup kitchens. It's one of the failures of our social system. And neither you nor I can pretend to alter that."

Maud rang the little silver bell for Ada, ending the conversation.

"Will you have a sweet, or just cheese?"

"Neither, thanks." Horace had gone to the sideboard to pour himself another large whiskey.

"Darling, aren't you drinking rather a lot tonight?"

"Yes."

"Is this because of Hessie? You are upset after all."

He swung around. His face was mottled red.

"Of course I'm upset. I'm going to miss her like hell. But I'm upset about other things, too. Maud, the truth is I'm in a jam. Will you help me?"

"A jam?"

"I'd have talked about it sooner, but I decided to wait until Hessie went. Maud, I've got to have some money."

"Oh, money!"

"Don't say it in that flippant way. The trouble is you've never understood about money. You've had what you wanted without effort. You haven't any conception of what it is to go without."

"Have you?"

"No," he said grimly. "But I will have if you don't help me now."

Maud's face went cold with surprise.

"You're not suggesting again that I sell Papa's pictures?"

"What else? You're sitting on a fortune, and I'm in serious trouble."

"Sell some shares, can't you?"

"I haven't any to sell."

"Don't be silly, Horace. You're a stockbroker. That's like saying a grocer has no sugar, isn't it?"

"Not exactly. I—but why should I explain? You're obviously not interested."

"I am interested, but you know I never did begin to understand the stock market or figures. We need Hessie for that."

"Yes. We need Hessie. And I need twenty thousand pounds rather quickly."

"Twenty thou— Horace, you're joking!"

He shook his head. "Not joking."

"But what have you been doing? Oh, don't be ridiculous! You can juggle something. Besides, if I put the pictures in Sotheby's, they wouldn't come up for sale for at least two months."

"You could sell them privately. A dealer would organize that."

Maud's eyes were full of pained reproach.

"Horace, you don't begin to understand me, do you? After all these years, living with me and knowing what those paintings mean to me, you can still ask me to sell them because you have made some bungle. It all just sounds sordid to me. You must find another way out."

Horace refilled his glass, spilling a little on the tablecloth. His hand was shaking. He must be drunk, Maud thought. That was why he was talking so wildly.

After a long time he said, "Very well. I'll find another way out. I only asked. You've never actually given me anything, have you?"

"I gave you Hessie."

"True. Sorry."

"And now she's gone, so you're being maudlin. But you agreed to this totally unsuitable marriage. You said she would be happy in her little shop, balancing her accounts each night. And going to bed with that beanpole. Not that I dislike Albie. Indeed, I rather like him, though not as a son-in-law, I admit. But he dislikes me, and Hessie isn't overfond of me, so that's it. End of a chapter. And you sit there and talk about money."

"Sorry," said Horace again. "I shouldn't have brought up the subject tonight. It's only that it's rather urgent." He stood up. "If you'll excuse me—"

"Where are you going?"

"To the office. I want to look at some things."

Maud sat for a while at the dinner table. She petulantly lit a cigarette, then put it out. This was ridiculous, feeling so badly treated because her daughter, whom she scarcely saw, and her husband, to whom she had so little to say, had both deserted her. What had Horace, with his eternal pessimism, been trying to tell her? She truly believed that he only wanted an excuse to get her beloved pictures out of the house. He looked for ways to hurt her. He was justified, of course. She was a terrible wife. She wasn't a wife at all. Then let him agree to divorce her. Living like this, now Hessie had gone, was going to be intolerable for them both.

Of course, one would have to persuade Ninian to divorce Honor, too.

Their love affair had, over the years, fallen into a pattern, two afternoons a week and an occasional evening, as well as the social occasions when they met in somebody else's house and played their private game of pretending not to like each other. It was an absorbing game, full of forbidden pleasure.

Did it deceive anybody? It didn't matter.

Would they have been happier had they been married? Sometimes Maud fretted and longed for conventionality, sometimes she was completely contented with things the way they were. Occasionally she was horrified at what she was doing to Horace and what Ninian was doing to Honor. But her conscience had always been an intermittent affair, and if Ninian had one, he managed to overcome it.

Tonight, however, alone in the house except for Ada and Cook in the basement, Maud found the situation unbearable. She sprang up from the table, ran up the stairs to her bedroom, snatched a coat, dabbed some perfume beneath her ears, and was off.

Sometimes Ninian was dazzled by her unexpected visits, some-times angry. She wouldn't forgive him if he were angry tonight, when she was so lonely and unhappy and deserted.

The one thing she hadn't expected was that he wouldn't be in his flat overlooking the river. She let herself in quietly and found the place in darkness.

A curtain moved in the breeze through an open window. The room was full of the familiar river smell. Lights twinkled from an-chored boats, their reflections quivering in the dark water. The breeze was cool on Maud's cheek as she sat disconsolately on the window seat. Where was Ninian? At some gay party she hadn't heard of? She imagined him surrounded by admirers—he was quite famous now—and angry tears came to her eyes. She felt suddenly lacking in confidence, an unpleasant and unfamiliar sensation. What if she had told Ninian she had to spend this evening after Hessie's wedding with Horace? He shouldn't have believed her. He should have waited here, knowing she would come. What was a love affair, if he couldn't anticipate her actions? He was growing in-sensitive. She would tell him so.

Was he growing tired of her?

That thought was not to be endured. Maud decided she wouldn't wait after all, in the hope of Ninian's returning here after whatever party he had been to. She would go home, go to bed, sleep, forget this thoroughly unpleasant day.

Before going to bed, however, it was calming to go up to the studio, switch on all the lights, and look at the precious paintings.

Portrait of Maud Lucie. *Circa* 1894, 1896, 1899, 1900, 1903, 1907, 1910 . . . Those brilliant long-ago days, when the sun shone all the time, in fields with her apron full of wild flowers, in the studio in her famous peacock dress, at the Royal Academy with her hand tucked in Papa's large warm loving one, riding on Papa's shoulders high above the crowd at Ascot or the Derby, solemnly pouring tea at the Ritz, hearing again and again the loved booming voice, full of inexhaustible pride. "This is my daughter, Maud . . ."

How could she part with any of these portraits, virtually her own flesh and blood, even if Horace's threat of impending bankruptcy was true? Which, of course, it wasn't. The pictures were her re-membered paradise, of which poor Horace was jealous, that was all.

The fight over them would have to go on forever, because she never intended to give in.

All the same, Maud turned from the youthful faces on the wall, putting her hands over her own forty-year-old face.

What am I growing into? she wondered.

Chapter 20

ADA SAID afterward that she had heard footsteps pacing about in the early hours of the morning and had gone upstairs to see who it was. She thought the master or the mistress might have been taken ill. Instead, she saw a light in the studio and found the mistress up there alone. It was after two o'clock.

She looked cold and was shivering, although she said she was perfectly all right. She was only walking up and down, thinking.

"I never saw her look like that," Ada said to Cook, and Mrs. Beauchamp's Pritchett, and others who had gathered to gossip. "She was sort of hunched up and thin, and all those pictures were blazing around her. She was like a ghost at a feast." The excitement had stimulated Ada. She was using wild metaphors.

"She was more upset than we thought at losing Miss Hester," Pritchett suggested.

"No," Ada declared solemnly, "she had a premonition."

"Had they quarreled?"

"Not so that I heard. Sometimes the master lost his temper and shouted, but he was ever so quiet last night. Sad. He was the one who was going to miss Miss Hester."

For it was Horace, not Hessie, who had finally run off. Or disappeared.

When Ada had found Maud, lost in her reverie in the studio, they both had thought that Horace was home and in bed. It wasn't until morning that Ada had found the note, propped conventionally on the mantelpiece in his bedroom, and had brought it to Maud.

It said simply:

My dear Maud,

It wasn't your fault that you couldn't love me. I have never blamed you for that. But I do blame you for your selfishness and lack of charity. I fancy you may not enjoy those pictures of your father's so much when you have nothing else.

Horace

"But what does it mean?" Maud cried, although she had enough sense not to show Ada the note. She didn't want this related around the Square.

"His bed hasn't been slept in, madam."

"I know that. You've told me several times. He's simply stayed away for the night."

"He's never done that before, madam."

"Well, it's time he did," Maud said.

She wasn't really alarmed. She was half-resentful, half-amused. But angry that he had left that melodramatic note so that the servants would talk.

She made herself wait until ten o'clock before phoning his office, so as to give him plenty of time to return from wherever he had been.

His secretary, Miss Collins, a middle-aged, efficient, garrulous woman, answered the telephone.

"Mr. Ponsonby isn't in yet, Mrs. Ponsonby."

"Oh! Isn't he rather late this morning?"

"Yes, he is. We were just wondering what had happened to him. Perhaps the traffic's bad. What time did he leave home, Mrs. Ponsonby?"

Ten o'clock last night after an argument . . . Maud said calmly: "He was staying away for the night. That's why I wanted a word with him."

"He never said anything to me about going away. He left here at midday yesterday for the wedding. Did it go off all right, Mrs. Ponsonby?"

"The wedding? Oh, yes."

"Perhaps he was celebrating," Miss Collins suggested absurdly. "Alone?"

"I didn't say alone. I mean—" The woman was abruptly flustered. Maud's fingers tightened around the telephone.

"What exactly do you mean, Miss Collins?" she asked coldly.

"Nothing. Really nothing. Shall I ask Mr. Ponsonby to ring you when he comes in?"

"Yes, do that."

Maud put the telephone down and stood staring at it accusingly, as if it were responsible for her feeling of utter indignation and fury.

How dare Horace leave a letter like that, carefully planned to make her feel full of guilt and remorse, when all the time he had been having an affair with some woman. Playing the injured innocent, swearing that he loved her eternally and sneaking off to his little typist or whatever she was. Probably he was short of money now because he had spent too much on his mistress. She must be the demanding sort. *If you won't marry me, I must have a flat. Or a house. Or a mink coat . . .* And Papa's pictures were to pay for *that!*

Horace, with his bowler hat, his rolled umbrella, his little protuberant stomach, his soft pale hands and pale face, his solemn humorless eyes.

Was there really some woman in some discreet bed-sitting room, nursing a passion for him? It wasn't possible. He just wasn't the kind of man to inspire passion. He should have been the solid reliable father of ten children. He should never have had the bad judgment to marry someone like her.

But having done so, Maud thought furiously, and having refused to let her go, he might have had the decency to remain faithful. Now everyone was going to know. The tittle-tattle would go around the Square. She would have to start divorce proceedings to save her pride.

And if Honor refused to divorce Ninian—or Ninian refused to leave Honor?

Maud clenched her hands. How dare Horace put her in this humiliating position!

It was half past eleven, and the telephone was ringing again.

"Oh, Mrs. Ponsonby, have you heard anything?"

Maud was haughty. "What should I hear?"

"About Mr. Ponsonby. He hasn't turned up yet, and he has an

important meeting in ten minutes. It just isn't like him to be late for a meeting."

"Everyone can do something unexpected sometime, Miss Collins."

"Not Mr. Ponsonby. I've worked for him for fifteen years, and he never once—"

"Then it's time he did whatever it is," Maud interrupted testily.

"But aren't you worried, Mrs. Ponsonby? I mean, he was upset about losing Hessie. I know. He said he didn't know how he'd get on without her."

In spite of her irritation and indignation, Maud felt her first stirring of uneasiness.

But Horace would never do anything desperate or melodramatic. He would conform until the end of his life and then die whatever death was ordained for him, correctly and with the least possible fuss.

Poor Horace . . .

Now one of her periodic attacks of remorse and softheartedness was making tears prick in her eyes. She was beginning to feel bad about Horace, and she hated that. Was he really in some kind of trouble? He surely couldn't have meant it about needing all that money. He had cried wolf so often that one took no notice.

She rang the office again and asked to speak to Mr. Dobbs, Horace's assistant, who had been with him even longer than Miss Collins. A little colorless man with eyes sharp behind pince-nez.

Yes, Mr. Ponsonby had been worried, he agreed. For the last few days he had behaved quite strangely. Mr. Dobbs didn't know exactly what business he had been doing; he would have to study the books, but it was end-of-account day today, and he knew Mr. Ponsonby had some big purchases of shares to settle.

"Isn't there enough money?" Maud asked uneasily.

"I'll have to go into it, Mrs. Ponsonby."

"What happens if you can't settle?"

"You mean if clients' money has been tampered with!" Mr. Dobbs said incredulously. "But I assure you Mr. Ponsonby—"

"Just tell me what happens."

"There could be a prosecution for embezzlement. The firm could be hammered on the Stock Exchange."

"Hammered! That sounds like a form of medieval torture. Like being put in the stocks."

"It doesn't happen often," Mr. Dobbs said unhappily.

"I'm sure it doesn't. What a ridiculous conversation we're having. Will you ask my husband to telephone me as soon as he comes in?"

She waited restlessly. There was nothing to be alarmed about, of course. Maud's feeling of pity had see sawed back to one of anger. Horace was being deliberately mysterious in order to give her a fright, to punish her for her unchanged intention never to sell the paintings.

Perhaps his wretched mistress was pregnant.

But he would never behave in this mysterious way, even then. He was so tediously, boringly predictable.

Oh, to hell with him! She would go to Chelsea.

No, she wouldn't. She wanted to punish Ninian a little. He hadn't been there last night, at a time when he might have expected her to need him. ("Don't be a hypocrite, Maud," she could hear him saying. "You won't miss Hessie a tenth as much as Honor will. And don't complain. Honor deserved your daughter, since you've taken her husband . . .")

"Oh, madam, you've scarcely touched your lunch," Ada said.

"I'm not hungry."

"It really is queer about Mr. Ponsonby, isn't it? Do you think you ought to get in touch with the police, madam?"

"Good heavens, no. What a thing to suggest."

Ada stood her ground. "I only thought it such an unusual thing, him going off like this. He always was so methodical about his movements, wasn't he?"

"Don't talk in the past tense."

"I beg your pardon, madam."

"You're saying 'was,' as if he were dead."

"O-oh, I didn't mean that, madam!"

"I should hope not. You'd better take the afternoon off and cheer yourself up. What with Hessie gone and now this, the house is like a morgue."

"I would never leave you, madam. Cook and I—"

In spite of the way Ada's stolidity irritated her (would she have put up with an erratic mistress for so long if she hadn't been stolid?),

Maud suddenly found herself crying. Whatever was the matter with everybody?

"It's all right, Ada. Don't *fuss!* I was only thinking of Hessie and that absurd young man like a starved tiger—I really can't think what my father would have said."

Twice during the afternoon Miss Collins rang. She had cherished the hope that perhaps Mr. Ponsonby had arrived home, suffering from a sudden illness or lack of memory or something. Then Mr. Dobbs rang, and Horace's mysterious absence was no longer a joke. If it had ever been that. It was something much more sinister.

"I find we owe twenty-four thousand pounds odd—I haven't the exact amount—to be paid today, and our bank account, unfortunately, seems to be in debit. In other words, Mrs. Ponsonby, our checks won't be honored."

It was nice of him to use the plural, Maud thought numbly. He was a good employee, loyally associating himself with his employer's troubles.

"We aren't the only ones, Mrs. Ponsonby," the anxious voice said in her ear. "The depression has been hitting a number of firms. When the market began to fall badly six months ago . . ."

But Maud was no longer listening. She was thinking that the depression, Horace's old bogey, had come face to face with him at last . . .

It was then that she knew she must take Ada's advice and go to the police.

After that, all the distasteful publicity began. "Mystery of vanishing Kensington stockbroker" . . . "Stockbroker husband of famous beauty missing" . . . "Missing stockbroker accused of fraud" . . . "Rumors that firm to be hammered."

A week, a whole interminable week later, the inevitable tragic conclusion came. "Body found in Savernake Forest, Wilts, believed to be that of missing London stockbroker . . ."

Horace Edward Ponsonby, aged forty-eight, had died of exhaustion and exposure, the doctors said. It wasn't that the weather was so inclement, but there had been a cold snap over the last few days, and he was not young enough or fit enough for sleeping out.

Flabby, they said. And he didn't seem to have eaten for some time.

The night wind blew cold through the beautiful high trees in the forest. In the day they were bird-haunted; at night the tawny catlike owls floated from tree to tree.

The dead man had not taken his life in the conventional sense. There were no drugs, no alcohol, no gunshot wounds. He simply seemed to have lain down in the wet bracken and died.

The body had been found by two small boys looking for rabbit burrows.

Hessie cried for hours. But she had her fierce-eyed young husband to comfort her. Once, Maud thought, she would have hidden away and done all that desperate sobbing secretly. Now she simply put her head on Albie's shoulder and cried openly.

Strangely, this, even more than her last visit to Ninian's empty flat, made Maud feel completely alone.

"Hush up, love," Albie growled tenderly, and Maud, feeling she was intruding on some sacred rite, retired to her bedroom. Why should she feel so frantically jealous of Hessie's happiness, when she could have the same tender attention herself?

Or could she?

There had been something guarded in Ninian's voice when he said, "I don't think Honor would stand in our way now, Maud. Give her a little time, shall we?"

Honor had already had six years. Did she need more time?

"Do you feel you have to do the gentlemanly thing?" Maud asked in a prickly voice.

"I don't understand you."

He didn't either. His sensitive face was perplexed. But he looked old. Iron-gray hair, deeply grooved cheeks, tired eyes. His tiredness gave him an ascetic look that was rather out of place, come to think of it. Maud wanted to laugh. She would have, but for the agony of loving that serious, sensitive, monk-like face too much.

"You'd hardly want to marry a murderess."

"Maud!"

"It's true. I regard myself as that."

"Then I share your guilt."

"No, no, no!" she said violently. "It's nothing to do with you. It's entirely me and my hardheartedness and meanness. I was the cause of Horace's death. But I truly didn't know he was in this trouble. He'd been pessimistic so often. Even if I had known—"

"You would have sold the pictures, of course."

"No! No, I wouldn't. That's the terrible thing. I know about myself."

"I think you would, Maud."

"Oh, I will now, of course. Enough of them to pay off every penny of Horace's debts. That's retribution, if you like. But it's taken his death to make me do it. And even now, I feel the most awful resentment."

She stood at the window, looking out over the mournful river. There was no sun; the gray mud, the water, and the sky met.

When Ninian put his arm around her shoulders, she said again, "It's too late. You're fifty and I'm over forty, and we've had the most wonderful, the most perfect love. But after this it will be spoiled. Don't argue, Ninian. I know it will be. I'll remember Horace and you'll remember Honor, and we'll go on hating ourselves. Perhaps each other."

"Maud, dearest. You're talking like bad fiction. Not one of your characteristics."

"I can't bear watching Hessie and Albie. They're so young and naïve, and I want to slap them. That's me. That's what I am."

"Maud, I'm thinking of going to live in Paris."

She was quiet suddenly, looking at him.

"Alone, if you don't come."

"Leave Honor?"

"Yes. Staying with her has been a mistake. A mistaken kindness. I'm still devoted to her, but I can't go on letting her pretend all the time. We've got to start being honest."

"Running away."

"Nothing of the kind. Only changing my surroundings before I get too old."

"I simply can't imagine living anywhere but Melbury Square."

"If you're on again about it being your parents' home—"

"I'm not on about anything. Anything at all."

The dusk was growing, the evening taking on the negative color of the sky and the river. His arm around her almost cracked her bones.

"Maud! Your face is like a white star."

"Now who's talking fiction?"

"Maud, come to bed."

She turned to him agonizedly.

"But don't you see, that's the thing I really don't believe I can do any more." Her shoulders drooped sadly. "I'm awfully afraid I believe in ghosts."

The sale room was crowded. The sun shone through the skylight onto the stacked paintings, some old dim scenes on dark canvases in dusty crumbling gilt frames, some full of color and light, as in the James Lucie series of portraits of Maud.

The auctioneer, impassive, bland, his little hammer in his hand, his eyes missing no smallest movement, recited his litany.

"Lot Number 26. I am bid two thousand pounds . . . two thousand five hundred . . . two thousand eight hundred . . . three thousand . . . three thousand five hundred . . . four thousand . . . five thousand—the bid is against you, sir— Have I any bid above five thousand? Going at five thousand . . ."

The little hammer cracked smartly.

Hammered in the Stock Exchange . . . Was that how the macabre procedure sounded? Maud wondered. Was it as agonizing as this?

"It's awfully pretty, though," a woman whispered.

"Terribly sentimental."

"How couldn't it be, when the artist was painting a child who looked like that? They say she's still quite lovely, although she must be middle-aged now."

"*And* she's supposed to have driven her husband to his death."

"S-sh! She might be here."

Thirty-four thousand pounds. She could pay Horace's debts, stay in her house, and keep her three most precious pictures—the peacock one, the Worth dress, and the Faces.

The finest examples of James Lucie's work, the experts said. In another twenty or thirty years they would be worth double or triple their present value. A good insurance for her old age. She was wise to keep them.

"I would wither away and die without them," Maud murmured,

wondering even now how she could go on living with the many empty spaces on the walls, in a house so denuded.

"Mother, what will you *do?*" Hessie demanded with her familiar intensity.

"Do? Why, I'll stay here, of course. What else would I do?"

Hessie looked relieved. Had she been imagining Maud weighing out pounds of sugar in her absurd shop?

"I'm not decrepit yet or incapable of living alone. Anyway, I won't be alone, since Ada wants to stay. Cook will have to be put in a home. I'm arranging that, before we're all accidentally poisoned. So off you go with your husband and be happy."

"Mother! You just pretend to be so cheerful, don't you?"

"Everyone pretends most of the time."

"Then go see Honor, because I know she's terribly lonely now that Ninian has gone to live in Paris. I can't think why he's suddenly being so cruel." Hessie's chin stuck out. "Albie and I intend to make a great deal more of a success of our marriage than either you or Honor did."

(Ninian had written: "Dearest Maud, Lovely Maud, I'm here and I'm not going down on my knees to you, but I truly believe you could lay your ghosts in Paris. Or find some much more graceful and beguiling ones. We could watch for Marie Antoinette in the Luxembourg Gardens . . .")

"Yes, I'll go see Honor," Maud said absently.

She didn't, however, for when the next day Honor saw her coming down the street, she deliberately crossed to the other side and turned her unhappy face away, refusing to look or speak. It was the only implicit accusation of Maud that she had ever made.

Time passed, the world moved on; there were new sensations, new tragedies. The whispers about poor Horace Ponsonby and his death by misadventure, as the coroner called it, lingered longer in Melbury Square than they would have in other places only because of his widow.

She had always been a talking point, for her dash, her style, her unashamed outrageousness. Now, still beautiful and only in early middle age, she was reputed to be growing a little eccentric. She rarely left the house. It was said that after the sale of her precious pictures, she refused to have the darker places on the walls, where the pictures had hung, papered over. So her famous peacock studio was marred. Not that it mattered at present, for the Sunday afternoons had stopped with her husband's death, and no one but Maud —and Ada (who told the story)—ever saw the room.

However, no doubt it would soon be refurbished and reopened. Someone as vital as Maud Ponsonby couldn't stay in eclipse for too long. Although there were rumors about the reason for Ninian Spencer's departure, too. If the rumors were true, Maud had suffered a double loss. She must be going through agonies of remorse, poor thing. One had to sympathize with her, for, even if rather wicked, she was so picturesque, like a gorgeous butterfly. The Square was very dull while she remained in her cocoon.

Maud's tragedy, however, could not stop the progress of the summer and the season. The Sylvester girls' coming-out ball was a great success. Or so their mother said. She called on Maud to tell her about it.

"It's all so different from our day, Maud. The gels won't stand for chaperones. I left them to come home by daylight, if you please. They said they had had eggs and bacon and champagne and strawberries for breakfast."

"Yes?" said Maud languidly.

"Not that I was worried about them. Edith and Grizel are sensible gels. I'm going to have more worries with Melinda. She's the wild one. But one has to make allowances, because of the way she was born after her father was dead. I'm sure a baby is affected by that. Oh, and we did miss Hessie last night. At least, Marcus did, I know. He always had a soft spot for her. He said she had more sense than all the other gels put together. But I don't suppose Hessie ever forgave him for that night they fell in the fountain. Gels of that age are so sensitive. But it's a pity she wasn't there last night. The Duke of Kent danced twice with Grizel. He is *so* good-looking. The prince himself didn't come, but he's so in demand. He can't be everywhere, can he? And, Maud, what's gone wrong between you and Honor? She won't say, but Mother thinks it's something to do with Ninian's extraordinary bolting. Had you anything to do with that?"

"No, I only killed my husband," Maud said in her weary voice.

"Oh, for heaven's sake, don't be so doomy! It isn't like you a bit. Why don't you pull back the curtains? Sitting here in the gloom like a goldfish in a bowl."

"It's peaceful. If you had been through what I have, you'd want quiet and gloom, too."

"Well, you can't spend the rest of your life doing that, can you? Actually, it isn't so bad being a widow. I ought to know. I have lots of fun. I keep it from the young, though. They think because you're forty, you're dead, though unfortunately not buried."

Daisy gave her exuberant laugh. She was growing, if possible, more garrulous and noisy and plump and highly colored. The supreme confidence she had acquired from having married an earl and being the mother of an earl had become too overbearing. Maud found that she almost preferred Honor's standoffishness.

"And you really needn't fret so much about losing your pictures. I know more than one family that has had to sell heirlooms to pay for their gels' season. Times are terrible. After the season's over, I intend to work in the East End in a soup kitchen. All my friends are doing it. You might think of that yourself, Maud, instead of sitting here moldering away."

"Yes," said Maud. She knew all too well about the soup kitchens, the queues of hungry, the unemployed, the sour smell of poverty. The whole situation, she felt, belonged uniquely to Horace. This was Horace's depression, and he was not here to see it. "Yes, perhaps I might."

"He didn't love me, I knew he never loved me," said the girl in the beige coat, with the beige-colored face and the nicely rounded figure, sitting so astonishingly in Maud's drawing room. "He only needed—well, to be frank, Mrs. Ponsonby, he only wanted to go to bed with me."

"Love's an overworked word," Maud said helplessly.

"Do please forgive me for coming, Mrs. Ponsonby," the girl went on, wringing her hands painfully in her lap. "Because I did love him, and I had to know why—I mean why he wanted me."

"Have you found out?"

"No. At least—"

"Come on, Miss Cobley. You're not shy. If you had been, you wouldn't have come here."

"Well, then—if you insist—I think it was that he felt comfortable with me. He was quite a simple man, and seeing you—"

Maud was silent.

"Oh, Mrs. Ponsonby, I haven't offended you!"

"Of course you've offended me," said Maud harshly. "By being here. By existing. What do you want?"

"Nothing, Mrs. Ponsonby. Really."

"You must have come for something."

"I suppose it was to see you—what you looked like. I grieve so much for him. I thought it might help—I really don't know why I thought that." The ridiculous creature was crying. Maud sighed in exasperation. If Horace had had to go to bed with someone, and of course he had had to, having the most frigid wife in the world, he might have chosen someone more decorative. Although he might just possibly have had enough of decorative women . . .

Maud rang the bell. When Ada came, she said, "Make some tea, Ada. Be as quick as you can."

"It might surprise you," she said to the girl pressing the genteel scrap of lacy handkerchief to her eyes, "that I grieve for him, too."

At the beginning of the next spring, when the mornings were getting lighter and Maud's tree in the gardens was putting out fresh green buds, the invitation came from Holland House.

Lady Ilchester requests the pleasure of Mrs. Maud Ponsonby's company at a White Ball . . .

It was more than twenty years since that other ball, when, drunk with champagne and youth and high spirits, Maud had danced in the gardens in the early morning and met Guy Beauchamp.

Another age. Her lost paradise . . .

She left the thick white gold-embossed card on the drawing-room mantelpiece because Ada liked seeing it there.

She came home from a long exhausting day in the East End, of brewing and handing out cups of poisonously sweet tea and washing dishes, and looked with incredulity at this echo of the luxurious past. She hadn't worn smart clothes, much less a ball gown, for so long. Each morning she put on a sensible gray coat and skirt, quenched her hair beneath a close-fitting cloche hat, and set out by bus for the sad gray streets, the grimy outstretched hands, the hollow faces.

A ball—music, gaiety, perfume . . .

Maud's attack of conscience was going on much too long for Ada's liking. Old Nanny had related how once she had shut herself in her room for days because of a disagreement with her father. Strong-minded, was Miss Maud. She did everything so thoroughly, whether it was having a good time or punishing herself for some misdeed.

But her self-inflicted punishment had gone on for long enough now. It was getting a bit boring. Only Ada's habit of loyalty made her able to stand the quiet house.

"You ought to go to the ball, madam," she said.

"Don't be fanciful," said Maud.

It was a very grand affair. As the shining black Daimlers, with royal standards fluttering, swept through the big gates leading to Holland House, people gathered on the footpath and leaned out of windows to watch.

His Royal Highness, the Prince of Wales. Their Royal Highnesses, the Duke and Duchess of York. Her Royal Highness, the Queen of Spain. The Maharaja and Maharani of Jaipur. The Duke and Duchess of Norfolk. The Duke and Duchess of Devonshire. The prime minister, the Right Honorable Stanley Baldwin and Mrs. Baldwin. The Earl and Countess of Rosebery. The Earl of Deepford and his fiancée, Miss Caroline Mansfield. The Lady Edith Sylvester and the Lady Grizel Sylvester and their brother Lord Marcus Sylvester. The Countess of Deepford . . .

All the ladies wore white, like angels.

The cars disappeared up the long drive, beneath the deep dark trees, and it was pure imagination that one thought one could hear the grinding of carriage wheels on gravel and the clopping of horses' hooves. Or have the sensation that one's hand was pressed by Papa's, proudly, as an onlooker exclaimed, "Look, there's Maud Lucie! 'Course you know who she is. The debutante of the year."

Hallucinations, Maud thought, pulling her hat further over her eyes. Not that anyone was likely to recognize her. Tall, thin, her hands stuffed in her pockets, her pale triangular face a blur in the dusk, she could have been any anonymous passerby catching a glimpse of the unfamiliar world of the rich and privileged.

Why had she come out here? She really didn't know. She walked back to the Square, to the trees fragrant with their spring leaves, to the quiet dew-silvered gardens, to the lighted windows in the pleasantly austere houses, to the sound of Honor's piano.

Everything was the same. Nothing was the same.

BOOK III

MAUD AND EVANGELINE

Chapter 21

THE TELEPHONE had not rung for so long that when it did so Maud sprang up, dazed. She thought the sound was a fire engine going past. Or perhaps another disturbance made by those horrid large Russian children, sons of minor embassy officials who had come to live on the opposite side of the Square. They whistled and shouted and made a great deal of noise, and called one another Dimitri or Stefan or Alexandrei. It was all so foreign, and not a bit the way Melbury Square used to be. One hardly dared go out, the streets were so full of strange apparitions, young girls dressed like grandmothers, their boyfriends looking like Tibetan yaks or other strange hairy animals. The whole world except herself, living her quiet solitary life, had gone mad.

Gradually, the incessant ringing of the telephone sank into Maud's consciousness and identified itself. Then there was the hurried stumbling journey on her stiff legs down the stairs to the sitting room, fearful all the way that the sound would stop, and her caller remain forever unknown.

It might be Hessie, of course.

But Hessie, prudent as always, seldom made a long-distance call from Devonshire. If she had done so, she would have had to enter the toll charges on the debit side of her neat account book. She wrote letters instead, once a month or thereabouts. Since Maud never answered the letters or acknowledged the parcels of food (that was Hessie salving her tedious conscience), one could hardly expect more frequent communications.

With a gasp, stumbling over a chair, she at last reached the telephone and snatched it up.

"Who is it?" she demanded.

"Is that Mrs. Ponsonby?"

The caller was a man with a quiet, courteous voice. Vaguely like Ninian's, Maud thought, and her heart gave a jolt.

But Ninian had died long ago, hadn't he?

Hadn't she read that somewhere? Certainly Honor behaved like a widow, but she had done that ever since Ninian had left England to live in Paris.

"Yes, this is Mrs. Ponsonby," she said.

"My name is Shepherd. I'm speaking from Sotheby's. We wondered, Mrs. Ponsonby, if we might ask your advice about a picture we've just received."

Her advice. But no one even remembered she was still alive.

Then her heart jolted again.

"One of Papa's?"

"Yes, it's been sent in as a Lucie. It's signed and dated."

"The subject?" Her voice was dry and breathless.

"A child in a white dress, sitting on a bank. I believe you were probably the sitter, Mrs. Ponsonby."

A white dress. A green bank scattered with daisies. Did she remember sitting for that portrait? There had been so many.

The stiff white organdie had crushed and got smeared with grass stains. No, that was another dress. Another time.

"Perhaps you would be good enough to come in and look at the painting. Or allow us to bring it out to you."

"Why do you want me to see it?"

"Because we have some doubts about its authenticity. It might be a copy."

Papa being copied! He would be livid with anger. She was hotly angry for him.

"Who would find it worthwhile doing that?"

"Anybody. Didn't you know that your father's paintings are bringing up to twenty thousand pounds nowadays?"

"I haven't sold one lately," she said dryly.

"Well, if ever you have occasion to, remember that. Especially if they are portraits of Maud."

She had only three left. Twenty thousand pounds. She seemed to be sitting on a fortune. But of course she would never sell them. Even if she were as near starving as Hessie thought she was . . .

"So could we ask your opinion, Mrs. Ponsonby?"

A touch of her old tartness returned.

"I thought you people knew everything."

"Not everything," said the voice gently. "In this case, we have divided opinions."

"Then you'll have to bring the painting out here. I'm too old to travel."

Bond Street, Piccadilly, Burlington House, the Royal Academy took quite half an hour by hansom cab with a fast horse. Of course, one traveled by taxi nowadays. But the traffic was so bad. It terrified Maud. She scarcely dared cross the High Street, especially at the corner where William Holman Hunt's widow, daft and eccentric, had been knocked down and killed. And that was years ago, before all the fast cars and trucks hurtled past. She only crossed the street when she wanted to walk in Holland Park, which wasn't often, since Holland House had been bombed and burned out during the last war. And all the artists' houses in Melbury Road and thereabouts had been turned into flats, and no one thought of William Holman Hunt or Luke Fildes or Lord Leighton or George Frederic Watts anymore.

The times were devastatingly changed, and not at all to Maud's liking. She could hardly bear the green glades, the nightingale-haunted woods of Holland Park, thronged with all kinds of vulgar people, the old house a shell (which sometimes gave forth strange hollow echoes), and the foreign students who occupied the recently built student hostel, walking through the Dutch gardens and the orangery, dropping their irreverent litter.

Maud's wandering thoughts came back to the present. Imagine Papa's pictures being so valuable that someone might even be copying them! The intriguing knowledge made her feel suddenly sharply alive. She was looking forward to the visit by the Sotheby's man. She would know instantly, by instinct, whether this picture was a forgery.

She must tidy herself. Where should she receive her visitor? The drawing room? The dining room? Her own small sitting room? The studio, if he didn't mind her slow progress up the stairs?

None of these rooms had seen a guest for a long time; consequently, none had made contact with a broom or a duster. It seemed such a waste of energy to go about doing housework just for herself. Besides, she had never been taught how, any more than she had been taught how to cook. It would have been out of the question to do anything so ambitious as having guests to dinner. One could hardly feed them on boiled eggs or on one of Hessie's tins of Irish stew. Besides, five courses had always been the minimum. That may not be so nowadays, but those were her standards. It was better to do nothing at all than to lower them.

In any case, since old Mrs. Beauchamp had fallen dead, in the act of waving her umbrella furiously at the German bomber that had dropped the bomb on Holland House, she had had no friends.

However, the man from Sotheby's would not need to be fed. One had only to tidy one's appearance and receive him in the little sitting room, where the light, owing to the ivy growing over the window, was quite dim. In this light, her hair still looked red, not the old vibrant red, but the color of late autumn leaves—faded, dry and dusty. It was still luxuriant, too. She was able to twist it into a heavy coil and secure it with pins. Then she dusted powder over her face, hung her fake Georgian turquoise necklace around her neck (the real one had been sold to a pawnbroker long ago), and threw a fringed Indian silk shawl over her shoulders to hide the shabbiness of her dress. (How could she go shopping in those great stores in the High Street, with their crowded lifts and escalators, and where did one find a clever dressmaker nowadays? Such as Monsieur Worth or even timid hardworking Miss Lavender? In any case, what would she do with a new dress?)

The shawl smelled musty. Or was it the room that still, stubbornly, held Mamma's fragile ghost? It seemed as if the cobwebs in the corner gave out a faint aroma of lavender water and stuffiness.

All the same, when she had finished dressing, Maud was pleased with her appearance. When she held her head up, she looked interesting, rather grand. A person of importance, as she had always been.

* * *

It was shattering to look at the portrait, because of the memories flooding back. Now she remembered that day so well. They had come by carriage to Barnes Common, bringing a Fortnum and Mason's picnic hamper, as well as Papa's painting equipment. She had been seven years old, and Papa had given her a glass of champagne with her pâté de foie gras and cold chicken. Consequently, she had been flushed and sleepy when he had begun to paint. He had caught her look exactly, the drooping eyelids, the rosy mouth, the slightly mussed red hair. He had called the picture "Windblown." It had been a wild success and had been sold to some rich manufacturer in Yorkshire.

In whose house it still was as far as Maud was aware, for she knew at once that this was a fake.

How did she know? young Mr. Shepherd persisted. She must base her certainty on some facts, other than intuition.

He switched on all the lights he could find, illuminating the dusty room. He was a young man, deeply interested in his job, and excited by the opportunity to meet the legendary Maud Lucie, who had so uncompromisingly retired from the world. It was certainly difficult to identify this skeleton-thin old woman, with the raddled-looking face, the heavy hair falling out of its pins, and the bizarre clothes, with the glowing child in the portrait.

She obviously did so, however, for her strange green eyes glittered. "I remember it all now," she said. "My father had given me champagne, and I was almost fast asleep. But this is certainly a copy. Oh, it's clever. The artist has talent. Whoever he is. But look at the fingers. Papa never painted carelessly like that. Every bit of his detail was meticulous. His hands were always particularly good. And look at those tendrils of hair. Half-finished. The artist is mean with his paint. It's too thin and has no quality. The whole thing is an outrageous fake, Mr. Shepherd. How long has it been in existence?"

"We don't know. Certainly, if it's a recent piece of work, the artist has known how to age a canvas."

"Where did it come from? Isn't that the clue?"

"It came from a small so-called antique shop in Westbourne Grove, whose owner purports to have discovered it. In the usual attic. She's a little deliberately vague."

"She!"

"Yes, a young woman. A Miss Evangeline Winter."

"Evangeline!" said Maud, on a long breath.

The young man looked at her curiously.

"Do you know her?"

Maud's hands were pressed to her breast. She could feel her heart thumping beneath her spread fingers.

"Know her? Indeed not. At least, if I do, she must be over sixty. You said young, Mr. Shepherd."

"She is young. I saw her myself. I'd say early twenties. Attractive. Reddish hair."

"Red hair!" Maud breathed. Abruptly, she sat down.

"Are you all right, Mrs. Ponsonby?"

"A little startled. Oh, for no reason I have to explain to you," she added rudely. She gathered herself together. "What do you intend to do about this young woman? Prosecute her?"

"Goodness me, no. We'll simply tell her we believe the picture to be a forgery and therefore can't offer it for sale."

"But she'll have to be stopped. She can't go about copying Papa's work."

"She, Mrs. Ponsonby! You don't think this is Miss Winter's work?"

"I must have her address. I'll deal with this myself."

"Really? But . . . I'm not sure . . . about divulging—I mean, if you're going to accuse her—"

"Don't stutter, young man. Give me the address."

"Well, I suppose there's no reason why I shouldn't. I must say I'd be interested to hear what comes of your investigations."

"You won't," said Maud.

"Sedge!" called Ginny. "I've just had the oddest letter."

"Okay. Be with you in a minute. I've got something rather nice here."

"What?" Ginny asked, coming through the doorway that led to the room at the back of the shop.

"George the Third tankard. Who's your letter from?"

"Someone called Maud Ponsonby. She says she's heard I'm interested in James Lucie paintings, and if I'll come see her at her house in Melbury Square, she can show me three particularly good ones." Ginny pushed the long, thick hair back from her eyes. "What do you think that's all about?"

"Haven't a clue. Will you go?"

"I'm curious. How does she know about me?"

"I'd be careful, love. She might be a friend of someone at Sotheby's."

"That couldn't matter. They only refused to sell my picture. They even sympathized with me for being had!"

Sedge gave his attractive, jaunty smile. He had eyelashes half an inch long. Whenever they lay on his sallow cheeks, Ginny's heart turned over. A smile and a pair of girlish eyelashes, and she had fallen in love. Otherwise, he was thin, hollow-cheeked, starved. When he was contemplating some new idea—and he had plenty of those—his eyes were hard, secretive, emotionless.

He was a will-o'-the-wisp, a fly-by-night, and she adored him.

Barry Sedgewick, known as Sedge to his friends, Sedgie to her in her most loving moments.

"What shall I do, Sedge?"

"I don't know. Melbury Square. Isn't that rather posh?"

"In Kensington. Very posh."

"It could be an idea to get into that house. Might be packed with valuables that this old dame will sell for a song."

"I'd thought of that, too."

"Maud. That name seems to ring a bell."

"'Come into the garden, Maud . . .'" Ginny said reflectively. "Don't tell me she's of Tennyson's generation. Sedge!"

"What's the matter, love? Are you having one of your intuitions?"

"I've been struck by lightning. Maud is the name of the sitter in all those sentimental child portraits my grandfather painted. This must be the Maud."

Even Sedge was unwillingly impressed.

"Good God, could she still be alive?"

"She probably could. She was only Edwardian, after all. That's not fighting the Battle of Waterloo, or anything. She'd have to be about eighty, of course. My grandmother used to talk about her. She said she was the most beautiful person she had ever seen. But of course, her father absolutely ruined her. He gave her everything and then wouldn't let her have the ultimate thing."

Sedge's thin black brows lifted.

"And what is the ultimate thing?"

"Love, of course."

"Oh, my Gawd! Couldn't she have found that for herself?"

"She could, but her judgment got all messed up or something. She was always half in love with her father."

"Incestuous! Those naughty Edwardians!"

"Sedge, if this is Maud, I've got to go see her."

"Then go. But take my advice."

"What's that?"

"Human antiques don't fetch money, but their possessions do. Take a good look at what's in the house."

"Yes," said Ginny thoughtfully. "Although—"

"Are we making contact, love?"

The brilliant eyes beneath the sweeping eyelashes melted her. She swayed toward him.

"After all, you're entitled to them if they were your grandfather's, him disowning you."

"Not me. He never knew me."

"Then you add up the bill for your mother and your grandmother. Compound interest."

"Sometimes I think you think of nothing but gain. Filthy lucre."

"Most of the time I do," he agreed amiably. His hands felt for her breasts. They held them hard, hurting. "Not all the time. Now leave me to get on with my modest George the Third tankard. When you come back, if you don't bring a James Lucie original, at least bring a Tang horse or something."

"A genuine Tang horse in this dump?"

"Well, we have to get out of this dump, don't we? Or have you lost that letter from the landlords?"

"Oh, Sedge, I counted on my James Lucie to pay all that back rent."

"Well, it's not going to, is it? So go see Maud."

Punctually at four o'clock, the doorbell rang. Hastily patting her hair, pulling her shawl straight, Maud looked toward the front door. Don't hurry. Don't look too eager, too nervous. The girl might be an impostor. Or she might be ugly. Papa would never have tolerated an ugly grandchild.

But it was nice that she was punctual. She had good manners. She had had a nice voice on the telephone too, with no trace of Cora's Cockney accent. She had said she would be delighted to come see Mrs. Ponsonby's James Lucie pictures. She had always admired James Lucie as an artist. That was why she was so deeply disappointed to find that the painting she had come by was only a copy. She should have been able to guess that herself. But she hadn't had too much experience. Mrs. Ponsonby was an authority on this artist's work?

Maud had smiled to herself, keeping her secret. The girl was clever. She liked that. Devious perhaps? She was less happy about that. But she could scarcely wait for the moment of recognition.

She opened the door to the late-autumn sunlight and the tall slender girl with the luxuriant lion-colored hair on the doorstep.

"Miss Winter?" she said. "Evangeline?"

"That terrible name. Everyone calls me Ginny. How do you do, Mrs. Ponsonby."

Maud stood back, motioning her to come in.

"My mother's name was Evangeline," she said vaguely.

The girl's face lit up most beautifully. She actually wasn't very pretty. She had freckles and a blunt nose, and the hair that streamed onto her shoulders in the current fashion (the Pre-Raphaelites would have loved this fashion) was a very watered-down red, but she did seem to have the most essential thing, animation.

"Then you *are* Maud!" she cried.

Maud was disappointed. She had wanted to make that dramatic announcement herself.

"Aren't you being a little familiar?" she said stiffly.

"I mean the Maud of all those glorious paintings. My grandfather's paintings."

"Ah! So you are going to make that claim."

"But it's true. Sir James Lucie was my grandfather. My grandmother's name was Cora, and she was a servant—why, in this house, I suppose."

"I have lived here for more than sixty years," Maud said enigmatically.

"Well, your father seduced my grandmother, and she had this baby called Evangeline, who was my mother."

"Was!" The cry of pain escaped Maud before she could close her lips.

"She died several years ago. She was really quite old. I was born when she was over forty. I was an afterthought. My two brothers were a good deal older than me."

"You have brothers?"

"Had. They were both killed in the war. I never knew them. I was supposed to be a comfort to my parents."

"And were you?"

"My father died before I was actually born. I did love my mother, though, but she had too many ambitions for me."

"Ha!" said Maud. "That's a word I'm familiar with. Why are we standing here? I have tea ready in my sitting room. Come this way. Later I'll show you the house."

"And the paintings?"

"Be patient, my dear." The endearment, like the cry of pain on hearing of Evangeline's death, escaped her also. She seemed to have lost her self-discipline.

She had taken great trouble with the tea, ordering Fortnum and Mason's special blend (she still had an account there, seldom used), also a rich dark fruitcake. But to her distress, all the good Royal Worcester cups and saucers seemed to be cracked or chipped. She hadn't noticed that before, since she so rarely entertained. Mamma would never have permitted tea to be served in chipped cups.

But there was no alternative. At least the silver tea service was undamaged, even though she hadn't been able to polish it as it should be polished. It had come from Mamma's family and was genuine, hallmarked, and crested. She noticed the girl looking at it and was pleased that she appreciated things of quality. The tray, however, was an old kitchen one. She simply hadn't been able to find a decent one, or a well-starched and ironed tablecloth. But she had dusted the mahogany table carefully. Fortunately, in the dim light filtering through the ivy-shrouded windows, the faded and frayed blue silk coverings of the chairs and sofa didn't look too disreputable. She hadn't noticed things like that herself for years.

"So your mother wanted to bring you up properly, did she? Did you have a season?"

"A what?"

"A season. Don't you know what that is?"

"You mean all that coming-out lark? Blimey, no!"

A little vulgarity? Disappointing, but not to be wondered at.

"Sorry," said the girl, instantly aware of her disapproval. "I catch Sedge's expressions."

"Sedge?"

"My boyfriend."

"Oh."

"He hasn't had my advantages, he says. He ran away from school." There was a twinkle of mirth in the blue eyes. It was so exactly Papa's twinkle that the shock was a sword through Maud's breast.

"And what were your advantages?"

"Oh, my mother saw that I got into a good grammar school, and I was supposed to have been properly educated. Anyway, I thought all that being-presented-to-the-queen stuff was over long ago."

"I believe it is. I'm out of touch. I know Daisy deplores it for her granddaughters. She has a brood of heifers. But of course, you don't know who Daisy is. The dowager Countess of Deepford. She's really grown grander than the queen herself these days. And she was only the daughter of a penniless major in the hussars. I never bother to see her. Nor her sister, although she only lives three doors away. Honor and I are the veterans of the Square, you know. We never speak."

"Why not?"

"Oh, an old quarrel. A very tedious affair. If one lives too long, one finally quarrels with everybody. How is your tea?"

"Lovely."

It wasn't. It tasted musty. How dare Fortnum and Mason's send her musty tea. But perhaps it wasn't the tea but the teapot, which, she remembered now, she hadn't washed out. It couldn't have been used for twenty years. Well, a little dust wouldn't hurt them.

"So you say you are Papa's granddaughter."

The girl leaned forward. "Look at me. Don't I look like him?"

"How do you know what he looked like?"

"I've seen photographs of him. I thought he looked terribly attractive. I'm not surprised my grandmother couldn't resist him."

"My mother was an invalid."

The frostiness in Maud's voice had to be acknowledged.

"How sad! Did she lie on a couch and pine away?"

"In this room. And took forever doing so."

Maud's unexpected change of mood from frost to sardonic humor bewildered, then amused, the girl. Her lips twitched. So, presently, did Maud's own, and suddenly she was laughing as she hadn't for years.

"Ginny," she said. "It sounds strange, but I'll call you Ginny. There was only one Evangeline for me. I adored her."

"My mother! But how—"

"When she was a very small baby. Then Cora took her away and took a piece of my heart as well. I always meant to find her one day. But I was prevented—by one thing and another. It would do no good, they said."

"Who were they?" Ginny asked, quite gently.

"People you don't know. They thought they were being wise. Perhaps they were. Since here you are now."

Something strange was happening in the dim room. Both women sensed it.

"Yes, here I am," said Ginny, a little uneasily. "You were going to show me the pictures, Mrs. Ponsonby."

"So I was." Maud sprang up energetically. "We must go up to the studio. At once, before the daylight goes. They're best by daylight, although when Papa gave a soiree in the evening, with gaslight, they looked very well, too."

"So you do believe your father was my grandfather," the girl said behind her, on the stairs.

"You fool! Of course I do. From the moment I saw the forgery you had made of his work. It was very naughty of you. And very clever. What did you do it for?"

The girl looked confused only for a moment. Then she looked straight at Maud and said, "Money."

"Ah. Honesty. I'm glad of that." Maud paused on the first landing, waiting to get her breath. "How long have you been painting?"

"All my life."

"Better and better. And where did you see that particular painting? It was one of my portraits, you probably realize."

"Yes, I guessed so. It's owned by an old woman in Yorkshire. I worked for her for a while, as a companion, secretary, car driver, you know the sort of thing. And she had this lovely picture, and I couldn't resist making a copy of it. When it turned out so well, I thought, why not have a joke with the experts and make some money as well. Which I needed fairly badly."

The wide blue eyes, with their outrageous candor, looked into Maud's.

"But when you were one of the experts, Aunt Maud, I guess my little joke collapsed."

"You said Aunt Maud," Maud said.

"That's what you are, sort of. Isn't it?"

"I suppose it is. Odd. My daughter's children call me Gran, which I find ludicrously undignified. Though I hardly ever see them. They're exactly like their mother. Cabbages. Fancy that painting of Papa's being in a house in Yorkshire, where you happened to go to work. That's fate, if you like. Well then, have you caught your breath, ready for the next flight?"

In the studio, with the dying sunlight coming through the big north window, the peacock picture glowed richly, drawing Ginny inevitably to it. She looked at it for a long time. Then she moved silently to the more formal portrait of Maud in the Worth dress and from it to the Faces. She looked at them longest of all.

At last she turned. "Something happened to you between that"— she pointed to the peacock figure—"and these two."

"Yes," said Maud dryly.

"I think you lost your innocence."

"I grew up, you could say."

"Yes. That's interesting. Truly interesting. They're lovely, Aunt Maud. All of them."

"I'm glad you think so."

"And so were you. I'd only seen your child portraits before. You were a celebrated beauty, weren't you?"

"So they said."

"I can believe it."

"I can still sit on my hair," Maud said, with sudden pride. "And it's never gone gray." She pulled the shawl over her bony shoulders and held up her chin arrogantly. All at once she felt the old confidence of her beauty returning to her. It was strange, like being resurrected. She had grown too used to the children in the Square sniggering or shrinking away from her. Someone had told her that they thought her a witch.

Once upon a time a young man had thought her a witch, too. But the comparison had been a compliment then. Did witches age more alarmingly than ordinary people?

Anyway, the children who played in the Square nowadays were rude, badly brought-up, spoiled little animals. Their nursemaids were casual creatures in their short skirts, looking like long-legged dolls. And most of the parents, even the rich ones (and they must be rich because the houses now sold at grossly inflated prices), had careers of one kind or another—films, television, publishing, the stage. They imagined themselves the new elite. Old Mrs. Beauchamp would have put them in their place with a few tart words. Mamma would never have received them.

A hand moved in front of her face. "Hey, Aunt Maud! Where have you gone to?"

She shivered a little. She was getting tired. She wasn't used to company. Her habit of daydreaming had become a vice.

"I do apologize. I'm old. I'm simply too old."

"Are these all you have of Grandfather's paintings?"

Maud looked at the girl sharply, suspiciously. "Isn't it enough? They're three of the finest."

"I somehow thought you'd have more. It was always said that you would never sell his paintings."

"By great effort, by starving myself, I have kept these. The others—that's a long story. One I'm not proud of. But these I'll keep to my dying day. They're my food and drink, my clothes, my warmth." She shot another sharp sideways look at Ginny. "You think I'm a little mad, don't you?"

"No, Aunt Maud. I think you're quite remarkable. And why should you sell your pictures if they mean more to you than physical comfort? I absolutely agree."

"It's not that old precious thing of having two loaves of bread and selling one to buy a lily to save my soul. Oh, no. It's simply that if ever these have to go, I'm afraid Papa will go, too. That's something I simply don't care to face."

And something she had never put into words before. When Ginny nodded slowly, Maud looked at her with the stirrings of a long-unused emotion. Gratitude.

"I believe you understand. My own daughter doesn't. She thinks any form of art is like groceries, something to be sold at a profit. She sold Mamma's miniatures to set up her husband in a grocer's shop. One was a Nicholas Hilliard, too. Can you imagine?"

"She's the practical type."

"She takes after her father."

"Tell me about him."

Maud's face closed. "My dear, it's getting dark, and we haven't all night." She started. "What's that noise?"

"It's only the telephone. Shall I run down and answer it?"

Maud was grasping her shawl about her, her fingers tense.

"But nobody telephones me. Until the other day. No, my dear, I must attend to this. It might be burglars. Sometimes, I'm told, they ring to see if a house is empty. Quickly, help me downstairs."

When at last, breathless, she reached the telephone, a man's voice spoke. Not the courteous one of the Sotheby's man. A rougher one, hard and flippant.

"Is Ginny Winter there?"

"Ginny—oh, just a moment, will you?" She turned to Ginny. "For you. A man." Her voice was accusing. "Who did you tell that you were coming here?"

Ginny had snatched the receiver.

"Sedge! Yes, I'll be leaving in a little while. Yes, I'm all right. What are you on about? In the High Street? Yes, I'll be there. Make it half an hour. Yes, yes, wait until then. You shouldn't have rung me here. I was coming straight home. I can't tell you now; wait till I come."

The telephone banged down.

"Honestly, he's the most possessive person I ever met. He wants to know where I am all the time."

"Your boyfriend?"

"Yes. Sedge."

"You said you were coming straight home. What is home?"

"Oh—two rooms over our shop in Westbourne Grove."

"You're a shopkeeper, too!" Maud cried disbelievingly.

Some tension caused by the telephone conversation that had made Ginny strangely uneasy vanished, and she laughed merrily.

"But not groceries, Aunt Maud. Antiques. At least, we glorify them with the name of antiques, but they're really junk. We can't afford to buy good things."

"And this Sedge. He lives there, too?"

"He's my partner. Silver is his specialty." The lion mane was flung back, with a gesture so like Papa's that again the sword thrust in her breast left Maud struggling for breath. "We live together."

"Do you love him?"

The nod was almost imperceptible, but not the dreamy tenderness in that vulnerable young face. That, Maud guessed, was irrepressible.

She spoke a little harshly. "And he?"

Ginny laughed, gesturing toward the telephone. "You heard, didn't you?"

"Are you going to marry him?"

"We don't talk about that. We like living from day to day, from week to week. We like this voluntary thing. No one's kept in a cage. I can walk out tomorrow, tonight, if I like. So can he."

"What about children?"

"Oh, Aunt Maud! Haven't you heard of the pill?"

"But one day."

"Who knows? Sedge is so restless. He'd make an awful father. Look, I've really got to go now. I'm not under his thumb, but I hate it when we quarrel. I've had a lovely time. Will you let me come again?"

Already, as if she had gone, the house was settling back into the familiar shadows, the familiar quiet that ever since Ada's death Maud had convinced herself she enjoyed. But now, suddenly, she dreaded it. When this rangy creature with her mop of hair, her candid eyes, her glorious vitality left, she knew that the loneliness would be suffocating and intolerable.

"Please!" she heard herself begging.

"Of course I'll come."

"I'll show you scrapbooks, cuttings of old Royal Academy exhibitions when your grandfather and I were always the absolute center of attention."

"I'd like that."

The girl was at the door. It was open, and the cold autumn wind was blowing in.

"And you can tell me why you're selling junk instead of getting on with your painting," Maud called, in a desperate delaying maneuver.

"Oh, that's force of circumstance," Ginny said gaily. "I can't live on tubes of paint, the way you can."

"I'll show you my tree in the Square gardens."

"Yes, I'd really like that, Aunt Maud."

"And we won't mention that naughty forgery, so long as you promise never to do it again."

"That's awfully generous of you, though I refuse to be ashamed of it. It was good."

"It was too good."

"Bless you, Aunt Maud. But now I've got to rush."

The light, quick footsteps went running over the uneven paving stones, anxious for lights, for one of those horrible plastic cafés smelling of coffee they called espresso, for her lover. The dead leaves, swept by the wind, rustled around Maud's ankles. Memory—painful, sweet—filled her mind. She could scarcely bear to go back into the house, filled with ghosts as it was. They hadn't worried her too much in the past. Papa's, golden and dominant, had kept the more troubling ones at bay. But now, in a scintillating flash, she had seen a way of getting rid of them altogether. Even before the sound of Ginny's footsteps had died away, the idea, complete and dazzling, was in her mind.

She had to find writing paper and pen and ink. She would go up to the studio to write the letter. What more fitting place?

It was irritating about that possessive young man, though.

Chapter 22

"So what was the period of the silver?" Sedge asked.

"I don't know. Victorian, I should think."

"Are you sure?"

"I told you I wasn't sure. I'm not an expert, and I couldn't pick up the cream jug and look at the marks, could I?"

"Was it overdecorated?"

"Not exactly. I suppose it could be earlier than Victorian. Her mother came from a stately home. It could have been an heirloom."

Sedge's tongue went around his lips, a sure sign of deep interest and excitement. Ginny knew what was coming. She tensed herself.

"But we're not going to do anything about it, Sedge. I warn you."

"Got you around her little finger already, has she?" he said blandly.

"Nothing of the kind. She's only old and alone, and if I didn't know her from Adam, I'd still stick up for her. I simply don't believe in cheating helpless old women."

"You didn't say that about Miss Fosdyke."

"She wasn't helpless. Far from it. But Aunt Maud is, in a strange way."

His hand was laid over hers on her lap.

"That's what I like about you. Your tender heart."

His tone was gentle, not mocking. She thought, with relief, that perhaps he wasn't teasing her after all. Or being serious about getting into that house in Melbury Square himself. She only wished she could twist him around her little finger.

But did she? Clever, unpredictable, fascinating, a little frightening. Did she want him different?

"What about the pictures then?"

"Oh, they're really gorgeous. Luscious. I wish you could see them."

"So she's sitting on a fortune."

"That's her affair, isn't it?"

"All right, all right. Don't be so touchy. Going again?"

"To Melbury Square. She wants me to. I want to, too. I want to hear more about my grandfather and things."

"So you should. Blood's thicker than water. I wouldn't mind discovering a rich aunt myself." His voice was still gentle, apparently sincere. "But remember I fell in love with you before I knew you had these grand relations."

Ginny flushed with pleasure. "One mad old aunt? And on the wrong side of the blanket."

"It gives you your style, love. Well, what shall we do?"

"Now? Or—"

"Now, stupid."

"Walk home through Holland Park. I love it as it's getting dark. The trees rustling and the leaves falling."

"Watch it. Your grandfather's showing."

Ginny laughed. "But you should have seen this old woman, Sedge. She was such a sight, I can't tell you. All bones, like a starved molting old bird. Muddly sort of clothes, a shawl slipping off her shoulders, and fake jewelry around her neck. And slits of green eyes and wonderful faded hair. She should have looked a mess, but she looked a real *grande dame*. I'd love to paint her. I'd call the picture 'Witch.'"

"Why don't you paint her?"

Ginny looked up, startled.

"You mean that, don't you?"

"Sure I mean it. You've probably always had a subconscious desire to be descended from a witch."

Ginny laughed again, the queer excitement boiling in her.

"Come on, I'll cook you kidneys and bacon for supper, and you can go out and get some wine. Let's have a party. Candles. Everything."

"Everything," said Sedge in the deep velvety voice that preceded love. He tucked his arm in hers, holding her close against his tough, neat body. "All the same, love, we have to be practical. Agreed?"

"I suppose so."

"It's a hard world for those who don't seize opportunities."

"Okay, okay."

"But not with this molting old bird, Aunt Maud?"

"No," said Ginny stubbornly. "It would be sort of incestuous."

"Incestuous or not, what does this old hermit bird want with a silver tea service, probably George the Second. At least George the Third."

"Sedge!"

He sighed heavily.

"Okay, love. It just happens I'm keen on my work."

Two days later the letter, written in immaculate copybook script, arrived.

My Dear Ginny,

It seems to me a very uncomfortable, not to say unsuitable, arrangement that you should live in two rooms in Westbourne Grove. Some of the worst slums in London were in that area in the last century. My father would have been most distressed to know that a grandchild of his lived in such squalid surroundings.

"They're not that squalid," Ginny muttered. She went on reading.

So I am going to make what may be a surprising suggestion to you. Why don't you come share this house with me? As you must have noticed, it's much too large for one old woman alone. Some of the rooms, my old nurse's and my late husband's, I haven't opened for years. You could have your own quarters on the second floor, and I would never interfere with you or your friends. So long as you don't have noisy parties, of course. This has never been a Square for noisy parties, although it's changing nowadays, like everything else.

However, I mustn't stray from the purpose, the second purpose, of this letter.

I can't tell you how delighted I am that you have such a genuine talent for painting. Papa would have been overjoyed. Not that I could ever expect you to be as good as he was. After all, none of the really great painters were women. But I think you could be very successful—judging from the one piece of your work I have already seen. So why don't you give up what you are doing—selling junk isn't a very worthy occupation for such an attractive girl as you are, and I shouldn't think it has any future—and let me send you to the Slade School for some good tuition? It would be what your grandfather would wish. He went there himself.

As for me, I could hardly believe that such a wonderful thing could happen to me at the end of my life.

Take time to think about this, but do think about it most seriously.

I only add that I think I would prefer you to come alone, although I would have no objection to your lover visiting you, since this would make you happy, and you must be happy. Besides, I would like to meet the young man.

The letter was signed formally, "Maud Ponsonby," but at the bottom was an impulsive postscript:

Do please come! I couldn't bear the disappointment of your saying no. I will sell something—though *not* a picture—to pay for your painting lessons. It is quite astonishing, things we thought so little of when I was a child are now proving to be quite valuable, and this old house still yields up its treasures!

"The thing is," Ginny said intensely to Sedge, "she's never criticized me at all for making that copy of my grandfather's picture and intending to sell it as a genuine Lucie. She simply gives me credit for my skill. I think that's quite wonderful."

"Don't be dumb. It only suits her not to say anything about that at present, while she's trying to get around you. She'll get to it someday."

"Then you don't want me to go?"

"Actually I do."

Ginny, contrarily, looked at him forlornly.

"You'd let me go, just like that."

"Don't be dumb," he said. "I'm not letting you go. I'll be in there, snug with you, before you know it. All that Victorian furniture and William Morris wallpaper. Just my cup of tea."

"Sedge, I said no funny business!"

"There won't be any funny business. The old lady will love it. Wait until I expose her to my charm."

"That's just what I'm afraid you'll do."

"And why not? She can't live that long. She'll make you her heir. We'll wait for that. And give her a bit of fun in the meantime."

"Sedge! You promise!"

"Sure. I can have patience. It's one of my qualities. Hadn't you noticed? Melbury Square!" He grinned. "I'll have to get a bowler hat."

Ginny hadn't noticed his patience. She had always been aware of, and secretly enjoyed, his great impatience. The day they met, for instance—when in the space of two hours they had planned their future.

It had been her twenty-third birthday, and she was feeling old, frustrated, aimless, and lonely. Loneliness was a condition to which she was accustomed. The other emotions were not so constant. Her mother had always said, "Make something of yourself. Don't be like me and Granny. Don't marry too young and find your husband's a stick-in-the-mud and bores you to death. Mind you, Gran did snatch at something with a rich lover, but the times were wrong for that sort of thing. She only got landed with me, and then that brute, my stepfather, who wanted her to slave for him and be grateful to him to his dying day. Marrying him was a big price to pay for respectability. But respectability was such a thing in those days, and she did it for me, she said. She was so scared I would follow in her footsteps she had me married off before I realized what was happening. So I'm saying to you, belong to yourself. You're clever, you'll be pretty enough, and you're lively. I never saw my father, but I suspect you're quite a lot like him. You can get somewhere in the world. Don't let yourself get bogged down in respectability, security, all those dull things. They said my father had mistresses in all the grand houses. He thought himself more royal than the Prince of Wales. Why he wanted to bother with my mother, I can't imagine. Except that she was there, and he was greedy. Anyway, she always told me she never regretted it. It was her bit of brightness to think about in her old age. A person needs something like that."

Certainly Ginny's mother hadn't had much brightness. Married at seventeen to a husky, good-looking young traveling salesman who proved to have no interests but football and beer, she had endured years of frustration and boredom, then tragedy when her two sons were both lost at sea in the last year of the Second World War. By some freakish chance, Ginny was conceived when she thought herself past childbearing. Before the new baby was born, her husband, leaving a pub in his usual intoxicated state, was knocked down by a car and killed. There was no money except the widow's pension and child allowance. Ginny grew up in conditions of the greatest austerity. Finally, she watched her mother slowly dying of chronic bronchitis, aggravated by years of quiet starvation, in order to give the best she could to her child. Her coveted grammar-school uniform, textbooks, a tennis racket, even, on Ginny's fifteenth birthday, when the art mistress told her mother of Ginny's exceptional talent for drawing and painting, an expensive box of oil paints and palette. The child was taking after her famous grandfather. She must be encouraged. She had died before she had seen Ginny's talent blossom or, fortunately, hear to what ends she was putting it. She had once been extremely pretty, animated, and merry. Ginny had never seen this. She had seen only a worn-out old woman, permanently anxious, painfully thin, always choking with her little suppressed cough.

Ginny had no illusions about life. It only gave to those who took, as, for example, her flamboyant rich famous immoral grandfather. She also intended to take. This was her reason, several years later, for going to work for rich Miss Fosdyke, who was known to have a small art collection, including a painting by Sir James Lucie.

Ginny's talent for painting had developed, although she had had no tuition except that of the enthusiastic art mistress at school. It was her only genuine love.

Until she met Sedge.

That was when he called at Miss Fosdyke's, saying he was representing a London dealer. Had she anything she wanted to sell, silver, china, bric-a-brac. Perhaps some old junk in the attic?

Miss Fosdyke might have been old and fragile and uncertain of memory, but she knew what to do with a strange man on her doorstep. She shut the door in his face. She called to Ginny to see that he left the premises. If he lurked about, the police were to be called.

So Ginny followed the neat, jaunty figure of the young man down the path to the front gate and felt his tension. She immediately identified it with her own. One lonely person can always recognize another.

"Hi!" she called softly.

She didn't really intend him to hear, but he had ears as acute as an animal's. She was to find that out later.

He turned, hope flaring in his eyes.

"Are you the daughter of the house?"

She giggled. "Of that old mothball!"

"Then what's up? Following me?"

"She told me to watch you off the premises."

"So you have."

"In another yard or so. The gate's behind you. All the same, it's a pity about that junk in the attics. She doesn't even know what's there."

His hand was on the gate. He regarded her with narrowed eyes.

"How about meeting me for a drink in the local tonight? What's your drink?"

"Scotch. When I can afford it."

He laughed suddenly, a taut, hoarse sound.

"She's so rich," Ginny said. "And she doesn't give a half-penny away. She's planning to take it all with her. Like an Egyptian mummy. She'll have her coffin lined with old-fashioned diamond brooches." She looked at the man with her wide innocent eyes. "I know I don't know you, but that makes it more interesting."

He began the slow smile that she was to come to look for. Even on the first occasion, she guessed it was rare. An accolade to the recipient.

"You're right. It does make it more interesting. See you."

He was gone, and Miss Fosdyke was on the doorstep, making vague movements like a very old fly trying to climb a wall.

"Miss Winter, what were you saying to that dreadful man?"

"I was just telling him he has no right to frighten defenseless women."

"Oh, I wasn't frightened," said Miss Fosdyke. "Just cautious. I was always taught to be cautious about men."

Sedge's drink was vodka. It suited him. It was like himself, innocent on the surface, but sophisticated, with a sharp unexpected impact. Ginny tried a vodka martini, and her head swam. Yet that was fine, that first night, because it reduced significantly the time they took to understand one another.

Sedge was a loner, like herself. That was the first thing to be established. Barry Sedgewick, the only child of a broken marriage. He had begun to go into his shell as a very small boy, when he had first heard his parents quarreling. It had become his permanent retreat when he realized that the last vicious quarrel was about himself. They were fighting for custody of him, not because either of them wanted him, but for the sole purpose of scoring off each other. He had gone through the motions of a normal youth, however. He had even gone to a fairly snob school until, at sixteen, he had run away. He was glad now about that school. It had given him the right accent although in his usual conversation he affected an informal slang. He really could have been working for a Bond Street dealer, or in a famous auction room. His appearance was right, too, the narrow head, the cool eyes, the long chin.

He ought to grow a Van Dyke beard, Ginny said, and he fingered his chin thoughtfully. "Would you like it?"

"It doesn't matter about me."

"I think it does," he said.

But that was after their long discussion about the objects in Miss Fosdyke's attics.

"There's a copper kettle, and a warming pan, blue and white china jugs and bowls that could be first period Worcester. A lot of papier-mâché, trays and tables, and things. And some old paintings which might be something if they were cleaned. Her grandfather fancied himself a collector, but when he died, they found most of his collection was valueless."

"How long ago?" asked Sedge.

"Oh, ages. Forty years."

"A lot of that old stuff has come back into fashion."

"I know. There are bound to be some of those awful Pre-Raphaelites. I do know she's got one lovely Lucie, but that hangs in the drawing room. I've been copying it."

Then the story of Ginny's own grandfather had to be told. Sedge listened with flattering interest. He ordered more drinks—the little dark country pub where they sat on a bench in the corner was ideal for this sort of discussion—and asked her if she could actually paint.

"Yes," she said.

He didn't dispute her confidence. That was what she liked about him.

"I've never had lessons, and only one of my schoolteachers ever praised my work, but I've been drawing ever since I could hold a pencil. Then my mother gave me a box of oils. I simply know I can paint."

"You must make use of a talent like that," said Sedge.

"How? Stand shivering on the Embankment in London?"

"No, we'll think of a better way." (*We*, thought Ginny.) "For instance, I decided I wanted to be a silver expert, and now I am. I challenge anyone to know more than I do. I should be on the telly really."

"Do you have a shop?"

"No. But I intend getting one. I'm just about ready."

Ginny leaned forward eagerly. "That's my ambition too. That's why I keep going up to Miss Fosdyke's attics and looking at all those old dusty things. There's enough there to start a shop. And I know for a fact that Miss Fosdyke never goes up there. She won't because she's scared. She thinks the attics are haunted. Once some wretched pregnant servant hanged herself from a hook in one of them. So now the doors are locked. And if Miss Fosdyke lives for another ten years, as she certainly will, she takes such care of herself, no one would know until her death that anything was gone. They wouldn't even know then, because nobody but me knows what is up there."

"It's a marvelous situation," Sedge said softly.

"Isn't it? I've often thought about it. I've been going slowly desperate lately, stuck in that moldering house. Yet I couldn't bring myself to leave because I thought something would happen." Ginny looked at the taut shadowy face opposite her, and something more than the vodka made the blood surge through her body. She had always known that when she fell in love it would be like this. Suddenly, like a thunderbolt.

He was dishonest. So was she. Or so she intended to be, which was the same thing. Yet from the first moment, they had both been completely honest with each other. She knew that. He had trusted her, and she had trusted him. It was a rare situation for her, and certainly for him. She knew that, too. Fate had sent him to Miss Fosdyke's door.

"Do you believe in fate?" she asked.

"Oh, God, let's be practical, love. Fate isn't always on your side, for one thing. It might be today, and it might not be tomorrow. Let's hear more about your plan."

"My plan?"

"You have got one, haven't you? Cards on the table, love. You've told me about yourself, and I've told you about myself. You say I should grow a beard, and I say in a dress by Pierre Cardin, or perhaps one of the Italians, or without a dress at all, you could look fabulous. But let's be practical right now."

"Well," said Ginny breathlessly, leaning forward, "Miss Fosdyke always goes to church on Sunday evening, and Cook gets the afternoon and evening off. There's only me in the house."

"Don't you go to church, too?"

"Sometimes. If I'm in the mood. But let's be practical, you said. If you could have a small van come up the lane to the back door just after the church bells start ringing, we could have the stuff out in an hour, and I could lock the attic doors again, and wham!"

"Clever," said Sedge.

"You could whiz it up to London and sell it. You'll know the best places to do that."

"Sure I know them. But what about you?"

"Oh, I'd have to take it quietly for a while, just in case there was any trouble. I'd give my notice, say in about three months. You'd have found a shop by then. I could be gathering up some more stuff around here. There are still bargains to be found. Then I'd join you."

"Ginny!"

"Yes?"

"Would you trust me that much? I mean, I could get off with this stuff, and you'd never hear from me again."

"But you wouldn't do that."

"You mean it would never occur to you not to trust me?"

"It occurs to me, but I don't entertain the thought seriously. Don't ask me why."

He studied her face for a long time.

"Then I have to be trustworthy, don't I?"

Chapter 23

"CHRIST!" Sedge swore as he bumped his head on the doorframe. Ginny began to giggle helplessly.

"S-sh! Don't move until I put the light on."

She drew him in, closing the door softly after him. Then she switched on the lights, showing the tiny passage and the small low-ceilinged room.

"This used to be a maid's bedroom. There's another one opposite, and the kitchen's in there. Do you want to see the kitchen? It's absolutely safe. Maud goes to bed at ten o'clock, and her room's on the second floor. She won't hear a thing unless you shout like that again."

"I hurt myself, damnit. This is a bit poky, isn't it?"

"Wait till I get it fixed up. Mind you, Aunt Maud can't understand why I insisted on living in the basement. I said if it was good enough for my grandmother, it was good enough for me."

Sedge peered up the narrow steep stairway.

"Did those poor wretches have to toil up and down that ladder with trays and things?"

"*And* with hot water and buckets of coal. Actually, not food. There's a dumbwaiter in the dining room. It still works. And the kitchen's gorgeous. At least, it will be when I finish with it. I'm going to paint the walls white, and you're going to red-raddle the tiles, and put in a new sink and cooker, and get rid of the cockroaches."

"Hey! You're making this sound permanent."

Ginny tucked her arm in his.

"Could be," she said dreamily. "I love it. I just love it. White frilly curtains for the windows, red geraniums in pots on the window-sills, steps up to the back garden. It's a little private world."

"A basement."

"Perhaps I take after my grandmother, and basements are my natural habitat. Anyway, the main thing is we might have to be here for a year or two, and it's nice to have our own entrance."

"Now you're saying we."

"Wait till Maud sees what a handyman you are."

"We start at the bottom, do we?"

"Why not? When we get to own the house, this part of it, at least, will have been fixed up. Actually, I've been thinking about it, and I believe you could stay here all the time. Maud never comes down these steep stairs. Luckily for us, she has shaky legs. She's been cook-ing, or what she calls cooking, on a gas ring in the dining room. You should see the mess."

"Something more for the handyman to clean up?"

Ginny ruffled his hair. "Sedgie, I adore you."

"Will that bed hold us both?"

"Want to try?"

He pulled her to him and with his tidy but urgent movements stripped off her sweater and unzipped her slacks.

"Don't put out the light. You might have that grandmother of yours tweaking your nose."

Ginny caught back a laugh of pure excitement. She threw her-self on the bed, holding out her arms.

"Didn't know you were scared of ghosts."

"I'm not scared of them."

"Well, that you respected them. I don't know why, but suddenly I feel gorgeously wicked. Abandoned."

"That's your grandmother again. Now shut up."

She knew what he meant. He liked silence. At this stage, he liked their bodies to do the talking. He was a fantastically good lover. For her, at least. She thought she was for him, too. She was abso-lutely certain that in two years he had never once been unfaithful to her.

Tonight, in this small austere room, the presence of Maud inno-cently upstairs and the house full of ghosts, even the illicit creaking of the bed, added to Ginny's pleasure, giving it an almost unbearable edge.

Afterward she lay very still, feeling the fire leave her body, trying to conceal the tears on her cheeks. Sedge was funny, sometimes he liked sentiment, and sometimes he hated it.

Tonight he said laconically, "Have to see to the springs on this bed. You might make that top priority on your list."

Ginny bounced up. "Will do. Actually, you're invited to dinner next week. The fifth of November. They have a bonfire in the Square. Maud thought it might amuse us."

"So I go up the basement steps and in at the front door?"

"That's it."

"And get a look at everything?"

His eyes were brilliant, with their mocking, teasing look. She was never sure what lay behind that particular expression.

"Hands off, Sedge. You promised."

"I'm not allowed to fill my pockets with silver! Not even a salt-spoon!"

She rolled over on him, tugging his hair.

"Actually, Maud's going to ask your advice about the tea service. She thinks that may be the thing to sell to pay my art school fees."

"You want this, don't you, love? This art school kick?"

"It's one of my dreams," she said intensely.

"Why didn't you tell me before?"

"There's hardly been time. We've been so busy."

"Going bankrupt?"

"I guess we'd have got by. What will you do with the shop now?"

"Give it up. Go free-lance again. Find stuff and sell it direct to dealers. No rent, no overhead, no worry."

"No bed," Ginny reminded him.

"That's right." He got up, humming, " 'Remember, remember, the fifth of November, Gunpowder, treason and plot . . .' That's it, love. That's the night I win the old lady over. You watch me."

Maud thought that she could never remember being so happy. Not even when she and Ninian were first in love. Or when she was nineteen and had had that wild spring romance with Guy. But things, even the most shattering events, faded in one's memory.

Which made it all the more of a luxury to be able to indulge in living in the present.

"I'm not dead yet," she said to her reflection in the mirror.

She rubbed rouge on her cheekbones with a lavish touch. Mustn't look too old and decrepit tonight. She was meeting Ginny's young man. Hadn't Mamma or Cousin Harriet known some Sedgewicks? Anyway, it was a name with a good reliable sound, very different from Hessie's Albie, which told you exactly what its owner would be like.

Thinking of Hessie, one must keep the advent of Ginny and Sedge from her; otherwise, she would come charging to London to see that Maud wasn't being murdered in her bed. Hessie had it firmly fixed in her head that in these immoral, lawless times an old woman living alone was an invitation to burglars or worse. Maud got bored with her constant injunctions—to keep the front door on the chain, to lock up properly at night, never to trust a stranger who rang the doorbell.

Well, Ginny was no longer, indeed never had been, a stranger. She was living in the basement as happy as a lark. She was fixing it up, she told Maud. When it was finished, Maud would be allowed down to inspect, but not until the last curtain was hung and the last piece of copper polished. In the meantime, between her bouts of cleaning and painting walls, she cooked meals and sent them rattling up to the dining room on the dumbwaiter. The unaccustomed nourishing food was giving Maud a vitality she hadn't had for years.

When she had done her hair in as near an imitation of Ada's triumphant formal style as she could manage, and had put on the long black velvet gown that she had last worn before Horace had died, and hung the ostrich-feather stole over her shoulders (feather stoles were in fashion again, Ginny told her; she must go to the Kings Road in Chelsea one day and see), she believed that she would make a very satisfactory impression on Ginny's young man.

It was a pity she couldn't find her long doeskin gloves and that her jewelry wasn't real. After Horace's death and all that nightmare of debts, she had had copies made of her best pieces and sold the originals. Mamma's diamonds, pearls, and amethysts and one valuable Georgian turquoise and gold necklace that Papa had given her on her eighteenth birthday had all gone. Now she wore paste, and in a dim light, she was sure that no one would know the difference.

Dinner was at seven so that later they could go into the Square gardens to watch the bonfire. Punctually at fifteen minutes to the hour, the doorbell rang, and Ginny, flying up the stairs from the basement, called, "I'll get it, Aunt Maud."

Then Maud found herself exasperatingly nervous. Supposing the young man didn't like her and took Ginny away.

She could hear low voices in the hall. The sudden explosion of a premature firecracker in the gardens made her jump convulsively. Ridiculous. When had she ever lacked confidence? She needed something to fortify herself, her brilliant-studded Spanish comb in her hair—bother, it was falling down already, she could never pin it securely as Ada had—another ring on one of her thin chicken-bone fingers. Props. Unfortunately necessary now. "When you're old," she remembered Mamma saying, "people look at your jewelry instead of your wrinkles."

But the dim, dusty glass of the mirror told her she looked magnificent. Tall, spare, upright, overwhelmingly feminine.

"Like a tatty old bird about to spread its wings and flap into a dead tree," Sedge said to Ginny afterward, down in the kitchen.

But his manners, on Maud's entrance, were impeccable. And she was delighted with the way he looked. He wore a white frilled shirt under a neat brown gabardine jacket that set off his neat, spare body, which gave an impression of whipcord strength. He had bright, jaunty brown eyes, and his long narrow chin was cleverly edged with a fringe of elegant black beard. He certainly had style, even if it was slightly bizarre. But all the young were bizarre nowadays. It was nothing new, after all. Papa had liked to wear a crimson satin cravat long after cravats were out of fashion because he said it was in character for him. People's clothes should express their personalities.

Of course, there was the possibility, nowadays, that all these oddly dressed young people were hoping their weird clothes would conceal their immaturity and lack of personality.

"Aunt Maud, this is Sedge," Ginny was saying, with a hint of aggressiveness, as if she had read Maud's thoughts.

Maud held out her beringed hand, and the young man promptly

lifted it and gracefully kissed it. Ginny made a slight sound, like a suppressed sneeze, but Maud was charmed and flattered.

"How do you do, Mr. Sedgewick. You look Spanish. Out of a Velásquez painting. A conquistador, perhaps?"

"If I look like that," he answered, in a deliberately casual, flippant manner, "then you must be the chatelaine of a palace on the Grand Canal."

Maud was delighted. She did like someone who could hold a conversation.

"Really, Mr. Sedgewick! How flattering!"

"I'm going to paint Aunt Maud's portrait, Sedge," Ginny said.

Sitting again on the peacock throne in the studio? Could she? Would the memories be unbearable?

"And sign it with my own signature," Ginny continued. "I was very silly when I thought I had to use my grandfather's signature to sell something, wasn't I?"

"Very," said Maud. "But we agreed not to speak of that. And you will have your own style. Isn't that right, Mr. Sedgewick?"

"Absolutely. Ginny's an original, if ever there was one. And clever."

Yes, thought Maud. *And so are you. Sharp. Observant. Amusing. Restless. A little wicked, perhaps. Everyone should be a little wicked. It gives such spice.*

"But you don't trust someone like that, Mother," Hessie would say.

"The children in the Square think I'm a witch," she said irrelevantly, as they sat at the table eating Ginny's delicious meal.

"But that's marvelous, Mrs. Ponsonby. I love witches."

"Ponsonby is a name I always particularly disliked," Maud said. She had already swallowed two glasses of the excellent wine someone seemed to have provided, and her head was swimming. "Why don't you just call me Maud?"

"So will I," said Ginny. "No one ever looked less like an aunt."

"A good witch or a bad witch, Maud?" Sedge was asking.

"Shall we wait and see?" Maud suggested blandly.

Although her head spun, she hadn't forgotten her skill as a hostess. She persuaded Sedge to talk about himself, learning, with deep interest, of his knowledge of antiques. He said he could dispose profitably of anything she wanted to sell. Porcelain, silver, knickknacks. He had his connections. He would see that she got a good price.

"Deducting your own fee, of course," said Maud.

"For you, Maud, I do it for pleasure. Because of what you're doing for Ginny."

"You approve of her taking lessons in painting?"

"I approve of anything that makes her happy. And she is happy. Look at her."

"Yes, I am, Maud," said Ginny, her face flushed, her eyes bright. She looked very pretty. Her hair, tied behind with a velvet bow, showed the good shape of her face. There was a little of Cora's fresh chubbiness. But her eyes and the way she held her head with that confident arrogance were Papa's absolutely.

It was a miracle.

"But have I deprived you of a housekeeper?" Maud asked Sedge.

"You have, but I'm giving up the shop and the flat. Aren't I, Ginny? I'll be traveling a good deal. About England and on the Continent. Have to keep moving to find stuff. When I'm in London, I'll park myself somewhere."

"Perhaps here, now and then," Maud heard herself saying. She was enjoying the evening so much it would be wonderful if it could happen again, frequently. Although she had intended to be much more cautious. Ginny, a blood relation, was one thing. A completely unknown young man, with mysterious "connections," was another.

But when had she ever enjoyed being cautious? Hadn't she then made her biggest mistakes? Such as being so stupidly puritanical with poor Guy on her elopement. He must have died hating and despising her. Horace, too, and perhaps Ninian as well. Ninian, whose grave in Paris she had never seen. And Hessie's attachment to her came only from duty. It was appalling when one added it up. At least let her be reckless, incautious, and loved in her old age.

She saw the two watching her, Ginny frankly eager, Sedge with his secret Velásquez face.

"Do you mean that, Maud?" Ginny asked. "Could Sedge stay here? There's another bedroom in the basement."

"Cook's. Would he mind?"

"As long as Cook isn't there," Sedge answered, and something sparked among them. They all began to laugh merrily.

"Oh, dear," said Maud presently. Her face felt stiff. She hadn't laughed like that for so long. "Cook was here for years. I can't remember how long, but she began to get unreliable in her old age. She either left the seasoning out or put in too much. She once served fish delicately browned in sugar."

"Not really!" Ginny said. "Did you eat it?"

"I had to. Her feelings were very easily hurt. She was afraid she wasn't useful anymore. Who wants to be useful all their lives? How dreadfully dull. Take me, I've never been useful at all. Papa once painted me holding a lily. We had a fresh one delivered by Harrods every day. But the picture wasn't a success. I remember it so well. It was the only mistaken interpretation Papa ever made of me."

"But about Sedge, Maud," Ginny reminded her. "I'd fix up Cook's room for him. He could use the basement stairs. He'd never need to worry you."

For a moment, suspicion flashed in Maud's eyes. It all sounded prearranged. Had they counted on her agreeing? What did it matter? They were young and in love. One should be kind to lovers.

"Why do you both have to live in the basement, like moles in a tunnel?" she grumbled. "At least you must come up and use the drawing room to entertain your friends. Indeed, we all might give a soiree. Wouldn't that be jolly? Although it would have to be done properly, with champagne and smoked salmon and cold turkey, and strawberries and cream, and Cook's very clever jelly shapes. She does one that looks like the Albert Hall. It's always a tremendous success." She stopped uncertainly. Her memory was playing tricks again. The jelly shapes had been for Hessie's parties. And, much longer ago, for her own.

"You're talking too much, love," Sedge said gently.

Maud looked at him gratefully. "It's because I haven't talked for years. I'm like a silly old parrot who's been left with a cover over its cage, and now I'm gabbling without making sense."

"You were talking of selling things," Sedge reminded her.

"So I was. I want you to look at some silver that was my mother's."

"These knives and forks? They'd fetch something. George the Second." Sedge weighed one in his hand. "Nice."

"But we must have something to eat with."

"Woolworths sells quite a decent line of cutlery. Cheap. Never needs polishing. Food tastes just the same."

"Oh, Sedge, it's a pity," Ginny murmured.

"She needs money, doesn't she? She's lucky she's got something to sell. Aren't you, love?"

Maud wasn't entirely certain that she liked his perky too-familiar voice. He was getting a little bossy. But her head was dizzy. She made an effort.

"Woolworths. How interesting!"

"This dinner set looks good, too. What is it? Let me guess. Derby?"

"Crown Derby. How clever of you! But it's only 1920. My husband never liked it, although when we bought it, we thought of it as an heirloom. Heirlooms have to start somewhere, after all."

"You'll need to keep it another hundred years for that, love. Then what about the furniture? I'd make a guess these chairs we're sitting on are Hepplewhite."

"Sedge! If Maud is to sell furniture, it must be something she doesn't use every day."

"Unless Woolworths sells chairs, too," Maud managed to say dryly.

Ginny ended the awkward conversation, exclaiming, "It's bonfire time. Look, it's after eight."

"Goodness me, yes, we must hurry. Mrs. Beauchamp so dislikes unpunctuality." The wooliness that came over Maud every now and then had been heightened by the wine. She really couldn't think at all. Woolworths' cutlery. Would Papa have been incensed or amused? One simply didn't know.

But the bonfire, with flames and smoke swirling into the night sky, was splendid. The cool air cleared her head a little, although at the same time the smell of exploded firecrackers revived other memories. She was able to warn Ginny and Sedge to keep well away from the south side of the Square: that was where those noisy Russians were. They had never been taught manners by good old-fashioned nannies.

She added that there had been a bonfire in the Square every Guy Fawkes Night for as long as she had lived there. The Sylvester children used to come stay with their grandmother especially for it. Marcus, the younger son, had had a fancy for Hessie. If Hessie had married him, she wouldn't have been a countess, but she would at least have had a title, and that still counted in these peculiar times. It would have been infinitely better than being the wife of a tradesman. Her children could have had some sort of a season, even though the old grand days of being presented to the queen were over.

"She enameled her face, you know. I thought she looked like an elderly china doll."

"Who?" Ginny asked.

"Queen Alexandra, of course. That was the year before I planted my tree. Come see my tree."

The light from the leaping bonfire showed clearly the rhododendrons, the syringa, and the tall oak tree standing in a pool of dropped leaves. Maud scuffed among the leaves, making them rustle.

"Would you believe that this great thing grew from the acorn I planted? I love it. It's part of me. I want to be buried among its roots." The light from the bonfire caught her gaunt face, her tumbled hair. "Promise me you'll do that for me."

"But—I mean, for what it's worth—shouldn't you be buried in hallowed ground?" Ginny said uneasily.

"I'm supposed to be a witch, so it's unhallowed ground for me." With a sharp cackle of laughter, Maud moved away. Sedge took Ginny's arm.

"The old girl really is barmy," he murmured.

"No. Don't you be fooled. She only pretends to be."

"You could fool me, then."

"She's a born exhibitionist, that's all. Her memory does wander a little. But not to the extent of her forgetting how many fish knives and forks she has."

Sedge pinched Ginny's arm. "Point taken."

"Come on, you two," called Maud, above the hiss and explosion of fire rockets and the shrieks of children. "I'm tired. Once I could dance until dawn. I actually did, on this very spot. But that was several lifetimes ago. Listen!" She came back to take Ginny's hand and draw her to the gate. "Do you hear that piano? That's Honor. She has spent practically all her life at that instrument. Frustrated, poor thing. She wanted to be a concert pianist, but, oh, no, said her mother, music was only a pleasant hobby, a girl's real purpose in life was marriage. So Honor remained only half a person, and she never made Ninian happy. Never."

"Is she the one you never speak to?"

Maud lifted her chin.

"We haven't spoken for thirty years. I took her husband, and she took my daughter. Are you shocked?"

"No," said Ginny. "But don't you think it would be a good idea to make it up now?"

"Listen!" said Maud. "Did you hear that? A distinct fumbling. She used to play much better."

"Well, at eighty—"

"Eighty-two," said Maud. "The same age as me. It's not that old. We're not dead and buried yet."

"You'll miss her if she goes first," Sedge said craftily.

"Not a bit of it. Good riddance to the old broomstick. Now, you two, you mustn't take away my last quarrel. It wouldn't be good for me. I would feel too deprived."

"You're very up in psychology, Maud."

"I don't know about psychology, but I am up, as you call it, in human nature."

Climbing into bed, laying her creaking bones on the clean sheet (that was Ginny again, she had gone through the house like a whirl-wind—polishing, dusting, washing), Maud thought drowsily that it was like going back to the dear protected days of Nanny, with clean sheets every night, and hot chocolate, and sweet-smelling bath soap. She was glad she had overcome her faint distrust of that strange young man and allowed him to stay. Ginny loved him and had no inhibitions about what love was. So let her, an old woman who had learned a few things at last, approve. She supposed she was making belated amends to Guy. If he knew about it, in heaven.

But she hoped things would be all right for Ginny. He had a cat-like tread, that young man, and a sharp, aware face that missed nothing. Yet she liked him. He had great charm. And Ginny was too sensible to be fooled, even while in the uncritical, unreliable state of being in love.

All the same . . . Woolworths' cutlery. Was it quite the thing?

Maud turned, humping the blankets over her thin shoulders. Weren't a few minor changes, such as cheap knives and forks, better than dirty sheets that she hadn't had the strength to change or wash?

Still a little dizzy from the unaccustomed wine, she dozed, then awoke to vague creakings overhead.

This silly old house, full of ghosts . . . She turned again, and fell soundly asleep.

"S-ssh, Sedge! You'll wake her," Ginny whispered.

"I will not. With all those fireworks going off in the Square. Anyway, she'll be dead to the world by now. I say, look at this chair. Queen Anne, or I'm a canary."

"This was Nanny's room."

"And this was Nanny's wing chair, where she dozed, poor old devil, while waiting for Miss Maud to come home from a party. I could get a hundred for it. And look at that basin and jug, that's worth a tenner. Even the po, God bless my soul! And for God's sake —give me the torch—this is a William Shayer. Look, signed and dated. Now I'd have that any day rather than one of your flamboyant Lucies."

"You haven't much chance of having a Lucie," Ginny pointed out.

"No, but this little dark picture would never be missed, would it?"

"Sedge!"

"Come off it, love. Since when did you pretend to be innocent? You didn't mind taking down old Fosdyke."

"Old Fosdyke doesn't know to this day that she was taken down."

"Lucky for us. And neither will Maud. Have some sense, love. We're only anticipating what we'll eventually get."

"We?"

He grinned, his narrow face full of confidence.

"That's what you've been saying. I don't remember changing our minds about our partnership?"

He put his arm around her waist and felt her subside against him.

But she made a mild protest. "Maud does have a daughter, you know."

"Who she doesn't care a row of buttons for. No, it's you who's taken her fancy. You remind her of her father. There's a Freudian setup for you. I reckon she was in love with her old man. But that's a piece of luck for us. Anyway, look at you slaving for her, cooking and cleaning and washing. Does her daughter do any of that? And look at how your grandfather treated your grandmother. Kicked her out as soon as he knew she was pregnant. You're owed all this, love. You're only taking a bit in advance. And you're not hurting the old girl. You're doing her a favor, being an audience for her. She's the kind that needs an audience. But she'll end by driving you up the wall."

"Don't you like her?" Ginny asked in a prickly voice.

"Actually I do. She's a marvelous character. She should be in Madame Tussaud's. But I'm not letting her turn me soft. And since when would she value a painting by William Shayer? She'd more likely throw it on that bonfire."

"That's true."

"Then let's press on. This is like a treasure hunt. Who slept in the room next to this?"

"Her husband. Horace."

"Poor bastard, was he kicked upstairs? That's one thing I'll bet Maud was capable of."

"It wasn't a happy marriage, she said."

"Obviously." Sedge opened the door, switched on the light, and stood looking. The austere room seemed to please him. He began to laugh softly, pulling Ginny to him again.

"Look at that bed, love," he whispered. "It's virgin territory. Shall we change that state of affairs?"

"Sedge! We're directly above Maud."

"Think a creaking bed would shock her?"

An explosion from the Square gardens made the old house tremble. A brilliant shower of sparks illuminated the room. Momentarily, Sedge's face, with its wicked, merry look, shone out. Then the soft gloom returned and Ginny, suddenly trembling with wild excitement, allowed herself to be thrown onto the hard narrow mattress of the brass-knobbed bedstead, where it was madly titillating to know that poor Horace had spent so many lonely nights.

Were she and Sedge a bit perverted? If they were, she had no complaints. It was a delicious state.

Chapter 24

How was Honor to write this difficult letter?

Yet it had to be done. Her foolish old enemy had to be saved from one more of her follies.

My DEAR HESSIE,

I am sorry that this is not to be my usual letter. I am afraid it will upset you. It upsets me to write it, but I promised to let you know if I were ever worried about your mother, and I am now, very much. It seems that two young hippies (although I confess I have never known the exact meaning of that word) have moved into her house. The girl, I am told, claims to be the illegitimate granddaughter of your grandfather, your cousin in some sort of way, and the young man is her lover.

I must be honest and say that Maud has taken a new lease of life. She walks out every day, which is quite an innovation. I believe, to encourage this, the young pair have given her a Pekinese puppy, so consequently she has to exercise it. She is also obviously having regular meals, as she has lost that starved look I told you about. Indeed, she and the little dog look to be flourishing. Which is all to the good. However, forgive me, Hessie dear, if I am a suspicious old woman, but I simply don't believe that this is all innocent. This couple are up to something. Why should they appear out of the blue like this and begin to pamper and spoil an old woman who can't mean a thing in the world to them . . .

But Maud had always been pampered and spoiled, Honor thought. Was it so strange that it should happen again? She looked weird, a scarecrow, but there was no doubt, that even in gaunt old age, she still had that mysterious essence—charm, style, originality, perhaps simply a superego—that made people admire her and forgive her even her unforgivable faults.

Love her? Honor's fingers clenched her pen. Yes, they did that, too. Knowing Maud, it was possible that she could still attract love, even from such an unlikely source as these two highly suspect young guests. To flatter them with the assumption that they had been invited to stay at Number 7.

Honor began to write again.

Just to put my fears at rest, I wish you would come to London and see your mother. Of course, this is not an entirely unselfish request. It means I also will have the pleasure of seeing you. I have always been convinced you work too hard. Even you, Hessie dear, are not as young as you were. Daisy is planning a visit soon, but this I do not look forward to. She wants to run my house for me and has become very pompous and grand since John's youngest daughter is marrying into a dukedom. What does that sort of thing matter nowadays? But I suppose England will be England, in spite of all . . .

At the end of the letter Honor wrote an impulsive postscript:

The girl certainly has quite a resemblance to your grandfather, a way of holding her head, and her hair is just as long and thick as Maud's was, although not such a beautiful red. But I saw with my own eyes the furniture being carried out of the house when Maud was away walking the dog.

"Oh!" said Ginny, answering the doorbell. "Who are you?"

The stout woman in the tweed coat and skirt and the sensible hat said, "I'm Mrs. Ponsonby's daughter. I'll come in, if you don't mind."

She walked past Ginny into the hall, saying over her shoulder, "I expect my mother is in," and then calling loudly, "Mother! Are you there?"

Maud came, in a flurry, to the first-floor landing.

"Hessie! Whatever are you doing in town? Why didn't you let me know you were coming? You know I don't like being taken by surprise."

"I did that deliberately, Mother," Hessie said, and gave Ginny a long significant stare. "I heard you had guests."

Maud came slowly down the stairs, holding up the tattered hem of her old gray velvet tea gown. Ginny was nagging at her to get a new gown, but something that had lasted thirty years would last another ten, which would be more than enough time for her. Although it would be rather fun to dress up in something new for Ginny and Sedge. They loved it when she talked of her tea gown. "You should be in Carnaby Street, Maud," they said.

And now here was Hessie to spoil it all.

"Yes, I do have guests, Hessie. I would have told you all in good time. Let me introduce you. This is Miss Evangeline Winter. Ginny, dear, this is my daughter, Hester. You're cousins in some sort of way, so I hope you'll be friends."

Nothing seemed more improbable, Ginny thought, taking the stout woman's hand briefly. She stared right back into those pale-blue shrewd-looking eyes and thought: *Maud's daughter!* It couldn't be true.

"And what do you do, Miss Winter?" Hessie asked.

"She's taking an art course at the Slade," Maud answered. "She's wonderfully talented. She's going to paint a portrait of me."

"Mother!"

Maud's eyes glinted.

"Why do you speak in that tone of voice, Hessie?"

"Only that I thought at your age you wouldn't still be vain enough to want your portrait painted."

"Maud has the most paintable face I have ever seen," Ginny said in her clear voice. "Do you want me to make some tea, Maud? Or shall I leave you to talk to your daughter?"

Hessie's mouth tightened. She obviously didn't care for the familiar way in which Ginny addressed her mother. Poor old-fashioned thing, she was out of her depth.

"Yes, make some tea, will you, Ginny dear? I expect Hessie has a train to catch."

"Mother, I've just arrived."

"I know, but you're always in such a rush, aren't you? I under-stand perfectly. Customers mustn't be neglected."

"That's perfectly true, Mother. We have a staff of twelve now. They take a lot of supervision. But I can stay overnight."

"Too generous of you. How is Albie? And the children?"

"Albie is well. So are the children, although they'd hardly care to be called children. George is thirty-eight and Betty thirty-five. Betty's having another baby in the spring, which is so nice, because I think only children are a mistake. I know I hated being an only child. But can't we sit down? I see you have another dog."

The little Pekinese had come snuffling out, and Maud scooped it up, cradling it in her arms.

"Bless his little heart. This is Ching. Ginny and Sedge gave him to me when they heard how much I had adored Han when I was young. But I don't suppose you remember Han. You were only a little girl when he died."

"I remember him perfectly well. He was elderly and bad-tempered." Hessie followed Maud into the familiar dim sitting room. "Now, Mother, what is all this? Is that girl preying on you?"

"*Preying* on me! Whatever do you mean?"

"Well, what's she doing here? And with a boyfriend."

Maud nodded slowly, her face sharpened with anger.

"Ah. So that explains your unheralded visit. You have an in-formant."

"Of course, I have an informant. I wouldn't have come all the way to London for no reason."

"Except, perhaps, to see your old mother."

"But you never want me. You never welcome me." Hessie stopped. The old argument had worn out long ago.

Maud switched on a table lamp and let the light fall on her face.

"Take a good look at me. See if you don't think my health has im-proved since Ginny has been cooking for me. No more of those tins of potatoes." She shot Hessie a malicious look. "As if I were an Irish peasant."

"But, Mother, Albie and I never knew if you ate at all. At least what we sent you didn't need cooking."

"Well, I eat now, if that's all that was worrying you. I have never been so spoiled in my life. And look at this room. Clean as a new pin. For all that she's doing for me, shouldn't I give Ginny some art lessons? Shouldn't she have the chance to be famous like her grandfather? Now don't you say anything against this, Hessie, because I simply won't listen to you."

"When did you ever listen to me?" Hessie straightened herself determinedly. "But this time you must. I'm staying the night, Mother. I'm not satisfied. I'll have Nanny's room. That's if it isn't already occupied."

"Oh, no, they're—Ginny's in the basement. She prefers it."

"I want to see this man, too," Hessie announced.

"Mr. Sedgewick."

"Don't be so formal, Mother. I'm sure Mr. Sedgewick wouldn't understand that language. What's he like? Long hair? Strings of beads?"

Maud gave a peal of laughter.

"Oh, dear, no. Beads are quite out. You are countrified, Hessie. Actually, Sedge is extremely well groomed. He has the most captivating beard. And I'm sure he will be delighted to meet you."

At that moment Ginny came in with the tea tray.

"Shall I pour, Maud?"

"Please, my dear."

"But where's your silver tea service, Mother?" Hessie demanded, eyeing the tray, her voice full of triumphant suspicion.

"Sold," said Maud laconically.

"Sold!"

"I'm sorry if you expected me to leave it to your Betty or your George, but I needed the money. I have been struggling to live on twopence a week for too long. Besides, Ginny and Sedge have been showing me how to enjoy life a little more."

"What else are you selling?" Hessie asked grimly.

"Oh, this and that. A little table silver. Who would have known there was such a demand for old silver? Or that Woolworths has the most practical cutlery for practically nothing."

"Woolworths! You, Mother! Are you catching up with this century at last?"

"Well, I still like to wear a tea gown," Maud admitted complacently.

"Are you going to sell Grandfather's pictures, too?" Hessie asked. Maud's complacency vanished.

A look, full of hostility, passed between the two women, and Maud said stiffly, "You ought to know better than to ask that question. It took me years to recover from the pain of selling the ones I had to, to pay your father's debts. I have only three left. It would kill me to part with them, as you very well know."

Ginny, calmly pouring tea, said to Hessie, "You mustn't worry, everything Maud has spent on me will be repaid when I sell my first paintings."

"Aren't you being optimistic?" Hessie said sarcastically.

"Oh, I know paintings aren't as easy to sell as tea and coffee and things like that. But Grandfather managed to do very well, didn't he? Do you take milk and sugar, Mrs.—"

"For goodness sake, call me Hessie, if you are my cousin."

"I am. That's perfectly true. And I'm also taking good care of your mother. You really mustn't worry."

"Hessie was always a worrier," Maud said. "Weren't you, darling? Do you remember your birthday parties? You used to think those Sylvester brats persecuted you. Did you hear that Daisy's cock-a-hoop about snaring a duke's son? Of course, Daisy always was a dreadful snob. But you're so buried in the country, aren't you? You had a good brain, too. Hessie had a passion for figures, Ginny. So strange. She took after Uncle Lionel, who had a bank and left it all to his dullest niece."

"You're forgetting again, Mother. You mean I took after Father."

"That's what I said. He owed the bank twenty-three thousand pounds, and I had to find it. That's really the beginning of why I have just had to sell my silver tea service," Maud finished triumphantly, and Hessie could only look baffled, realizing that her mother, for all her muddled memories, was as devious as she had always been.

"Sedge," said Ginny into the telephone, in a low voice. "Better not come home tonight."

"Why?"

"Hessie's here."

"Hessie?"

"The daughter."

"Can't I charm her?"

"Not this one. You're not a bloody miracle. Someone's told her about us," she added.

"She's suspicious?"

"You can say that again. But Maud and I are doing a good job." He laughed softly. "Maud's on our side?"

"Absolutely. She's enjoying herself like mad. Hessie's going to sleep in Nanny's room."

"Gawd!"

"I'm not sure how much she remembers. I'll cope."

"I trust you, love."

"I trust you, too. But don't let anyone ring up this evening. And Sedge. I'll kiss your half of the pillow."

"Mother!" called Hessie from the second landing.

"Yes. For goodness sake, what is it now? I'm just going to take Ching out."

"Mother, there's practically no furniture in this room. Where have you put it?"

"What furniture?" said Maud vaguely. "You are a trial, Hessie. How ever did I have a daughter who always counted things?"

"There was a very nice old wing chair in here. Don't you remember, Nanny's chair?"

"Oh, that. I believe it went to be covered."

"But everything in the house is falling to pieces. Why cover Nanny's chair?"

"Because I'm sentimental about it," Maud snapped.

"Then where are the pictures from Papa's room? There are faded places on the wallpaper, showing where they hung. I believe one was by Shaver or Shayer, or something. Aren't Victorian paintings suddenly fashionable?"

"I haven't the least idea, and I've never heard of anyone called Shaver or Shayer. Who is he? How did I come to have pictures by a man I've never heard of? I suppose I got rid of them years ago."

"Very recently," said Hessie. "Judging by the wallpaper."

"That old William Morris wallpaper? Yes, I know it should be replaced. But I'm rather attached to it. Now, Hessie, if you're going to criticize everything, I'd rather you didn't stay. This is my house, and everything in it is mine. If a chair isn't where you expected it to be, it's none of your business. I don't come to your house and accuse you of deciding to make changes, as if it were a crime. I simply don't like your attitude."

"But, Mother, I'm only trying to protect you."

Maud drew herself up regally.

"And what sort of protection do I require from people who love me?"

"Love you! So you do know what I'm talking about? Mother, I never thought you of all people could be so gullible."

"Senile, I suppose you mean," Maud said icily.

"If you prefer that word." Hessie's face was red with distress.

"I don't care for either word. They're nasty words, and if you don't withdraw them, I must ask you to leave my house."

Hessie came heavily down the stairs. "How can I withdraw them when they're true! Look at you, in that dreadful old dress, thinking you still look so grand. Well, you don't, Mother. It's time someone told you. You just look—"

"Mad?" Maud suggested.

"I didn't say *that*."

"No, but I'm afraid you meant it. So we really have grown beyond communicating with one another. Oh, I don't blame you. I blame that woman in Number Nine. She has put you against me ever since you were a child. So go ask her to give you a bed. And tell her to stop interfering in my life or I'll sue her for molestation."

"Mother, Honor—"

"Don't mention her name!" Maud screamed.

Hessie stood silent, pressing her hands to her hot cheeks. Then she straightened her shoulders, tightened her mouth—Albie had taught her long ago not to be so thin-skinned—and said quietly, "Very well. If that's your wish, I will go. It is true that we can't communicate. I should have given up trying long ago."

She retrieved her handbag and her overnight case from Nanny's room and walked heavily down the stairs. A stout middle-aged countrywoman, nothing whatever to do with her, Maud thought, standing rigid to let Hessie pass.

Nothing whatever to do with her . . . Although it was a great pity that Hessie would never know how to be a little frivolous and gay in her old age.

"Ginny," said Maud, "how clever of you to know how much I disliked those dark old paintings! What did you do with them? Give them to the dustman?"

Did the girl's eyes flicker slightly? Did Maud have to believe those outrageous insinuations of Hessie's? Never! Ginny's eyes were as wide-open and innocent as they had always been.

"No, I didn't do that, Maud. I'm too much of a respecter of junk. To be honest, Sedge sold them to someone he knows for a few pounds, and that's what we used to buy Ching for you. I know that's an awfully backhanded way to give a present, but I didn't have any money, and Sedge was pretty short. We did so long for you to have another Pekinese. Actually, I was thinking of myself, too, because I want him on your lap when I do your portrait."

Maud felt tears pricking at the back of her eyes. Imagine these two young things trying so hard to make her happy. If Ginny spoke the truth. And of course, she did!

"Nanny's chair?" she asked casually.

"Oh, that was to be a surprise. Sedge will be mad when he hears it's been spoiled. He thinks the chair is Queen Anne, and it's being sold by auction. We were planning to give you a wonderful Christmas party with the money. We thought we might even have champagne, and smoked salmon and grouse, and all those things you used to have when Grandfather was alive."

Maud couldn't help herself. She was trembling with pleasure.

"But who will we ask? All the people I cared about are dead."

"Sedge and I will find plenty of people," said Ginny gaily. "Nobody old."

"Except me, unfortunately."

"You old, Maud! You'll be the belle of the party. You'll have everyone sitting at your feet."

"I'll wear my peacock dress," Maud exclaimed excitedly.

"Not the one Grandfather painted you in! You haven't still got it?"

"Indeed I have. It's been wrapped away in camphor for fifty years."

"Maud, you're fantastic! Shall we have the party in the studio? You can sit on the throne."

"And don't stint the champagne," said Maud. "That was always Papa's most important rule."

"But, Ginny," she decided to say in the morning, as she was falling asleep that night, "don't you and Sedge sell anything more without asking me." She dreamed delightedly of the Christmas party and in the morning had quite forgotten the admonition she had intended to make.

"She says she's having fun!" Hessie stormed to Honor. "It's her vanity. She simply can't believe that everyone doesn't still admire and love her."

"Then I shouldn't have interfered," said Honor. "It's kinder not to disillusion her."

"Even if these two completely fool her? Well, I suppose she'll have to pay for her vanity in the end."

"Not only in the end, Hessie dear. She's been paying for it all her life. And it wasn't her own fault. Her father made her what she is. And still is. He was a very overpowering man. Vital and radiant, like the sun. He bewitched Maud. I believe nowadays it's called a father fixation. You were lucky he wasn't still alive when you were a child."

"Oh, he'd have paid no attention to me, from what I've heard of him. Honor, how can you still speak so charitably of my mother, when she did that unforgivable thing to you?"

"Took my husband? But she couldn't have taken what wasn't takable. He was. That was my fault." Honor gave a slight sad smile. Then Hessie was pleased to see her face regain its serenity. For a long time after Ninian's departure to Paris and his subsequent death, Honor had looked dreadfully tormented and unhappy. Then, slowly, she had grown serene and quiet, as if, after a long struggle, she had come to terms with herself and life.

"It's all so long ago," she said. "It's not my wish to prolong this stupid quarrel with Maud. But she enjoys it, so I say nothing."

"Enjoys it!"

Honor shrugged. Her face was delicately carved ivory.

"Your mother always wanted life to have drama. She had a great gift of it. It would be very unkind to deprive her of one of her last sources of amusement."

Chapter 25

MAUD had forgotten what she was looking for. She sat on the floor, cramping her old bones, her lap full of half-remembered things. Old dance programs—who were all those young men, Algernon, Bertie, Charles, Ninian, Guy, Hamish Drood, what an extraordinary name! A pair of long kid gloves smelling of perfume, an ivory and lace fan, a green satin hair ribbon, a jester's cap and bells. She remembered that cap: she had worn it at one of her studio parties just after the war—her war, not that later noisy, untidy one when bombs fell all over London.

A shabby red leather dog collar (beloved Han's). A jeweled mask shaped like a butterfly. Goodness, a tiny scuffed baby's shoe. Not Hessie's surely. No, Evangeline's. She remembered that much. She had stolen it when Cora wasn't looking. After all, Cora was taking Evangeline away from her, so she must have a small painful memento. A lock of thick blond curly hair in a little morocco jewel box. Papa's, darling Papa's! She had kept it under her pillow every night until she had married Horace. Even then, it had only been removed when Horace had gently but firmly protested.

She sat back. What was she to do with all these treasures, so deeply personal, so meaningless to anyone else? Suddenly she had an inspiration. She would dig a hole and bury them under her tree. That way she would leave a piece of herself permanently in the Square. Ginny said the Square was unhallowed ground, but a fig for that. She would have to avoid the gardener, Bates, seeing her, of course. He was a cantankerous old fellow who didn't like anyone interfering with his arrangement of the lawns and gardens. ("Miss Lucie, you know you didn't ought to pick my roses." "Oh Bates, just one bud. It smells so delicious. I wanted it for Papa's buttonhole.")

She struggled to her feet, holding up her skirt with its precious burden. Mamma's little trowel that she had used for her window boxes. Where was that? She would take Ching with her. He could provide an excuse if anyone observed her actions.

The ground was damp after late-November rains. The dead leaves crackled like the sound of Nanny's starched petticoats. The earth scooped up easily and allowed her to make a shallow oblong grave. She stood up and shook out her skirts, the little collection of treasures falling into their intended resting place.

A hand was laid on her shoulder.

"Mrs. Ponsonby, whatever are you doing?"

Damnation, it was that cross Bates. No, it wasn't Bates, it was someone else, a gardener certainly, but a stranger to her. Or had she seen him before?

"One buries oneself bit by bit," she said vaguely. "I have taken as little space as possible."

"But what have you hidden there, Mrs. Ponsonby?"

"Hidden? You make it sound like a crime. Is it a crime to bury old memories?"

His eyes told her that he thought she was mad.

Was she mad? A cold shudder went over her. She had to get back to the house quickly, to Ginny and Sedge and their gay youthful laughter. At all costs, one must remain able to laugh.

"But what did you do between your husband's death and now?" Ginny asked as she worked at her easel. "That's a long time. Forty years."

"Papa never talked while he was working," Maud said. She moved her head tentatively. In her youth she had been trained to sit for hours without stirring, but she was really too old now. Her neck was aching severely. She was also a little chilly. There was no warmth in an ostrich-feather stole. She couldn't think why Ginny had wanted her to wear it over her rusty black dress.

"All that cascading black with your hair," Ginny had enthused. "Isn't it marvelous that you haven't a gray hair. And I'm mad about your bones. We'll have Ching on your lap, picking up the color of your hair. This is going to be a masterpiece."

Of course, Maud thought without surprise. Her portraits always were masterpieces.

But what had she done since Horace's death? The years had run into each other and blurred.

"I worked for charities in the East End," she said vaguely. "The East End always meant something to me, after your mother was born there. I was even moderately happy, I believe, although now and then I wondered if I would have been happier in Paris with Ninian."

"Your lover?"

"How did you know I had a lover?"

"Maud, Maud! Someone like you. How couldn't you have?"

Maud examined the small pain in her heart. It had dwindled to almost nothing now. A melancholy, that was all.

"He was a famous writer in his day. I believe his books are out of print now. I asked once. People forget so soon."

"And you? Did you forget him soon?"

Maud pressed her lips together.

"He was buried in a cemetery at St.-Cloud. I always meant to go and see his grave, but I never did." She frowned. "Really, Ginny, you ask too many questions."

"You'll have plenty of time to answer them while I'm working," Ginny said blithely. "I'm going to spend weeks on this portrait. I do want to do you justice. Life is going to be marvelous, isn't it? And why should you make yourself sad, going to see your lover's grave?"

Ginny's face, when radiant, was quite arresting. The imperious air, the stubborn chin, the vitality were all poignant echoes of Papa. Yes, life was going to be marvelous.

"Then the war came," Maud went on, "and I worked in hospitals again. After that I had an illness—the doctors said I'd worked too hard and not eaten enough, but who had at that time? They also said I had had too precocious a childhood, whatever that had to do with it. I had always been too stimulated. Anyway, my illness seemed to go on for a long time, and I got out of the habit of seeing people. Later Ada died. Ada, my maid. Then, luckily, I had a sum of money left to me by my mother's cousin Harriet, who was ninety-eight when she died. She hadn't stirred from her country house for thirty years. I was advised to buy an annuity to provide me with an income so that I could keep this house. Though my income has become ridiculously inadequate now that everything is so expensive. I have had to be most economical."

"But what happened to all your friends?" Ginny asked. "Why have you become such a hermit? Why didn't you go to Ninian in Paris, not when he was dead, but when he was alive?"

"That was a matter of conscience."

"How boring!"

Boring? A little startled, Maud reflected on the word. Had she pretended her guilt over Horace and Ninian all these years? Had it been nothing really but a tedious bore?

"Go on," said Ginny. "Tell me more. Was Ninian a wonderful lover? Illicit love is always the most fun, isn't it? Though Sedge and I"—Ginny gave a small secret smile—"illicit isn't exactly the word for us. We have other ways of making it exciting. If I began to bore Sedge, I'd run as fast as I could."

"I've buried my memories," Maud said.

"Oh, please, Maud. Try to remember more things. I'm fascinated."

"Under my tree in the gardens. Here lie the memories of Maud Lucie." She gave a short harsh laugh, her head thrown back.

"You look wonderful," Ginny breathed.

"Mad?"

Ginny didn't seem to hear the apprehension in her voice.

"Splendidly. Don't move. Keep your head like that."

But Maud stood up, spilling Ching out of her lap. She stalked across the studio, crying, "I may be mad, but I prefer not to have it recorded for posterity."

"Oh, Maud! I wouldn't want to paint you if you were ordinary. It's your eccentricity that makes you so fabulous."

"That's only another word for madness."

"Well, whatever it is, it's what makes you interesting. Sedge says so, too. He says you're unique. Did I tell you that Sedge and I have decided just the three of us will have Christmas dinner together? Everyone else can come later to the party. But we three will have a cozy quiet dinner, in case you get tired. Candles on the table, brandy on the pudding. Maud, whatever is the matter, honey?"

She had forgotten how to cry. That was the trouble. Her lips trembled violently, her hands were wrung together, but her eyes stayed staring and dry.

Anyway, she wasn't touched to the heart by this knowing little hussy with her impertinent probing questions. She was plainly and simply angry.

"I've changed my mind about sitting for my portrait," she said stiffly.

"I've kept you there too long," Ginny exclaimed, full of remorse. "You're tired. I am a thoughtless beast. Look, let's not have another sitting until after Christmas. Okay? Anyhow, there are a thousand things to do. Tell me, how long is it since there was mistletoe hung in the hall?"

"Mistletoe! Let me think!" Diverted, her mind went seeking again. For Hessie? For Horace? For Guy? For Papa, who had made a point of kissing the maids, even staid Cook and Nanny and Bertha? "I don't believe since Papa died. He liked to kiss everybody."

"I'll bet," Ginny murmured.

"But Horace thought it was frivolous, and Hessie was only terrified the Sylvester boys would want to kiss her."

"Well, there's going to be some this year," Ginny announced. "Because, to tell the truth, Sedge and I have never had a really proper Christmas. I mean with a tree and candles and mistletoe and everything."

"Why, you poor children!" Maud exclaimed, her anger—if it had been anger—quite vanished.

"Of course we're doing it for Maud," Ginny reiterated.

"You sure, love? Sure it's not for yourself?"

"Well, maybe partly. I honestly didn't know I could be so sentimental."

"Don't get soppy."

"Of course I won't. It's only because I can't remember Christmas in anything but crummy rooms with my mother. It's so wonderful having a home."

"Better not think of it as permanent," Sedge warned.

"But why not? Maud will leave it to us. I'm absolutely certain."

"That's fine. I never said I despised a legacy. But not to live in, love. Imagine us, respectable residents of Melbury Square! Next thing I'll have my bowler hat and umbrella! And you'll be getting one of those sexy *au pair* girls for the kids. Not that I'd object to the *au pair* girl."

"I never said anything about kids," Ginny protested.

"I know you didn't. But there's been a look in your eye lately. It's not old round-the-bend Maud doing it to you either. It's this damned snob Square. Well, I suppose I could call myself an antique dealer and mix with the best of them, but I'm not going to. Hear me? That's flat."

"You can't stop my pretending," Ginny muttered under her breath. She was almost crying. That would be disastrous. Sedge would put up with a little sentiment now and then, but never tears.

From excitement, or the slight incontinence of old age, Maud found that she needed to go to the downstairs bathroom after she had come down, dressed in the resurrected peacock dress. ("Didn't you attend to that before you came out?" she could hear Papa's testy voice.)

The mistletoe was hanging in the hall, and there was cleverly looped greenery and scarlet ribbon up the stair rail. The house was as festive as it had ever been, from the lighted Christmas tree in the drawing-room window to the long red candles in the old china candlesticks on the dining table. The silver candlesticks seemed to have got lost, but Ginny said it didn't matter, porcelain was prettier.

After more lonely Christmases than she could remember, it was not surprising that Maud found an extra visit to the bathroom necessary. She hurried in, impatient to get back, to call down to the basement to Ginny and Sedge. She was ready, and couldn't they begin the celebrations?

But in the narrow space of the little washroom, she stubbed her toe severely on some excessively hard object. Grimacing with pain, she switched on the light and found a half-filled sack in the middle of the floor. It looked like a sack of potatoes. How very odd. She opened the top to peer in.

Not potatoes, she realized dazedly. Not her missing candlesticks either, but other silver pieces which she had never seen before. She pulled some out to examine them. Six soup ladles tied together, a cruet set, a salver with a piecrust edge—Georgian, she knew that much—a sugar shaker and two small milk jugs, a christening mug, and a charming tea caddy. What an extraordinary find!

Forgetting her purpose in coming to the bathroom, Maud burst out, calling, "Ginny! Do come quickly! I have something to show you."

"And what have you been doing snooping in there?" came Sedge's voice behind her.

She stopped abruptly. A queer little cold trickle went down her spine. She wasn't afraid of Sedge, of course. He was always so gentle and courteous and gallant. But just for a minute his voice had sounded menacing.

She had to stiffen her back and hold her head up haughtily.

"I haven't been snooping, as you call it. I merely went in there for the usual purpose and stumbled over a sack."

Ginny had come hurrying up from the basement. Her face was flushed and startled.

"Sedge?"

"It's all right," Sedge said in his normal voice. "Maud's only fallen over Father Christmas' sack and all the presents."

Soup ladles, the little salt and peppers . . . She supposed there had been nothing particularly large and valuable.

Just Christmas gifts for Ginny's and Sedge's friends, who would be arriving shortly. But expensive, all the same, for young people who had been having money problems. Perhaps not so expensive for Sedge, with his mysterious "connections."

"What a ridiculous place to put them!" Ginny exclaimed, strangely angry.

"It was only for a couple of hours," Sedge replied. "Sorry, Maud. Did you bruise your shins? Come in here. Your present's on the tree. Anyway," he added, "it wasn't me, it was Father Christmas who put them there. Probably he wanted to take a leak—sorry, Maud, what was the polite expression in your day?"

"Nanny would ask me if I needed to be excused," Maud said vaguely. "As it happens, I do. Will you excuse me?"

"Don't be long," Ginny said. "The turkey's ready."

"I'll be with you in a moment," Maud said, carefully skirting the bulging sack. Father Christmas, indeed!

When she came out, Sedge was waiting under the mistletoe, and he promptly took her arm and drew her to him and kissed her very skillfully. An old woman like her! As if she still had appeal. How clever he was. Yet when Ginny appeared, still flushed, but smiling now and looking very pretty in a remarkably short pink dress, and carrying a tray with three glasses of hot punch, she forgot about Sedge's cleverness and was only grateful that he and Ginny were there.

Sedge raised his glass and said, "Happy Christmas to us all! Drink up, Maud. You look marvelous in that dress. Doesn't she, Ginny?"

"Fabulous," said Ginny.

"My peacock dress," said Maud. "I told you I still had it."

Ginny turned out the lights, leaving only the candles alight on the Christmas tree.

"Stand over there, Maud, by the fireplace," and as Maud obeyed, she said breathlessly, "Yes, that's it. If you move, your skirts will rustle, and you'll really be a ghost. Won't she, Sedge?"

"Smelling strongly of camphor," said Sedge.

"Oh, dear, I am sorry. This dress has been packed away for so long—"

Ginny gave herself a little shake.

"Mood gone. Come on, lights, more drinks, food—and haven't you noticed, Sedge, that I've been lingering under the mistletoe?"

So there they were, the two young faces looking at her across the table. Her family. They had given her an elaborately wrapped parcel, and she had opened it to find a ring, a circle of purple garnets around a clear crystal.

"It's Victorian, Maud," said Ginny. "It's a hair ring. We thought you'd like it." Maud looked at it for so long that Ginny burst out anxiously, "*Don't* you like it?"

"The trouble," said Maud slowly, "is that I have no lock of hair to put in it. What a pity. I buried Papa's only the other day." She caught the sharp look that passed between the two and said very sanely and sensibly, "But I like it so much. It's perfectly charming."

"Then we must give you a lock of hair to put in it," Sedge said gaily. "Here, Ginny, clip off one of your curls."

"But I wanted Maud to ask me herself," Ginny pouted.

"I was going to!" Why hadn't that brilliant idea occurred to her sooner? She was in such a mixed-up state of emotion and happiness. The gift of the ring had touched the hard spot in her heart and nearly melted it. "And I have such a little thing for both of you," she added. "I searched so hard and could only find this."

It was one of Mamma's small treasures, an enameled box which Maud had used for years to keep her hairpins in. She had washed and polished it, and it really was very pretty, with its inset painting of cupids and white clouds.

"Sèvres," she heard Sedge murmur.

"Eighteenth-century?" Ginny breathed.

"I rather think so. Maud, this is a smashing present."

"Is it?" Maud said doubtfully. "I thought Hessie got all Mamma's nice things. She certainly got all the miniatures. But if you like that small trifle—"

Ginny flew around the table to throw her arms around Maud.

"We didn't want anything. Look at all you've done for us. But we adore it. What an absolutely gorgeous Christmas this is."

Maud thought so, too. Afterward, in the studio, when the other guests had arrived, and she was seated on the peacock throne where they had all insisted she be, she was so happy that she was frightened. In a moment this gay scene would vanish. She would find she had been dreaming of these boys and girls (very strangely dressed, long-haired, some bearded, some with naked faces that seemed tenderly young and vulnerable), and would awake to find herself alone in the lonely, dusty room.

One young man had brought a guitar. He sat on a cushion at Maud's feet and asked her earnestly what songs she had sung in her youth.

She had to think very hard. What was that catchy tune that Papa had whistled until Mamma had begged him to learn another one?

"The man who broke the bank at Monte Carlo," she exclaimed triumphantly.

There was a tremendous roar of laughter. "Did you know this guy who broke the bank, Maud?"

"No, of course I didn't. He was only in a song."

"What a pity! You could have invited him here tonight. Be useful, wouldn't he, Sedge?"

"Shut up," said Sedge. Was that his menacing tone again? No, it couldn't have been, for he was saying, "Maud wouldn't have known that sort of person. She was a debutante, weren't you, Maud? The deb of the year, weren't you? Curtseyed to the queen. That's more than the lot of you have done."

"I wore white satin with a train and carried an ostrich-feather fan," said Maud dreamily. "The thing was to scoop up one's train gracefully as one backed away from the queen."

"Did it do you any good, all that stuff?" one of the girls asked.

"I imagine so. It opened doors. One went to a great many balls and parties and met suitable young men. At least the kind one's parents thought suitable."

"We don't need to ask the queen's permission to open doors," someone said, and someone else retorted, "No, only the judge's," and again Sedge said sharply, "Shut up."

Then the young man with the guitar began strumming and singing in a low melodious but mocking voice, "After the ball was o-o-over . . . After the break of dawn . . ."

. . . And one danced on the dew-wet grass, and a strange young man leaped over the railing to have a conversation . . . Someone put a glass in Maud's hand. She automatically lifted it and drank. Her head was beginning to swim. This extraordinary collection of young people in their motley garb began to merge together like a patchwork quilt. But it was lovely, lovely. She had never had such fun.

"Say, Johnnie, that's a fantastic tune. Couldn't you reset it? You'd have a hit. Well, look at old Doddy with 'Tears.' Let's try it again. Let's all sing."

When was Sedge going to give them their Christmas gifts? Maud wondered vaguely. She began to sing herself, in a hoarse, quavering voice, and when she stopped, everyone applauded wildly.

"Didn't I tell you?" said Ginny, as if she were proud.

And someone else said, "Isn't she fantastic! Is her hair really her own? And those emerald eyes. Maud, your eyes slay me."

But then it was all spoiled by a very long-haired young man with a thin, ferocious face, who was obviously unimpressed by the remnants of her beauty. He stabbed a finger at the peacock portrait hanging behind her and said, in an unpleasantly incredulous voice, "Say, Maud, is that really you?"

"Of course. You could see that for yourself if you would use your eyes. This is the selfsame dress I am wearing."

"Holy Mother of God!" the young man murmured, in a tone so far from flattering that Maud belatedly wished she had kept her head clear so that she could have annihilated him. How she could have done so once! But now, suddenly, she was trembling-tired, and she had drunk too much wine. She would also have to excuse herself again. In any case, on second thought, she didn't think the young man had meant to be insulting. He was simply a stranger to tact and good manners.

"Maud," said Ginny in her ear, "time for bed."

"Yes, I think perhaps you're right, my dear."

"You've had quite a party for an old lady."

Damn being an old lady. Damn, damn, damn!

She stood up unsteadily.

"I'm afraid—yes, your arm, dear. My rheumatism—"

"Or the wine," said Ginny cheerfully.

That was the virtue Ginny and all these young people had, complete candor. One had to accept what they said on those terms.

All the same . . . At the door, Maud couldn't resist turning and pointing at the rude young man who had dared to doubt her identity. She said in Papa's best cutting manner, "If I am not exactly an oil painting in my old age, my imagination entirely fails me when I try to think what you will be in yours."

There was a momentary silence—stunned, she hoped—but as she went down the stairs, clinging to Ginny's arm, the laughter burst out and rang in her head for long afterward. She thought she heard someone say, "What attic did you find her in, Sedge? She's hardly the portrait of the year; she's more like an old master in need of a good cleaning."

They were laughing at her—Maud Lucie. Age had made a fool of her. How could Papa permit it?

"Your Papa is not God, you must remember," said Nanny . . .

In the small hours the doorbell rang twice. The second time Sedge called into her room, "Not to worry, Maud. It's only the neighbors complaining. I said we had a famous pop singer here, and they shut up."

Who were the neighbors? Dr. Burns? No, that was long ago. There had been a nice elderly couple, retired from the colonial service in India. She fancied they had moved, or died, some years ago. Now there were several small children, she thought. And one of those long-legged *au pair* girls, with blond hair hanging in her eyes.

Sedge's head was around her door. "Don't tell me you didn't used to enjoy shocking the neighbors, Maud," and was gone before she could answer.

She would have had to agree with him. But somehow, shocking the neighbors in her long-ago youth had seemed so much more innocent than this. Whatever it was . . .

After the Christmas party, in the New Year, the telephone calls began. Strange voices asking to speak to Sedge.

"Is Sedge there?"

When she said no, the caller hung up, refusing to leave a message.

Sinister voices. Or so she thought.

She tried not to think about it. She never mentioned it to Sedge.

He was as charming as ever, although occasionally she heard raised voices in the basement.

"It's Sedge getting restless," Ginny explained. "I tell him he's like a gypsy. He likes moving. But he's going to Amsterdam next week. That'll keep him quiet for a while."

"Why is he going to Amsterdam?"

"Oh, he has some connections there. They might have things for him to buy."

"And to sell again at a profit in London," Maud said, pleased with her sagacity. There was always a simple and logical answer to everything.

"That's it."

"I expect he has customers to satisfy." Much as she liked Sedge's company, she would enjoy having Ginny to herself. "Cheer up, dear. You can get a lot of work done on my portrait while he's away. Now I remember something else. There's an exhibition of nineteenth-century paintings at the Royal Academy. All Papa's old friends—

Whistler, Holman Hunt, Alma-Tadema, and so on—will be there. I have an invitation to the private view. It came yesterday."

"And you thought you'd go?"

"If you would come with me, dear. It would be good for your education."

Ginny's blue eyes were reflective. Suddenly they sparkled.

"Why not? I'll come with you. We'll have a ball."

Chapter 26

It was mid-January, with tardy daylight and the familiar winter-time lavender-colored haze hanging about the bare trees. The gardens were quiet, the noisy children indoors. Maud could walk with Ching gamboling at her heels without half a dozen small boys following her, stopping when she turned, then creeping up behind her again with loud whispers and giggles. It was their latest game, which she found very tiresome.

But they would have forgotten it when the sun shone again. She was so happy herself that she was almost able to feel charitable toward them. True, Hessie had taken to telephoning once a week and inquiring if those hippies were still in her house and repeating boringly that Maud must get in touch with her immediately if she were in trouble.

What trouble could she be in that Ginny would not take care of? Hessie had been startled enough by Maud's account of the wonderful Christmas party, but was even more so when she heard of the intended visit to the Royal Academy.

"But, Mother, you haven't been for years."

"No, dear."

"Then why now?"

"Because I want to take Ginny."

"That girl! I would hardly have thought she would be interested in Victorian artists."

"Oh, I'm quite aware that there will be some hopelessly bad paintings. But the private view is an important social event."

"Really, Mother, you'll have her at the palace next."

"So I would, if there were still presentations. Ginny hasn't had the advantages that you threw away."

"Mother, can't you see that she's fooling you?"

Maud looked at the charming garnet ring on her finger. She could hear Ching, her adorable little companion, snuffling about in the sitting room. Who but Ginny would have thought of these clever things to please her?

Her voice was cold. "I'm afraid I don't understand what you mean, Hessie."

Hessie's deep sigh was audible. "At least, if you're serious about going to this private view, do get some decent clothes. Don't be a laughingstock."

"I have a wardrobe full of clothes," Maud said stiffly, very offended.

"That's what I mean!"

"So why should I be a laughingstock? Do stop interfering, Hessie. It's very tiresome of you, especially when you don't know what you're talking about."

Ginny certainly had no criticism when Maud, after having tried on and discarded half a dozen garments, finally appeared dressed for the great occasion.

She had decided on her picture hat with its wreath of French silk roses, a little faded and crumpled to be sure, but still becoming. She had last worn it to a garden party in the gardens of Holland House and had been much complimented. The pale-green chiffon dress that went with the hat had long ago disintegrated, so she must wear her old black lace, always so right, as Horace used to say. For a wrap, she had had an inspiration. She would wear Papa's opera cloak, which she had preserved all these years, thinking it much too grand and romantic to give away.

She spent a long time making up her face, using rouge and lipstick lavishly; otherwise, in all that black, she would look like an old crow.

When she presented herself to Ginny, Ginny made her turn around slowly, then gave a delighted grin.

"That's fabulous, Maud. Bang up to date. Half the girls I know dress exactly like that."

"Is it too young?" Maud asked anxiously.

"No, I expect it's us who are too old. The funny thing is, we look like grannies, but you certainly don't look like anybody's grandmother. You look fantastic."

"Do I?" said Maud, pleased but unsurprised. She had always been accustomed to such compliments.

Ginny herself wore a skinny red coat over skinny black trousers. Her lovely tawny hair hung free.

"How'll I look, Maud, among all the nobs?"

"You mustn't use that expression, dear. You *are* one of the nobs, as you call them. And you look very nice. Are we ready to go? Are we traveling by bus?"

"Not dressed like that, Maud. You're so gorgeous you'd stop the traffic. We'll get a cab."

It was ridiculous to be nervous. She, Maud Lucie, nervous of going back to her old triumphant haunts. But she hadn't been in the West End for so long she was bewildered by the traffic and by the crowds pressing into Burlington House. She hated to be jostled. Her legs were unsteady, and she was afraid she would fall.

She was not jostled, however. When, with Ginny holding her arm, she approached the entrance, the people fell back on each side to allow them through. Almost as if they were royalty. Though there were odd expressions on some of the faces and she fancied she heard echoes of the tittering small boys who pursued her in the Square gardens.

"Smile, Maud," Ginny whispered. "These are your old friends."

They were not old friends. She knew better than that. But this was familiar ground. Suddenly the old memories took possession of her. She was Maud Lucie, and the center of attention, as always. She held up her head proudly, giving the smallest regal nod here and there, since all these staring people obviously expected some recognition.

And then the pictures claimed her whole attention. Goodness me, there were so many of her old favorites. Millais' "Autumn Leaves," Lord Leighton's "Garden of the Hesperides" with its luscious cornflower-blue sea, that wretched "Scapegoat" of Holman Hunt's, one of Frith's racecourse scenes.

And there—she gave a gasp of incredulous pleasure—hung on the line where he would have expected it to be, was one of Papa's early pastorals, with herself a small figure in a white dress, stooping to pick daisies.

"Maud!"

"Yes, my dear?" She was vague, dreamy, lost in that sunny landscape.

"Someone wants to take your photograph."

Her dreamy mood vanished. She turned, imperious, proud, unsmiling, ten feet tall.

"You can have two minutes, young man," she said. That was what Papa had used to say, and the anxious photographer had hastily disappeared under his black velvet cloth.

But this young man held a strange contraption to his left eye, said laconically, "Ten seconds will do," and a light exploded in her face. "That's it. Now one with your granddaughter beside you."

The light flashed again. The young man was gone; the crowd surged around.

"You are not exactly my granddaughter, dear," Maud said complacently, "but no one will notice."

Then three or four elderly people came up to shake her hand. Some of them remembered Papa. They all, they swore, remembered her, but she hadn't the faintest idea who they were, the Algernons or the Percivals or the Berties of those long-ago summer evenings.

"And everyone of you thought me dead," she declared triumphantly. "I've noticed you staring at me as if I were a ghost. But I'm not. I expect to see you all out." She gave her famous brilliant smile, softening the effect of her words. But they were true words. These people were all so old. And deaf, it seemed. Or was it she who was deaf, in all this babble? She couldn't hear what they said and turned away to take Ginny's arm. Ginny, her refuge. "Come, my dear, I must show you the spot where I arranged to elope. Or was that where I met Ninian? I'm afraid all this noise is addling my wits. Anyway, I mustn't be a bore with old memories, and we must give the pictures a little attention. One never knows if the artist isn't standing right behind one at these affairs."

"Not this time, Maud. All these chaps are dead."

"Of course! How sad!" A small coldness settled on her. She was becoming confused again, and very tired. Her brief triumph seemed to be over, for her elderly admirers had dispersed and other groups of people were being photographed, judging by the dazzling flashes of light.

Someone said, "Are you still living in Melbury Square, Mrs. Ponsonby?" and as she nodded vaguely, she noticed a young man scribbling in a small notebook.

"And this is your granddaughter?"

"This is Miss Evangeline Lucie Winter."

Ginny drew her away. "Don't let him bother you, Maud."

"I put that Lucie in. Did you mind?"

"No, I loved it."

"But I think I'm a little tired now. It's time for tea at the Ritz."

"Blimey!" said Ginny. "We are being posh."

Maud winced, then was ashamed of herself. After all this was Cora's granddaughter, as well as Papa's. There was a great deal to teach her. And all the rest of her life to do it in. Wasn't she a remarkably fortunate old woman?

"Maud, we're famous!" Ginny shouted the next morning, charging up the stairs.

Maud sat up in bed and took the newspaper from Ginny, who was saying excitedly, "Look! It's us! Where are your spectacles? Put them on and look."

Maud was not unduly surprised to see the photograph of herself and Ginny against the background of Papa's picture. She had frequently had her photograph in the newspapers as "among those present" at private views. Though not for a very long time, of course.

And not so unflatteringly. She experienced a queer shock. Was that strange tattered old woman her? Beside her, Ginny's youth and freshness was almost an affront.

"Why didn't you tell me I looked like that?" she asked indignantly.

"Like what, Maud?"

"Such an old fool, such an old frump."

"You look distinguished and eccentric," said Ginny.

"Do I?" Maud peered again, nervously. She remembered once laughing a great deal about the spectacle that doddery old pair Holman Hunt and his wife made.

But at least she was tall and upright and her bones were good, as Ginny frequently told her. One didn't want to be tame and medi-ocre, after all.

"What do they say about us?"

"I'll read it to you. 'Visitors at the Royal Academy included Mrs. Maud Ponsonby of Melbury Square, Kensington. Here she is seen with her granddaughter, Miss Evangeline Winter, standing against an early portrait of herself when she was Maud Lucie and as fa-mous in her own way as Elizabeth Siddal, Jane Morris, and Effie Millais.'"

"Do they think I'm a hundred years old?" Maud grumbled. "I was long after those Pre-Raphaelite women."

"But you're still famous, Maud. Isn't that something?"

"It's nothing to make a fuss about. I've always been accustomed to fame."

"Well, I'm not accustomed to it," said Ginny. "I never thought I'd get my picture in the paper. Wait till I show Sedge."

"Is he coming back?"

"Tonight. I'm cooking a special dinner. We'll have a party to celebrate."

"What a lot of parties we do seem to be having."

"Why not? Sedge has had a good trip. Anyway, I'll always want to celebrate when he comes home."

Maud's pang of jealousy that the softness in Ginny's eyes was not for her had to be repressed. The child was in love. One had to understand.

"So decide what you're going to wear, Maud. Make yourself glamorous."

"Do you really think I look distinguished in that photograph?" It was not that Maud required reassurance, only that she loved to hear flattery from Ginny.

"Absolutely. I'm an artist. I ought to know."

"And it's true I haven't a gray hair," Maud said. "How many women of my age could say that?"

"Then don't let Sedge and me give them to you," Ginny said lightly, dropping a kiss on Maud's forehead before she left the room.

Now whatever had made her say that?

It was a sparkling frosty morning. Maud was suddenly energetic and restless. Since Ginny was too busy with her plans for welcoming Sedge to do any work on her portrait that day, Maud decided to take Ching for a long walk in Holland Park. She was still in a nostalgic mood after yesterday's outing. She would like to see her old haunts, the ruined shell of Holland House, the unspoiled woodland walks, the sheltered Dutch garden where she could rest.

It was a pleasant hour, and she was stared at, as usual. When people failed to look at her, she might as well be dead. Old memories filled her—the time when the king had danced with her and not the queen but that possessive Mrs. Keppel had frowned, the time, much earlier, when Papa had filled her shoe with champagne at the Café Royal and drunk it (when she had put the little red shoe back on, it had been sticky and wet, and Nanny had been extremely cross), the time that she and one of her young men had screamed down the High Street in a de Dion Bouton and all the hansom cabs and plodding tradesmen's carts had had hurriedly to get out of their way, the time she and Guy had had that race in Kensington Gardens and she had fallen and got green stains all over her skirt and he had kissed her, the time Papa had made her sit at the head of the table at a meeting of Royal Academicians and called her Madam Chairman and none of the other gentlemen had been amused, nor Mamma when she had been told . . .

Had she told Ginny any of these things? She must hurry home to do so. Ching was slow, just as Han had been. Halfway home, he sat, refusing to walk another step. She stooped to gather up the little amber bundle, and a pain shot through her back. Bother, couldn't she walk even half a mile without her body reminding her of its age? She would have to rest when she got home. Ginny would make her some delicious hot chocolate.

Passing Number 9, she was even able to feel sorry for Honor, who had no devoted young relative to care for her. Poor old thing, attached to her piano like an elderly lichen.

To her surprise, she found her own front door standing wide open. Hessie wouldn't approve of that. "Always keep your door locked, Mother, don't let any strange men in . . ." Ginny, not having heard these instructions, had done both things. There were two strange men standing in the hall.

Ginny, talking to them, had that attractive flush in her cheeks, but this time it came from agitation, not happiness. Maud realized at once that she was extremely agitated.

"What is it, Ginny?" she asked. "Who are these men?"

The two men turned. One, who had a round, slightly pop-eyed face, a little like Horace's, Maud thought, said, "Are you the owner of this house?"

"I am. What is it you want?"

"I'm Detective Inspector Brackett of the CID. This is Detective Sergeant Watkins. We have a search warrant."

Maud stared uncomprehendingly at the piece of paper held out to her. "You mean to search my house! What impertinence!"

"I'm sorry, madam, but we have a job to do. Will you just go and sit down somewhere quietly while we get on with it. Why don't you make her a cup of tea, miss?"

Ginny, her knuckle in her mouth, suddenly began to cry. This was the most alarming thing of all. Maud hurried to her side.

"What is it, my dear? Have these men been bullying you?" She turned on the men. "You ought to be ashamed of yourselves. Couldn't you have waited until I got home? If you say you must search the house, I suppose you must. But you'll do it in my company. Why should I be expected to sit drinking cups of tea like a charwoman while you go through my treasures?"

"Okay, madam. Whatever you like. Just let us get on with the job."

Maud's indignation gave way to complete interest and fascination before the men had finished what they had set out to do. She had never imagined anything so thorough. In every room, cupboards, beds, wardrobes were gone through, pictures moved, walls tapped (for false panels, she presumed, as if she were hiding the crown jewels). The men worked from the basement up, Ching snuffing curiously at their heels and herself panting up flights of stairs after them.

She volunteered information occasionally. "That's the original William Morris wallpaper from my father's day. You don't need to suspect that." Or, "My mother locked treasures in this wall cupboard, but the key was lost long ago, and anyway my daughter Hester got most of her bibelots. I don't suppose you know what bibelots are."

"That's not what we're looking for, madam."

"What *are* you looking for? Or is that an official secret?"

"Just keep quiet, would you mind, madam."

Finally they reached the studio. And then it was nonsense for them to expect Maud to keep quiet.

"If you're looking for treasures, there they are. On the wall. Three of the finest examples of my father's work."

"So we gather, madam."

"Then you know who my father was?" Maud said, in a friendlier tone.

"Can't help it, after seeing your picture in the paper, madam."

"Oh, so you saw that," Maud exclaimed, pleased. Imagine policemen being interested in her photograph. She certainly had not been forgotten, even after all these years.

"Saw the young lady with you," said Detective Inspector Brackett. "Well, what do you think, Sergeant?"

"Nothing here, sir. Looks like we came the wrong day."

"Afraid so. We'll be off, madam. Sorry for the inconvenience."

They went clattering down the stairs; the front door banged behind them. Ginny came slowly up from the basement, her eyes red.

"Maud, how absolutely awful!"

"I confess I found it rather interesting," Maud said. "Intriguing. They do love to be secretive, don't they? Now what *were* they looking for? It wasn't drugs because they didn't sniff anything. Wasn't it clever of me to notice that?"

"Yes," Ginny murmured.

"Then why are you crying?"

"Because I'm frightened."

"Frightened! Whatever for?"

"They saw that picture of me in the paper, saying you were my grandmother and that you lived in Melbury Square. They came out to see if I was here, and I opened the door to them!"

The vague signals of alarm were touching Maud again. Suddenly, for no logical reason, she was remembering that bumpy sack in the bathroom.

"Well, what do they think you are?" she demanded angrily. "A criminal! What dreadful poppycock!"

"They know I'm Sedge's friend," Ginny said flatly. And Maud sat down, because her legs all at once gave way beneath her.

After a long time, she said, "Ginny! You must tell me. What is it that Sedge does?"

"Nothing! At least, it's awfully harmless. I mean it doesn't really hurt anybody. It's—no, I can't tell you, Maud." Ginny was beginning to cry again. "You must wait until he gets home."

"Very well," said Maud grimly. "I'll wait."

It was a long afternoon, and she was remembering, among other things, the extremely clever copy Ginny had made of Papa's picture and tried to sell through Sotheby's. A harmless deception that wouldn't hurt anybody—except the buyer, who would have been duped and defrauded.

And no one had ever told her how much money that nasty dark little William Shayer landscape had fetched.

Hippies, Hessie had said in her worried voice.

Gay, fun-loving, kind, warmhearted, original, exactly the kind of people she enjoyed. Her family . . .

Chapter 27

THE TROUBLE was that Sedge arrived home in the highest spirits. He burst into the house, calling, "Where are my beautiful women?" threw his leather jacket across a chair, and paused at the door of the drawing room, where Maud was sitting.

"Hello, lovely Maud. How's the famous face?"

"Too famous," Maud replied briefly.

"Hey? Something wrong? You didn't sound as if you meant to be funny. Where's Ginny?"

"Downstairs, I imagine. Waiting for you. Though no one could less deserve that attention."

"There is something wrong," said Sedge, standing very still.

He looked so attractive, damn him, with that lean rakish face and the flippant eyes masking what Maud had once thought was vulnerability, that she waved her hands at him despairingly.

"Oh, go find Ginny. I know you're longing to. Then both come up here. Immediately."

"Maud—"

"Do as I say."

"You sound as if you're giving us our marching orders. What's Ginny been doing?"

"Breaking her heart over you. That's all."

He went then, quickly. All the time he was gone Maud sat tense, listening for the doorbell. She had been afraid all day that those policemen might have remained in the Square, strolling about looking like everybody else in their treacherously ordinary clothes, but waiting to pounce on Sedge the moment he appeared.

However, the doorbell remained silent, and she had only five minutes to wait before Sedge and Ginny came up the stairs and into the room to stand before her.

In that short space of time, Sedge's attractive lightheartedness had vanished. His face had narrowed and gone sallow; his eyes were hard with fury. He had Ginny by the arm and was shaking her roughly.

"But how could you let her do such a bloody stupid thing, Maud? Getting photographed and giving her real name. She might as well have stood in Piccadilly and shouted our affairs to the whole world."

"I didn't know they knew I was your girl," Ginny wailed. "Anyway, I told them you didn't live here. I said you had left the country."

"Do you think they believed you?"

"I don't know! I don't know!"

"But they went on searching the house?"

Ginny nodded, her face bleak with misery.

Sedge's hard eyes rested on Maud.

"And what did they ask you, you crazy old prima donna?"

"Me! They weren't interested in me. They told me to be quiet."

"Thank God for that."

Maud stood up slowly, holding on to the arms of the chair. Her legs felt so stupidly weak. But she had to overcome that. She had to stand straight, to tower over this angry little bantam cock of a man.

"However," she said, "I have remained quiet long enough. Now I have a great deal to say."

"Can it, Maud. There's no time—"

"There's time." The cool authority in her voice made Sedge hesitate. "And you'll listen to me and answer my questions."

"You've got another think—"

"Be quiet!" she thundered, and momentarily Sedge's eyes flickered, showing that trace of apprehension and vulnerability.

Maud saw Ginny's hand slip into his, and something twisted in her heart. The anger failed to stay in her voice, although the unexpected cool sanity that seemed to disturb this young man more than anger remained.

"Now," she said, "I'm perfectly aware that you have been cheating me. Various pieces of furniture didn't walk out of this house. Perhaps

I didn't need them. Perhaps I do have too much for an old woman. But it's very possible I would have given them to you if you had asked."

"Maud—" Ginny began.

"You be quiet, too, my dear. I'm speaking now. I imagine Sedge financed his trip to Holland with the proceeds from the sale of Nanny's old chair, which Hessie tells me was valuable. There was also a small dark picture I didn't like, but which I imagine fetched much more money than the cost of a Christmas party. Never mind. All this is rather petty and foolish. But why should two policemen search my house? That isn't petty and foolish. So what else is it you are up to, young man?"

Sedge took a step forward. Maud drew herself up another two inches. The back of her neck ached agonizingly.

"I'm not afraid, you know. My daughter imagines I am a gullible old woman who might be murdered in her bed. But I'm no longer gullible, and I know you won't murder me."

"How do you know?" Sedge asked in a tight, ugly voice.

"Oh, don't be ridiculous, you silly boy. No granddaughter of my father would fall in love with a man capable of murder. But all the same, Ginny has made a pretty fool of herself. She's just like I was at that age, much too impulsive with the wrong men."

"Maud, it isn't only Sedge doing this," Ginny cried painfully. "I've been helping him. I made him promise never to hurt you, but for the other things I'm as guilty as he is."

"The silver in the sack at Christmas?" Maud asked stonily.

"I knew about it."

"Then perhaps one of you would enlighten me."

"Tell her," Ginny said to Sedge.

"Come off it, love, what do you take me for?"

"*Tell her!*"

"Gawd, you two! Chips off the same block. All right, the silver in the sack was from a robbery. I took it to Amsterdam last week. Sold it very well."

Maud thought she would have to sit down, her legs trembled so badly. Somehow she managed to stay upright.

"So you are a receiver, as I believe it's called."

"Maud, you mustn't judge. Sedge—"

"Let him speak for himself. And I'm not judging. I'm asking."

"Yes, that's it, Maud. I'm a receiver, a thief, I suppose you could call it. The police want me even though they didn't find anything today. We'll have to move, Ginny love."

This time Maud did sit down, her legs simply folding under her. Strangely, his confession seemed to have restored Sedge's aplomb.

"It isn't really fair," he said. "I know so much more about that silver than its owners ever did. It had been badly neglected. I cleaned it with the right stuff and got all its beauty back. I deserved something for that. I don't just take at random; I select the best."

"Steal."

Sedge shrugged. "If you insist. Someone else does the actual job. Anyhow, half the world preys on the other half. Which side do you think gets the biggest kicks?"

"Are you using that as an excuse?"

Ginny went to kneel beside Maud, taking her hand. Her big blue eyes were full of that deceptive innocence.

"Maud, Sedge has had a horrible life. So have I. You can't blame either of us."

"Who said anything about blame?"

"Well, you have every right. But neither of us has ever hurt anyone. Physically, I mean."

Maud leaned back, very tired.

"I suppose mentally doesn't matter. I suppose you think an old, eccentric, half-mad woman doesn't have feelings."

"Oh, honey love, we've cherished you! We've adored you! Haven't we, Sedge?"

"Sure, Maud. You've been great. We've loved making a fuss of you, but now we have to move on."

"You keep saying 'we,' " said Maud.

"Well, naturally, Ginny's coming. That's if she wants to."

Swiftly, Ginny had deserted Maud and was at Sedge's side, her arm possessively in his.

"Naturally, you dope."

"But your lessons at art school! My portrait!" Maud wasn't sure if she said those words aloud. She was suddenly so confused; the pain twisting in her heart was so sharp.

"I'll come back and finish it when it's safe. I'm sorry, Maud. But you have been painted an awful lot of times. Perhaps you won't mind this last portrait going wrong."

Sitting on the peacock throne with every bone in her body aching, trying not to show it, enduring for this dishonest young woman who had never loved her, after all.

"Perhaps I won't," she said slowly. "Perhaps I don't even mind having been a pawn in your sordid little games. But one thing I'll give you credit for. I've been happy. I've had marvelous fun. I've felt loved. It has all been more than I deserved or expected."

"Oh, Maud!" Ginny cried. "I mustn't cry. Sedge hates me to cry."

"So you really do love this man?"

"What do you think, you daft old woman? Doesn't it stick out all over me?"

"And you, Sedge? Do you love Ginny?"

"Gawd, you sound as if you're saying the marriage service over us."

"Which wouldn't do either of you any harm. All right, I have no criticism to make of loyalty. So I give Ginny my permission to go with you. But where to?"

"Somewhere abroad," said Sedge, the urgency coming back into his voice. "Tonight, if we can. I've got some money from my Dutch trip. Can you be ready in ten minutes, love?"

Ginny nodded. Her eyes had grown hard and bright. The emotion was over.

"I'll have to leave the geraniums in the kitchen for you to look after, Maud. And you will look after yourself as well, won't you? Eat properly?"

"How long will your money last?" She could show them that she could be practical, too.

"A while. Until—"

"Until you do something else dishonest." Her eyes flashed. "I won't have it! I simply won't have it! Papa's granddaughter—I don't mind the stealing so much. I only can't contemplate her being put in jail, and that will be inevitable if she goes on like this." She began to get up, painfully. "I know it's no use asking two people like you to promise me anything unless you have a suitable bribe. So can you spare a few minutes of your precious time to come with me?"

She took their assent for granted, leading the way to the stairs.

"Once I eloped," she said over her shoulder. "It wasn't a success."

"This isn't an elopement, Maud," Sedge said.

"And it *is* a success," Ginny added. "We've had long enough to prove that. Where are you going, Maud?"

"Up to the studio, of course."

She climbed the stairs, panting, her stiff legs dragging. She could manage this climb once more. It would be the last time. After this, there would be no reason to go up.

In the studio, she switched on all the lights.

"I'd suggest you change your plans about Europe and go to America," she said cryptically. "I believe Sir James Lucie paintings fetch the best prices there."

"What are you *saying?*" Ginny whispered.

"I'm saying you could sell these three pictures and make a fresh start in life. Honestly, perhaps, though I'm not making conditions."

"But, Maud!" Ginny had given up the losing battle with tears. She was crying unashamedly. "You said you'd starve rather than ever sell these."

"I will be starving," said Maud. "Starving for company and care and affection. Oh, for heaven's sake, don't let's waste time on all this boring talk. Take the canvases out of the frames. Roll them up. Ginny, you do it. Sedge might understand silver, but he doesn't understand paintings. If there's any damage done, you must promise me to repair it before you sell the pictures. I'll give you a letter setting out their provenance. Not that they have one. They have always been Papa's and mine . . ."

But not any longer. The great empty holes in the frames were holes in her heart. The house seemed to be shouting with silence. Although once, surprisingly, she thought she heard Cora laughing. Cora! That must be sheer imagination. Actually it was as quiet as it had been the night Papa lay dying and straw muffled the streets outside his bedroom window.

Long ago, Ginny and Sedge, carrying hastily packed bags (the biggest containing the rolled canvases), had left. Ginny had kissed Maud tenderly; Sedge had said that Number 7 Melbury Square had been the first real home he had known. But their footsteps had been full of haste and eagerness. They couldn't wait to be on their way, to start something fresh, to pursue their untidy optimistic lives.

It was four o'clock in the morning, and Maud was still in the denuded studio, trying to recover from the growing traumatic knowledge that Papa was dead at last. As she had feared it would, that great dazzling presence had vanished out of the house with his pictures.

What she hadn't expected was the enormous relief she herself would begin to feel.

Sitting there, looking at Ginny's half-finished portrait, the ravaged ancient face, the slitted emerald eyes, the disordered dusty red hair, she felt less and less shock at Ginny's clever, merciless interpretation of her.

The situation was perfectly simple and logical. The Maud Lucie Papa had created would have had to go out of the house with him. The one who was left might be old and ugly, but at least she was entirely herself. That inhibiting shadow would no longer fall over her or that suffocating love restrain her, whatever she decided to do.

She was free.

But what could she do with freedom at her age? the mad green eyes in the portrait asked her.

Plenty, she said aloud vigorously, gathering herself up. Plenty. It was not too late to experiment with this novel sensation. If only, she thought, with a sly chuckle, for the satisfaction of shocking Hessie.

A surprised and sleepy Ching made it clear that he thought walking in the Square at four o'clock on a winter's morning was the height of folly. Moreover, Maud walked with unaccustomed speed, her body full of restless nervous vigor. She was enjoying the sharp taste of frost and smoke, the black tree trunks gleaming in the light of streetlamps, the pavement echoing to her footsteps. The quiet deserted Square gardens, in the early morning, were peculiarly her territory. She turned the key in the iron gate and let the gate clang behind her.

A bird fluttered in a tree, its wings clapping fretfully, then settling. Ching showed the greatest distaste for the crackling frosty grass.

"What are you afraid of, you silly creature?" Maud chided. "A little thing like cold feet? You'll have to face more than that in life."

If she were to sit on that seat and close her eyes, she might see Guy coming across the wintry grass.

Then she realized, in her new freedom, that she didn't want to see Guy or anyone else from her past. Good gracious, she might even find she could no longer maintain her quarrel with that tiresome Honor. For she would have to conserve both her physical and mental energy if she were to make the most of her new life.

She wished she were young enough to fall in love . . .